PRAI...N

Only Randy Ingermanson could blend science and riveting historical detail into a fascinating read. The breadth and scope of Randy's knowledge of the lives of first-century Christians is amazing. I loved this book!

> Colleen Coble, author of *Without a Trace* and *Beyond a Doubt*

Retribution, Book Three of Randy Ingermanson's genre-bending City of God series, takes up where *Premonition* left off—a perfect blending of science fiction, well-researched first-century history, realistic human drama, and gripping action. Bravo!

> DeAnna Julie Dodson, author of *In Honor Bound*,
> *By Love Redeemed*, and *To Grace Surrendered*

Retribution is a convincing page-turner, full of compelling, distinctly voiced characters. I devoured the book and wished it were longer.

> Kathy Tyers, Author of *Shivering World* and the *Firebird* trilogy

Fiction by Randy Ingermanson

Transgression (2000)
Oxygen (2001) *
The Fifth Man (2002) *
Premonition (2003)
Retribution (2004)
Double Vision (2004)

* = coauthored with John B. Olson

RETRIBUTION

CITY OF GOD SERIES

RANDALL INGERMANSON

ZONDERVAN™

GRAND RAPIDS, MICHIGAN 49530 USA

ZONDERVAN™

Retribution
Copyright © 2004 by Randall Ingermanson

Requests for information should be addressed to:

Zondervan, *Grand Rapids, Michigan 49530*

Library of Congress Cataloging-in-Publication Data

Ingermanson, Randall Scott
    Retribution / Randall Ingermanson.
        p. cm.—(The City of God series)
    ISBN 0-310-24707-1
     1. Church history—Primitive and early church, ca. 30–600—Fiction.   2. Jews—
History—Rebellion, 66–73—Fiction.   3. Palestine—History—To 70 A.D.—Fiction.
4. Rome—History—Nero, 54–68—Fiction.   5. Americans—Jerusalem—Fiction.
6. Jewish Christians—Fiction.   7. Time travel—Fiction.   8. Jerusalem—Fiction.
I. Title.
PS3609.N46R48 2004
813'.6—dc22

                                         2004005344

The website addresses recommended throughout this book are offered as a resource to you. These websites are not intended in any way to be or imply an endorsement on the part of Zondervan, nor do we vouch for their content for the life of this book.

Published in association with the literary agency of Alive Communications, Inc., 7680 Goddard Street, Suite 200, Colorado Springs, CO 80920.

Interior design by Nancy Wilson

Maps: Jane Haradine

Printed in the United States of America

04 05 06 07 08 09 10 /❖ DC/ 10 9 8 7 6 5 4 3 2 1

AUTHOR'S NOTE

On April 30, A.D. 66, Gessius Florus, the governor of Judea, randomly selected hundreds of Jews from the streets of Jerusalem and crucified them in the public market.

In retribution.

For an insult.

Two time-travelers from the far future, Rivka Meyers and her husband, Ari Kazan, were present in Jerusalem to witness this horror. This is their story.

If you are interested in how Rivka and Ari got trapped in ancient Jerusalem, you can read about their earlier adventures in my previous novels, *Transgression* and *Premonition*, but neither of these is required reading for this story.

Most of the characters in this book are real historical characters, and their names can be infuriatingly similar, but I can't really change them. If you get confused, please consult the list of historical characters at the back of the book. You will also find a glossary of Hebrew words there.

For more information on me and my books, please visit my website at www.rsingermanson.com. You may email me directly at retribution@rsingermanson.com.

R0019981873

ACKNOWLEDGMENTS

I thank:

- My friends the Beckers, the Hymans, the Kasdans, the Lundgrens, the Magees, the Poages, the Walkers, the Wearps, the Wilsons, and many others at the Coast Vineyard and Kehilat Ariel.
- My fellow writers/artists, John Olson, Brandilyn Collins, Kathy Tyers, Mike Carroll, John DeSimone, Rene Gutteridge, Janelle Schneider, Angela Maust, and my many friends in Chi Libris. Special thanks to Meredith Efken for her detailed and valuable critique of the story.
- My agent, Chip MacGregor.
- My editors Dave Lambert and Karen Ball, my marketing wizards Sue Brower and Cindy Wilcox, and all the others in the extraordinary Zondervan team.
- My Mom and Dad.
- My three girls, Carolyn, Gracie, and Amy.
- My Eunice.

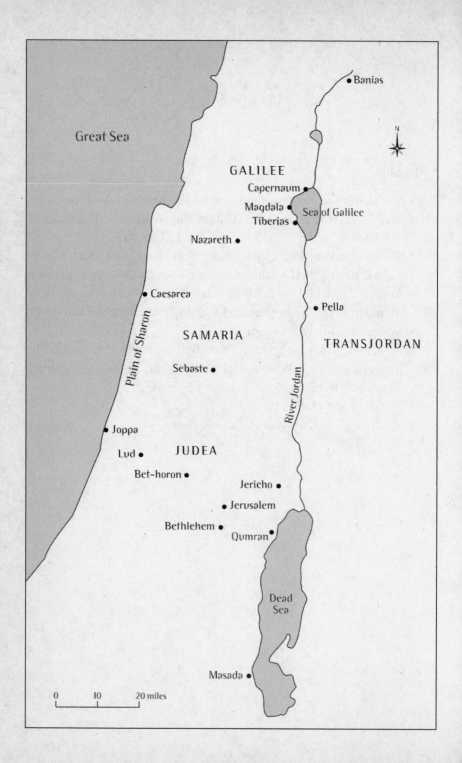

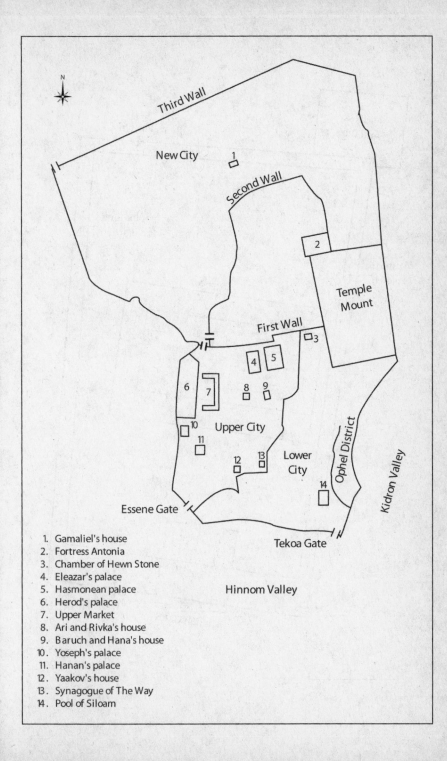

N

Third Wall

New City

1

Second Wall

2

Temple
Mount

First Wall

3

4 5

6 7

8 9

10

Upper City

11

12 13 Lower
City

Ophel District

14

Kidron Valley

Essene Gate

Tekoa Gate

Hinnom Valley

1. Gamaliel's house
2. Fortress Antonia
3. Chamber of Hewn Stone
4. Eleazar's palace
5. Hasmonean palace
6. Herod's palace
7. Upper Market
8. Ari and Rivka's house
9. Baruch and Hana's house
10. Yoseph's palace
11. Hanan's palace
12. Yaakov's house
13. Synagogue of The Way
14. Pool of Siloam

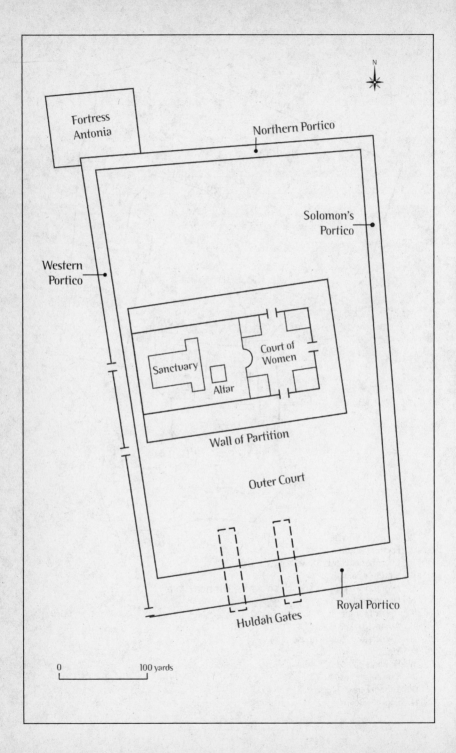

Fortress
Antonia

Northern Portico

Solomon's
Portico

Western
Portico

Sanctuary

Altar

Court of
Women

Wall of Partition

Outer Court

Huldah Gates

Royal Portico

N

0   100 yards

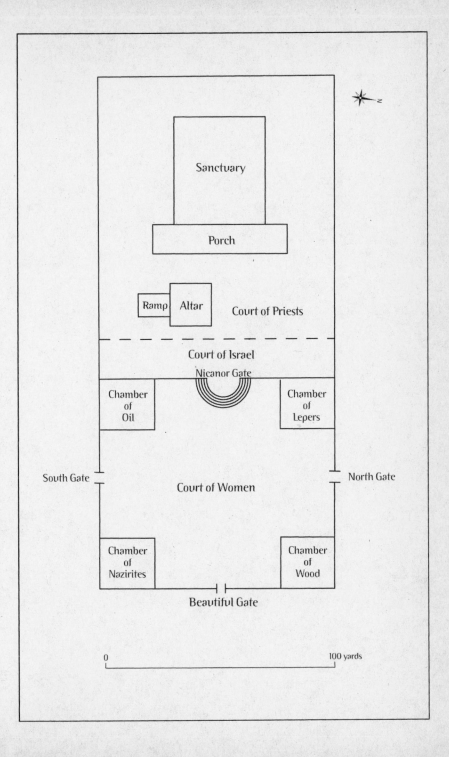

PART ONE

BLESSINGS AND CURSES

Fall, A.D. 62

Today I set before you a blessing and a curse:
  The blessing if you hear the commandments of Yahweh your God,
    Which I command you today.
  The curse if you do not hear the commandments of Yahweh your God,
    If you turn from the Way
    Which I command you today.

— Deuteronomy 11:26–28, author's paraphrase

ONE

Rivka

Rivka woke from a light sleep, her heart aching. The room was pitch black and smelled of incense and sweat and cheap wine. Like her apartment building back home in Berkeley.

A dull sigh caught in Rivka's throat. She was not in Berkeley. Not even in America. She was in Jerusalem, a city of shimmering white stone, simmering with rage. And she was in the biggest trouble of her life.

Beside her, Ari moaned quietly. Dear, sweet, opinionated, lovable, infuriating Ari Kazan. They had been married for five years, and she knew now why people said it was a mistake to marry an unbeliever. More accurately, a half-believer. Ari believed in God. He did not believe in Yeshua. Three days ago, that unbelief had saved his life.

Deep grief welled up in Rivka's heart. She felt so very grateful Ari had been saved. But not that way.

She could smell him in the deep darkness, the stale sweat rank on his naked body. Rivka touched a gentle finger to his jagged back. Thank God, Ari had survived the flogging. Blessed be HaShem, as they said here in Jerusalem, where they were too polite to say God's name, but they had no qualms about torturing in his name.

"Rivka, are you awake?" Ari's voice was a tight whisper.

"I'm sorry, did I hurt you?"

"A little." Ari rolled to face her. His labored breathing rasped in Rivka's ear. "Please forgive me for bringing you to this city."

"There's nothing to forgive." Rivka clutched his hands to her chest. "It was my fault, not yours." She closed her eyes, too late to stop the hot tears.

Five years ago, thanks to a physics experiment gone horribly wrong, they had come through a wormhole and ended up trapped forever in a world they could never have imagined. First-century Jerusalem.

It was a world that treated women like children. Rivka had hated it at first. Slowly, slowly, she had gotten used to the men who would not deign to speak to a woman, the women who looked askance at her. But she would never feel at home in this world.

Unlike Rivka, Ari had quickly found a niche in this city of God. Trained as a physicist at the Hebrew University, MIT, and Princeton, Ari had floundered when he first came to this primitive culture. Then certain young men had found him a job with a builder, and before long, Ari's talents as an engineer had blossomed into a lucrative consulting career. Now he had a great many friends.

Plus one very powerful enemy. Hanan ben Hanan, leader of the great and powerful House of Hanan, a man with no conscience at all, a conservative who despised the unorthodox, the strange, the new. Most of all, Hanan hated a stranger named Ari the Kazan, a "magician" who knew deep secrets of the universe that were surely forbidden by HaShem.

A few months ago, Hanan ben Hanan had been appointed high priest. This past week, he had arrested fifteen men he hated and tried them in his kangaroo court. Thirteen of them were now dead — killed in a stoning pit in the Hinnom Valley. One, Brother Baruch, had escaped entirely. The fifteenth — Ari — had received a flogging intended to kill him.

A flogging that *should* have killed him. Ari would be dead now, except for a miracle. Wracked by fever and loss of blood, Ari had slipped into unconsciousness, had found himself before the Throne, had exchanged words with HaShem, and then . . .

. . . and then had been sent back because of the intercession of Brother Baruch, a man gifted in healing. HaShem had sent Ari back, but he had asked Ari to do some great and mysterious task. Neither Rivka nor Ari had any idea what that task might be.

Rivka felt a spasm of rage rush through her body. She hated Hanan ben Hanan. The man was evil, pure evil. She would never breathe easily until she saw him dead.

Ari sighed deeply. "Your thoughts are dark."

"I'm scared." Rivka felt nausea well up in her throat. She'd been trying not to admit it to herself, but now she couldn't keep quiet anymore. "Please, don't be mad at me, but . . . I think I might be pregnant again."

A sudden intake of breath. "Are you sure?"

"Not a hundred percent," Rivka said. "I was due to start my *niddah* uncleanness three days ago. Last time I was this late, I was pregnant with Rachel. We need to get out of this city — go somewhere safe."

"Perhaps a son this time." Ari's voice sounded thick, husky. Thrilled. "Rachel has been asking for a brother."

"You're not angry?" Rivka couldn't believe he was taking this so calmly. She was furious with herself. They did not *dare* get pregnant at a time like this. She would love to have another child — but at the right time. Not now.

"It is a gift from HaShem." Ari pulled Rivka's hands to his lips and kissed them.

"Are you crazy?" Rivka felt so relieved, she wanted to cry. Ari wasn't angry. But he would be if he understood. "This is the worst possible time to get pregnant."

"My grandfather's sister became pregnant four months before they put her on the train to Auschwitz. She went straight to the showers. Please, you will remember that there is always a worse thing than what you are enduring."

Rivka knew all that, but Ari was wrong. In Berkeley, she had specialized in the history of this time period, and she knew that a thing worse than Auschwitz was coming to this city. "Listen, we have less than four years until the war begins. Eight years from now, the Romans are going to slaughter everybody in this city. Everybody. I want you to take me away from here. Now."

"And will we abandon our friends to die?"

Panic shoved a dagger into Rivka's heart. "If they won't come with us."

"We must persuade them." Ari's voice was infuriatingly calm. "You will tell them what is to come."

"Ari, nobody believes a word I say, remember? They call me the witch woman." *And I am a witch woman. Everytime I turn around, I'm using my knowledge to manipulate people. I'm a scheming, deceitful —*

"Our friends will believe you now." Ari's voice sounded tired and sad. "You foretold what would befall at the hands of Hanan ben Hanan, and none believed you. Now thirteen good men are dead."

"Will you talk to Shimon for me?" Rivka knew no man would listen to her, but they would listen to Ari, because he was a man. It wasn't fair, but she couldn't fight the system anymore.

"Which Shimon should I speak to?"

"Sorry, I guess I haven't told you about that yet. Shimon ben Klopas will be our new leader. According to Eusebius, he'll lead our people to safety."

"When?" Ari's voice sounded tight.

"I don't know. I'm assuming we'll leave before the war. For sure before the Romans destroy the city. You'll talk to Shimon?"

A long pause. "Yes, I will speak with Shimon, but I must know what to tell him."

"I'll try to figure it out, but . . ." Rivka felt her throat tighten. She could not imagine giving birth to another child in this wretched city of God. "Ari, if I'm really pregnant, then I want you to take me somewhere safe right away."

"I will pray on the matter."

Rivka had never heard Ari say he would pray about anything before. It caught her like a slap, because . . . she hadn't prayed about it. What was there to pray about? Of *course* God wanted them to get away from here. It said so in the Bible. Yeshua said to leave.

"You will pray on the matter also, Rivkaleh?"

Rivka held her breath for a long moment. "Yes."

"Then sleep." Ari kissed her fingers again. "All is in the hands of HaShem."

Which was exactly what Rivka was afraid of.

Rivka, wake up! There is trouble."

Rivka forced her eyes open. Her best friend Hana knelt over her, holding an olive-oil lamp, her face tight with anxiety.

Hana handed Rivka a tunic and cloak. "Please, you must come. Do not wake Ari the Kazan."

Rivka felt her heart thumping against her ribs. She pulled on her tunic and slid out onto the cold stone floor. Hana flung the cloak around her. Rivka stepped into her stiff camel-leather sandals, wrapped her hair in a head-covering, and followed Hana out into the corridor.

Surprise sparked through her. Where was Hana's husband? If there was trouble, they would need him. "Where's Baruch?" Rivka whispered.

"Hurry!" Hana pattered down the hall.

Rivka hurried. She reckoned it was still an hour before dawn. Every few feet, olive-oil lamps flickered in small insets in the stone walls. Rich tapestries of silk hung on the walls. The floor was inlaid with polished marble. The owner of this compound was an extremely wealthy man named Mattityahu, one of the most powerful men in Jerusalem. He had sworn to protect them all. Rivka was not sure he could keep his oath.

They reached the door and went out into the early morning chill. Rivka snugged her cloak tighter around her shoulders. Hana led her across the large courtyard toward the outer gate of the palace. Outside the iron gate stood two dozen men in the linen garb of Temple guards. In their center, Rivka spotted a sixtyish-looking man in aristocrat's clothing. Hanan ben Hanan, the high priest. Her heart skipped a beat.

Hanan ben Hanan was the reason they had taken refuge here. Now he must have come for Ari. Rivka would scratch his eyes out first.

Hanan ben Hanan took absolutely no notice of Rivka or Hana. In this city, women were of no consequence. Empty heads, vessels for bearing children, property to be hidden from the eyes of other men. A man of honor did not speak to a woman. Rivka bit her lip to keep from shrieking at the stupidity of a culture that made so much of wretched honor.

Flickering shadows sprang out in front of her. Rivka turned and saw several torches hurrying toward her from the palace. Shapes behind them. Men. Ari's friend, Yoseph. Yoseph's father, Mattityahu, the master of this palace. Several other men followed them, and in their center was . . .

Hana's husband, Baruch.

Rivka's heart lurched. Suddenly, it was all clear. Her breath began coming in short gasps, and her head felt strangely light. Rivka stumbled over to Hana and put her hand around her shoulders. "Hana, they're not going to — "

"Why have you disturbed my gate, Hanan ben Hanan?" The old man, Mattityahu, stopped just inside the iron gate and put his hands on his hips, his gray beard quivering with anger. "I have sworn protection to these. What is the meaning of this?"

Hanan ben Hanan stepped forward, and the bitter gleam in his eyes frightened Rivka. He gave Mattityahu a cold smile. "You have sworn protection to certain women and children and to Kazan, is this correct?"

"You know it is," Mattityahu said. "I have sworn by the Temple of the living God. Leave now. I will not violate my oath."

"I do not ask for those under your protection." Hanan turned and pointed his finger at Baruch. "You are harboring this man who stands under sentence of death. I know with certainty that you have not sworn to protect him. He entered your palace yesterday, not at your invitation, and not under promise of protection. He stands under the curse of the court, and you will give him to me now."

Mattityahu said nothing. In that moment, Rivka saw that Baruch was lost. Everything Hanan ben Hanan had said was true.

"Baruch!" Hana screamed and ran to clutch him.

Baruch's face was calm, placid. He threw his arms around her. "Hanaleh, Hanaleh." He stroked her head softly and held her for a long moment. "Kiss my son Dov for me."

"No!" Hana shrieked. "Take me instead!" She flung herself at the iron gate. "Take me and leave him alone!"

Baruch signaled to Rivka. "Please, you will give comfort to her."

Feeling sick with rage, Rivka hurried to Hana's side.

Hana screamed a long wail of despair.

Baruch put his hands on Hana and calm seemed to flow from his fingers. Hana stopped screaming. Her frame shook with silent sobs.

Baruch turned to Rivka. "Please, you and Brother Ari will take care of Hana and my son."

Rivka stared at him and she read in his eyes that he had seen this coming, had known all along when he came back into the city to heal Ari that he would die. And yet he had come. To save Ari.

Hanan ben Hanan spit at her feet. "Mattityahu, you will give me the man called Baruch now."

Cold fury stuck a sword through Rivka's heart. Boldness welled up inside her. She jabbed a finger at Hanan ben Hanan. "You . . . you son of Satan! Hear now the curse of the seer woman. Before the third month of your high priesthood, you will be deposed. Before seven years have passed, you will see the destruction of all you hold dear, and you will die in your own house at the hand of an Edomite!" Rivka put her face up to the bars in the gate and spat in Hanan's beard. "I am unclean with *niddah* uncleanness, and now you also are unclean until evening!"

Black rage slashed across Hanan's face.

For an instant, Rivka felt certain he would slip a dagger through the bars into her heart. Instead he spun away and stalked into the blackness of the night.

Rivka sagged against the iron gate. What had she done? Cursing the high priest — that was foolishness.

Hana put a quivering hand on Rivka's cheek. "You were very brave."

Rivka heard whispering behind her, and it was clear that the men thought she had acted foolishly. One did not antagonize Hanan ben Hanan. Shame pierced her heart. She had done it again — used her knowledge of the future to manipulate people. That was wrong, but what else could she have done? Hanan ben Hanan was an evil man, a murderer. Had she done nothing, he would have killed Baruch tonight — right now.

"Sister Rivka." Baruch's voice, very strong, unafraid. He was looking directly at her, contrary to the customs of this city. Baruch put a hand on her arm.

Rivka felt a little shiver run through her. In this society, a man did not look a woman in the eye, nor talk to her in public, not even to his wife. Certainly, a man would never touch another man's wife in public. Rivka could not remember Baruch ever doing any of these things, though he often spoke to her in private, knowing that the customs were different in the far country from which she came. But to touch her now in public? That was dishonor. Furthermore, she had said she was unclean. Therefore, Baruch had now made himself unclean. What could have got into him? Baruch had always been a man of honor.

Baruch took both of Rivka's hands in his and knelt before her. "I have spent much time in prayer since Brother Yaakov was murdered, and HaShem has told me that I must ask a thing of you."

Rivka felt her ears glowing as hot as the torches in the hands of the men around her. She risked a look at them. They were all staring at Baruch as if he had a demon.

"Please, my sister . . ." Baruch began weeping. "I ask your forgiveness for treating you as the men of this world treat women, as less than a child. I beg your forgiveness."

Rivka felt a rush of heat in her frozen heart.

Baruch fell on his face before her and . . .

. . . and kissed her feet.

A horrified hiss ran around the circle of men. Baruch had just destroyed his reputation for all time among these men. Ruined his honor, his precious honor.

Baruch kissed her feet again.

Rivka felt something melt deep inside her soul. Love flooded her heart. Tears murked her vision. A great lump rose in her throat. She smeared the sleeve of her tunic across her eyes. "B–brother Baruch, please." She reached down and pulled at his sleeve. "Please . . . yes, of course I forgive you. I . . ."

Now she could not speak. It seemed that all heaven broke open in that moment, that somehow, the universe changed, that the Kingdom of God flooded in on her. Rivka clutched at Baruch's arm. "My brother, yes, please stand."

Slowly, Baruch stood up. Dust smeared his beard, and his eyes gleamed red with weeping.

Rivka threw her arms around him. "Yes, my brother. Yes, and I also ask your forgiveness."

Baruch hugged her — a strong bear hug, such as no Jewish man would ever give a woman in this city. No man except a *tsaddik*, a man so righteous he could not be tempted by the desires of the flesh.

Rivka laughed for joy. Whatever Hanan ben Hanan did, he could not take away this moment, not if he came back and took Baruch away now. Only days ago, Hanan ben Hanan had killed Yaakov the *tsaddik*, the holiest man in all Jerusalem.

But HaShem had raised up another *tsaddik*. Blessed be HaShem.

TWO

Ari

"You spit on Hanan ben Hanan?" Ari stared at Rivka, feeling a cold knot in his belly. "That was unwise."

Rivka sighed and snuggled up to him under the covers. "I'm sorry, I know it was stupid, but . . . it saved Baruch. I told Hanan ben Hanan I was *niddah*."

"But you are not."

"He doesn't know that," Rivka said. "He thinks he's unclean."

"He can immerse and come back within the hour," Ari said.

Rivka shook her head. "He could if he played by the Pharisee rules. But the Sadducees don't recognize the *tevul yom* rule. According to them, if you're unclean, you have to immerse, but you're still unclean until evening. I got the idea from a Talmudic story about somebody who spit on the high priest." She bit her lip. "I also cursed Hanan."

Ari's heart flip-flopped. "Cursed him?"

"I told him when he's going to die. I'm sorry." Rivka buried her face in his beard. "Ari, I'm scared. Now he'll be after you and me like a mad dog."

Ari stroked her hair gently. "All is in the hands of HaShem. What can Hanan ben Hanan do to us? If he kills me . . ." Ari felt a rush of heat in his heart. "I have seen the World to Come. Hanan ben Hanan is a fool if he thinks to punish me by sending me there."

Rivka gave a deep sigh and her breath tickled Ari's neck. "I don't want to die . . . not yet. I don't think HaShem wants us to die, either. He put us here to live."

"Of course." Ari caressed her cheek. "But one cannot live if one is afraid always of dying. I meant only that I am not afraid of Hanan ben Hanan."

"I think he's afraid of you." Rivka pulled back her head and looked into Ari's eyes. "He's terrified of this monster named Kazan. He won't rest until you're dead. And if that means killing me and Racheleh, he won't hesitate for a second."

Ari shivered. It was one thing not to fear his own death. But if Hanan ben Hanan touched his wife, his daughter ... "Tell me what is to happen next. Hanan will be ousted soon, but he is to come back to power when the war comes, yes?"

Rivka nodded. "Four years from now, he'll be named head of the provisional government. Your precious friends Eleazar and Yoseph are going to start a war, but it's people like Hanan ben Hanan who'll get the power."

Ari sighed. He did not know what to do about his friends. They were fools, of course, wishing to throw over the Romans, hoping to bring in the age of *Mashiach*. There would be no age of *Mashiach*, and instead they would bring destruction on themselves, the Temple, and this city of God, Jerusalem the Golden.

And he could do nothing to prevent it. Yes, he had free will. No, he could not change the historical facts which he and Rivka had learned in a far country, growing up in the twentieth century, on the other side of the wormhole that brought them here. Now they were trapped, and nothing he could do would change the disaster to come. And yet he could act — must act — so as to minimize that disaster.

He would do what he could. HaShem had allowed him to live for just such a reason, to do one great thing. Ari did not know what that great thing might be, but he felt sure that it would be here in Jerusalem, that he would recognize it when he saw it. He would do that great thing gladly, and then he would go free. That was why he did not wish to leave yet. He owed a great debt to HaShem, and he would repay it at the cost of all. His own life. Rivka's. Even Rachel's.

A knock sounded at the door. "Brother Ari, are you well?" Baruch's voice.

"Come in, Brother Baruch," Ari said.

Baruch stepped in quietly, his eyes glowing in the light of an olive-oil lamp. "Brother Ari, Sister Rivka." He walked around to Ari's side of the bed and kissed him on the cheek. Then he leaned over further and kissed Rivka's forehead. Ari felt a little shock spasm through his body. Rivka had not been joking. Something had changed in Baruch. Radically.

Baruch knelt beside Ari. "How are your wounds?"

Ari pulled aside his covers. Long scars lashed his chest, but they were healing rapidly. "I will be well enough to stand in a few days."

Baruch nodded and looked straight at Rivka. "Sister Rivka, your heart is not right on the matter of Hanan ben Hanan." He put a hand on her cheek. "You will pray for him, please."

Ari stared at him. "Hanan ben Hanan tried to kill you an hour ago. He would kill all of us if he could."

"It is true." Baruch said. "Sister Rivka, you will pray for Hanan ben Hanan, yes?"

"Y–yes." A strangled whisper.

Ari cleared his throat. "Baruch, there is still the simple fact that Hanan ben Hanan will come back tonight to take you. You must go into hiding again."

Baruch shook his head. "The master of this palace, the man named Mattityahu, has sworn an oath not to give me into the hand of Hanan ben Hanan." He smiled at Rivka. "In the first place, he thinks that I have lost my wits in touching a *niddah* woman. In the second place, I prayed to HaShem just now for him in the matter of a fogginess in his left eye. It is healed."

Ari was not surprised. Baruch had great skill in healing. That was why Ari believed in HaShem — because he had seen Baruch do things that were not possible according to the laws of physics.

Baruch knelt beside the bed. "We will have nothing to fear from Hanan ben Hanan. Please, Sister Rivka, you will pray for him each morning and each evening."

"Why don't *you* pray for him?" Rivka said.

Ari also wondered this. Nobody could pray like Baruch.

Baruch merely smiled. "I have prayed many hours for Hanan ben Hanan. He is a man with much fear. But HaShem wishes that you especially, Sister Rivka, should pray for him also. Please do not ask me why. I am only the messenger."

Baruch had changed very much in the last three days. Ari liked this new Baruch even more than the old. "My brother, there is a matter of great importance which Rivka and I have been discussing. We need your advice."

Baruch closed his eyes. "Speak."

"War is coming," Ari said. "Within four years, men of violence will take control of this city. The Romans will come and destroy our people and our city and our Temple."

Baruch nodded. "Yeshua prophesied that a day would come when the Temple would be thrown down."

Ari did not think it required a prophet to see that evil was coming, but he did not wish to argue this point. "Before the evil day comes, we must leave. Rivka says that The Way is to leave the city and travel across the

Jordan to a new place, but she does not know when this is to happen. Please, you will ask HaShem."

Baruch stood up. "I will go inquire now." He went to the door and stepped out.

Ari felt a sense of peace wash through him. It was good to know a man such as —

Baruch strode back into the room, his face knotted with surprise. "Sister Rivka, HaShem says that you must ask this thing of him yourself."

Ari felt Rivka's body tense. "But I'm not a seer woman," she said. "Not a real one. All I know is what I've read in books. I'm a fraud."

Sorrow filled Baruch's eyes. "HaShem says that now you must become a seer woman in truth. No longer may you lean on your books. You must learn to look past the veil to the Other Side. A day is coming when many will stand or fall in Yisrael because of your hearing of the word of HaShem."

Ari gaped at Baruch. *Rivka? A real prophet?*

Baruch turned to Ari, and now there was steel in his eyes. "Brother Ari, I fear for you."

Ari felt a wave of cold run down his spine. Since when was Baruch afraid of anything?

"You think to walk together with the men of violence, and you do not know your hazard. These are the men who will bring destruction on the land, and they are your friends? No. What has good to do with evil?"

Ari frowned. "Brother Baruch — "

"There is another matter also." Deep pain filled Baruch's eyes. "You have been my friend now for five years, and still your heart is not right in the matter of Rabban Yeshua. You will pray on this matter, please."

"I — "

"You will pray on this matter, please." Baruch turned and went out.

Ari did not wish to pray on this matter. Baruch did not know what he asked. Ari conceded that Rabban Yeshua had been a good man, a prophet, a healer. A *tsaddik*.

But Ari would never believe Rabban Yeshua was HaShem, nor that he was *Mashiach*. Ari had grown up in the twentieth century. His grandparents had come through Auschwitz and Bergen-Belsen. But the camps were only the last chapter in a long tale of Christians murdering Jews. French Crusaders. Spanish inquisitors. Polish peasants. Italian Catholics. German Lutherans. Russian Orthodox. Killing Jews was an ecumenical enterprise.

For Ari to believe in Rabban Yeshua after so many centuries of murder — in the name of Jesus, under the sign of the cross — that would be an abomination, a desecration of those who died. A spasm of rage ran through Ari's frame. Never!

Baruch, a man of this century, could follow Rabban Yeshua.

But not Ari the Kazan. This was a simple matter of principle.

He would not do it to save his life, nor his wife, nor his daughter. If HaShem could not understand this, then he was not HaShem.

Rivka

Late that afternoon, Rivka walked in the courtyard with Hana, watching Dov and Rachel playing chase with Baruch. Baruch would stand quietly, pretending not to notice the children sneaking up behind him. At the last second, he bolted away. Rachel shrieked with glee. Dov shouted, "Abba!" Then they would do it all over again.

Hana's face wore a look of dreamy content. Not a flicker of fear on her face revealed that they were all prisoners in this palace, so long as Hanan ben Hanan ruled as high priest.

Rivka's mind was still buzzing from what Baruch had told her this morning. A long time ago, when she first came through the wormhole into this strange century, Rivka had been pretty sure of herself. Pretty sure HaShem had sent her to fix things up, to save the world.

And she'd spent the last five years learning that it just wasn't so. She wasn't God's solution to the problems of the world. She had gone running so far ahead of God that she'd lost her credibility. Nobody listened to her anymore.

Now, HaShem wanted her to go the prophet route? After she'd already ruined her good name? When every snotty little kid in the city pointed at her and shrieked, "Witch woman!"?

Rivka sighed. Great timing too. If she was pregnant now, wouldn't that just crack the camel's back?

Rivka looked at her friend. "Hana, I need help."

Hana raised an eyebrow.

Rivka hesitated. "Did Baruch tell you the word from HaShem that he gave me this morning?"

Hana smiled. "How wonderful, that you are to be a prophet! I am glad."

Rivka pursed her lips. "I don't know the first thing about being a prophet. I can't do it."

"If HaShem asks you to do a thing, then he will show you how."

Rivka sighed. Hana had an infuriating way of getting to the nub of the matter. "What he's asking is *dangerous*. People already think I'm a witch woman."

"In the arms of HaShem you will be safe wherever you go."

Right. In theory. In practice, Rivka wasn't very good at staying in the arms of HaShem. She shook her head impatiently. "It isn't going to work. I don't know how. If HaShem wants —"

"No." Hana's eyes pierced her. "Please, no more talking. Why must you always talk?"

"Listen to me —"

"No more. Be silent. It is your turn to listen." Hana folded her arms across her chest and glared at Rivka.

Rivka waited for several long seconds. "Well? I'm listening."

Hana shook her head. "You must learn to be silent and listen to HaShem."

"That's it?" Rivka stared at her. "Just sit there quietly and listen for a voice from heaven? I don't know how to do that."

"Then you must learn."

"You don't understand! I don't want to be a prophet."

Hana smiled. "Perhaps that is why you were chosen."

Rivka could not think of an answer to that. Apparently, she was going to be a prophet, whether she wanted to or not.

THREE

Ari

The next day, Ari felt strong enough to get out of bed. He sent his friend Gamaliel with Rivka's key to their house to fetch clothes for him. Rivka went off alone to try "listening to HaShem." Ari waited impatiently in bed, wondering what the day would bring. He did not think Hanan ben Hanan would return for Baruch. Evidently, Hanan had a spy in the palace. By now, he would know that Mattityahu had sworn an oath to protect Baruch. Hanan ben Hanan could not force Mattityahu to open the palace. Therefore, he would not risk losing honor by asking.

Ari threw back the covers and examined his body. Long scars lined his chest in parallel rows. They had healed almost completely — a miracle. Baruch's powers of healing had only increased since the terrible night last week. Rivka was right. Baruch had become a holy man, a *tsaddik*. His presence brought with it an electric freshness, like morning in summer when you are nine years old and there is no school and you have the whole day for marvelous adventures.

But Baruch had lost all sense of honor. Before, he had been overconcerned with his honor. Suddenly, he seemed to care nothing for it. Now, he would speak to a child or a man or a king in exactly the same way. He would kiss a woman in public as if she were a man. Such things were not done in Jerusalem. Only a *tsaddik* cared so little for his honor.

A loud knock on the wooden door interrupted Ari's thoughts. "Ari, my friend, may I come in?" Gamaliel's voice, cheerful as always.

Ari covered his body — Gamaliel, like any Jew, would be embarrassed by his nakedness. "Enter!" he shouted.

Gamaliel burst through the door carrying a stack of tunics. "I did not know what you would wish to wear, so I brought them all!" He dumped the armload on Ari's bed. A small wooden object tumbled out.

Ari snatched it up and hid it in his hand.

Gamaliel raised an eyebrow. "You keep a toy in your clothes?"

Ari shrugged. He had hidden it where Rivka would never find it, because her questions would be unbearable, but ... Gamaliel would not know the significance of the thing. Ari opened his fingers. Nestled in his hand lay a small cross made of olive wood. It was very thin, but carved with much ornamentation at each of the four ends. At the top was a small metal ring. As Ari understood it, Christians in America hung these small crosses on a tree at Christmas time. He did not know what a tree had to do with That Man, but of course he knew why a cross would be considered significant.

For him, this cross meant something else.

Gamaliel leaned in close to look at it. "What is it used for?" He poked a thick finger at the tiny ornament, which looked nothing like a real cross.

Ari closed his hand and pulled it away. Heat flooded his chest. "It is for remembering," he said in a thick voice. "It means much to me." He blinked rapidly several times.

Gamaliel straightened. "You will dress swiftly, please. Brother Eleazar and Brother Yoseph wish to speak with you on a matter of some importance." He crossed to the door and went out.

Ari slipped out of bed and began dressing. Sunlight streamed in from a window slit overhead. It must be already midmorning. He had been in bed for four days, and he felt stiff and sore. And lucky to be alive. No, not lucky. He had been chosen by HaShem. Chosen to do a task he did not yet know, a task to be revealed at the appointed time. Very well, he would wait. He pulled a scratchy wool tunic over his head and let it drop around him. The rough cloth caught at the scarred skin on his back. Ari tugged it down, wincing at the pain. Perhaps he would live with residual pain all his life. Better life in pain than none at all.

He selected a long linen cloth belt and wrapped it twice around his waist. Inside it, he hid the small ornamental cross. It was precious to him. He had treasured it for more than twenty years, but he had never shown it to Rivka.

Ari rummaged through the stack, found a pair of leather sandals, and slipped them on his feet. Now he was ready to face whatever Eleazar and Yoseph and Gamaliel had to tell him.

Yoseph's father had a room in his palace that he used as a library. Neat racks of acacia wood held many dozen scrolls. Ari's hands itched to look at some of these scrolls, but reading was not his business today.

Brother Eleazar sat on an ivory couch. Ivory! Yoseph's family must be fabulously wealthy, that they had a couch made of ivory. Eleazar was a massive man, as tall as Ari, but much more powerfully built. Ari had not seen a larger man in all Jerusalem, where the average man stood barely taller than Rivka. Eleazar's thick black beard billowed out from his face, a great mass of steel wool. Behind him stood Gamaliel and Yoseph, his two lieutenants, ready to do his will. Gamaliel was short and stocky and always grinning. Yoseph was taller, slim, aristocratic, with clever eyes that revealed a potent intellect. Ari knew from Rivka that one day, Yoseph would be the famous historian Josephus. But that was years in the future.

Eleazar's piercing black eyes studied Ari with keen interest. "You are recovered already, Ari the Kazan?"

Ari shrugged. "The prayers of a righteous man are powerful. Brother Baruch is a very righteous man."

Eleazar's eyes narrowed. "This man Baruch seems to me to lack sense. He is a child."

"Then perhaps we need more children," Ari said.

Eleazar leaned forward. "No, Ari the Kazan. We need *Mashiach*. We need *Mashiach* now."

It was so like something Ari's ultraorthodox stepfather would have said that Ari flinched. He had spent most of his life running away from such foolishness. But he could not run away from Eleazar, who was *sagan*, second in command of the Temple hierarchy. Eleazar was an aristocrat like Yoseph, and his father had once been high priest.

"Do you disagree?" Eleazar's eyes probed Ari. He stood up, filling the room with his massive presence. He was as tall as Ari, but outweighed him by at least fifty kilos, all muscle.

There was something frightening in Eleazar. He seemed to wear danger all about him, like a suit of armor. Ari had always felt a little discomfited by him. But not today. After standing before HaShem, Ari would never fear any man again.

Eleazar took a step toward Ari. "My friend, I have asked you many times and you have never yet answered me. Now let me speak plainly. The revealing of *Mashiach* depends on you."

Revealing? Ari wondered if he had missed something these last five years. Eleazar had often spoken of the *coming* of *Mashiach*. To speak of *revealing* implied that *Mashiach* was already here, but hidden.

Hidden in plain sight.

The thought hit Ari like a thunderbolt. Eleazar intended to be *Mashiach*. That was the only explanation. That fit with what Rivka had told of Eleazar's future actions. It fit with his machinations in the past. And it fit with his impatience now.

It did not make sense. Eleazar was a priest, and therefore of the tribe of Levi, whereas *Mashiach* would come of the tribe of Judah, the House of David. Eleazar could not be *Mashiach*, and yet clearly he meant to be. No doubt, Yoseph's fine lawyering mind would find a way to interpret the prophecies as needed. Ari had seen enough of the messianics, both now and in the future, both Christians and Jews, to know that facts were of small consequence when a determined man wished to see a prophecy fulfilled.

Eleazar's eyes suddenly glowed hot. "So!" He rubbed his enormous hands together. "You understand us at last!" He turned to Gamaliel and Yoseph. "Ari the Kazan knows our secret. He understands." He returned to the ivory couch and sat down again. "So you will help us?"

Ari sighed, exasperated. This was *meshugah* — foolishness most profound. Helping Eleazar would not turn him into *Mashiach*. Nor would opposing him prevent him from destroying the nation. "What is it you wish me to do? There are yet four years before —" Ari clapped his hand to his mouth.

A hiss of astonishment filled the air. Brother Yoseph's face quivered with disappointment. "Yet four years? You know this from your woman? It is still four years until *Mashiach* comes?"

Ari saw that the three men were expecting *Mashiach* much sooner than that. They were children if they thought they could oppose Rome now. He closed his eyes and said nothing.

Ari heard excited whispering, but the only words he could catch were "seer woman" and "four years." He felt sick at heart.

"Ari the Kazan, you will help us then?" Eleazar's voice, deep, booming, an irresistible force in the small room.

Ari said nothing. If he helped these children, he could not take Rivka away to a safe place.

"I will tell you a tale," Eleazar said. "Then you will understand my rage. Once there was a small boy. So young that he did not know better than to mock a Roman soldier in the street. The soldier caught the boy. Did he scold him? Did he beat him?" Eleazar's voice quivered with fury. "No, he did not. He cut off the boy's ear and threw it in the street. The boy was of a priestly family, and he grew up to be a brilliant man, Hizqiyahu by name. Have you heard of this man?"

Ari shook his head. A great lump had grown in his throat and he could not speak.

"He is my uncle, my father's brother. He should have been high priest, but he is unfitted to serve in the Temple of the living God. Why? Because a filthy Roman *mamzer* violated him. A man without an ear cannot serve as a priest. My father, who is a fool, cares nothing of the matter. When I was a boy, my uncle showed me this ear. And I swore that I would one day avenge my family, that I would exact retribution from the dogs who violate our land." Eleazar pointed to Yoseph. "Now you will tell Ari the Kazan your tale of rage."

Yoseph's eyes turned hard and bright. "When I was a young man, in the sixteenth year of my age, I was a Torah student studying with Rabbi Yeshua ben Gamaliel, the greatest of the Sadducee teachers. Do you know of this man?"

Ari nodded. "He is allied with Hanan ben Hanan, and he sat on the tribunal that condemned me to be flogged."

Yoseph's hard face softened. "Then you will understand my tale. There came a night when we studied together and he was summoned to a council meeting. He brought me also, and there I saw a sight I do not wish to see again. A Jewish man, a bandit, so-called. He was captured by Jews and flogged and handed over to the Romans to be killed. His name was Eleazar ben Dinai, and his crime was avenging the death of certain Jewish pilgrims slaughtered on the way to Jerusalem for *Pesach*. I saw then that our fathers are in league with the Great *Zonah*."

"The great . . . what?" Ari said.

"The Great *Zonah* — the whore of Babylon," Yoseph said. "Rome."

"I see." Ari did not see at all.

Yoseph gave a deferential nod to Eleazar. "That same night, I met Brother Eleazar, and he showed me a way that is better than the ways of our fathers. The way of retribution."

Eleazar nodded to Gamaliel. "You will tell Ari the Kazan your tale of rage."

Gamaliel flexed his large and powerful hands. "Three days before I became a man, I was in the Temple with my father. By an evil misfortune, we saw a vile deed. A Roman soldier, standing guard on the portico roofs, exposed his nakedness and turned his hind parts to the Temple and made a disrespectful noise. The people cried out and made a riot, and the soldiers attacked us, and many ten thousand of our brothers were crushed in the press at the gates."

Something seemed to be squeezing in on Ari's lungs. He fought to breathe. "And your father . . . ?"

"My father was trampled and he died." Gamaliel blinked twice. "I swore to exact retribution on the man . . . on the great Dragon."

An uneasy silence passed between Gamaliel and Yoseph and Eleazar. Ari wondered what Gamaliel had intended to say.

"And so he joined us," Brother Eleazar said. "And all the forty men in our brotherhood, the Sons of Righteous Priests, have such a tale. There are many like us in Jerusalem. Ari the Kazan, we are men of zeal, awaiting *Mashiach*. He is coming and then the Dragon will be slain. We will need weapons such as Rome uses, machines of war. You are skilled in matters of machines. You will help us."

Ari's brain was buzzing. Of course he must refuse. It was foolishness to battle Rome. A band of zealous young men stood no chance against hardened legions. He could not dissuade them from this foolishness, but he could not join them either.

And yet . . .

Ari looked again at Gamaliel, whose father was murdered by Romans. Felt a righteous anger bubbling up in his heart. Turned and stumbled toward the door, fumbling through a haze that clouded his vision.

"Ari the Kazan, you will think on it?"

Ari staggered out and slammed the door. Rage welled up from a deep abyss in his soul. He would not help these children in their foolish quest for retribution. Never. But if he did . . .

If he did, HaShem would understand.

Gamaliel

The door slammed. Gamaliel flinched. He had been certain that Ari the Kazan would be persuaded by his story.

"He wishes to join us," Brother Eleazar said.

Brother Yoseph began pacing. "He needs a reason. We must put him in our debt."

Gamaliel thought that Ari the Kazan had every reason he needed already.

"We must have him," Brother Eleazar said. "He is worth ten thousand ordinary men. With the weapons he will build, an army will flock to us."

Gamaliel shook his head. "He is distracted, that is the problem. He will be caged in this palace so long as Hanan ben Hanan is high priest."

Brother Eleazar glowered. "My father says that King Agrippa has no intention to depose ben Hanan."

"Then we must persuade the king." Yoseph pointed a finger at Gamaliel. "You are a witness to what ben Hanan did. Will you testify?"

Gamaliel was mystified. "King Agrippa has heard already from the rabbis on the matter. If Rabbi Yohanan ben Zakkai and Rabbi Shimon ben Gamaliel could not convince him, then how will I?"

Brother Eleazar jumped up. "That fox Agrippa will not be persuaded by Jews. Therefore, he must be persuaded by Romans."

Gamaliel stared at him. "Romans? What Romans?"

"The new governor," Eleazar said. "We will persuade the rabbis to lead a delegation to him asking for justice. I am second in command under ben Hanan — therefore I cannot go. But you can, Brother Gamaliel. You will tell him what you saw, and the rabbis will appeal for justice. A Roman governor wishes first and always to be known for justice. He will force the issue with Agrippa."

"You want me . . ." Gamaliel swallowed back his fear. "You want me to testify against Hanan ben Hanan?"

Eleazar put a huge hand on Gamaliel's shoulder. "If the governor rules in our favor, then you will gain great honor. And if he rules against us, you will gain more honor. It is a rare man who spits in the eye of Hanan ben Hanan."

Gamaliel sat down and put his head in his hands, resting his elbows on his knees. Honor. Yes, there would be very great honor in this, if Hanan ben Hanan did not kill him. And Ari the Kazan would be much in his debt.

"I ask you as my brother to do this thing," said Brother Eleazar. "For me and for our brothers in that other city."

For five years, Gamaliel had known that someday Brother Eleazar would call in this debt. For the six brothers in Rome and the one who was dead. He could not deny it now. To deny Brother Eleazar would be to bring the blood-guilt back on his head.

Gamaliel sucked in his breath. "I . . . will testify against Hanan ben Hanan." A great wave of fear washed through him.

The tension in the room broke. Brother Eleazar began pacing, and when he spoke, there was triumph in his voice. "Brother Yoseph, you will meet with the rabbis and arrange a delegation. I will ask my father to send messengers to find out who will be the new governor and where we can find him. When Ari the Kazan is in our debt, then he will stop his foolish dithering."

"We have time," Brother Yoseph said. "The seer woman said four years."

"Four years is nothing." Brother Eleazar strode to the door and yanked it open. "We need Ari the Kazan now if *Mashiach* is to be revealed in four years."

Gamaliel sighed and stood up. The lots were cast, and now it remained to be seen if they would win or lose.

FOUR

Berenike

Berenike peered at her reflection in the polished brass mirror. Her features were dull and indistinct in the uncertain image. What a tragedy that she would never see her own beauty. But it could not be helped. She opened her poison chest and took out a small alabaster jar full of white arsenic powder. Berenike pinched a tiny amount between her fingers, dropped it into the crystal goblet of wine on her one-legged marble table, and stirred it gently.

When it was ready, she raised the goblet and drank it down in one long draft. It was a daily ritual that could save her life. She had raised her dosage high enough that she would be immune to an amount that would kill several strong men. It was a necessity for one born of royal blood. Arsenic was tasteless and readily available and it had killed more kings than the sword. If Papa had been more careful in his own dosage, he would still be alive, still be the Great King of Judea, Samaria, Galilee, and parts north.

And she would still have a chance to be Queen of All the Earth.

That was the dream Berenike had envisioned for herself since the age of five, when her father's best friend put a riddle to her and she solved it on the spot and discovered that she had a mind, a deep, subtle, conniving mind like Papa's. She was not an empty head like her mother.

Like her brother.

Berenike seized her goblet and flung it against the wall. It shattered into many ten thousand shards.

Even so, her life.

She would never be Queen of All the Earth now. Her marriage to King Polemon had failed and her foolish brother Agrippa — empty of mind, but male of body — now despised her. She hated him for despising her. And for ... that other thing he had done. On account of his sin, she had done a greater sin, destroying the child of her womb. For Agrippa's honor. So that she might someday be Queen of All the Earth.

Well, it was done, and her life was ruined, and every night was torment because of the evil dreams that clawed at her heart. And because of it, she would never rule.

HaShem was making an evil game with her. She would continue to play, with hope or without it, because one never knew what the dice might bring on the next roll.

Even HaShem could be beaten.

"Mistress?" Shlomi's voice, behind her.

Berenike turned and scowled at her. "What is it?"

"I heard a noise."

Berenike waved her arm at the wall. "Another goblet has thrown itself at the wall. You will see to it."

"Yes, mistress." An empty-headed reply from —

A loud pounding came from the door of Berenike's bedchamber.

Berenike gestured with her head toward the door. Shlomi went to answer. For a moment, she stepped outside and held a whispered conversation with someone. Shortly, she returned.

"Mistress, your brother the king sends word by his servant Andreas that you will come to see him at once."

Berenike did not wish to see her brother ever again. "Tell him no."

"Mistress, Andreas told me that you would say so. He said to give you this note." Shlomi held a scrap of papyrus out in a trembling hand.

Berenike snatched the papyrus and scowled at it. One word in Latin. *Albinus.*

A rush of excitement shot through Berenike's soul. Less than a week ago, the seer woman had predicted that Caesar would name a certain man to be the new governor, a man who would punish Agrippa for allowing Hanan ben Hanan to commit murder in the name of HaShem. Agrippa had laughed then, but he had marked the name, as had Berenike. It was a name neither of them had heard before — Lucceius Albinus.

Berenike began pacing. "Fetch my *palla* and put it on me. Quickly, quickly! We are going to speak with Agrippa."

Shlomi found the beautifully woven fine woolen outer garment and draped it over Berenike's shoulders.

Berenike's mind was already racing down a thousand corridors of the great maze that HaShem had set before her. The dice were thrown and had gone against Agrippa. Excellent! It was far too soon to see if the game would turn in her favor, but ... this was something. She could not work with nothing, but with this she could employ her wits.

Berenike went to the door and waited impatiently for Shlomi to open it. With a little luck, she might yet outplay that old fox, HaShem.

Agrippa handed the letter to Berenike and slumped onto a low couch.

Berenike scowled at him in disgust. Agrippa had the lean, aristocratic face and dazzling good looks of all the Herod men. But where Papa's eyes had been those of the fox, warm and clever, Agrippa's eyes were those of the wolf. Papa had wanted to be king so as to govern his people well. Agrippa wanted to be king so as to plunder the people.

He pointed at the letter in Berenike's hand. "Read."

Berenike held it up to the light and read it aloud. "Lucceius Albinus, procurator of Judea, to Marcus Julius Agrippa. I am informed by a delegation of ranking men from Jerusalem that one Ananus the son of Ananus, head priest appointed by you, has encroached on the rights given by Caesar to myself alone — namely, the right to put men to death. Why have you allowed this, fool? I will arrive in Jerusalem shortly and deal with this man Ananus. As for you, I intend to send a letter to Caesar regarding your incompetence before shipping closes for the winter. You will be permitted to make your defense when I arrive."

Berenike fought to repress a smile. "The seer woman spoke true."

Agrippa's eyes burned red with fear. "What else did the seer woman tell you?"

Berenike went to the window and looked down on the public square below. "Are you now ready to depose Hanan ben Hanan?"

Quick as a tiger, Agrippa was standing beside her. "What message did the seer woman give you for me?" He put a quivering hand on her shoulder.

She brushed off his hand as if it were a rat. "You will keep your claws off my person, fool. I told you to remove Hanan at once. And you said — "

"I know what I said. Now I concede that you were correct. This man Albinus exists. He will be here in a few days. What else did the seer woman tell you?"

Berenike enjoyed hearing him grovel. But she was not going to tell him this choice bit in exchange for nothing. He had treated her like a woman all her life. Now let him suffer. "I may tell you. I may not. It is of no consequence to me whether you know it or not."

"I can compel the seer woman to tell me."

Berenike laughed in his face. "And I can warn her to make up an idle tale. How would you ever know the difference?"

He glared at her. "What do you want?"

Was he such a fool? If he did not know what she wanted after thirty-four years of life together, then he could not be helped. Berenike turned away from him. "What are you going to do about Hanan ben Hanan? That is our immediate problem."

She realized at once that she had said more than she intended.

"*Our* problem?" Agrippa said. "You mean it is *my* problem."

"Of course." *Fool.*

He began pacing. "I will depose him at once and appoint a worthier man."

"And what excuse will you give for taking no action when you first heard of his crime?"

Agrippa's silence told her that he had not thought of this yet.

Berenike wanted to shriek. Papa would have thought of a dozen lies in the first instant she asked the question. Papa would have anticipated the question. He had been a real man, the most wonderful man in the world, a man worthy of the name Herod.

"What do you suggest?" The tone of Agrippa's voice told Berenike that he now realized the gravity of his situation. He was a client king of Caesar. If the governor wrote an ill report, then he would lose his kingdom.

"I suggest you allow me to discuss the matter with him."

Agrippa was sweating now. "What will you tell him?"

Berenike had a hundred ideas. It would take time to choose one that was suitable and develop it into a plan. "When you have named me as your co-regent, then I will tell you."

His eyes gleamed. "Do you think me a fool?"

Berenike smiled. "I think you are wise enough to know that half a throne is better than none." She spun on her heel and went to the door.

Agrippa's cold voice pursued her. "I did not give you leave to go."

Berenike laughed and marched out.

Hanan ben Hanan

Surrounded by six Temple guards — his personal bodyguards — Hanan ben Hanan threaded his way through the streets to the palace of King Agrippa. A messenger had come to the Temple shortly after midday bringing word that the king wished to see him on a matter of extreme importance. It could not wait until after the afternoon sacrifices.

Hanan was furious. The high priest of the living God should not be required to come and go at the whim of this half Jew, this son of a dog, this ... Herod. The Herods were scum, and Agrippa was the lowest of a long line. But fortunately, weak. The fool had no stomach for governance. Hanan would scorch him with the heat of his anger, and Agrippa would lie down and whimper like a dog.

The outer gate of Agrippa's palace was open to the plaza. Hanan's lead bodyguard announced him to the gatekeeper. "Hanan ben Hanan to see the king."

The gatekeeper sent a boy running into the palace. Moments later, Agrippa's chief of staff came out. He strode stiffly across the court and made a small nod with his head. "You will follow me." He spun around and marched away.

Leaving his bodyguards at the gate, Hanan followed. They went up several steps, through the marble-paved receiving room, and into the Hasmonean throne room, the room from which the Maccabean kings had ruled. Men whose feet Agrippa was not fit to slobber on.

Agrippa stood behind the throne with his back to Hanan. On the throne sat Agrippa's sister. Hanan's belly knotted. The woman dressed and acted like a Roman senator's wife. Which was to say, like a *zonah* — a whore. She was a vile woman and had no right to sit on this throne.

Hanan marched toward the throne, feeling the rage rise within him. He would tell this filth that he must control his sister —

"Hanan ben Hanan, you are deposed." Berenike stood up and walked out through a side door.

Without even looking at Hanan, Agrippa followed her.

Hanan gaped at them, feeling as if a great hole had been scooped out of his chest. Deposed from the high priesthood? By a *woman?* "Dogs!" he shouted at the door. "Filth!"

Agrippa's chief of staff stepped in front of him. "With respect, the king and queen have completed their business. You will leave now."

Hanan would have slapped the man, but he refused to soil himself by touching a *goy*. He stalked back out the way he had come. At the palace gate, he curtly ordered his bodyguards to take him back to the Temple. Then he remembered that he was no longer the high priest. His reign had lasted barely three months and now he was deposed.

A great, aching rage welled up in Hanan's chest. Three months. The curse of Kazan's woman, who called herself a seer woman. She had said three months, and now it was so. Fear wrapped a giant fist around Hanan's heart.

Kazan's woman had also put a curse of death on him. Seven years, she said, and he would die at the hand of an Edomite.

Hanan stopped. Since he was no longer high priest, these Temple guards were no longer under his command. Without these men to guard him, his life was at hazard in these very streets. Because of the dagger-men, who had killed his brother and many others.

The guards clustered around him, awaiting orders.

Hanan realized he had only one choice. "Home."

The group turned and began moving back uphill toward the upper city. Within an hour, all Jerusalem would know that Hanan ben Hanan, head of the great and mighty House of Hanan, had been deposed by a woman, after the curse of another woman.

Such affronts could not be forgotten. He would avenge himself. Not on the women. One did not take notice of acts of women. Women were nothing. Puppets.

Hanan ben Hanan would avenge himself on this fool Agrippa. And on Kazan. Vengeance on Agrippa would be simple justice.

Vengeance on Kazan would be . . . sweet.

FIVE

Berenike

Two days after Berenike deposed Hanan ben Hanan, the new governor Albinus arrived in Jerusalem. He promptly sent a message to King Agrippa that his presence was required instantly in Herod's Palace to answer for his inaction in the matter of Hanan ben Hanan.

Within an hour, Berenike and Agrippa stood outside the palace, surrounded by ten of their finest German bodyguards. Berenike could almost smell the fear that enshrouded her brother. She felt giddy with joy. The great game had begun and she was a player. At last.

Agrippa's chief of staff stepped forward and spoke to the gatekeeper in Greek. "King Agrippa and Queen Berenike to see the governor Lucceius Albinus at his request."

An honor guard of smartly dressed Roman soldiers already stood waiting for them in the courtyard, sweating in the bright noonday sun.

Agrippa saluted the soldiers Roman fashion, and the centurion returned his salute. The group of men turned as a unit and began marching into the heart of the great palace. Agrippa and Berenike followed, leaving their bodyguards at the gate.

Berenike had dressed carefully, in a green silk *chiton* of Greek manufacture. The tight sleeveless garment displayed her figure perfectly. She wore slippers cunningly woven with gold threads, showing off her fine feet and ankles. In her hair, a modest silver tiara.

Herod's Palace was enormous. The huge central courtyard was large enough to hold footraces like those at the Olympian Games, large enough to race chariots even. The entire court was paved in marble. A central fountain, surrounded by the best in Greek statues, filled Berenike's heart with delight. And desire. If she played her chances well, someday this palace would be hers. Now, it stood empty for nine parts of the year, housing the Roman governor on those few occasions when he came to visit from his headquarters in Caesarea.

The soldiers led them toward the north end of the courtyard, where the magnificent northern wing stood. It was roughly the size of her own palace, yet it was barely a fourth part of the buildings in this complex.

They walked up a series of low, broad marble steps and past a statue of a naked Zeus wrestling with some legendary beast. They continued through a receiving room large enough to hold two centuries of men, and entered the throne room of Herod the Great.

Lucceius Albinus sat on the great throne of Herod, eating grapes and scratching his nose. He was a thickly built man with a ruddy face and white eyebrows and no hair. He wore a cynical smile and had the eyes of a ferret. His toga bore the thin purple stripe of the equestrian class, and Berenike wished at once that Agrippa had not worn his toga displaying his broad purple senator's stripe. It was an ill moment to show up Albinus.

Albinus did not stand when they entered the room. By design or chance, Agrippa was now half a step behind Berenike. The centurion announced them. "King Agrippa and Queen Berenike to see the governor."

Berenike paced up the long white silk runner and stopped before the governor. His bulging eyes told her that she had chosen her costume well. With a slight bow of her head, she said in Greek, "Grace and peace to you, Excellency. It is a pleasure to meet you at last." She could feel Agrippa trembling beside her.

Albinus popped a grape in his mouth and chewed it languidly while studying her. He spit out the seeds on the silk runner. Finally he turned his eyes on Agrippa. "You will explain about the matter of this priest, this man Ananus. Why did you not punish him at once? I will not have such things again. If men are to be executed, it will be at my orders, not those of Jewish swine."

Agrippa stank of sweat now. He took a small step forward. "Excellency, of course you alone have the right of execution. As you may have heard, this man Ananus is insolent above all men, and very ruthless. Such insolence demanded a punishment fitting of his crime, and it required some time to think of one appropriate to the situation. My sister and co-regent, who is very clever and intelligent for a woman, finally suggested the perfect solution."

Albinus let his eyes stroll lazily down her body and then back up to her face. "So the tales are true that you have the mind of a philosopher in the body of a prostitute. What was the punishment you devised for this head priest, Ananus?"

Berenike swallowed her fury and gave the governor her most politic smile. "As you may know, pious men of Jerusalem do not speak to women, considering us beneath their dignity. So my brother the king summoned Ananus to our palace and allowed me to depose him. The streets have rung with songs of mockery since then. Ananus dares not show his face in the street, so great is his dishonor to be deposed by a woman."

Albinus pursed his lips and narrowed his eyes, studying her. "Your sister Drusilla must be a great beauty indeed if she exceeds you, as the rumors tell." He took another grape. "But I hear also that she is a fool, and I see that you are not." He spit the seeds on the floor.

Berenike wanted to strangle him. She favored him with a thin smile.

Albinus turned his eyes back on Agrippa. "I have heard reports of the meager tribute which my predecessor extracted from this province. Has there been a drought in Judea?"

Agrippa shook his head. "No, Excellency."

"Earthquake?"

"None, Excellency."

"Disaster?"

A pause. Berenike could almost hear the thought forming in Agrippa's mind that the only disaster in Judea was the Roman government.

"No, Excellency."

Albinus stood up and belched magnificently. "Then what?" he roared. "What is the difficulty with this people? A man does not accept the burdens of governing a people of ill renown without some hope of recompense. I am told that Festus had accumulated but a few silver talents for himself after three years in office! What insanity is this?" Albinus sat down and shoved another grape into his fat red face.

Agrippa was breathing hard now. Berenike put a hand on his arm and stepped forward. "Excellency, if I may be permitted to answer?"

He nodded at her curtly.

"There is a matter which we had intended to bring before you at your earliest convenience," Berenike said. "Governor Festus, who was a good man and governed well, came to Judea after it had suffered some six years of the most monstrous behavior by a man, Governor Felix — "

"I have heard of this Felix," Albinus said. "One of Caesar's freedmen?"

"No, but he was brother to one of them — Pallas." Berenike hesitated. Pallas was now out of power in Caesar's court, but he was still one of the two or three wealthiest men in the world, after a career of official thievery unlike any ever seen. When Pallas left office, it was stipulated by all that his books were officially balanced. That was the price of being rid of him, and well worth it.

A gleam came into the eyes of Albinus. "Pallas — now *there* was a man." He sighed deeply and leaned back into the great throne. "But you were telling of Felix."

Berenike realized at once that it was hopeless, but there was no way to back out now. "Governor Felix drew off more wealth than the province could bear, causing many of the peasants to fall into banditry. Now the countryside is overrun with thieves and it has not recovered. Governor Festus made some attempts to seize the bandits, but matters have only gotten worse."

Albinus's face turned a deeper shade of red. He leaned forward and jabbed a finger at Berenike. "You are telling me that this province is worthless? Old bones, picked over until nothing is left?"

Berenike felt a little thrill of relief. Good, he understood. "Yes, Excellency."

"But . . ." Albinus stood up and gestured at the magnificent palace surrounding them. "Judea was once wealthy, am I mistaken? Who built this palace? Your grandfather?"

"Great-grandfather," Berenike said. "Yes, Judea was once a fat land. But greedy men have picked it clean. Now there is little left, and much of that is stolen by bandits who — "

"Bandits." Albinus spit the word through clenched teeth.

"Excellency, if I may make a suggestion?" Berenike's heart was beating so hard she could see it pulsing through the thin fabric of her *chiton*.

"Say on." Albinus picked up another grape and glared at it with distaste.

Berenike could feel Agrippa tensing, but she did not care. "Judea could return to fruitfulness. Quickly," she added, though this was a lie. "It is a matter of capturing the bandits by whatever ruthless means comes to hand, restoring order in the province, and allowing the land to produce its bounty. Of course, there must be a short period in which the tribute is lessened — "

"Ruthless." Albinus leaned forward. "I like that."

Footsteps clattered outside on the marble steps in the grand receiving room. Berenike cringed to hear the iron cleats of a soldier's leather boots scraping the floor.

Albinus stood up and looked to the door. A centurion entered, anger scrawled across his face.

"What is the meaning of this?" Albinus bellowed.

The centurion strode down the silk runner, ruining it with his cleats. He saluted the governor and spoke in rapid Latin. "Excellency, a Jew was caught outside the walls of the palace shouting insults in the Hebrew language. We arrested him, but he refused to stop. Some of the soldiers say that he has an oracle, a *pythonic* spirit."

Albinus grunted and strode past Berenike and Agrippa toward the door.

Berenike seized Agrippa's arm. "Follow him." They hurried after the hulking Albinus into the receiving room and then outside into the afternoon sunshine.

A man dressed in rags stood in chains in the middle of a circle of soldiers. "A voice from the east!" he shouted in Aramaic. "A voice from the west!"

Berenike scowled. This man, Yeshua ben Hananyah, had been venting his foolishness on the city now for a week, and he refused to be silenced, day or night.

Albinus stopped before the man, then turned to Agrippa. "Translate. What is this fool shouting?"

Agrippa translated his words into Greek, then shook his head with an exasperated look. "Excellency, it is foolishness. The man is insane. He has been doing this for some days and will stop for no man."

"I am not just any man," Albinus said. "Tell him that Rome commands him to stop."

Agrippa shrugged and moved to the edge of the circle.

The man continued shouting. "A voice against the bridegroom and a voice against the bride!"

Agrippa put both hands to his mouth and shouted, "The governor of Rome commands you to be silent!"

"A voice from the west!" shouted the man.

"Silence!" Agrippa bellowed.

"A voice against this place!"

"The governor of Rome —"

"A voice against the Temple and a voice against the palace!"

Agrippa turned to the governor and raised his hands. "Excellency, you see —"

"A voice against the king and a voice against the queen, his consort!"

Berenike's head whipped around to stare at the man. Fury lashed her veins. Of course the soldiers and the governor would not understand this wicked tale, but if he was shouting this through the city . . . Sick rage cut through her. Agrippa had not touched her in many months. Nor would he, ever again. But rumors live forever, and who could outrun them?

"Flay him." Albinus pointed toward the palace gate. "Take him to the public square in front of the market and flay him there." He turned to Agrippa and Berenike and intensity lit up his eyes. "You will join me to enjoy the spectacle."

Not an invitation. Not a request.

A command.

Berenike did not like watching public floggings, not even with a Jewish whip. But a flaying—with a bone and metal-tipped Roman *flagrum*—that would leave her nauseous for days.

Agrippa nodded. "Of course, Excellency."

Berenike gritted her teeth.

The insane man continued to shout his mindless words as the group proceeded out through the gates and into the public square. Stone benches ringed the perimeter. Children played in the dust. Mothers sat and gossiped. Men stood in their own circles, chatting in the lazy autumn warmth. Heads turned all around the square as they approached.

"A voice from the north! A voice from the south!"

Berenike wanted to vomit.

The soldiers led the way to the far edge of the square. Two matrons sitting on a bench saw them coming and scurried away, their eyes white with fear. The soldiers stopped before the bench. One of them unchained the prisoner.

"A voice against this city!" shouted the man.

A soldier yanked at his ragged tunic. It ripped down the middle. He wore nothing underneath. "A voice against the bridegroom and against the bride!"

Another soldier took leather straps and bound them around the man's wrists. All the while he continued bellowing his absurd oracle. The soldier bound his arms to the bench. Another tied his ankles together, fastened the strap to a spike, and drove it into the hard ground.

"A voice against the king and his consort, the queen!"

"Flay him," said Albinus. "Ruthlessly."

"A voice against the Temple!"

A trained *lictor* stepped to one side of the man, shook the tangles out of his *flagrum*, and then swung it high overhead in a great circle. The lashes wrapped around the man's back. The embedded bits of bone and iron bit into his chest. Blood spurted to the ground.

"A voice . . . from the west!"

The *lictor* jerked on the *flagrum*, yanking out the embedded ends. More blood.

"A voice from the east!"

The *lictor* gathered his *flagrum* and made another stroke.

"A voice from the north!"

Berenike turned away. Behind her, Albinus stood, all his attention focused on the flaying. Smiling.

SIX

Rivka

Rivka set down Rachel in her bed and held her breath. At four years old, Rachel thought she was much too old to take an afternoon nap. But she was worn out from playing chase all morning with Baruch and Dov.

It felt strange to be back in her own home again. Rivka had gotten used to the exorbitant pleasures of living in Mattityahu's palace, a home that was almost civilized. She walked back downstairs and tried to think what to do first. Ari had gone to the market to buy some food. Maybe she should do some cleaning. They'd been gone for a full week and the house smelled musty.

She went through the house opening the wooden shutters at all the window slits. The afternoon breeze felt warm, with a hint of autumn. The days were getting shorter now and soon it would be cold at night.

Rivka went into her room and began putting away the stack of clothes she had brought back from Yoseph's palace. Ari had made a lumpy mess of his shelf, wedging everything in. Typical man. She dumped the whole stack on the bed and began refolding. Honestly, you'd think a guy who could design a crane —

Something small and brown leaped out from one of the tunics. Rivka screamed, thinking it was a mouse. It lay unmoving on the bed. A small olive-wood cross. She inspected it closely. No doubt about it. One of those cheap touristy things people from the States bought in Bethlehem and took home to put on their Christmas trees.

This one had a shiny, polished feel to it, like it had been rubbed smooth by the touch of many fingers. But where had it come from? They didn't *do* Christmas trees here in this city, this century.

Ari must have brought it with him through the wormhole. But why? It didn't make sense. No way would Ari Kazan, the great Christian-basher, carry around a *cross*. Rivka put it on Ari's pillow where he would find it. She finished folding his clothes, stretched out on her bed, and closed her eyes.

All right, HaShem. Baruch says I'm supposed to listen to you. Learn to hear your voice. I've been trying. And I hate to be rude, but you're not following through. It's been several days and so far I haven't even heard a dial tone. Are you there or not?

Rivka waited.

Nothing.

The ridiculous part was that there was nothing she could do to fix this problem. No AT&T guy she could call to come out and climb the telephone pole and make it all right. If she couldn't hear God, it was his fault. Or was it? Baruch had said HaShem wanted to talk to her. So was it her fault if she couldn't hear anything? Was she the one who was broken?

Or was the problem that she wasn't broken enough? An image formed in her mind. Baruch on his face in the dirt, kissing her feet. Which was just plain gross. Disgusting. Even she wouldn't kiss her feet.

Rivka put her hand over her mouth, nauseated. If she had to go around kissing people's feet, she was going to pass on the whole repenting thing. Kissing feet was Baruch's style. She would find her own way to repent. Something meaningful that —

The door downstairs clicked quietly open.

Rivka's heart jumped into orbit. If Hanan ben Hanan had sent somebody to get her and Rachel . . . Rivka jumped up and looked around for something heavy she could swing. Nothing. She rushed to the head of the stairs and collided with . . . Ari.

He held her tight, and she heard his heart pounding in his chest.

He sighed deeply. "Rivkaleh."

"What's the matter?" She leaned back and looked at his face.

Sorrow filled his eyes. "I was in the upper market buying food. They were flaying a man there — the man we saw in the Temple last week, the crazy man who shouted the woes to the Temple."

Rivka shuddered. Josephus had said something about that man. How Governor Albinus flayed him until his bones showed through his skin. How he showed no pain. How he lived another seven years, shouting his weird prophecy of doom.

Ari told her what he had seen. Deep pain etched his voice. He knew what it was to be flayed. "I would have brought him home with me," he finished, "but they took him back into Herod's Palace."

"And he never screamed at all?" Rivka could hardly believe that a man could endure that kind of pain in silence.

"He only shouted his strange oracle." Ari gripped her tight. "The new governor was watching it, the man called Albinus. He enjoyed the sight. He licked his lips when he saw the blood of a fellow man."

Rivka shut her eyes tight, wondering how anybody could be so evil. "Why don't you lie down? I'll get you a nice drink and you can relax for a little. It's been an awful day."

Ari kissed the top of her head and lurched to the bed.

Rivka turned to go downstairs, and heard the sharp hiss of his breath. She spun around and saw Ari scoop something off the pillow and stuff it into his belt. He looked at her, guilt written across his face.

Rivka took a deep breath. *What was that all about?*

Ari lay down on the bed and turned his face away from her.

Rivka went downstairs, found a clean stone cup, went to the pantry, lifted the top off a huge stone jar, and scooped up a cupful of beer. Her InterVarsity friends back in Berkeley would have a cow if they knew that Rivka Meyers had a vat of *beer* in her house. Rivka had quit worrying about the alcohol thing a long time ago. There wasn't any choice. The drinking water here simply wasn't safe unless you added in some beer or wine to kill the germs.

Rivka walked upstairs, checked that Rachel was still asleep, then went into their room.

Ari hadn't moved.

She knelt beside him. "Ari?"

He jumped as if she'd slid a knife into his back.

"Do you want some beer?"

He rolled over and downed it in one long draft. "Thank you." His voice sounded thick.

Rivka took the cup downstairs and put it on the kitchen table. She tip-toed back upstairs and lay on the bed beside Ari. Took his hands in hers. Snuggled up to him. "What's the cross about, Ari?"

His eyes gleamed in the half-darkness. "You would not understand."

"I want to understand."

Long silence.

"Is it about some girl? Somebody from your past?"

"Not a girl, no. My mother gave it to me." Ari blinked rapidly. "On the day of my *bar mitzvah*."

Rivka waited. "And?"

Ari gave a deep sigh and rolled onto his back. "When I was very young — younger than Rachel, my mother and I lived together in Haifa with my father. He was a tall man with a very neat beard. He smelled much of tobacco. I do not remember more of him."

Rivka had never heard Ari talk about his real father. Every time she had asked about him, Ari changed the subject. She put a hand on his chest. His heart was pounding.

"He was in the reserves, like every Israeli. That year, he drew duty in Bethlehem in the week before Christmas." Ari stopped, swallowed hard. "It was quiet that year. Very safe. In those days, Christians still outnumbered Muslims in Bethlehem. You knew this, yes?"

"Yes."

"There was an incident." Ari put his hand on Rivka's and gripped hard. Two tears formed at the corners of his eyes. "It was never established how it happened, but a gang of young Palestinians caught him alone. Arab Christians. They disarmed him and . . ."

Rivka found that she had stopped breathing. She forced her lungs to draw breath. "I'm so sorry."

"They kicked him to death in an alley. They stomped in his face, on his body. They . . ." Ari fished the small wooden cross out of his belt. "They forced this halfway down his throat. It was found in the autopsy. The doctors gave it to my mother."

Rivka was staring at him, feeling deep horror inside her. Rage. "And so she gave it to you."

"So that I would never forget what Christians do to Jews. What they have done to Jews for two thousand years."

Rivka was weeping now, weeping because she was finally beginning to understand.

"My mother's parents survived the Holocaust," Ari said. "Her father was liberated from Auschwitz, weighing forty kilos. Her mother came out of Bergen-Belsen. They made *aliyah* after the war. To Israel, to a homeland where Christians would not send mobs to murder and burn on Easter, on Christmas. To Israel, where a Jew could be a Jew without fear. To a land free of the blood curse."

"The blood curse?"

Ari closed his eyes. "It is a thing written in the Christian Bible. It was preached in Europe for many hundred years. The priests would gather the whole city into the cathedral at Easter. They would bring the Jews of the city to sit on the front row, wearing dunce hats. Then the bishop would preach about how the Jews gave Jesus a crown of thorns. How the Jews flayed Jesus. How the Jews murdered Jesus." Ari's voice cracked.

Rivka did not trust herself to say a word. She had heard all this before and yet she had never heard it. Not like this.

"The bishop would tell how the Roman governor offered Jesus back to the people. Would they take him free? No. The Jews shouted that he must be crucified, that his blood must be on them and their children to all generations. This is the blood curse. It is in the New Testament. It was repeated for many hundred years at the famous play in Oberammergau. It is the reason that a Jew who hears the words *Christ-killer* knows to run first and ask questions later. It is the reason Christians killed my father. Because he killed Jesus. Because he, personally, murdered God."

Ari held up the tiny cross. "The cross is the blood curse and the blood curse is the cross. My mother gave this to me to remind me that a Jew must never forget that he is safe nowhere, not even in his own land, his own city, his own home."

Rivka was crying so hard she could not see. She smeared the sleeve of her tunic across her eyes and pulled herself up so that she was kneeling on the bed beside Ari. She put her face on his chest and just wept. "I . . . I'm so sorry. I didn't know. No, that's not true. I read *Exodus*. I read *The Source*. I must have read twenty books about Christian anti-Semitism. But it all seemed so . . . far away. So medieval. Another galaxy. I'm sorry. Will you . . . forgive me for not listening to you? For just blowing it off like it was just a little religious tiff? For not understanding what the cross means to you?"

Ari's big hands patted her softly on the head, stroking her hair gently. "Yes, I forgive you. Only . . . never forget. Never, ever forget, please."

Rivka lifted her bleary face and fumbled with Ari's hand. She folded back his fingers. Pulled out the small wooden cross.

Kissed it.

"I won't forget. Ever again."

Hanan ben Hanan

Late at night, ten Roman soldiers came to Hanan's palace with a message from Governor Albinus. When Hanan's steward showed them into his receiving room, they calmly informed him that his presence was required by the governor at Herod's Palace.

Immediately.

Hanan realized at once that he was a dead man. Albinus had sent him a threatening letter while on the road from Egypt. Now the governor meant to make good on it. Hanan knew he could not fight the soldiers. He had no Temple guards anymore. The governor would kill him, and few would mourn him. He asked permission to kiss his eleven-year-old daughter. The soldiers granted this request.

Hanan went to her room. Sarah was asleep. He kissed her head. She did not stir. He came back out. The soldiers led him outside. At the door, Hanan's steward hovered, anxiety on his face.

"A secret meeting," Hanan said. "I will return shortly. Tell no one of it." The steward nodded. Perhaps he even believed this lie.

Hanan strode out into the night. He steeled himself for his ordeal. Kazan's woman was wrong. He would not live another seven years. Tonight he would go to the long sleep of his fathers, to rest forever in the outer darkness of the grave. A Sadducee did not believe in an afterlife. Angels, demons, souls, spirits, pah! Pharisee foolishness. Torah said nothing of Paradise or Gehenna.

They marched through the dark streets without a torch. The month was nearly ended, so there would be no moon until near dawn. The stars lit the way. They walked north to the upper market, then turned west to Herod's Palace. The governor had flayed a man here today — that foolish man who cursed the Temple at *Sukkot*. Hanan's insides quivered at the thought that he would endure such a punishment also. As he had done to Kazan, so it would be done to him. He would not cry out nor beg for mercy.

The main gates of Herod's Palace were shut, but the men entered through the heavy iron door next to it. The governor was staying in the palatial residences on the west side of the compound, in the great edifice that butted up against the city walls. The soldiers marched rapidly across the broad outer court and through the doors into the main receiving room. They led Hanan into a large side office. The governor reclined on a long low couch. Before him was a marble table with an assortment of vile foods, unclean meats of the *goyim*.

The governor pointed to a couch. "I am told your Greek is excellent. Recline with me here. I wish to discuss a matter with you frankly."

Hanan gaped at him, then lowered himself onto the couch.

The governor waved the soldiers out of the room. "Be ready when I ring for you."

Hanan's heart slowed to a gallop.

The door shut behind the soldiers. Hanan and Albinus were alone.

The governor pointed to the table. "Eat, if you like."

Hanan shook his head. He would not defile himself with the food of a *goy*. "Thank you, Excellency."

"I have heard tale of you from the king and queen." Governor Albinus cut a slice of a small roasted bird of a type Hanan did not recognize and popped it into his mouth.

Hanan bristled. "The king is a weakling and his sister is a whore."

"They say you are ruthless." Albinus leaned forward, his eyes gleaming.

Hanan did not know what to say, so he said nothing.

"It is said you killed a man with your own hands." Admiration shone on Albinus's face.

Hanan felt a shock run through his body. "Who told you that?"

Albinus smiled. "An eyewitness. He saw you push the man into the stoning pit when the nerve of your executioners failed."

An eyewitness? Impossible! Hanan's throat felt painfully dry. "Which eyewitness?"

"One of your Temple guards." Albinus took a handful of raisins and shoveled them into his mouth. "A very short man with a large head and an honest look to him. On account of his testimony, I ordered King Agrippa to put you out of your office."

Hanan fought to show no reaction, but his heart pulsed with fury. The description could fit only one man. Gamaliel ben Levi had testified against him. Had disgraced him. But Gamaliel was a nobody. He would not have testified without a powerful backer. That could only be Eleazar ben Hananyah, leader of the Sons of Righteous Priests.

"I am informed that Judea is overrun with bandits," Albinus said. "What do you know of this?"

"It is the fault of Governor Felix," Hanan said. "He strangled the countryside for his own profit, driving the people to banditry."

"I mean to rid Judea of bandits." Albinus took a small bite of a melon, made a face, and spit it on the floor. "And I mean to do it quickly. You know this people and this country. I want you to make a plan. Some ruse to allow me to capture many bandits. A ruthless plan that will terrify the whole country."

Hanan narrowed his eyes. Why should he help this disgusting corpse of a man?

Albinus gave him a cruel smile. "Do this and you will be reimbursed fairly for your efforts. And I will not send you to Caesar in chains as you rightly deserve. Nor will I be forced to extract this year's tribute from the Temple treasury."

Hanan said nothing.

Albinus popped a candied fig in his mouth. "It would be a pity to have you flayed and your young daughter sold as a slave, do you agree?"

"Yes, Excellency."

"I will be here in this miserable city for three more days. Before I leave, you will devise a plan for me." Albinus picked up a bronze handbell and raised an inquiring eye at Hanan.

"Yes, Excellency."

Albinus rang. The soldiers came back into the room. One of them carried a *flagrum*.

"You will escort this man Ananus back to his palace," Albinus said. "He has been most pleasant and cooperative."

On the way back to his palace, Hanan's mind spun furiously. He must devise a plan that could never be traced back to him. It must capture as many bandits as possible. It must enrage the people against the bandits, not against Rome or the Temple.

And if it could be contrived to entrap Kazan and the Sons of Righteous Priests, so much the better.

Ari

Y ou wished to speak with me, Ari the Kazan?"

Dawn was breaking on *Shabbat* morning, and Ari had been dreading this moment all week. The early-morning prayers were ended and now men were speaking together in small clusters all around the synagogue. Ari was watching Baruch pray for a cyst on Brother Yonatan's eye, when he heard the voice of Shimon ben Klopas at his elbow.

Ari turned to look at him. Shimon was a gray-bearded man, thin from much fasting, with a quick step and a straight back. He lived in Magdala, a town on the Sea of Galilee, where he was a leader of the followers of Rabban Yeshua. Just as Rivka had predicted, the brothers of The Way had decided that Shimon must come and live here in Jerusalem as replacement for Yaakov the *tsaddik*. Ari knew Shimon to be honest, pious, serious of heart, with a good intellect. A fine man, though not a *tsaddik*. Earlier this week, Ari had passed word through a friend that he wished to speak with Shimon on a matter of high importance.

Ari bowed his head slightly. "My father, yes, there is a thing I must ask you privately."

Shimon pointed toward the door. "Please, you will follow me."

Ari followed, wondering how to explain himself. Too soon, they were outside in the street, alone in the chilly dawn. Shimon gave him a warm smile. "What is it, my son?"

Ari rubbed his damp palms on his tunic. "My father, you may have heard tale of my woman. HaShem has given her knowledge of some things that are yet future."

Shimon nodded sagely. "I have heard of Rivka the Kazan. Some say she is a seer woman and some say she is not."

"She sees some things darkly and some clearly," Ari said. "She foresaw the murder of Yaakov the *tsaddik*."

"She saw this darkly or clearly?"

"Clearly."

Shimon gave him a shrewd look. "And yet she could not prevent it."

Ari shook his head. "It was not a thing that could be prevented. Yet there is a greater hazard that can be prevented, and she asks me to warn you of it."

"She knows this darkly or clearly?"

"Clearly. I myself also have some knowledge of the matter, but I know it only darkly." Ari sketched out the course of the next few years. Evil governors would suck out Judea's marrow. Drought would shrivel the province. Rome would burn in a great fire. A Roman governor named Florus would arise, more evil than the others, too harsh to be endured. The city would rise in revolt. Then death, destruction, defeat. The Temple would burn and the people be killed or enslaved.

"How long until this happens?" Shimon said.

"Not four years before our people will rise against Rome. Not eight years before the Temple burns."

Shimon's face had gone chalky pale. "She knows this clearly? All of it?"

"Yes, just as she knew clearly a week ago that you would be chosen to lead us here. She asked me then to speak with you."

"And we may prevent these great disasters?"

"No, my father. We may only choose whether to die in them or to escape to another place. My woman says that you are to lead the people to safety, to a place called Pella, across the Jordan."

"She knows this clearly or darkly?"

"Clearly."

Shimon began pacing in the street. Ari had not expected Shimon to like this news. He had only just arrived in the city, and now he was expected to persuade many hundred people to leave? A man required years to build authority for such a move.

After some time, men began coming out of the synagogue in twos and threes. Baruch strode out. "Brother Ari! Blessed be HaShem! Our brother Yonatan is restored."

Ari gave him a weak smile.

Shimon stopped pacing. "When does your woman say we are to leave?"

Ari shrugged. "That is yet dark to her. Brother Baruch had a word from HaShem that Rivka will receive a prophetic word when the time comes. She believes we must leave soon."

Shimon gave an impatient sigh. "You ask much. I have heard rumor of your woman. She is quick to give warnings, and always she is off the mark."

Ari did not know what to say. Shimon had heard true.

"I knew Rabban Yeshua in the flesh," Shimon said. "He was my cousin and he told me things in private that I have never told to another."

Ari looked at him sharply.

Shimon put a thin, strong hand on Ari's shoulder. "I will not tell you these things, except to say this — that your woman knows clearly of matters that Rabban Yeshua told me thirty years ago. I am no prophet and the thing is dark to me. I do not know the day or hour. When your woman hears this clearly from HaShem, then you will bring her to me and I will do what I can. Only not soon, please. *Shabbat shalom!*"

Ari bowed slightly. "As you say. *Shabbat shalom!*"

Baruch tugged on Ari's sleeve. "Come, Brother Ari. I wish to know more of this man Riemann and his strange geometry."

Ari joined Baruch and they walked home together discussing Riemannian geometry. He found it a great challenge to explain without using tensor calculus. Baruch was not at all satisfied when they came to the splitting of their ways. "You must explain it again tomorrow," he said.

Ari trudged home. Rivka would be displeased to hear that Shimon would not soon agree to leave the city. He unlocked his door with a clumsy iron key and climbed the stairs.

Rivka was still in bed, which was not usual for her.

Ari knelt by the bed. "I have some good news and some not so good. Shimon agrees to meet with you, but only when you know the time clearly that our people are to leave the city."

Rivka rolled away from him. "Don't touch me."

A rock formed in Ari's heart. "Are you sick?"

"I started bleeding this morning," Rivka said. "I'm *niddah.*"

Ari stared at her. "Then you are not pregnant."

"Thanks be to HaShem." Rivka gave him a dazzling smile. "I've been so scared all week. We dodged a bullet."

Ari did not know whether to be happy or sad. He did not wish to take Rivka away from Jerusalem.

But he had wanted a son so very much.

PART TWO

MEN OF VIOLENCE

Summer, A.D. 63

In those times many will stand against the King of the South,
And men of violence among your people will rebel
To make the vision stand
But they will fail.

— Daniel 11:14, author's paraphrase

From the days of John the Baptizer until now
The Kingdom of Heaven has suffered violence
And men of violence lay hold of it.

— Rabban Yeshua, Matthew 11:12, author's paraphrase

SEVEN

Rivka

For seven months, Rivka tried everything she could think of to learn to hear from HaShem. Nothing happened, and anxiety gnawed at her heart with each passing month. She desperately wanted to leave Jerusalem. She wanted even more desperately to be obedient to HaShem. On a warm morning in late spring, Rivka strolled down the street with Rachel toward the house of Hana and Baruch.

Rachel clutched Rivka's hand with a chubby paw. "*Imma*, tell me again, why do we eat the feast of *Shavuot?*"

This was a ritual they went through before every feast. And for every feast but one, the answer was pretty much the same. As some wag once observed, all Jewish holidays celebrated the same three things — "Somebody tried to kill us. HaShem saved us. Let's eat!"

But this feast, *Shavuot*, was different. *Shavuot* was the feast Greeks called Pentecost, because it fell fifty days after *Pesach*. It had an agricultural significance — the beginning of the wheat harvest, seven weeks after the end of the barley harvest. And by tradition, *Shavuot* was the day when HaShem gave the Ten Commandments on Mount Sinai. Rabbinic Judaism would someday fix it to always fall on a Sunday. Not so in this century, at least not among the Pharisees, who controlled the majority view. They reckoned *Shavuot* to be on the fiftieth day following the first day of *Pesach*. Therefore, it could fall on any day of the week. This year it would fall on a Monday, the second day of the week. Tomorrow.

Which meant that today marked six years since Rivka had blundered through a wormhole into ancient Jerusalem. She had been awed then. Excited to see this ancient world. Eager to go back and get her videocam so she could do *research*.

It wasn't research now. She wasn't a tourist anymore. This place was home, this century was her life. She was still a stranger in a strange land, but she no longer felt homesick for California. No longer wished that God or the physicists or whoever would fix the wormhole. No longer thought that she was God's little avatar, sent in to save the day. She was —

"Witch woman!" A girl's voice.

Rivka turned to look. A little girl, maybe ten years old, stood pointing at her from the safety of a crowd of other girls. Rivka glared at them.

The girls ran away. By the time they disappeared around the corner, Rivka's heart was thumping in her chest and her eyes were blurring.

Rachel was looking up at her, big question marks filling her eyes.

Rivka pulled on Rachel's hand and began walking again, breathing deeply to calm herself. "So you tell me. Why do we eat the feast of *Shavuot?*"

"Somebody hates us, don't they *Imma?*"

Yes, for no reason except that some other person told them I'm a witch woman. Rivka bit her lip. "HaShem will protect us." She smiled at Rachel. "What shall we eat for the feast?"

"Uncle Baruch says we should pray for people who hate us."

Rivka looked down sharply at her daughter. Rachel was not yet five years old, but sometimes she said the most amazing things.

When they arrived at the house of Baruch and Hana, Rivka was still shaking. She touched the *mezuzah* and closed her eyes. In three years, just as the war broke out, those silly girls would probably be getting married. *May HaShem have mercy on them and protect them.*

Rachel banged on the wooden door with her tiny fist. "Dov! Open the door, Dov!"

Rivka heard Dov stampeding down the steps. The door flung inward.

"Rachel!" Dov threw his arms around her and kissed her cheek. "Aunt Rivka! Come and look! *Abba* is teaching me the arts of the scribe!"

Rivka bent down and gave him a hug. Dov was tall and stocky for a five year old, full of energy and unaware how strong he was. A tiny leather black box — an imitation *tefillin* — was strapped to his forehead. Not a real phylactery, since he was not yet a man. But he insisted on wearing one every waking hour, because Baruch did. He also wrapped little black linen straps on his left hand exactly like the real leather ones Baruch wore.

Dov turned around and raced up the stairs, bellowing, "*Abba!* Aunt Rivka and Racheleh have come! Show them what I wrote!"

Rivka stepped inside with Rachel, shut the door, and followed him up the stairs. Baruch stood at a tall wooden scribe's desk, copying a Torah scroll. Dov had a small desk next to it, identical in shape. A sheet of old parchment lay atop it, written over many times and scraped just as many. The surface had been rubbed smooth again with pumice. A small inkwell lay beside it, along with a tiny reed pen.

Dov snatched the leather sheet and held it up. "See what I wrote!"

Rivka studied the letters. The first was a recognizable *bet*. The second was a slightly sloppy *dalet*. Or maybe a *resh?* The third was a mangled *shin*. And the fourth was a very diseased-looking *tav*.

"How wonderful!" Rivka said. "Racheleh, look what Dov wrote! *B'reshit!* The first word of Torah!"

Rachel looked at Dov with adoring eyes. "Dov can write! Will you teach me to write, *Imma?*"

"Girls are not allowed to write," Dov said. "Are they, *Abba?*"

Baruch smiled. "Perhaps we should ask one. Sister Rivka, please, you will show Dov whether a woman may write."

Rivka picked up the pen, dipped it in the inkwell, and wrote, *Dov hu tov v'hu ohev Rachel.* "Read this for me, Dov."

Dov took the sheet and puzzled over the letters for a full minute, working out the words. "Dov . . . he is good . . . and he loves . . . Rachel!" He let out a whoop and began dancing around the room with Rachel, hollering something about how he would teach Rachel to read and then they would get married and have many sons.

Rivka turned to Baruch. "Where's Hana? She and I were going to go shopping for the feast."

"She went to fetch water." Baruch studied her. "You are troubled, Sister Rivka."

Rivka told him about the girls.

"You will pray for them, please."

"I did already," Rivka said. "Those poor little things. In a few years they'll be married, maybe pregnant — just when terrible things fall on the city."

A broad smile creased Baruch's beard. "I am glad that HaShem is speaking to you."

"Well . . . no." Rivka sighed. "I still don't hear a thing from him."

"You returned mercy to those foolish girls instead of rage. Therefore, you are most assuredly hearing the weeping of HaShem's heart. Soon you will hear his voice also. You have been praying for Hanan ben Hanan also, yes?"

Rivka said nothing.

"Rivkaleh?" Baruch studied her closely. "Please, you must pray for this man."

"He's evil." Rivka felt her heart pounding with rage.

"Therefore, you must pray for him. HaShem has told me that much depends on this."

"Why?" Rivka glared at him. "Why couldn't HaShem ask me for something easy? Like walking on water or raising the dead? I don't *want* to pray for Hanan ben Hanan."

"And therefore you must. If you truly wish to hear the voice of HaShem — "

Downstairs, Hana called out, "Baruch! Dov! There is news!"

"*Imma!*" Dov tore down the stairs. Rivka took Rachel's hand and followed him. Baruch came last.

Hana's face was shining. "I was at the outflowing of the aqueduct near the synagogue and I heard a wonderful thing."

Dov seized Rachel's hand and began jumping up and down, shouting, "A wonderful thing! A wonderful thing!"

Baruch pulled out short wooden stools and they all sat down around the one-legged stone kitchen table. "Please, you will tell us this wonderful thing, Hanaleh."

Hana's eyes shone with happiness. "There is a rich man who lives in Shushan, whose gold is as the sand of the seashore . . ."

Ari

There is a rich man who lives in Shushan, whose gold is as the sand of the seashore." Brother Eleazar held up a beautifully written letter.

Ari inspected the document, wondering what this was about, and why Eleazar had invited him to the synagogue of the Sons of Righteous Priests this evening. The letter was of the finest vellum parchment. Real gold had been mixed in the ink. A faint whiff of some wonderful scented oil clung to the leather. Ari looked around the synagogue at the shining faces. "We have rich men in Jerusalem."

"This man's name is Mordecai ben Hanina, and he will come to Jerusalem at the going out of the year, bringing many armed men and much gold to contribute to the Temple and to the comfort of the citizens of Jerusalem and to those who burn with zeal for the living God." Eleazar gave a significant nod around the room. "Mordecai ben Hanina writes to me, the captain of the Temple, asking for an honor guard to escort him from Jericho to Jerusalem one week before Rosh HaShanah. He asks also that any leading citizens, men of zeal, should accompany us."

Ari sighed and sat down on one of the wooden benches against the wall. So. Eleazar wished to annoy him once again with his talk of zeal. This was foolishness. But one did not tell Eleazar ben Hananyah, the *sagan*, the captain of the Temple, that he was a fool.

Eleazar began pacing. "We have yet time before we will require the machines of war. But you, Ari the Kazan, must begin giving thought to their construction now. We will need ballistas for throwing great stones. Also, catapults for firing great spears. The Romans have such machines. We will require better ones, along with means of neutralizing theirs."

Eleazar stopped in front of Ari. "You, my friend, are the key to such machines. Why do you hesitate? Do you love Rome?"

Ari shook his head. He hated the arrogant brutes who ruled his country. "Do you fear Rome?"

Ari swallowed a great knot in his throat. "No. I fear only HaShem."

"Then why do you delay?" Eleazar's black eyes glowed. "Yet three years until *Mashiach* comes, do you agree?"

Ari closed his eyes, wishing he had never let those words slip out.

"Why will you not come to our aid?" Eleazar demanded.

In Ari's mind's eye, he saw great flames spring up around the city. His city. Flames high and terrible, consuming all. Flames fed by the zeal of this man, Eleazar ben Hananyah.

Brother Yoseph murmured something.

Ari looked up and saw him speaking quietly in Eleazar's ear.

Eleazar nodded and began pacing again. "Ari the Kazan, Brother Yoseph reminds me that Mordecai ben Hanina is a man like yourself, born in a far country and very learned. He owns great riches. I ask you this, as a friend. Will you not go with us to Jericho to meet him?"

Ari had never been to Jericho. Not in this century, anyway. He had gone once, in the twentieth century, to see the site of the legendary victory, the first in the land of Canaan, three thousand years and more ago. As a boy, Ari had been something of an amateur archaeologist, following the exploits of Yigael Yadin, Meir ben Dov, Nachman Avigad.

Now he had an opportunity to see something none of those men ever had. In this century, Jews still lived in Jericho, one of the most ancient cities in the world. What harm could it do to go to Jericho and meet this rich man whose gold was as the sands of the seashore?

"Will you not come with us?" Eleazar asked again.

"I wish to go to Jericho with you."

Rivka

If you're going, I'm going." Rivka lay snuggled up with Ari late that night. "Jericho! Good grief, Ari, do you know how old that city is?"

"I know."

"I'm going." Rivka leaned up and nibbled on Ari's ear. "Tell me you're taking me."

Ari's forehead wrinkled. "I am puzzled on one point. Why does your Josephus say nothing of this man Mordecai ben Hanina?"

Rivka had given up trying to understand what was in Josephus and what wasn't. "Ask him thirty years from now when he writes *Antiquities of the Jews*. But while we're waiting for that, I want to go to Jericho and see this Mordecai. You're taking me, right?"

"Please, you will not antagonize Eleazar."

Rivka smiled. That was Ari's way of saying yes. "I'll be good. Who's going? Eleazar and his whole synagogue, right?"

"Yes, all."

"So I'll just avoid Eleazar. Everything will go fine." A horrible thought struck her. "Hanan ben Hanan isn't going, is he?"

Ari shook his head. "Hanan is much out of favor with the Temple authorities. The high priest would never allow Hanan to go on such business."

"Then everything will be perfect." Rivka's heart raced with glee. Jericho! "We'll take Rachel too. It'll be good for her to see the city."

"Rivkaleh, you have done as Baruch told you in the matter of Hanan ben Hanan?"

Rivka hesitated. "Baruch is asking an awful lot."

"I wish you to do as Baruch has asked you."

Rivka's heart spasmed. "I don't want to pray for that creep."

"Please, you will do as Baruch asked. It is a word from HaShem."

"Do *you* pray for Hanan ben Hanan?"

Ari's face twitched. "Baruch asked you specifically to do so."

Rivka knew she had scored a point. "I will if you will."

Ari's eyes narrowed and his whole body quivered. Rivka put her arms around him, letting her hands run over the long parallel grooves in his flesh where Hanan's men had flayed him. What kind of a horrible person was she, to ask a thing like that? "I'm sorry, that was cruel—"

"Very well," Ari said. "I will pray for this evil man. And you will also."

Something hot broke loose inside Rivka's belly.

Rage.

Rivka gasped. She had not realized until now just how *much* she hated Hanan. Now she had to pray for him.

It was going to be a very bad summer.

EIGHT

Ari

After *Shavuot* the full heat of summer bore down on Jerusalem. The city shriveled under the merciless sun. Because the second rains had failed in the spring, the barley harvest had been poor. The wheat harvest was likewise a disappointment. Jerusalem ran thick with rumors of the coming visitor, Mordecai ben Hanina. Such a visit had not been anticipated with so much fervor since the arrival of Queen Helena from Adiabene, twenty years ago during the drought. But this year the drought was harsher and the population greater and the need deeper.

Ari gave away many *dinars* in alms over the course of the summer, but he felt like a man who empties an ocean with a teacup. Two weeks before Rosh HaShanah, he took Rivka with him to the workshop of Shimon the stonecutter, one of the men in Gamaliel's synagogue. Ari had ordered an ossuary to be made, a stone bone-box. In just a few weeks, they would reach the one-year anniversary of the death of Yaakov the *tsaddik*. Then they would go to the burial cave where they had taken his body after his death and "gather his bones" into the ossuary. That would free up the scarce burial space in the cave for another body, and the ossuary could then be stacked with the many hundred others. It was a strange and bizarre solution to the problem of space. Many Jews, foreign and native, wished to be buried in this city of HaShem. But the city was growing, and therefore the available land for burial was shrinking.

Ari led Rivka into the shop. "Shimon, my friend!" He clasped hands with the thick-bearded artisan who had done many jobs for him around the city. "You will show my woman the bone-box, please."

Shimon hefted the box up onto a stone table. Ari studied the ossuary. It was half a meter long and constructed in the usual proportions of a coffin. The dimensions were chosen to just contain the longest bones in a man's body.

Rivka read the Aramaic inscription aloud. "Yaakov bar Yoseph." She looked disappointed. "That's awfully plain, don't you think?"

Ari raised his eyebrows at Shimon. "It is the custom, yes?"

Shimon nodded. "Yes, the custom. Is it not enough? I spent much time carving the rosettes."

Rivka shook her head. "It seems like it needs something more. There must be a hundred Yaakovs with fathers named Yoseph. Can't you be a little more unique? Something like, 'Yaakov bar Yoseph the *tsaddik*'?"

"It is Yaakov who was the *tsaddik*, not Yoseph," Ari said.

Shimon picked up his chisel and knelt beside the box. "It is nothing to add more words. The limestone is soft. What shall I carve?"

"Yaakov bar Yoseph, leader of The Way," Rivka said.

Shimon raised an eyebrow. "Ari the Kazan, it is you who are paying. Do you agree? What shall I add?"

Ari shrugged. "Brother of Yeshua." He looked at Rivka.

"Fine." A smile slid across her face. "Yes, that's perfect."

Shimon tapped out the letters. "*Akhui d'Yeshua*."

Ari peered at the inscription. "*Akhui*. That is a strange way to spell *brother*."

Shimon looked defensive. "It is the way I spell it."

"It's fine." Rivka tugged at Ari's arm. "Nobody's ever going to care if it's spelled a little funny."

Shimon put his hammer and chisel away on a shelf. Rivka knelt beside the inscription, putting her fingers on the freshly cut letters.

Ari took his purse out of his belt. "So then, Shimon! How much for this work of art?"

Shimon shrugged. "For you, my friend, one *dinar*."

Ari never bargained with his friends. "So little? You worked hard on the box."

"Half a day, no more," Shimon said.

Ari took out two *dinars* and pressed them into Shimon's hand. "A small gift then for you. You will buy something special for your woman next week when we go down to Jericho, yes?"

Ari heard Rivka gasp. He turned and saw a strange look on her pale and clammy face. Tears filled her eyes and she tilted her head to one side as though she were listening.

"Rivkaleh . . ." Ari could not think what to say. He had never seen Rivka looking like this before. So frightened. So distant.

So lost.

Rivka

Rivka stumbled blindly through the streets, clutching Ari's arm. Through a dense fog, she heard him saying her name, over and over. When they reached home, Ari carried her upstairs and put her on the bed. Rivka huddled into a knot.

Ari lay down beside her and held her in his arms. "Rivkaleh. What happened?"

Rivka fought for air. "I heard a voice."

Ari's arms tightened around her. "A voice? My voice?"

"No." Rivka shuddered. "I heard another voice. Not you. Not Shimon. Someone else. Talking about . . . a man who went down to Jericho." Cold fear filled her stomach.

"That was my voice," Ari said. "I was telling Shimon to buy something for his woman when he went down to Jericho."

Rivka flinched. She was hearing Ari's words. And something more. Something hollow and deep and immensely . . . old. Words behind Ari's words. Words from beyond the veil. Words from the Other Side.

Ari stroked her hair. "Rivkaleh, only rest."

Rivka rubbed her bleary eyes. "When I was looking at Yaakov's bonebox, I was thinking about him. And Hanan ben Hanan. So I said a little prayer for Hanan and then you said that thing about Jericho and I remembered a story Rabban Yeshua once told. A certain man went down to Jericho. Do you know that story, Ari?"

"Please, you will tell me."

Rivka shuddered again. "A certain man went down the road from Jerusalem toward Jericho. It is a steep road, lonely and dangerous. Bandits attacked the man, took all his money, and left him for dead. A priest came along and hurried past without helping."

"Rivka, nobody travels that road alone. It is too dangerous."

"It's just a story. An allegory. Yeshua had a point to make."

Ari said nothing.

"Then a Levite came by and he also hurried past without helping." Rivka felt her whole body tensing up. "And then a Samaritan came by and he helped the man. He put him on his donkey and took him to an inn and paid many *dinars* for his keep."

"A Samaritan?" Ari sounded skeptical. "That is not possible. Samaritans hate Jews."

"I told you, it's an allegory. In real life, the Samaritan would have kicked the Jew in the face and hurried on. And the Jew would have spit at the Samaritan." Rivka sighed. "When I heard the voice, I also saw something. I saw the body of Hanan ben Hanan lying in the road."

Ari's breathing rasped, harsh and heavy in the hot room.

"Ari, I finally understood that story. I finally put myself in it. You know how much I hate Hanan. Yeshua's point was that we have to treat our worst enemies as that Samaritan treated the Jew."

"And for this, you nearly fainted?"

"No, there's more." Rivka gathered her will and said the last thing she wanted to say. "I don't know how to explain it, but I'm not going to Jericho."

"But you were the one who—"

"I was wrong." Rivka sighed deeply. "I wanted to go see the sights. To see the Jericho where Joshua fought the battle. But there's death on that road."

"Death? Going which way?"

"I don't know." Rivka hugged him tight. "All I know is that I'm not going. Neither are you."

"I must go. I have given my word to go with Brother Eleazar and the Sons of Righteous Priests. They have made plans all summer and—"

"Ari, you're not going. Let *them* go. I could care less about Brother Eleazar. Let him get killed if he wants to. But you're not going. And you've got to talk Gamaliel out of it too. I don't want him to die."

"And what shall I tell him?"

"Tell him . . ." Rivka didn't want to say it, but there was nothing else. "Tell him I heard from HaShem."

"This is hearing from HaShem?" Ari's voice was laced with deep skepticism. "You hear my voice and see a picture in your mind's eye and recall a story of Rabban Yeshua, and from this you deduce . . . something else? Rivkaleh, with respect, this is not logical. This is not the way in which HaShem speaks to Baruch. It is not the way HaShem spoke to me."

Rivka didn't know what to say. Ari was right. It was all totally illogical.

But it was also the word of HaShem and she was not going to let Ari talk her out of it.

Ari

Do you think this word is from HaShem?" Ari asked. He and Baruch were on the way to the synagogue of The Way for the morning prayers. No hint of dawn yet painted the night sky.

"Brother Ari, you must obey this word." Baruch's voice sounded troubled.

"But it is not logical. There is no reason for it."

"HaShem always has a reason when he gives a word."

"So it *is* from HaShem?"

"I do not know." Baruch shook his head. "HaShem speaks in one way to me and in another way to another man. Why should he not speak in this strange way to Sister Rivka?"

"And what if she is wrong?"

Baruch shrugged. "Then she will learn humility and you will learn obedience. It is good to obey a prophet, whether she is right or no."

"Obey?" Ari stared at his friend. "Since when does a man of honor obey a woman?"

"Brother Ari, I think you concern yourself overmuch with honor."

Ari felt stung. This was foolishness. Brother Eleazar expected him to go to Jericho next week. Mordecai ben Hanina would be expecting to meet him. He would be a guest of honor.

Honor. Against honor, he had the word of a woman, who claimed that she now heard from HaShem. She was not in the custom of hearing from HaShem. She had never heard from HaShem until now.

Ari sighed. "Baruch, will you ask HaShem if he wills that I should go to Jericho?"

Baruch gave him a mysterious smile. "HaShem wills that you should listen to the voice of your woman."

"And if she is wrong?" Ari did not know which was worse — for Rivka to be right or for her to be wrong.

"Then she is wrong. But you will have obeyed the will of HaShem."

NINE

Rivka

I*mma*, someone is knocking at our door!"

Rivka sighed and opened her eyes. She had spent the last hour trying to hear from HaShem. She hadn't heard a thing. This was frustrating. A week had now passed since her vision or whatever it was. Ari was upset with her, and she was worried about that. Baruch would have to talk some sense into him.

But the important thing was that Ari had agreed not to go to Jericho with that horrible man Brother Eleazar.

"*Imma!*" Rachel tugged again at Rivka's sleeve. "I'm scared."

Rivka sighed and rolled off of her bed. She knelt beside Rachel and gave her a hug. "There's nothing to be afraid of, Racheleh. Let's go see who it is. Maybe Dov?"

Rachel clutched her hands. "It sounds like a big man, *Imma*."

Rivka went downstairs. Probably somebody looking for Ari. She unlatched the door and pulled it open.

Brother Eleazar's massive frame filled the doorway. The cords in his thick neck stood out. Sweat glistened on his forehead. His mouth was set in a straight, angry line.

"Oh!" Rivka gaped at him. Eleazar was *sagan* of the Temple, and she didn't know the proper way to address him. Finally she lowered her head submissively. "Ari the Kazan is not here. You will find him —"

"I did not come to speak to Ari the Kazan." Brother Eleazar's voice sounded thick with menace.

Rivka took a step backward, then jutted her chin at him. "I will not speak to you without my husband present." She began closing the door.

Eleazar slid an enormous foot forward, wedging it against the door.

She pushed on it. "Take your foot out of my door."

"You have poisoned the hearts of my men." Eleazar's voice came out in a low growl.

"What are you talking about?" Rivka pulled the door open a bit and then rammed it forward. "You will discuss the matter with my husband, please."

Eleazar punched the door with the flat of his hand. It rocketed inward. Rachel began wailing.

Eleazar leaned forward and his hot breath scorched Rivka's face. "Because of you, Ari the Kazan refuses to go to Jericho. Because of him, none of my men will go either. Now I will lose honor in the eyes of Mordecai ben Hanina and all Jerusalem."

Rivka felt hot all over and she could not seem to get air into her lungs. Honor! For honor, he was trying to steamroll her?

"Witch woman, you will change your foolish prediction and inform Ari the Kazan at once that you were wrong."

Rivka wiped her damp face with the sleeve of her tunic. "No. And don't you ever call me a witch woman again, you evil man."

Eleazar flinched as if she had slapped him. Rivka wondered if any woman had ever stood up to him before. His black eyes gleamed with rage. "Do you know that I have power — "

"I know how you will die," Rivka said. A preternatural calm fell over her. Eleazar had overstepped, and she was *not* going to let him bully her. "Shall I tell you?" A voice in her head was shouting, *no, no, no,* but she was too furious to pay attention. She jabbed a finger at him. "Shall I tell you the year and place of your death?"

Eleazar took a step back and uncertainty clouded his eyes.

"Get away from here and don't come back!" Rivka shouted.

"Zonah!" Eleazar spat at her feet. "You will pay for your insolence." He turned and strode away. When he reached the corner, he threw a glance back at her.

Rivka read fury in his eyes. And fear. She collapsed against the door frame, shaking. Her heart was thumping so hard in her chest she thought it might break loose. Rachel was crying inside the house.

Rivka put her hand on the *mezuzah* on the doorframe. *I'm sorry, Father — that was wrong. What have I done?*

"Imma! I'm afraid!" Rachel wailed.

Rivka stepped back into the house and shut the door. She had offended the second most powerful man in Jerusalem, that's what she had done. Wouldn't Ari be tickled pink when he heard about that?

Two days passed and nothing happened. Ari had apparently not heard about Eleazar's visit, because he said nothing. Rivka was afraid to tell him, afraid to tell even Hana, who would tell Baruch, who would tell Ari. She had blown it, made a mess of things, and she had no idea how to make amends. She spent much time praying, hoping to hear from HaShem.

She heard nothing.

Finally, on the third morning, after Ari went off to work at a construction site in the New City, Rivka decided to go ask Baruch what to do. She took Rachel by the hand and walked over to Baruch's house. It was now only a week before Rosh HaShanah. Excitement tingled in the air, the same excitement Rivka had felt years before in San Diego during the week before Christmas. It was a hot day in late summer. The blue sky hung cloudless overhead, a reminder of the drought that gripped Judea. In a month, the rains would come. Or so Rivka hoped, so she prayed. Most people in the city had a cistern in their house to catch rainwater. Virtually all of them were now dry and the city depended on water from the aqueducts and the Gihon spring.

A legless beggar lay in the street. Rivka rummaged in her belt and found a couple of *lepta*. She dropped them into his hand and stepped around him.

"*Imma*, why did HaShem create him without legs?" Rachel asked.

"Because." It was a stupid answer, but Rivka was feeling stupid today. She was fresh out of answers.

When they reached Baruch's house, Rivka didn't bother to knock. She pushed open the door and went in. "Hana?" she shouted. "Baruch?"

Hana was sitting at the table sewing a tunic for Dov. "Racheleh!" Dov shouted. "Come see what I wrote today." He seized her hand and led her upstairs, shouting, "*Abba!* Rachel wishes to see what I wrote!"

Rivka had never seen a boy with so much *life* in him. She sat down across from Hana.

"You are troubled." Hana continued pushing the bone needle through the thick unbleached wool cloth. "Please, you will tell me what troubles you."

A tread on the stair told her Baruch had come down.

Rivka told them about Eleazar.

Baruch paced back and forth while she talked, asking the occasional question. Had she heard anything further from HaShem on the matter of going to Jericho? What had Brother Ari told Eleazar? Did she know how Eleazar meant to make good on his threat?

Rivka had no answers. "Do you think I heard rightly from HaShem?" she asked. "I feel like such a fool."

Baruch smiled. "Better a fool in the house of the Lord than a wise man in the congregation of the unrighteous."

Rivka sighed. That was nice, really nice, but it didn't change anything. She still didn't know if she had heard from HaShem. And she had a new enemy.

"You will pray for this man Eleazar," Baruch said.

Rivka wanted to shriek. Baruch seemed to think that was the answer to all her problems — to pray for her enemies. At the rate she was making enemies, pretty soon she'd be on her knees twenty-four hours a day.

Baruch opened the door. "Sister Rivka, you will go home now and pray for this man. We will watch over Rachel until you have done what you must do."

Rivka sat staring at him.

Hana looked up from her sewing. "Go, Rivka! You must thank HaShem for putting this wicked man in your life."

Rivka saw she wasn't going to get any sympathy from either of them. She stood up and went outside, feeling very alone. Nobody understood her.

Baruch gave her an encouraging smile. "Sister Rivka, Rabban Yeshua says this — that he has walked in your sandals and he understands."

He pushed the door shut, leaving Rivka alone in the street.

I can't pray for that horrible man Eleazar.

I have to pray for him.

Why is my life so hard?

Ari

Ari the Kazan!"

Ari turned to look across the large construction site. His friend Gamaliel stood waving both arms. Ari sighed and stepped away from the circle of workmen assembling the crane — a new design that he had developed with Levi the bronzeworker. The iron gears allowed for a higher mechanical advantage than could be achieved with bronze. The experimental design showed much promise, and Levi was excited about developing new skills in ironwork.

It had not escaped Ari's notice that such skills would make Brother Eleazar very happy. He himself cared nothing for the military applications of his work. Iron was stronger than bronze. With it, he could build machines stronger and lighter, and that was his only consideration. Yes, the only one.

"Ari the Kazan!" Gamaliel's face was an unreadable mix of anger, confusion, astonishment, and joy.

Ari approached his friend and grasped his right forearm, clasping it tightly for a moment. "My brother, are you well?"

"There is news," Gamaliel said in a tight voice. He looked all around them. "A word with you privately?"

Ari nodded and waved his workmen away. Gamaliel shouted to Levi the bronzeworker to join them. Levi belonged to the Sons of Righteous Priests, and clearly Gamaliel trusted him to listen to whatever secret news he had brought.

Gamaliel led Ari and Levi to the far corner of the site. "My brothers, a merchant party just arrived from Jericho."

Jericho? Ari's throat tightened and he flinched. Because of Rivka, he had missed out on going to Jericho, on meeting with Mordecai ben Hanina. He had made Eleazar angry also.

Gamaliel's eyes misted. "My brothers, a terrible thing has happened. Bandits attacked the caravan of Mordecai ben Hanina and ..." His voice broke.

Ari put a steadying hand on his shoulder. "And ...?"

Gamaliel sighed deeply. "And massacred them all, taking his gold."

Ari's mouth felt very dry. "All? How? Hanina's men were many and well-armed."

"An ambush," Gamaliel said. "In a steep ravine, the bandits made a rockslide on the caravan. Two parts of Mordecai's men were killed by the rocks, and the others were overwhelmed by many hundred bandits. There were no survivors. All the gold that was meant for the city is gone."

Ari felt like his head was filled with cotton. If he and Rivka and Racheleh had been in that caravan ...

Gamaliel gripped Ari's hand. "Your woman heard rightly from HaShem, Ari the Kazan. And you also did well. It required courage for you to ask us to obey the word of a woman."

Ari nodded, mute with emotion. He felt astonished that Rivka had been right. Grateful that he had listened. Grieved for the death of Mordecai ben Hanina, a righteous man.

And enraged beyond words that the gold meant for the relief of Jerusalem had gone to the bandits.

TEN

Berenike

Behind her palace in Jerusalem, Berenike had a private garden filled with flowering plants taken from all over Judea, Samaria, and the Galilee, and chosen so that some of them were always in bloom. The light blue speed-well, the yellow spurge, and the purple mandrakes blossomed in winter. In spring, the bee-colored orchids, the brilliant red tulips, the pastel violet irises, and a dozen others lit up her garden. In summer, she had pink ole-ander and huge orange horned poppies. But now, as summer edged into fall, an ill time of year, Berenike had nothing except trefoil, a short bushy plant with small orange and yellow flowers.

All such flowers grew easily at her winter palace in Jericho, which was warm all year round. Here in Jerusalem, where it sometimes snowed in the winter, it required much skill and care to keep these plants thriving. Berenike employed a small army of gardeners to keep her precious flowers alive. It was a haven of peace and luxury in a mad city.

Today, two days before Rosh HaShanah, her heart burned inside her, driving away all thoughts of peace. The fool should have warned her. Should have —

"Your Highness, the seer woman has arrived." Berenike's chief of staff, Andreas, materialized at the edge of the garden. Behind him the seer woman hovered, looking upset.

Berenike remained reclining on her satin couch. "You may go, Andreas. We are not to be disturbed, not even by my brother."

Andreas bowed and backed away. The seer woman stepped closer. Berenike had not seen her in almost a year, not since the unpleasantness over that man, Yaakov called *tsaddik*.

The seer woman bowed. "Grace and peace to you, Your Highness."

Berenike snapped her fingers. "Come and recline with me on the couch." She kept her voice low and cordial, masking the fury in her heart.

The seer woman's eyes went wide. Berenike had never invited her to recline on the same couch with her. She would not have done so today, but she wanted the seer woman close. The fool deserved a slapping.

"I said, come and recline with me. There is room." Berenike patted the spot beside her.

The seer woman lay down on the far edge of the broad couch, her body tense as a coiled cobra.

"Closer." Berenike said.

The seer woman edged closer. Berenike saw new lines in her face. Lines of worry. Grief. Deep pain.

Berenike leaned toward the seer woman, and now at last she let anger into her voice. "Why did you not warn me, fool?"

Shock slashed across the seer woman's face. "I was not sure myself."

"Not sure?" Rage burned in Berenike's heart. "Not sure? You were sure of many things when you told me my fortune four years ago. Or were those lies also?"

"No!" Panic filled the seer woman's voice. "I was sure of the things I told you. But much is hidden from me."

"And yet you knew of this thing and you did not tell me." Berenike grabbed the seer woman's tunic, yanked her close, and slapped her face hard. "You will not withhold such information from me again."

Tears stood out in the seer woman's eyes. And anger. She blinked many times before she answered. "I will tell you what I knew. My husband meant to take me and our daughter to Jericho to meet this rich man, Mordecai ben Hanina. I saw a vision two weeks ago. HaShem told me that there was death on the Jericho road. Therefore, I refused to go, and I forced my husband also to stay home."

Berenike narrowed her eyes. "You should have warned me, fool. My cousin Saul traveled down to Jericho that same day and might have been killed."

The seer woman's face went pale, and something like panic filled her eyes. "I'm sorry. I don't understand what happened. I had thought by this time Governor Albinus would have captured many bandits."

Berenike laughed in her face. "Fool! Albinus cares nothing for capturing bandits."

Shock. Berenike could read faces as easily as she read a book. The shock on the seer woman's face was complete.

"Please, you will explain how you know this," the seer woman said. "I know with certainty that Albinus will capture many bandits. So many that they will fight back by taking hostages."

"Then your knowledge is lies," Berenike said. "Governor Albinus arrived in town yesterday for the coming feast. My brother and I invited him to a banquet. You have seen the governor?"

The seer woman nodded. "He is an evil man."

"And easily read," Berenike said. "My brother spoke much of the massacre of this man Mordecai ben Hanina on the Jericho road. Already a year ago, I warned Albinus about the bandits and urged him to do something about them. Do you know what he said when we told him of this massacre?"

The seer woman waited, her face tight.

"He said it was a terrible tragedy." Berenike closed her eyes and saw again the easy way Albinus said this, as if remarking on the fine weather or the excellence of the wine. "Then he smiled." Berenike studied the seer woman. "He smiled! Albinus cares nothing about bandits. If he wished to capture bandits, you will explain why he smiled."

"Smiled?" The seer woman's eyebrows twisted down. "I do not understand. Something is very wrong."

Berenike sighed. Yes, something was terribly wrong, but the seer woman was no help at all. "You may go now. You will come to see me if you learn anything new."

The seer woman rolled off the couch and stood up, her face dark and closed.

"You will come see me again, yes?"

The seer woman backed away and bowed her head slightly. But she did not answer Berenike's question. Then she turned and fled.

Berenike bit her lip, feeling foolish. She should not have slapped the seer woman. It was a tactical mistake. The seer woman had done nothing wrong, and had been punished unfairly. Berenike regretted her error.

But no queen of the House of Herod would ever apologize. Never, ever, ever.

Ari

On the day after Rosh HaShanah, as Ari returned from the morning prayers, he saw a small boy standing in front of his house. The boy looked to be about nine years old and his face was very dirty.

When Ari reached his door, the boy thrust a piece of papyrus at him. Ari took it. "What is this?"

The boy shook his head. "You will read it and then you will come with me, please."

Ari scanned the writing. It was written in very clumsy Aramaic letters.

Menahem ben Yehudah, son of David, to Ari called Kazan: peace to you. It is said throughout the city that you are a man of honor, honest and respected by all. If you are willing to serve as go-between on a matter of life and death, you will come with the boy to meet with me. I swear on my honor that no harm will come to you, unless you bring violence with you.

Ari rolled up the papyrus. "And who is Menahem ben Yehudah? What is this matter of life and death?"

The boy shrugged. "Come with me and you will see. But you must not bring a weapon."

Ari narrowed his eyes. In his experience, those most fearful of weapons were those who carried them. "Why should I trust this Menahem ben Yehudah?"

"Menahem ben Yehudah has sworn on his own honor that you will be safe," the boy said. "Therefore, you will be safe."

That was foolish logic. Ari considered the matter for a moment. The boy lacked any hint of guile. This Menahem claimed that it was a matter of life and death. Ari did not see how this could be, but it would be wrong to do nothing in such a case. "Lead me."

The boy turned and began walking south. Ari followed. They walked all the way to the Essene Gate and out of the city. Ari did not like leaving the safety of the city, but he followed.

The boy led down the dusty path to the road running along the southern edge of the city through the Hinnom Valley. Ari hated this road. Ash heaps stood on both sides of the road. Burning pits smoked. Wild dogs raced among the garbage heaps, fighting for scraps of refuse.

When they reached the crossroad at the southeast corner of the city, the boy turned north. He walked half the length of the Kidron Valley and then plunged into the jumble of tents on the shoulders of the Mount of Olives. Ari felt his suspicions rising. Why had they come the long way around?

The boy snaked his way through the welter of tents. Dozens of dirty children raced past him, shrieking, laughing. Women huddled inside their tents, eyeing Ari with hostility, as though he were an invader. Finally, the boy disappeared into one of the natural caves in the side of the mountain. Ari hesitated for a moment, then followed him in.

It took a moment for his eyes to adjust to the smoky darkness.

"*Shalom* to you, Ari the Kazan." A man's voice, deep and powerful. "My name is called Menahem ben Yehudah."

Ari squinted into the haze but could see nothing. "*Shalom.*" He heard movement behind him and looked back. Two men had stepped between him and the entrance of the cave. They bore short curved daggers and neither looked friendly. A sick feeling clutched the pit of his stomach. What had he done?

"You will sit, please, Ari the Kazan," Menahem said. "There is no danger here except that which you bring with you."

Ari sat. Slowly, his eyes made out the shape of a stocky man of about sixty with a dense gray beard and piercing eyes. Ari drew in a deep breath and slowly released it. "What is this matter of life and death?"

Menahem smiled. One of his front teeth was missing, and a crooked scar ran diagonally across his forehead. He wore *tefillin.* Ari did not know if this was a good sign or not. In his experience, the most violent men were very religious.

"First, I will tell you a story," Menahem said. "Every man likes a story, yes?"

Ari thought he had little choice in the matter now. "Yes."

"My father Yehudah was a pious man," Menahem said. "He came from Galilee, which was then under the control of the evil king. Then the evil king died, leaving his lands to his three sons. One son's line failed and his land went instead to the Queen of Heaven."

Ari blinked. None of this made the least sense to him. "I do not understand. Who is this evil king?"

Menahem looked astonished. "Everybody knows who is the evil king. His great-grandson is now king."

Ari lacked Rivka's knowledge of history, but even he had studied about Agrippa's great-grandfather as a schoolboy. Herod the Great, the last great king of Judea. A vile man, but a great architect and leader. "And who is the Queen of Heaven?"

Menahem stared at him in disbelief. "The Great *Zonah* who rules our land now."

Ari remembered Brother Eleazar saying something like this once. The whore of Babylon. A metaphor for Rome. "Very well. Please continue your story."

"My father led an uprising against the Queen of Heaven." Menahem scowled. "He was captured and crucified, but his sons lived. Many years later, we also fought against the Queen. Two of my brothers were captured and crucified, but I lived."

Ari stared at him. "And you still fight against the Queen?"

"Always." Menahem's eyes pooled with deep pain. "And now it is not I who am captured, but my son." His voice cracked. "My son will be crucified and my line ended and the Queen of Heaven, who spits on HaShem, will violate the holy land of our fathers for all time." He leaned forward and gripped Ari's hand with shocking strength. "Ari called Kazan, you are a man of honor. You will help me."

Ari found that he could not breathe. "How? In what way could I help you?" Of course it was foolishness to think of helping this outlaw. This bandit.

Menahem's nails dug into Ari's hand. "We have taken a hostage of the house of the chief priest Hananyah ben Nadavayah."

Ari was sweating now. That was Brother Eleazar's house. Had they captured —

"We will kill the hostage," Menahem said. "We must kill him, unless Hananyah intervenes in the matter of my son and those others who were captured by the Queen."

It was all clear now. Ari felt appalled. These bandits, these dagger-men, wanted him to broker a deal. Of course he could not do it. These men of violence were evil. Murderers, robbers, outlaws. Such men as these had once taken Rivka for ransom and would have killed her.

Menahem's eyes hardened. "You will help us, yes?"

Ari wanted to say no, but that seemed to be a quick way to be killed. Yet how could he say yes? A man of honor would not lie.

"You will not allow my son to be killed," Menahem said. "He was taken by the lies of the Queen."

Ari blinked. "What lies?"

Menahem's eyes flickered with anger. "Surely you have heard the lies concerning a certain rich man from Shushan who was to bring gold as the sand of the seashore for the comfort of Jerusalem?"

"I have heard of this man." Ari's throat felt painfully dry. "I have heard he was murdered by men such as you."

"Lies!" Menahem spat in the dirt and glared at Ari. "We were fools to believe in this man Mordecai ben Hanina."

Ari felt his heart hammering in his chest. "I do not understand. Bandits ambushed him and took his gold on the Jericho road."

Menahem glowered at him. "And you believe this lying tale? You believe in this Mordecai? Bah!" He spat again, then waved Ari away with his hands. "Go! I will not make business with a fool."

Ari leaned forward. "You are telling me there was no Mordecai ben Hanina?" His breath was coming in tight little gasps now. Something was very wrong and he must know what had happened. "You will tell me what happened, please."

Menahem's eyes narrowed like a cat's. "Many dozen men were gathered in the hill country to ambush this man Mordecai. Men of my clan and some others we are allied with. Good men, who love HaShem and have never bowed the knee to the Queen of Heaven."

Good men. Ari had heard that often used of men who were not good. "And?"

"It was a trap!" Menahem said. "We chose a spot to wait for this man Mordecai. He had spies in the hills, and they signaled him to retreat. He lured us into pursuit along the road, back toward Jericho, and there we were trapped ourselves."

Ari stared at him. "Trapped? By men of Shushan?"

"No, fool!" Menahem's face bristled with rage. "Mordecai was an idle tale, designed to lure us in. These men did not fight as Jews. They were the Queen's men."

"Romans?" Ari said. "Roman soldiers?"

"As I said." Defeat filled Menahem's eyes. "My men know many escapes in those hills. We ran a hundred different ways. By the will of HaShem, I escaped, but my son was taken. My own son, who swore when he became a man to bow to no Lord but HaShem, is now taken by filthy idolaters, the Queen's men."

Ari sat in deep thought for a long time. He had never felt any sympathy for these dagger-men, these outlaws who terrorized their own countrymen. And yet he had a strange feeling. If Mordecai was nothing more than a lie, a lure to draw in these dagger-men, then . . . he was also a lure for Ari the Kazan. This ambush had been intended to catch him also. All the Sons of Righteous Priests. Rivka. Racheleh. That was the only explanation. Cold sweat bathed Ari's forehead. An old Arab proverb crossed his mind. *The enemy of my enemy is my friend.*

Which made no sense. Such men as Menahem ben Yehudah murdered chief priests in the streets. They had killed many already, including two men of the House of Hanan.

The enemy of my enemy is my friend.

No. Ari would not fall into that cycle of retribution, that blind hatred. He shook his head. He could not help these men.

Menahem snapped his fingers. "Yoav! You will guide Ari the Kazan out of the camp."

"I can find my own way," Ari said.

Menahem gave him a thin smile. "You would be killed if you were found alone in the camp of Menahem ben Yehudah. By the women."

Ari stood up. His knees felt wobbly.

Yoav led him outside the cave and began leading Ari through the tent village. "Will you help us then?"

Ari felt his skin crawling, imagining a murderer in every tent. "Please tell me about your clan. Are you related to Menahem?"

Yoav shook his head. "I am an orphan. Syrians raided our village in Galilee. They killed my father with hammers. They raped my mother many times before she died. They killed my brothers, stole my sisters, and burned our fields. I escaped by hiding in a cave. When I am a man, I will avenge myself on the Queen."

"But . . ." Ari felt his mouth hanging open. "Syrians are not Romans."

Yoav's eyes narrowed to slits. "They were Syrian auxiliaries, soldiers of Rome. I saw their insignia. They were the Queen's men. When I am a man, I will kill such men and avenge the name of HaShem, which they dishonored."

A wave of dizziness washed over Ari. Partly it was the matter-of-fact way in which this small boy described horrors unimaginable. And partly . . .

Ari reached inside his belt.

Felt the small wooden cross, the token of his own father's murder.

Stopped walking.

Yoav turned and looked up at him. "Please, you must follow me."

Ari felt a wave of revulsion inside his throat. No, he could not do this. Yes, he must do this. How would he ever explain this to Baruch, to Rivka?

"Take me back to Menahem ben Yehudah," Ari said. "There is a thing I must tell him."

ELEVEN

Rivka

Y ou're going to *what?*" Rivka shrieked at Ari.

"Please, you must not wake Racheleh." Ari's voice sounded very quiet, very calm. It was late at night and they were snuggled together in bed.

Rivka felt the thin edge of panic sliding under her skin. *Please, God, no!* "Ari, do you know who those men are? Menahem ben Yehudah — he's a revolutionary! He's the son of Judas the Galilean, who led the revolt in the year A.D. 6."

Ari nodded. "Perhaps he has his reasons for hating Rome."

Rivka thought she might throw up. "Ari, you can't help this creep! He's a murderer. He robs Jews. Kills women and children."

"You know this from your own experience?" Ari said. "Or you know it from someone else?"

"I . . ." Rivka stopped. "I read it in Josephus."

Ari said nothing.

"Ari, please, don't have anything to do with Menahem."

Ari clenched his eyes shut tight. "Perhaps I should tell you the tale of one of this Menahem's warriors. He is a boy of perhaps nine years old . . ." Ari told her the story of the boy, Yoav.

By the time he finished, Rivka was crying. "Ari, do you think it's true?"

"He is a boy, an innocent, unskilled in deception." A deep sigh shuddered through Ari's frame, rocking Rivka. "I do not believe he is lying."

"And you think Menahem was telling the truth about the ambush? We could have been on that road with Mordecai."

"There was no Mordecai," Ari said. "They were Roman agents, probably Syrians or Samaritans dressed as Jews." A long silence. "We would have been killed if we were there. It was a trap for us also."

Rivka felt nauseous. She clutched Ari and closed her eyes, wishing she could make this horrible story go away.

"Rivkaleh." Ari held her tight. "I believe that I must help this man Menahem. Yes, he has blood on his hands. But yes, he and his people are also victims of much evil. He wishes me to help him regain his son. If Racheleh were taken, what would you do to regain her?"

Rivka took a deep breath. "There's something in Josephus about this. He says bandits kidnapped the secretary of Eleazar ben Hananyah and held him for ransom. Hananyah paid a large sum of money to Governor Albinus, who released some of the bandits."

Ari's arms tightened around her. "You know for certain that Hananyah will pay this ransom? That Albinus will release the men?"

Rivka nodded. "This incident is well-known. One of the earliest recorded acts of terrorism."

Ari's whole body shuddered. "What do you think we should do?"

Rivka didn't know what to say. The last thing she wanted to do was to collaborate with terrorists. But one man's terrorist was another man's freedom-fighter. Which were these dagger-men? Satan's spawn? Or righteous agents of HaShem?

"I believe I should help these men, Rivkaleh. But perhaps I am wrong. Please, you will pray on this matter."

Rivka felt cold sweat all over her body. "Of course." *You better believe I'm going to pray about it. If ever I needed to hear from HaShem, it's now.*

Ari

Two days later, Ari was sweating when he went with Brother Eleazar to meet his father, Hananyah ben Nadavayah. Eleazar also seemed jittery, and that was not usual.

"You will let me do the speaking," Eleazar said for the third time that morning as they walked through the great iron gate into the palace compound where Eleazar lived with his father's clan.

"Of course." Ari did not wish to talk to Hananyah at all. Yesterday when he woke up, the whole idea had seemed very foolish. But yesterday afternoon, Rivka had another vision. When Ari returned home from work, she had told him he must speak to Hananyah as soon as possible. So Ari had gone to find Eleazar this morning and told him what he must do in order to recover his secretary.

"You are certain he is still alive?" Eleazar said.

"I spoke with him yesterday," Ari said. "He was terrified but alive. They have said they will kill him after the feast unless the Romans release ten certain bandits. I have their names on a list."

"I could take Temple guards and seize him by force," Eleazar said. "Tell me where they hold him."

Ari shook his head. "A man of honor does not break confidence. I am sworn to keep secret their location. Besides, they know where I live, and retribution on my house would be swift."

Eleazar led the way into the great palace and spoke to his father's steward. The servant nodded and hurried away, leaving them to wait in the receiving room. Ari had never been here before, and he studied the interior with interest. It was sumptuously decorated, like Brother Yoseph's palace, but on a much grander scale. A mosaic abstract pattern covered one whole wall of the receiving room, and some of the tiles were real gold. A representation of the Temple *menorah* was scribed into the plaster of another wall. An extraordinary tapestry with glittering threads covered a third wall. None of the art had representational forms of animals or humans. There were no furnishings to sit on. Ari stood and sweated. Eleazar paced.

A quarter of an hour passed, and then the steward returned. "He will see you in his scriptorium. Follow me."

Ari wiped his forehead with the sleeve of his tunic, then followed Eleazar and the steward down a long plastered hallway, lit every few meters with an olive-oil lamp. Again, there was much art, all abstract. The floors were marble tile, cut in many geometrical shapes and cleverly fitted together in a mosaic pattern that never repeated.

At the end of the hallway, Eleazar stopped before a great oaken door. "You will let me do the speaking."

Ari nodded. Eleazar pushed open the door and they went in.

Eleazar's father looked to be about sixty. Like Eleazar, he was a large man, not as tall as Ari, but thickly built. He had a dense gray beard and the deadly black eyes of a cobra, eyes that pierced Ari with keen suspicion. Ari knew that this man, Hananyah ben Nadavayah, was a malicious old man, hated even by the other Sadducees. Hananyah stood at a tall writing desk made of ivory.

Ari caught his breath. Hand-carved ivory was more valuable than gold. He had never seen such extravagant waste.

Hananyah did not make any move to clasp hands with Ari. "I have heard tales of you, Kazan. What is it you want from me?"

Brother Eleazar's breath hissed in his throat. "Father, my secretary—"

Hananyah turned his malevolent eyes on Eleazar. "I asked Kazan."

Eleazar seemed to shrink visibly. Ari clasped his hands behind his back, wishing he were somewhere else. A den of lions would be an improvement.

Hananyah pointed at Ari. "Speak, Kazan. I have little time for foolishness."

Ari told of his visit with Menahem ben Yehudah, leaving out details of where his camp might be found.

Hananyah looked unimpressed. "When a man chooses to become a bandit, he takes certain risks. I am not concerned with this Menahem and his son."

Ari told of the boy, Yoav.

Hananyah scowled. "Galilean swine! They are no concern of mine."

Ari did not know what to say. Hananyah had not a milligram of compassion in his body. This was the man who had stolen tithes from the poor priests a few years ago. His thugs had beaten up several men, and Ari had gotten his arm broken. All because of this man, who had more wealth than any man could need, more gold, more ivory, more slaves—

Something tickled at Ari's brain. Slaves. Slaves were wealth. Eleazar's secretary was a slave, a trained scribe with facility in three languages. Ari turned to Eleazar. "How much did your secretary cost?"

Eleazar grimaced. "More than a talent. Fifteen thousand *dinars*. But that was seven years ago. To replace him in this market—it would be eighteen thousands."

Hananyah blanched. "You should have protected the man better. Such waste . . ." Rage crossed his face.

Ari took a step forward. "With respect, nobody could have known this man was at risk. The dagger-men have never kidnapped a slave before. Until now, they have been killing men such as yourself."

Ari saw at once that his words struck home. Hananyah's face hardened and he stared into space for a long moment. "Eighteen thousand *dinars*," he muttered.

"The governor could be persuaded for much less than that," Ari said. "If you were to offer him a silver talent, he could be persuaded to release the bandits."

Hananyah's eyes bored through Ari. "You know this with certainty?"

Ari knew it because Rivka had gone to talk to Berenike yesterday, who had told her that the governor was much displeased with the yield from the province so far. In Berenike's judgment, a silver talent would buy the release of the prisoners. Ten thousand *dinars*.

Hananyah's eyes gleamed. "Seven thousand *dinars*. I will offer no more to this pig, this Albinus."

Ari did not know if that would be enough. "With respect —"

Hananyah froze him with a stare, then turned to his son. "Eleazar, send in my steward and I will see to it. You are dismissed."

Eleazar took Ari's arm and backed out of the room. Outside in the hall, Ari dared to breathe again. He had faced the old lion and won.

Or had he? Ari shook his head. It was impossible to say. He had done what he thought right, what history told him would happen. HaShem could not ask him to do more.

Rivka

Three weeks passed with little news. Eleazar reported that his father had paid seven thousand *dinars* to the high priest, Yeshua ben Dannai, who took it to Herod's Palace and gave it to the governor in person.

And then . . . nothing.

All the city seemed to hold its breath through Rosh HaShanah, then the Ten Days of Awe, then the Fast, and finally the seven days of *Sukkot*. If the bandits were not released by the end of the feast, Eleazar's scribe would be returned in pieces. So said the tales on the street, and so said Ari.

Rivka worried that she had done something wrong. Menahem and his men were criminals. Helping them was like helping the Mafia.

On the last day of the feast, Shimon ben Klopas and the other elders came home with Ari after the morning prayers to get the bone-box. Tomorrow, on the anniversary of the death of Yaakov the *tsaddik*, they would go to gather his bones and take him to his final resting place.

Two burly elders trundled the ossuary out. The other elders gathered around them and they all proceeded back toward the synagogue. Shimon remained behind. "A word with you and your woman, Brother Ari?"

Rivka was so surprised she nearly fell over. In years past, she had often spoken with Yaakov the *tsaddik*, but Shimon was a different sort of man. He was not unkind, but just traditional. Rivka could deal with that.

The three of them came inside. Rachel's eyes widened when she saw them.

"Run upstairs and play," Rivka said.

The three of them sat on wooden stools around the one-legged kitchen table.

Shimon looked at Ari. "Has Sister Rivka heard a word from HaShem yet on when we are to leave the city?"

Rivka shook her head. "I've been trying to listen. It's very hard."

Shimon still did not look at her. "And yet Sister Rivka has heard from HaShem."

"HaShem warned me that we should not go to Jericho."

"It saved many lives," Ari said.

Shimon's eyes filled with deep sadness and now, finally, he turned them toward Rivka. "It is said in the street that Rivka the Kazan heard another word from HaShem."

"I . . . yes." Rivka studied the knuckles of her hands.

Shimon shook his head. "And as a result, Ari the Kazan now bargains with the men of violence."

"To save an innocent man." Ari spoke in a very soft voice. He put a hand on Shimon's gnarled fist. "Did we do wrong, Father?"

"I do not know." Shimon sat in silence for a very long time. "But if Sister Rivka intends that the brothers of The Way will hear her words on the day that HaShem tells her that we must leave Jerusalem, then please she must guard her reputation. If her words now cause evil on account of the men of violence, then who will believe her on that day?"

Rivka didn't know what to say. She could not make HaShem speak to her, but neither could she make him not speak. If she heard from him, wasn't she obligated to tell people?

Shimon stood up and went to the door. "My children, be wary of the men of violence. Retribution is a sword which cuts both ways." He went out, leaving Rivka and Ari staring at each other.

"Do you believe we did right?" Ari asked.

Rivka felt a sick churning in her belly. "I think so. I know what I heard from HaShem. All we can do now is pray."

Ari nodded. "Yes, we must — "

A heavy fist pounded at the door. "Ari the Kazan, are you home?" It was Yoseph's voice, and it sounded distraught.

Ari

Ari opened the door, his heart thumping. "Brother Yoseph, has something gone wrong?"

Yoseph's face showed pain and fear. "You must come to see Brother Eleazar."

Ari stepped outside, then looked back at Rivka. "Bar the door. There may be trouble. The dagger-men know where we live." He pulled the door shut and waited until he heard the heavy wooden bar thumping into place.

Yoseph and Ari hurried through the streets to the palace of Hananyah ben Nadavayah. The guard at the gate admitted them and they strode through the outer courtyard to the palace and down the corridor to Hananyah's scriptorium. Ari felt a sense of dread rising inside him. He had failed. He did not know how, but he had failed.

Yoseph knocked at the door and murmured something. The door opened. Ari saw several men inside.

Brother Eleazar. Eleazar's father. The scribe who had been kidnapped.

Ari's heart jolted. The scribe was alive and unmarked. Menahem ben Yehudah had returned him after all. But Eleazar's father did not look happy, and that made no sense.

Behind them stood Hanan ben Hanan, and his face was a mask of rage. "You, Kazan, are to blame for this. And you also, ben Nadavayah."

Ari felt cold shock through his system. "What has happened?"

Hanan took three quick steps and seized a fistful of Ari's tunic. "Fool! The dagger-men returned this scribe, but now they have stolen the chief steward of my house. They left this note." He thrust a piece of papyrus in Ari's face.

Ari took it and read.

Menahem ben Yehudah, son of David, to Hanan ben Hanan: peace to you. We have taken a servant of your house to a hiding place where he will be kept safe. You will arrange for the release of certain men of mine, taken prisoner by those who pollute the land, or I will kill your man without mercy. I will send word to you by the hand of Ari the Kazan, a man of honor, who will act as go-between.

Ari's hand was shaking so badly now that he lost his grip on the papyrus.

"Fool!" Hanan said. "All of you are fools. Now these dagger-men have gained power over all of us. They will not stop until they have emptied the prison and our purses!"

Brother Eleazar glowered at Hanan. "You would leave your servant to be killed?"

Hanan's eyes narrowed to dagger points. "You should have left *yours* to be killed. Now you leave me no choice." He pushed past Ari and stalked out.

Then all the men were talking at once. Ari could not focus on their words. He had made a terrible blunder. And yet he had obeyed what HaShem told Rivka. Caught between the hammer of justice and the anvil of mercy, he had chosen mercy.

What more could a man do?

TWELVE

Hanan ben Hanan

Three weeks after his steward was kidnapped, Hanan went to the Hasmonean Palace, surrounded by a dozen bodyguards. Under his arm, he carried a leather bundle. In his heart, rage beat like a storm. The sun hammered down from a cloudless sky. The rains were overdue, but in this pitiless year, Hanan expected little.

The great iron gate was locked. Hanan stopped at the stout wooden door next to it and shouted through the small iron grate. "Hanan ben Hanan to see the king."

The door swung open and Hanan slipped inside. He left his bodyguards outside, knowing that the king would not allow armed men in his palace. Hanan strode across the courtyard and into the palace. Agrippa's chief of staff stood waiting for him. Hanan had sent a curt message that morning to expect him at noon.

"The king and queen await you." The chief of staff spun around and led the way into the throne room. Agrippa and Berenike sat on twin thrones.

Hanan wondered what the queen might have done in order to be named co-regent with Agrippa. There were scandalous tales about these two.

The chief of staff stopped before the thrones and bowed at the waist. "Hanan ben Hanan to see the king and queen."

Hanan stepped forward and gave a slight nod to the king. His eyes flickered toward the queen, and his pulse quickened. She was a woman who did not hide her great beauty from the eyes of men. Vile woman.

The queen's voice purred softly. "You may speak, Hanan ben Hanan."

Hanan felt sure that the events of the past few weeks were familiar by now to both Agrippa and Berenike. He reviewed them anyway. How dagger-men captured a servant of Eleazar ben Hananyah. How Kazan was chosen as a man of honor to mediate. How Hananyah ben Nadavayah paid a ransom to the high priest, Yeshua ben Dannai, who transmitted it to Governor Albinus, who freed ten certain prisoners. How the dagger-men then kidnapped Hanan's chief steward.

All this was known to the king and queen. All but the ending.

Hanan drew the leather bundle from under his arm. He saw the king and queen lean forward, curiosity lighting up their eyes.

Hanan flicked open the bundle and threw its contents on the floor.

A left ear. A right hand. Two feet. The private parts of a man.

Berenike gave a small shriek. Agrippa's face whitened to the color of chalk.

Hanan wadded up the leather wrapping and threw it aside. "The House of Hanan does not negotiate with bandits."

Agrippa made a motion to his chief of staff. "Andreas, you will remove these things."

Andreas scooped up the leather wrapping and rapidly bundled the body parts. He threw a vicious look at Hanan, then stalked out.

"You are a hard man, Hanan ben Hanan." Agrippa folded his arms across his chest. "You should have paid the ransom."

Hanan shook his head. "The dagger-men will not trouble my house again. It is a shame about the servant, but better that one man should die than many be endangered."

Berenike's eyes glittered with anger. "What do you want from us? We cannot make the dagger-men end this evil."

Hanan clasped his hands behind his back and stood up straight. "Hananyah ben Nadavayah showed weakness. He and his lackey, the high priest Yeshua ben Dannai. You must punish them. Their weakness has put all our servants in danger, including yours. And you must speak to the governor to put a stop to this foolishness. If he releases bandits for a price, then there is no law in the land."

Agrippa scowled at him. "You know nothing at all. This governor is not concerned about bandits. The more hostages these dagger-men kidnap, the more ransom he will collect. We can do nothing with the governor. And we have no jurisdiction over Hananyah ben Nadavayah."

"Then make an example of the high priest," Hanan said.

Berenike laughed out loud. "You amuse me, Hanan ben Hanan. I suppose we should replace Yeshua ben Dannai with you? Leave us." She waved him away with her hands. "Go! You weary me with your constant machinations."

Hanan backed away, her laughter mocking his ears. When he reached the door of the throne room, he turned and stomped away, bile burning his throat. He had sacrificed his chief steward.

To no gain, except the mockery of a woman.

Berenike

Berenike stood to leave. Hanan ben Hanan was a horrible man, and she was glad to have dishonored him.

"You should not have laughed." Agrippa's voice arrested her.

Berenike turned to look. "He is a humorless, merciless, wretched—"

"He showed strength of will. The dagger-men will not kidnap more of his servants." Agrippa stood and began pacing. "Better that Hananyah ben Nadavayah had shown such courage first. Then it would not have been necessary for Hanan to do so."

Berenike shook her head. "These bandits are desperate. If kidnapping fails, they will turn to something else."

"And therefore the governor must not be bribed to release more of them." Agrippa stepped over a bloodstain on the floor. "Hanan ben Hanan showed courage in refusing them."

Berenike could not believe she was hearing this. "Hanan is an arrogant and violent man. We are not going to reappoint him."

Agrippa said nothing.

Berenike grabbed his sleeve. "We are not going to appoint Hanan ben Hanan high priest again."

"*We* do not have the power to appoint and depose the high priest," Agrippa said. "*I* have this power. Caesar gave it to me alone."

Berenike could not argue with that. She waited. It was obvious that Agrippa meant Yeshua ben Dannai must go, but it was not obvious who should succeed him. Agrippa needed her analytical mind, and he would remember that, so long as she did not press him.

"This man Yeshua ben Dannai is weak," Agrippa said. "He should not have taken the ransom to the king. It was not his servant who was kidnapped. He should have been strong."

Still Berenike said nothing. Agrippa would talk until he ran out of words, and then he would ask her help.

"Yeshua must go," Agrippa said. "But I will not have Hanan ben Hanan back as high priest. He is a harsh man. Too harsh."

Berenike bit her tongue to keep from speaking.

Agrippa continued pacing. "We have exhausted the men of the principal houses." He gave Berenike a sharp look. "You agree? The last few years have seen many high priests, but none good."

Berenike shrugged and threw him a small morsel. "There are other houses."

Agrippa mulled that for some time. "None that are houses of high honor."

Berenike had considered this. All of the senior men of the four principal houses had already served as high priest, and most had been failures, but there was another option. "Tales tell that Yeshua ben Gamaliel is to marry Marta, of the House of Boetus."

Agrippa's eyes gleamed with a golden light. "Marta is wealthy."

Berenike knew that Yeshua was also an intelligent man. He was a protégé of Hanan ben Hanan, but he would be no puppet. Naturally, Hanan would serve as his advisor. But Yeshua was a scholar, and even the Pharisees acknowledged his wisdom. Such men were not ruled by their own passions or the will of other men. Yeshua ben Gamaliel would not yield to foolish rage, like Hanan ben Hanan. Nor would he be ruled by foolish mercy, like this Yeshua ben Dannai.

Agrippa was studying her. "You agree? Marta is wealthy?"

Berenike nodded. "Very wealthy." She wanted to say more, but decided that was enough. Agrippa might be thinking of the size of the gift Marta would give, but the important thing was that Yeshua ben Gamaliel was the best choice to be high priest.

Agrippa smiled. "Then I will see to it."

Hanan ben Hanan

Late that evening, Hanan's new steward ushered in two visitors to his receiving room. Hanan stood to welcome them. The younger man was his nephew, Mattityahu ben Theophilus, a fine man who served the Temple well as treasurer. The other was Yeshua ben Gamaliel, a brilliant man of an otherwise unaccomplished Sadducean family. Yeshua was Hanan's favorite among the younger generation, like a son to Hanan, who had only one child of his own, Sarah.

Yeshua's face was shining. "I have news. My betrothed woman Marta has been contacted by Agrippa, who solicits a contribution. The king hints strongly that I am being considered for high priest."

"And?" Hanan narrowed his eyes. "Agrippa takes contributions but does not always follow through."

Yeshua smiled. "Marta offered him eight silver talents, on condition that he consider no other candidates."

Hanan was staggered. Eight talents! That was far more than he had paid a few years ago. But he had not been canny enough to add a stipulation, and his bid had lost. "The king accepted this?"

Yeshua tapped the side of his nose. "He says he will think on it. I do not believe he will think long, but he must make a pretense of considering the matter so that he does not seem too eager."

Hanan began pacing. "Have you given thought to who will be your *sagan*? That young fool Eleazar ben Hananyah must go. Because of him, the dagger-men kidnap our servants with impunity and the prisons are emptied. It was a mistake for me to appoint Eleazar in the first place."

Yeshua inclined his head toward Hanan's nephew. "I will appoint Mattityahu, who is like a brother to me. And I would be honored if you would serve as my counselor."

Hanan smiled. "A privilege. You will inform me as soon as the king makes it official. It is a shame about your woman."

Yeshua looked at him sharply. "What is a shame?"

Hanan raised his eyebrows. Surely Yeshua must know of this matter. "Your woman is a widow."

"It is well known she is a widow. What of it?"

Hanan realized that Yeshua did not know of certain very foolish rules. "The Pharisees interpret Torah to say that the wife of the high priest must be a virgin."

"She is a woman of high repute."

Hanan sighed. "She is a widow. A high priest does not marry a widow."

Yeshua's face hardened to iron. "I am not concerned with the rules of Pharisees. They bend Torah to their will. She is a woman of good family. If I marry her, I will have deep ties to the House of Boetus. And it is her silver talents that are paying Agrippa. I do not have eight talents to give him."

"You could divorce her and marry my daughter," Hanan said. "The House of Hanan has more honor than the House of Boetus." *But I do not have eight silver talents to give Agrippa either.*

Yeshua's face flushed. "Your daughter is how old?"

"Twelve." Hanan felt a knot in his throat. He remembered the day Sarah was born. It seemed only yesterday. Now she was almost of marriageable age. "She will be thirteen at *Pesach*, and then she will be of age. When she was four, I promised her to a young man of the House of my brother Yonatan, but the dagger-men killed him and I have not found another match yet."

Yeshua began pacing. Hanan could see that he was much disturbed. This was only natural. The woman Marta was very wealthy, and Yeshua would not wish to lose that. Hanan's father had also been very wealthy, but his wealth was divided between five sons. Hanan had done well with what he inherited, but times were hard and he could not make miracles.

Finally, Yeshua shook his head. "She is well offered, but I have a daughter only a few years younger than yours. I am more suited to a mature woman such as Marta than a high-spirited girl like your daughter, who is not a third my age."

Hanan knew this was nonsense. Yes, Sarah tended to be outspoken. She was young and more intelligent than most females and therefore she sometimes spoke out of turn. She would learn sense from a good and wise man, such as Yeshua. Therefore, it was only a matter of the money. The wealth of Marta's family was legend. Hanan could not compete with that, but Yeshua would never cause him to lose honor by saying so. "Very well," he said. "But the Pharisees will call you a law-breaker if you marry Marta."

Yeshua curled a lip. "Pharisees! They are nothing. Idle talkers. We have allowed them too much freedom. I will pay no attention to these fools. Let them say what they will say. I will marry whom I will marry."

Hanan saw that there was no arguing with him. It made no matter. Yeshua would become high priest with Marta's money. Then he would marry her and the Pharisees would make an outcry. If Yeshua could shout them down, then all would be well. If not, then he would divorce the woman and remain high priest and still all would be well. If he managed things wisely, he would gain many talents during his tenure in office, and then he would have no need of this widow of the House of Boetus. Then he would be more willing to ally himself with Hanan by marrying his daughter.

Hanan put a friendly hand on Yeshua's shoulder. "We will deal with the Pharisees harshly if they cause trouble. And also Kazan. It is because of him —"

"I am little interested in Kazan," Yeshua said in a sharp tone. "He is a dangerous man, but only to one who pursues him. And these Pharisees who worry you so much will raise a far greater outcry if I touch Kazan than if I marry Marta, yes?"

"Yes." Hanan felt a burning in his belly. He had hoped that Yeshua would see the wisdom in eliminating troublemakers. There was rebellion in the air, and Kazan was at the heart of it. He was friends with the Sons of Righteous Priests, and they were bolder now than in years past. The reason must be Kazan, who consorted now with the dagger-men.

Yeshua took Mattityahu's arm. "Come, my brother. Tomorrow we shall hear from the king, and then the Temple is ours."

Hanan saw them to the door and out into the courtyard, wondering what had gone wrong. Yeshua was no longer young, almost forty, and a man unusually intelligent. Yet he was victim now to the same foolishness that fell on other men when they came to power.

Yeshua thought his newfound power meant that he could do as he wished, that he could ignore the wise counsel of older men. He would soon learn.

A few months from now, bruised but wiser, Yeshua would be readier to listen to Hanan's advice. Then he would put away this widow of his and do something about the young hotheads like Kazan who were pushing this city toward the abyss.

THIRTEEN

Baruch

Baruch woke before dawn with his heart thumping in his chest. He had dreamed a dream of Brother Ari, and it frightened him. Brother Ari walked a narrow line before the throne of HaShem. On the one side stood the men of violence, whispering words of zeal. On the other side stood Baruch and the men of Rabban Yeshua, and they were silent.

This dream frightened Baruch. Brother Ari was in danger and Baruch had been silent. Yaakov the *tsaddik* would not have been silent. Baruch curled up to Hana. She stirred in her sleep and clutched his arm to her chest. Baruch held her until the pounding in his heart eased and he knew what he must do. He kissed Hana's cheek softly and then rolled out of bed. He dressed quickly, pulling his four-cornered tunic over his head. He stroked the blue and white tassels of the *tzitzit* at each corner, taking comfort in their perfect symmetry. He wound a cloth belt around his waist, slipped on his sandals, and put on his *tefillin*. Hana and Dov remained sleeping.

Baruch eased open the door and descended the stairs. He took his sword from its hook on the wall and put it in his belt, then threw his cloak over his shoulders.

The voice of HaShem tickled his heart, stopping him.

No. This was wrong. Yesterday, yes, he had worn a sword on account of the bandits. Tomorrow, yes. Today, no. Today, he must trust in HaShem. Baruch put the sword back in its place on the wall. He lifted the thick wooden bar, unlatched the iron lock, and stepped outside into the morning chill. Black night hung over the city like a shroud.

Baruch swallowed his fear, pulled the door shut, and locked it. He strode down the street toward the house of Brother Ari, wishing that HaShem had chosen some other man to be a *tsaddik*.

One street over, he met Brother Ari coming the other way. A sword dangled from his belt. "*Shalom,* Brother Baruch."

"*Shalom*, Brother Ari." Baruch waited, but Brother Ari said nothing on the matter of Baruch's missing sword. Perhaps he had not even noticed.

They walked in companionable silence toward their synagogue. This was their custom and Baruch usually felt grateful for the silence. It was a time to enter the *Shekinah* — the Presence of HaShem — before the beginning of the morning prayers.

But this morning, the silence burned in Baruch's ears, a fire, a storm. Today, to remain silent was sin.

Baruch slowed his pace and caught Brother Ari's arm. "Brother Ari, there is a matter we must discuss."

Ari turned and gave him a puzzled look.

Baruch wondered if he had heard from HaShem correctly. His throat tightened. He did not know what to say. Yet how could he remain silent longer, when the men of violence did not? No, he must speak. If he had heard wrong, he had heard wrong, but a man could do no more than obey the word of HaShem as he heard it.

Ari

Ari studied his friend. Baruch was not himself this morning. He had forgotten his sword and that was not usual, but Ari had his own and there was no need to mention the matter. The dagger-men would not bother two men, even if only one of them was armed.

"Brother Ari, have you given thought to the matter of Rabban Yeshua?"

For a moment, Ari could not think what Baruch was talking about. Then he remembered the day a year ago when Baruch asked him to pray on the matter of following The Way of Rabban Yeshua. Ari had not done so. Rabban Yeshua was a very fine man, but he was only a man. A prophet, yes. A healer, yes. A *tsaddik*, yes. But he was not *Mashiach* and he was not HaShem. He was a man and Ari would never worship a man, no matter how good. Especially not a man who symbolized the deaths of many millions.

Baruch tightened his grip on Ari's arm. "Brother Ari, you have walked with us during the day. When night comes, will you walk with us, or will you go another way?"

Ari felt his whole body going rigid. "What way?"

"The way of the men of violence. The *anshei hamas*."

Ari recoiled with an almost physical pain. *Hamas*. That was a word no Israeli could ever love. It was the name chosen by Palestinian terrorists. In

Arabic it meant *courage*, but in Hebrew it meant *violence*. No, he would never choose that way. And yet . . .

And yet what was the alternative? The Way of Rabban Yeshua? In coming years, that would lead also to the way of violence.

"Ari, my brother." Baruch gripped Ari's arm and his voice burned. "Do not follow in the way of the men of violence. An evil time is coming, when all men must choose. You will follow the way of the men of violence, or else you will follow The Way of Yeshua. There is no middle way."

Ari had never seen Baruch in such an intense mood. The sight unnerved him. Ari leaned against a stone wall, breathing heavily. "I have not said yes to the men of violence."

"You have not said no to them." Baruch's eyes pooled with deep sadness. "And you have not said yes to Yeshua."

"He was a good man," Ari said. "His teachings were wise and—"

"He was the *Pesach* lamb and his blood atones for many."

Ari said nothing. This again. He did not believe this foolishness. Yes, Rabban Yeshua had died tragically. Yes, he was a good and admirable man. No, his death had no magical properties to take away the sins of other men. For that, HaShem had given men repentance. If a man repented from his sins, then HaShem would forgive him. HaShem did not require a bloody sacrifice to persuade him to show mercy. HaShem was not a God of violence, but of peace.

Baruch seemed to read his heart. "Brother Ari, you do not believe that Yeshua's sacrifice atones for many?"

"No." Ari began walking toward their synagogue. They would be late if they delayed any longer. "I do not see why HaShem should require a sacrifice. A sacrifice is for the benefit of men. It does not influence HaShem."

"Brother Ari, you are wrong." Baruch hurried to catch up with him. "Sacrifice releases power. This is a deep principle of the universe, and even HaShem cannot change it. You did not know this, that sacrifice releases power?"

Ari thought about that. The sacrificial death of a good man could inspire love in another man. Hope. Courage. Mercy. Yes, there was power in sacrifice, of a sort. Power over men. But no, it did not require a sacrifice in order to raise up hope or courage or mercy in the heart of HaShem. HaShem had all those in infinite supply. "No, I think you are mistaken, Brother Baruch. Now let us hurry or—"

"The prophet says that Yeshua was wounded for our transgressions. By his stripes we are healed."

Ari knew this verse. Jewish commentators applied it to the Jewish nation, suffering for its own sins. Whereas the Christians applied it to Rabban Yeshua who supposedly died for the sins of the whole world, for all men who would be born through all eternity. An infinite sacrifice by a finite man, a logical impossibility.

But this was not merely a matter of poor logic, it was a matter of deep evil. For many hundred years, the guilt for this sacrifice — the blood curse — would be laid on the heads of Jews by Christians. Torture, rape, arson, murder, all in the name of Christ. In coming centuries, it would become clear that the way of Rabban Yeshua was the way of violence, the way of evil.

Therefore, Ari could never follow Yeshua. To do so would be to dance on the graves of his forefathers, to shove the cross again down the throat of his dead father. Black rage rose up in Ari's heart, and the heat of it burned him like fire.

"Come, let us go to the prayers." Baruch pulled on Ari's hand. "I am sorry, Brother Ari. I see that I have offended you and I ask forgiveness."

Ari followed him toward the synagogue in despair. His life was shards again.

Ari strapped his *tefillah* to his forehead. The small black leather box held a fragment of Scripture inside, containing the command of HaShem to "bind these words between your eyes."

Next, he wrapped a second *tefillah*, a long black leather strap, around his arm and down to his fingers. The same Scripture commanded the faithful Jew to "bind it upon your hands." The *tefillin* were a literal reminder of these commandments.

Ari took out his prayer shawl, his *tallit*, and draped it over his head. There was nothing he wanted more than to follow the commandments, to be a good Jew, a man of peace.

The voice of Shimon ben Klopas rose up like a song. *"Baruch Attah, Adonai! Eloheinu, v'Elohei Avoteinu!"* Blessed are you, O Lord, our God, and God of our fathers!

Ari found that he could not join in the words today. Something was burning now in his belly, a terrible realization. His work required him to meet men in every corner of Jerusalem, and therefore he had his finger on the pulse of this city of God.

Men of violence were rising up all over Jerusalem. Not merely Menahem ben Yehudah and his bandits. Ordinary, honest citizens. Brother Eleazar and his Sons of Righteous Priests were one of many hundred groups of angry young men preparing for war. A vast horde of priests seethed in the Temple, all zealous for Torah, all eager for HaShem to deal retribution against Rome. Many men who prayed with Ari in this very synagogue of The Way spoke with hatred in their voices of the Whore of Babylon.

Life under the Roman boot was becoming a living death.

In a few years, every Jew must choose between two unthinkable options. If they refused the way of violence, they would be crushed by Rome. If they chose the way of violence, they would become evil themselves.

An image formed in Ari's mind. Years ago, when he was a small boy, he had received from his uncle Zev a long strip of paper, glued to form a loop. Uncle Zev was a teacher of high school mathematics and he had made a Möbius strip, a loop with a half-twist. Uncle Zev wished to teach Ari the peculiar topological properties of the Möbius strip, so he gave Ari two crayons. "Color the one side blue and the other side red, Ari."

So Ari dutifully began coloring, first on one side, then on the other. His mother and aunts came to watch. Then a horrible thing happened. There came a point where blue met red on the same side. The task could not be completed, because the Möbius strip had only one side. Ari cried when he understood the trick that Uncle Zev had played on him.

Now he saw that HaShem had played a like trick. Good and evil were intertwined in this universe. There came a day in every man's life when he must choose whether to fight evil with violence, or to renounce violence and let evil overcome good.

That day was now for Ari.

He did not wish to join with the men of violence, but . . .

. . . he did not wish to let evil triumph either.

HaShem had put a knot in the universe, and who could unloop it?

PART THREE

QUEEN OF HEAVEN

Spring, A.D. 64

In her heart, she says,
  "I sit as a queen,
  and not as a widow,
  and sorrow I will never know."
Therefore, in one day the plagues will overcome her:
  Death, sorrow, famine.
  And fire will consume her.
For mighty is the Lord God who judges her.

— Revelation 18:7–8, author's paraphrase

FOURTEEN

Ari

Ari awoke from an evil dream, exhausted. A thin shaft of moonlight slid in through the window slits. From the angle of the light, he saw that the moon was still well up in the sky. Today was the third day of *Pesach*, therefore three days after the full moon, and therefore . . .

Therefore it was several hours yet before daybreak.

For six months now, he had been wrestling with the knot HaShem had set for him. Would he join with the men of violence and make a stand against evil, or would he sit peacefully by and let evil destroy all that was good?

Ari sighed. His sleep had become shards now. A few hours per night, every night, with no relief. It would be so until he made his choice.

Ari rolled over and put an arm around Rivka. She lay with her back to him, sleeping soundly. He pulled her into the curve of his body and she snuggled closer in her sleep.

Sleep. He would give all his silver for one night of good sleep. But there was nobody to accept the money. Baruch had prayed for him, to no effect. Rivka also. Still, his sleep was shards.

Rivka mumbled something in her sleep. Ari realized that he was holding her too tight and released her. He put his hand on the narrow part of her waist, enjoying the simple delight that any man has in touching his woman. He put his face into her hair and inhaled its fragrance. She was all that he could ever want, but she was not enough.

Ari closed his eyes against the moonlight and thought of all the people in his life.

Rivka. *Please, HaShem, give her peace from those who call her the witch woman. Teach her to hear your voice.*

Racheleh. *HaShem, let her grow up into a woman who loves you, whose life is not shards.*

Baruch. *May he be a true* tsaddik *to his people and live many years in peace.*

Hanan ben Hanan. Ari did not know what to pray for Hanan. The man was evil. For no reason Hanan hated a monster called Kazan. Yet Ari had promised Rivka to pray for Hanan. *HaShem, please you will give peace to Hanan ben Hanan and reconcile him to his enemies.*

Ari sighed. He did not know if such prayers were foolishness, but they passed the long hours until morning, and they brought peace to his own heart. Whether HaShem would answer any of his prayers, Ari could not say, but HaShem could not escape hearing them.

After the morning prayers with Baruch and the brothers of The Way, Ari had breakfast at home, played with Racheleh for an hour, and then went out. It was a fine spring day and the streets bristled with people, many of them visitors for *Pesach*. Ari felt glad that this year, there was no prophet or wild-eyed leader to harangue the people and make a disturbance. If such a man meant to attract a following, he usually came at *Pesach* or *Sukkot*. And he always met a quick and violent death. His followers soon forgot him, fading into the background until the next zealous fool came along.

Ari walked quickly through the streets. Near the Hasmonean Palace, a blind beggar lay in a ragged heap against a wall, calling out for alms in a half-hearted voice. Ari gave him a few *lepta* and kept walking. In the square, many young men stood in little circles, talking and keeping sharp eyes out. As he walked by them, he heard many whispers of "Ari the Kazan," felt many desperate looks piercing his back.

He knew what these men wanted. They were day laborers, men who needed work. Men who had worked on various construction projects in the Temple. Men now unemployed, because the Temple was finally completed. After more than eighty years of continuous work, the massive renovations begun by Agrippa's great-grandfather were done. The chief priests had proposed a new project on the Temple Mount but Agrippa refused to permit it, on the grounds that the Temple was truly finished. As a result, a fourth part of the city was unemployed, and these young men had little to do but stand in the square all day and hope for work.

Ari hired as many as he could on various construction projects in the New City, but what could he do for so many thousand men? Times were hard just now, because the first rains last fall had been meager, and the second rains in the spring also failed, and so Judea had entered its second year of drought. Money was tight and food expensive, and this made a dangerous combination. The city was ready to burn, if the slightest spark struck it.

Ari hurried through the square and down past the market to the southern side of the Temple Mount. This was the short side of the Temple Mount, and yet still it was three hundred meters long. Near the center were the public baths, standing before the enormous Huldah Gates that led up into the Temple Mount. On the far side of the baths, the long row of steps continued the full length of the mount.

Towards the eastern end, at the foot of the stairs, stood a small man with wispy gray hair and a thin beard and a small crowd of students. Rabbi Yohanan ben Zakkai.

Ari hurried toward him. Rabbi Yohanan was standing, which meant he had not yet begun to teach. As a schoolboy growing up in Haifa, Ari had heard about this man. In coming centuries, he would be given the honorific title Rabban Yohanan and he would be credited with founding rabbinic Judaism, with saving his people from devastation after the war that was coming. But in this year and this city, he was merely Rabbi Yohanan, a Torah sage like many others, teaching a few students and attracting little attention.

Rabbi Yohanan was a man who made no secret of his distaste for the young and zealous fools who dreamed of war with Rome. According to Rivka, Rabbi Yohanan would lose all popularity and most of his students during the war. Therefore, Ari felt attracted to this man. Such a rabbi was a man who saw far and was not fooled by the winds of zeal that blew through the city. Such a man might be able to loose the knot in Ari's mind.

When Ari reached the group of students, he took a seat on the topmost step. Most of these students were very young, ranging from thirteen up to about eighteen. A few in the front row were Yohanan's disciples, twenty-something young men who might someday be rabbis themselves, men who attached themselves to Rabbi Yohanan, immersing themselves in his mode of thought. Ari did not know which of these would survive the war that was coming.

One of the disciples brought a wooden box and set it at the foot of the stairs. Rabbi Yohanan sat down to teach. An expectant hush settled over the young men. Ari felt his heart racing. This was the famous Academy, of which he had heard legends growing up. Ari's stepfather told of many marvels that happened in the Academy of Rabban Yohanan ben Zakkai. Ari had never seen a marvel here, but he had seen greatness in Rabbi Yohanan, and that was —

Ari heard shouts from the western side of the plaza. He turned and saw Brother Eleazar and Brother Gamaliel running toward Rabbi Yohanan.

The old rabbi turned his head, then stood up. Gamaliel and Eleazar arrived, panting. Rabbi Yohanan greeted Gamaliel warmly and gave Eleazar a stiff nod. Ari could not hear what they were saying so he went down the stairs.

". . . leaves immediately after *Pesach* for a far country, but he is too sick to travel," Gamaliel said.

The old rabbi tugged at his beard and then turned to the front row of students. He crooked an ancient finger at a very young boy who appeared to be no more than nine years old. The boy leaped up and joined the old rabbi, grinning with delight.

Rabbi Yohanan hunched down to the boy's level. "My son, you will go with these men and do as they ask."

The boy nodded. "Yes, *Abba*."

Ari did not think the boy was literally the son of Yohanan, but it was clear he was one of the rabbi's inner circle.

Gamaliel came around next to Ari. "Brother Ari! Come with us. Brother Yoseph is very sick." He lowered his voice. "Perhaps you have heard tales of this young boy? It is said that the spirit of Honi the Circler lives in him."

Ari had never heard of Honi the Circler, but Gamaliel seemed very excited.

Rabbi Yohanan patted the boy's shoulders. "Go with the blessing of HaShem, and then hurry back when you are finished."

The four of them began walking back west along the line of the stairs. Ari felt a sliver of disappointment. He had hoped to hear Rabbi Yohanan speak on the meaning of *Pesach*. Yet this thing with Yoseph seemed to be a matter of some importance.

The young boy walked between Gamaliel and Brother Eleazar. Ari walked on the other side of Gamaliel.

Gamaliel wore his usual cheerful grin. "Brother Eleazar, the boy has your name. He is called Eleazar ben Arakh and he works with me in my shop when he is not studying with Rabbi Yohanan. Perhaps we should call him Baby Eleazar, yes?"

Brother Eleazar looked down at the boy and gave him an appraising look. "*Shalom* to you, Baby Eleazar."

The boy did not seem offended by this. He looked Brother Eleazar squarely in the eye. "Why do you hate your father?"

Brother Eleazar's eyebrows shot up and his mouth tightened to a thin line. "Brother Gamaliel, what have you told him?"

Gamaliel shook his head. "Nothing. Baby Eleazar hears many things from HaShem."

"Apparently." Brother Eleazar licked his lips. "Baby Eleazar, please greet Ari the Kazan."

The boy looked up at Ari. He had a smooth, innocent face, untroubled by either beard or care. But his eyes were ancient. Deep pools of seeing lay in those eyes.

Ari said, "How old are you, Eleazar ben Arakh?"

"I am thirteen," Eleazar said. "I became a man last month. My father sent me here to learn with Rabbi Yohanan, because I had learned all that my village teacher could teach me."

Ari nodded. A prodigy. Jewish history knew many of them. "I am glad to meet you, my son. Rabbi Yohanan is a great teacher and you must learn all that he has to teach you."

The boy smiled. "You have eyes that see more than most men, Ari the Kazan. Will you teach me what you know of numbers?"

"Numbers?" Ari said.

Gamaliel gave a short laugh. "Eleazar ben Arakh loves numbers. I have seen him add up the accounts in my shop faster than most men can speak them aloud, and he makes no mistakes. Ari the Kazan, if you have anything to teach him about numbers, he will be glad of it."

"Of course," Ari said. "What is the matter with Brother Yoseph?"

"He is taken ill with a sharp pain in his side," Gamaliel said. "He was to leave on a long journey after *Pesach* and we fear he will not be able to go."

"Pain?" Ari said. "On which side?"

"The right side." Gamaliel pointed to a spot on his own abdomen.

Ari's heart double-thumped. He was no expert in medical matters, but he had nearly died of appendicitis in his teens. "How long has the pain lasted?"

"Since the night before last," Gamaliel said. "He is vomiting and in much pain."

A wave of cold washed over Ari's flesh. "I do not think Brother Yoseph will be taking a long journey."

"He must," said Brother Eleazar in a tone that told Ari that Brother Yoseph was going, sick or not sick.

"Where is he going that is so important?" Ari had heard nothing about a long journey.

"We must hurry." Gamaliel's face suddenly looked very red. "Please, you will ask no more questions on the matter."

They walked the rest of the way to the palace of Yoseph's father in silence. At the gate, the gatekeeper ushered them through the courtyard and hurried them into the palace. They went down a hallway, up some stairs, and into Yoseph's chambers. Yoseph's father and brother hovered over him.

Ari saw at once that Yoseph was in great distress. The look on his face spoke of much pain, and a sheen glistened on his forehead. He wore a linen tunic that stank of sweat. Ari knelt beside the bed and pressed the right side of Yoseph's abdomen. "Brother Yoseph, does it hurt here?"

"Aughhhh!" Yoseph pushed at Ari's hands.

Ari stood up, convinced that his initial guess was right. There was only one chance now. He must go and find Baruch.

"Ari the Kazan, you will stay, please." Baby Eleazar knelt beside Ari and took both of Yoseph's hands in his own. He leaned in close. "Yoseph! Can you hear me?"

Yoseph moaned and his eyelids flickered.

Baby Eleazar shook his head and looked up at Ari. "We are very late. Please, you will take me up on the roof."

"The roof?" Ari stared at him, feeling stupid.

"Quickly." The boy seized Ari's hand and tugged at it. "You will show me the way."

Ari did not know the way to the roof. "Brother Eleazar, take us to the roof."

Brother Eleazar backed out of the room, his eyes dark and hooded. "What does the boy intend?"

Baby Eleazar pulled Ari over to Brother Eleazar and took hold of the big man's hand. "Take me now."

No response.

"Quickly!" the boy shouted.

Both men jumped. Brother Eleazar led the way back outside and around to the back of the palace. They reached a stairway that ran up to the roof. Baby Eleazar bounded up the stairs. Ari looked at Brother Eleazar, then shrugged and followed.

When he reached the flat roof, Ari saw that the boy had walked to the center and knelt down, putting his head between his knees. When Ari reached him, Baby Eleazar was crying out in pain. Praying.

Ari did not know what to do. Should he leave the boy and go find Baruch? Much time had already been lost, but if he hurried, he might find Baruch in time. Soon Brother Yoseph's appendix would rupture and then no amount of prayer would help him.

But Ari could not simply leave the boy, who was clearly in such agony. Ari knelt beside him. "Baby Eleazar!"

The boy continued wailing.

Ari touched his back, then yanked his hand away.

Baby Eleazar's body felt hot to the touch.

Ari's heart was racing now. He wanted to do something, to speak, to comfort, to pray. But he did not know if any of these would do any good.

Something fluttered past Ari's ear. He turned to look.

A pigeon lay lifeless beside him. In the sky, a flock of birds wheeled away south. Ari's mouth went very dry.

Baby Eleazar's voice was a great column of sound now, rising up to heaven. Ari stared at him, wondering if there was still time to find Baruch.

Sudden silence. Baby Eleazar fell forward on his face and lay like a dead man. Ari leaned over him. "Baby Eleazar! Are you well?" He put a hand on the boy's thick mop of black hair.

Baby Eleazar pushed himself up from the roof a few centimeters at a time. Ari saw that his face was red with effort and he looked exhausted. Baby Eleazar stared up at him through bleary eyes. "We must go to Yoseph and see . . ." His eyes focused on the dead bird behind Ari.

Baby Eleazar's breath made a hissing sound. "Yoseph is healed."

Then he burst into tears.

FIFTEEN

Rivka

Rivka stared at Ari in astonishment. A bird fell out of the sky? Dead?

Ari nodded. "This means something?"

Rivka felt a rush of excitement. "There are some Talmudic legends about a man named Honi."

Ari looked puzzled. "Gamaliel said something about Honi the Circler."

"That's him." Rivka began pacing back and forth. "Honi was a famous rabbi credited with enormous miraculous powers. They called him the Circler because . . . long story on that one. I'll tell you sometime. He was a man of prayer. It was said that sometimes when he prayed, birds flying overhead fell out of the sky."

"*Abba!*" Rachel held up her hands. "Hold me!"

Ari reached down and scooped her up. She nuzzled her head into his beard. Ari joggled her on his hip. "What does Honi have to do with Eleazar ben Arakh?"

Rivka didn't know, but she wanted to find out. "All I know is a few stories. Honi lived maybe a century or two ago — nobody really knows. He had the power to heal, power over nature. And Eleazar ben Arakh was similar. Do you know about the five famous disciples of Rabban Yohanan?"

Ari shrugged. "Maybe."

"All five of them will be buried with him in Tiberias," Rivka said. "Unlucky for them, they'll be in the same cemetery as the Rambam's tomb, which is where all the tourists will go. Eleazar ben Arakh will be considered the greatest of the five. But I remember reading that there was something different about him. I think he was excommunicated late in life and nobody knows exactly why."

"A mystery then," Ari said.

"What's a mystery, *Imma?*" Rachel said.

"Something we don't understand, sweetie." Rivka had wondered about Eleazar ben Arakh for years. He was supposed to be a great expounder of

Torah, a man who could make the trees of the field clap their hands when he taught on the mysterious chariot of HaShem in the book of Ezekiel. A man to whom even the angels listened when he expounded the deep mysteries of Creation. But the stories were few and they raised more questions than answers. The truth was, nobody knew diddly about Eleazar ben Arakh, the greatest sage of his generation, a man whom even Rabban Yohanan would someday hold in awe.

"Yeshua understands, doesn't he?" Rachel said. "Rabban Yeshua knows everything! He'll tell you if you ask him."

"I'm sure he will." Rivka pinched Rachel's fat little cheek. "Ari, I want to talk to Eleazar ben Arakh. How do I find him?"

"He works for Gamaliel in his olive-oil shop." Ari set down Rachel and put a hand on Rivka's arm. "You will be careful, yes?"

Rivka pursed her lips. "Careful?"

Ari wrapped his arms around her. "Anyone who can kill birds when he prays is . . ." He stopped.

"Spooky?"

"Yes, Rivkaleh. Spooky."

That afternoon, Rivka left Rachel with Hana and went to see Eleazar ben Arakh. Her heart was thumping in her throat when she approached Gamaliel's shop. What did she expect, anyway? He was a little kid, according to Ari. Sure, he could pray up a storm. Was that enough to make her come running like some kind of groupie?

Rivka didn't know. She didn't care. She was going to see Eleazar ben Arakh and that was that.

When she reached the shop, her hands were quivering. Inside, a little old lady was buying olive oil from a boy. Of course. Ari had said he was a boy. Rivka just hadn't expected a *boy*.

"Thank you, my son," said the woman in the shop.

The boy said, "Come again soon, *Savta*."

The woman practically skipped out, her face shining. Rivka stood aside for her, then stepped inside the tiny shop, about the size of one of those cubicles in American office buildings.

"*Shalom*, sister," said the boy. His eyes took her in with surprise. "From what country do you come?"

"A far country." Rivka smiled at him. His eyes were deep. She could not believe how deep they were. Like bottomless wells, filled with wisdom.

"You have not come for olive oil."

Rivka blushed. "I'm sorry. Of course I would like some olive oil." She fumbled in her belt for a *dinar*.

Eleazar ben Arakh shook his head. "What is your name called and why have you come?"

"My husband is Ari the Kazan, whom you met this morning. My name is called Rivka." Rivka's voice caught. She did not know why she had come. Only that she wanted to see Eleazar ben Arakh, the greatest sage of his generation.

"I am very glad of meeting you, Rivka the Kazan." Eleazar's eyes sparkled as he studied her. "I wish that you were my sister. You have very kind eyes and you see things from the Other Side."

"Other Side?"

"Gamaliel has told me about Rivka the Kazan. He said you are a seer woman, but there are wicked rumors about you. I see that you are a seer and the rumors are lying tales."

Rivka bowed her head. She wished she could see things like that. Wished she could just magically look at people and know things about them. Her eyes blurred. She was never going to be a real seer woman. She would always be a fraud, or worse, someone with just enough gifting to see something, but never enough to make out what she was seeing.

"Sister."

Rivka smeared the sleeve of her tunic across her eyes. "Y–yes?"

"You see many things clearer than I ever will. Please, you must not cry. Be thankful for the gift HaShem has given you."

She sighed deeply. "I see nothing."

"That is not the tale Gamaliel tells. He says you have saved many lives. You feel sad because you see less far than some. Yet you see more than most. Give HaShem thanks for what you see. Give him a sacrifice of praise. Then be glad for what you see and do not be troubled for what you cannot."

A *sacrifice of praise*. Rivka felt lightheaded with surprise. Was it really that simple? She felt a powerful urge to go home and find out. "Thank you, Eleazar. Thank you very much." She turned to leave.

"Sister?"

Rivka spun around. "Yes, little brother?"

"Would you bless me?"

Rivka laughed out loud. The idea seemed absurd. Eleazar ben Arakh was a great man, a sage, a master, a seer.

But he was also a little boy, far from home, perhaps missing his mother. "Of course." Rivka stepped closer and put her right hand on his forehead. She noticed that he did not wear *tefillin*, and that seemed strange. Wasn't he a Pharisee?

Eleazar closed his eyes and raised his hands toward heaven.

"Blessed are you, HaShem, God of our fathers." Rivka hesitated. She didn't know what to say. He would think she was a fool. She swallowed and said the first thing that came into her head. "Eleazar ben Arakh, I bless you to know the deep things of HaShem, to pass through fire and not be burned, through flood and not be drowned, through deep wisdom and not be destroyed. May HaShem hold you always in the palm of his hand, though all men desert you. May you never fall victim to pride, or rage, and may you forgive those who wrong you and may you give back good for evil. In weakness, may you find the strength of HaShem."

Rivka pulled back her hand, terrified. Where had all that nonsense come from?

The boy remained still as stone. Rivka didn't know what to do. Was she finished? Was he?

Nothing happened.

Rivka tiptoed backward toward the door. Maybe the best thing to do would be to simply leave. She backed out through the doorway and squinted into the harsh afternoon sunlight. She was crazy, an idiot for coming here. It was all just her vanity, trying to be somebody she wasn't. She should leave now and never come back.

Rivka risked one more look inside.

Tears gleamed on the cheeks of Eleazar ben Arakh. His lips moved. "Thank you, sister. Please, you will come see me again sometime."

"Of course." Rivka turned and fled.

SIXTEEN

Ari

Ari walked to the back of the workshop of Levi the bronzeworker. "Show me the new chisels."

Levi smiled with pride and reached up on a shelf. "You were right, Ari the Kazan. The new process makes the iron much harder." He took down an oily cotton rag and unfolded it, revealing three chisels.

Ari pounded Levi's shoulder. "Excellent. It is the real thing. You have created Damascus steel. You will keep them covered in a thin layer of oil, except when the workmen are using them. Then they will not rust."

Levi nodded.

Ari spotted something on a lower shelf. He bent down to pick it up. "Brother Levi, what is this?"

Levi moved quicker than Ari could have imagined, stooping to cover it with his large callused hands. "That is something Brother Eleazar asked me to construct for Brother Yoseph."

"I will examine it."

"No." Levi's voice had an edge to it that worried Ari. Levi had never hidden anything from him before.

Ari heard the door of the workshop open. Brother Eleazar's voice called out. "Brother Levi! Are you finished —"

Ari turned to look. Brother Eleazar stood there, his mouth gaping open. It seemed best to take a small gamble. Ari said, "Yes, it is finished. He was just showing it to me."

Levi's voice stuttered. "B–brother Eleazar . . ."

Eleazar's great strides devoured the distance between them. He snatched the bundle. "You were not to show him."

"The workmanship is very fine," Ari said, hoping this would induce Eleazar to open it.

Eleazar thrust the bundle on a stone tabletop and unwrapped it. A short dagger clattered out, forged completely of Damascus steel. Damascus steel was a composite of many fine layers of steel having varying amounts of carbon. The many layers gave it both strength and flexibility — and an exotic-looking grain, almost like wood, but coarser.

The naked beauty of the dagger took Ari's breath. The long irregular grain of the steel made the flat of the blade look almost alive. That same grain gave it a fine serrated edge that would rip flesh on contact. Eleazar reached down and picked it up, his eyes glittering. "Very fine, yes." He looked at Ari. "So. How long have you known?"

Ari gave him his most mysterious smile. "For some time." Which meant for five seconds, but Eleazar did not need to know that. A sick feeling wormed its way into Ari's stomach. All this technology that he had been developing with Levi — for peaceful purposes — would go to war. Technology was technology, and the same steel that made chisels could make daggers, swords, spear tips, arrowheads, and more.

"Yet two years until *Mashiach*." Eleazar hefted the dagger in his hand. "Brother Ari, you are a man who does not choose quickly, and yet soon you must decide. Have you given thought to the matter?"

Ari had given much thought to the matter. "No."

Eleazar held up the dagger and sighted down the straight line of the blade. "I will give you a little longer to think on it. When Brother Yoseph returns from his journey, then you will tell me whether you wish to remain my friend."

"Where is Brother Yoseph going?" Ari asked.

Eleazar looked at Ari and the windows of his eyes snapped shut. "To search out the land of Canaan."

Rivka

That night after Rachel went to bed, Rivka sat praying in her wooden rocking chair, wondering if it could really be so simple. A *sacrifice of praise*.

Thank you, HaShem, for giving me Ari to be my strength. For Rachel. For Hana and Baruch and Dov. For Hanan ben Hanan.

"Rivkaleh."

She opened her eyes. Ari had seemed preoccupied all evening. Now he looked sick to his stomach. "Ari, are you feeling okay?"

"Brother Eleazar is pressuring me again. He has given me a deadline, after which I will be his enemy."

Rivka sighed. "You should have nothing to do with that man. He scares me."

Ari pulled the second rocking chair close to Rivka's and folded his big frame into it. "I also am frightened. He has given me until Brother Yoseph returns from a certain mysterious journey, of which he refuses to speak. I do not know how long this journey will last."

"Journey? Why didn't you ask me?" Rivka began rocking. "Yoseph is going to Rome."

"Rome?" Ari sounded skeptical. "Brother Eleazar said he was going to search out the land of Canaan."

Rivka felt heat in her throat. *Canaan?*

"Please, you will tell me what you know."

Rivka had long ago read *Life of Josephus*. In Greek. "Josephus says that in the twenty-sixth year of his age, he went to Rome. We know he was born in the winter of A.D. 37 or 38, and this is now the year 64. So he's twenty-six. Therefore, he's going to Rome this year."

"What does it mean to search out the land of Canaan?"

"It means he's a spy. Moses sent twelve spies into Canaan to spy out the land." Rivka rocked faster in her chair. "Josephus went to Rome to beg the release of a number of priests. They were very pious men who kept kosher even in prison."

"Priests? In prison? On what charge?" Ari said.

"That's the strange thing. He doesn't say, exactly. He calls it a trifling charge, but he doesn't bother to explain it at all. It's almost like he was embarrassed about it."

"There was some tension this morning between Gamaliel and Brother Eleazar when they told me of it."

"Maybe you should ask Gamaliel," Rivka said. "It sounds like Yoseph intends to spy out Rome. Which is really strange." Rivka closed her eyes and concentrated. "Josephus claims that in Rome he was awestruck by the military might he saw there, that he came back and urged his zealous countrymen not to pick a fight with Rome."

"With respect, Rivkaleh, Yoseph is not the kind of man to back away from a fight."

"I'm just telling you what he wrote in his book. You can believe it or not. I've caught him in plenty of fibs already."

Ari's eyes clouded. "He is going as a spy then. The reason is clear. He knows that time is short and he wishes to learn the ways of the enemy."

Rivka felt her whole body tensing. There was no stopping the war that was coming. "We'll have to leave the city. Soon."

"Do you know when?"

"I've been praying about that. We can't leave during this drought. Trying to find a new home in the countryside during a drought—that's just suicide. I was hoping to ask Baby Eleazar about that today, but I forgot all about it."

"Was he the great man of HaShem you were expecting?" Ari sounded amused.

"Yes. Well, he was the great boy of HaShem." Rivka smiled. "You've met him. He has these incredible deep eyes. He sees right through the veil, sees the Other Side as plain as sunlight. He knows HaShem. And he told me to make a sacrifice of praise."

"A what?" Ari's voice sounded tight, intense.

Rivka opened her eyes. "A sacrifice of praise. It's in the psalms."

"What does that mean, a sacrifice of praise? In what sense is praise a sacrifice?"

"I don't know." Rivka studied him. "What's this all about?"

"It is something Baruch told me last fall. He said that sacrifice releases power. Have you heard this thing? Is it in Torah?"

Rivka tried to remember. She hadn't heard any such thing, at least not explicitly. And yet it was all through the Torah, implicitly. Blood sacrifices. Atonement. "Was this about Rabban Yeshua?"

Ari nodded. "Baruch said that Rabban Yeshua is the *Pesach* lamb, that his blood atones for many."

Rivka held her breath. They had had so many arguments over this matter that she had long ago decided to let it rest. She wanted with all her heart for Ari to come to Yeshua, but she couldn't force him. And pressuring him only backed him up against a wall.

Ari put a hand on hers. "I am sorry for mentioning the matter. I do not wish to make a fight with you."

She patted his arm. "I love you, Ari. I don't want to fight with you either, but I do want you to follow Yeshua, if you can do that. Someday. When you're ready."

Ari reached inside his belt and took out the small wooden cross he always carried there. "I think you understand why that is not possible."

"None of those bad things have happened yet."

"They have happened in my reference frame and in yours," Ari said. "Not in Baruch's. Therefore, I do not condemn him as a false Jew."

"What about me? Am I a false Jew?"

Ari shook his head. "You are an American. My family came to Israel through the camps of Europe. It is different. For me to follow Yeshua ... no, to do that would make me a false Jew."

Rivka sighed.

"Will I burn in hell if I do not follow Rabban Yeshua?"

"You would be happier following him." It was an evasion and Rivka knew it.

"Rivkaleh, I do not think it is meant for me to be happy. Enough that I should do the will of HaShem. He has a thing for me to do, and if I do that, then all will be well."

"I think he wants you to enjoy his friendship, Ari. Not just do some great thing, but live in his presence. Don't you want that?"

"Do I require Rabban Yeshua for that?"

"I think so."

"And what of Baby Eleazar?" Ari asked. "Does he know nothing of HaShem? Does he live outside of HaShem's presence? He does not follow Rabban Yeshua."

Rivka had no answer to that. She just didn't know. She wanted desperately to understand, to figure it out. There were lots of good men throughout history, deeply spiritual men who weren't Christians. Were they unsaved?

She could quote a hundred verses from the New Testament that said Yeshua was the only way to God. But Ari would not accept an answer based on the New Testament. He would accept only logic, and logic was not enough.

"Rivkaleh." Ari held out his arms to her.

Rivka sighed and rocked forward to stand up. She nestled into Ari's lap. He wrapped his arms around her, rocking, rocking. The chair groaned under their combined weight.

Hot tears formed in Rivka's eyes. Ari wasn't ever going to come to Rabban Yeshua. No matter how smart she was, no matter how good her answers, he wasn't going to do it. He'd always have some reason not to, some logic. She couldn't make him, and HaShem wouldn't make him, and he was just going to live his whole life like that, was going to die like that. Separated from Yeshua. Separated from her, maybe for all eternity.

Rivka wept.

SEVENTEEN

Berenike

On a sweltering midsummer day in Caesarea, Berenike met the new governor of Judea, whom the seer woman had warned her about five years ago. Governor Florus was bald as an egg, with thick jowls and moist, meaty hands. Berenike instantly hated him.

"So." His eyes traveled up and down her body and he licked his lips. "You are the famous Berenike." He gave Agrippa a leering wink. "You are a lucky man."

Berenike's pulse pounded in her neck. She did *not* want to know what he meant by that. She had put the ugly rumors behind her long ago. Once, those rumors had been true, but never again. Never again.

Florus glared at Berenike. "Well? Is it true?"

"Is *what* true?" She gave him her frostiest glance.

"Do not be coy with me." Florus stood up from his marble chair and paced back and forth in front of the alcove that opened west to the Great Sea. "Everyone in this accursed city is talking about it."

Berenike wanted to spit on him and walk out, but she did not dare. Florus had been here in Caesarea for weeks now, having arrived to replace Governor Albinus, who was recalled to Rome. She pulled out her ivory fan and whiffed her face. The day's humidity made her drowsy, but this horrible lecher had woken her up.

Agrippa said nothing, of course. He would be useless in standing up to Governor Florus. And somebody *must* stand up to him. Berenike knew from the seer woman that this man would destroy all unless she could find a way to stop him.

Florus spun on his heel and rubbed two fingers of his right hand before Berenike's face. "Is it true that Albinus made a tidy little business of releasing outlaws for money?"

Oh, that. Berenike felt a rush of relief that he did not know her dark secret. "Yes, it is true. We wrote to Caesar about the matter when the first ships sailed in spring." *And if we had known it would result in you, we would have said nothing.*

The governor's florid face brightened a shade. "Well? Where are they?" he bellowed.

"Where are who?"

"The outlaws!" Florus began pacing again. "I want my share of this business. My aides tell me there is nothing to be made from this wretched province, short of selling outlaws their freedom."

"Excellency." Agrippa coughed lightly. "Your predecessor had few skills, but he was most efficient in this one business. When he heard you were detained in Egypt, he emptied the prisons, taking every *drachma* he could get. I understand there are none left."

Florus looked ready to erupt.

Berenike raised her fan to hide her smile. Florus had not been *detained* in Egypt. He had dallied there overlong, enjoying the legendary houses of prostitution in Alexandria. By tradition, a governor came direct to his new posting a month before his predecessor left office, so there would be continuity. Florus had arrived here in Caesarea mere hours before Albinus left. So if he had missed out on Albinus's miserable scheme, it was his own fault.

"Then tell me something." Florus began pacing again. "How is a man to make an honest living in this miserable little province? I am told the taxes are reduced by a fourth part since Albinus came here. That leaves little for Caesar and nothing for me."

"There is a drought," Berenike said. "Furthermore, bandits raid the countryside. The peasants have nothing to pay."

"A drought," Florus muttered. He jabbed a fat finger at Agrippa's face. "Are you aware that Caesar has changed his policy? He will be changing governors more frequently from now on. I have two or three years to make my fortune in this rat's nest and then I go back to Rome. I do not have time for a *drought!*"

"The people are starving," Berenike said. "One cannot squeeze blood from —"

"They are lazy." Florus glowered at her. "Filthy Jews! Liars and thieves, all of them."

"You are aware that *we* are Jewish?" Berenike gave him her coldest voice.

"They trade wives also," Florus said. "In Rome, there is not a Jewish man who knows if his son is his own."

Berenike bit back her rage. The seer woman had understated the matter. Florus was a disaster. She wondered whether she could find a way to poison him.

"I want to meet those head priests of yours in Jerusalem," Florus said. "I hear they are the ones who have been paying the best prices for the outlaws."

Berenike would pay money to see Florus in the same room with such as Hanan ben Hanan. She put on a regretful look. "No, they will not meet with you."

Florus looked ready to bite her head off. "What do you mean, no? I am the governor! They have to meet with me."

"It is a matter of ritual purity," Berenike said. "They are very pious and do not touch unclean men."

Fury lit up Florus's eyes. "What does this mean, *unclean men?*"

Agrippa looked thoroughly alarmed. "Excellency, of course they will meet with you."

Florus stepped directly in front of Berenike. "Explain this to me. What does it mean, *unclean men?*" Flecks of spittle flew out of his mouth.

Berenike stepped away from him. "Uncircumcised men."

Florus spun around and jabbed a finger at Agrippa. "Unclean?" he roared. "*We* are unclean because we do not mutilate ourselves? Is this some form of sick humor?"

"Excellency, I am sure our chief priests will meet with you." Agrippa was stuttering now.

Berenike thought that he could not have played this part better if she had rehearsed him for it.

"They *will* meet with me." Florus punched a meaty fist into his open palm. "These filth with their disgusting customs! Who are they to call Romans unclean?"

"They *may* agree to meet with you," Berenike said, twisting her face into a doubtful expression. "Only do not expect them to meet with you on the *Sabbaton*. They will not meet with you then, not under any circumstances."

Florus stomped over to a tall wooden desk where his secretary stood. "Make ink and take a letter!" Florus barked. He waved a fat hand at Agrippa and Berenike. "Dismissed!"

Berenike swept out of the chamber, past the great pool, admiring the marble statues commissioned by her great-grandfather. Outside the

Praetorium, she favored Agrippa with a gleeful smile. Florus was a horrible, horrible man. It would be such *fun* to see how those terrible chief priests handled him.

Hanan ben Hanan

Five days later, Hanan and the other chief priests gathered in the Chamber of Hewn Stone just across from the Temple Mount, awaiting the arrival of the new governor. It was midmorning, and already Hanan was sweating fiercely.

Yeshua ben Gamaliel leaned close to him. "He is more than an hour late! Perhaps we should go."

Hanan shook his head. "He is dishonoring us on account of yesterday." The day before, a *Shabbat*, they had all ignored the governor's order to meet with them in Herod's Palace. Of course that was a simple misunderstanding on his part. Somebody should have warned the governor that Jews did not conduct business on *Shabbat*. Now Florus was angry, but Hanan would explain the matter when—

A clatter of iron boots outside.

Hanan looked to the huge oaken door in time to see it swing open. Dozens of Roman soldiers poured in. Hanan felt deep annoyance. These common soldiers were swine. The governor needed some as protection, perhaps, but not so many.

A stout, jowly man in a toga strutted into the room. A thin purple stripe along the straight edge of the toga told Hanan that Florus was a man of equestrian rank, not a commoner, but also not of the high aristocratic families who populated the Roman Senate. Another minor noble, sent to govern the city of the living God. Absurd!

Governor Florus strode directly to the center of the room. "Who is the head priest here?" he asked in somewhat stilted Greek. Hanan spoke Greek fluently, having learned it from an Egyptian Jewish nursemaid as a very young boy. Greek was a vile language, fit only for dogs and *goyim*.

Yeshua ben Gamaliel stood up. "Excellency, my name is called Yesous the son of Gamaliel and I am the high priest of the living God." Yeshua's Greek was quite polished, because he had studied it as a young man, but he was not as fluent as Hanan.

Florus scowled at him, then snapped his fingers. "Come here, Jew."

Hanan pushed back his fury. This Florus had the manners of a pig, but he was governor. They needed his cooperation if they were to solve—

"Quickly!" Florus shouted.

Yeshua scurried forward, his face turning very red.

Florus thrust a thick hand toward Yeshua. Yeshua hesitated, then slowly reached forward. Florus seized his wrist and they clasped arms. Florus did not let go. "Am I unclean, then?"

Hanan could not believe this man's lack of manners. As a *goy*, of course he was unclean, but it was useless to dwell on such matters.

Yeshua said nothing.

"Let me tell you what I think of you." Florus thrust Yeshua's hand away. "You Jews are all dogs. Whining, filthy, thieving dogs. When I see a dog digging in my refuse heap, I have it beaten."

He began pacing. "This entire province is a refuse heap! Albinus failed to meet the requirements for collection of taxes. He is short more than four talents and —"

"Excellency." Hanan stepped forward beside Yeshua.

Florus's eyes bulged. "You dare to interrupt me?"

"Excellency, with your permission, there is a drought, very severe." Hanan met his eyes without blinking. "Taxes are reduced because the people are distressed by —"

"What is your name?" Florus said.

"My name in Greek is called Ananus the son of Ananus."

Florus studied him with malevolent eyes. "Sit down and be silent, Ananus. I did not give you leave to speak, and if you interrupt me again, I will have you flogged."

Hanan sat. He would never have believed it, but he regretted the loss of Albinus.

Florus put his right hand behind his back. Hanan saw that his left arm was permanently cocked at an angle, supporting the folds of his toga. A most inconvenient garment, the toga.

"As I was saying, receipts of taxes are down," Florus said. "Caesar's policy has changed recently. He means to assign governors for short periods — two years, perhaps three. This means that I have only a short time in which to earn my rightful fortune. I am not interested in foolishness about a *drought*. You men are the rulers of this city, and you will see to it that the province pays its rightful share."

Hanan felt his jaw sagging. Florus was mad. The man could not mean what he was saying. The Temple was not responsible for overseeing tax collection in Judea, not even in Jerusalem. That was the responsibility of Rome and her agents.

"There is another matter," Florus said. "When I send for you, you will come, whether it is your *Sabbaton* or no. I will not be delayed by your foolish superstitions."

Hanan wanted to tell Florus that these things were not possible. Wanted to tell him that *Shabbat* could not be violated on any account, that the Temple could not raise taxes, that anyone who thought so was a fool.

But a man who tried to talk reason with a fool would be twice a fool.

Hanan slumped into his chair and watched Governor Florus stalk out of the Chamber of Hewn Stone. One thing was very clear.

Governor Florus had to be killed. Quickly.

Ari

Ari had never felt so discouraged. It was a bright summer afternoon, and he was walking down the long market street in the shadow of the Temple Mount. Around him, many hundred shoppers chatted gaily. Shopkeepers barked, women bargained, children shrieked at play. The smell of roasting goat meat and pickled vegetables and sharp cheese filled his nose. Ari felt physically sick.

All Jerusalem was awash in rumors about the new governor, Florus. It was said he was greedy for silver, that he despised Jews, that he would stop at nothing to line his purse.

But Ari knew more. Rivka had spent an hour last night telling him all that she knew about Governor Florus. Soon enough, people would say that Albinus had been an angel by comparison. Florus would pursue his reckless road to wealth and drive Judea to war.

Ari hated this man. He wanted to kill Governor Florus. That was foolishness, of course. Ari was a pacifist, had always been a pacifist. And yet . . .

Ari had read a book once about the famous Christian theologian, Dietrich Bonhoeffer. He too was a pacifist. Yet during World War II, Bonhoeffer had conspired in the famous assassination attempt at Wolffschanze. Had the bomb been placed six inches further in, had the blast not been partially blocked by the stout wooden table leg, Hitler would have been killed. In 1944. A million Jews would have been saved.

Less than two years from now, Governor Florus would provoke a revolt that would destroy this city and make captives of its inhabitants. Hundreds of thousands of Jews, possibly millions, would die. On account of one evil man.

Ari would kill him if he could, pacifism or no pacifism.

But that was foolishness. He could not get close enough to Governor Florus to kill him. Furthermore, history said that Florus would live and Jerusalem would die. Ari could not change that, but he could do *something* to oppose evil. He did not know exactly what. HaShem had given him his life back to do a great thing. He would do that great thing, and then if he died, it would be enough.

Rivka would give birth to a cow if she heard such things. She hated and feared the coming war. Every day she cried out to HaShem to make a way for them to leave the city. If Ari stayed, it would crush Rivka's heart. So for the sake of Rivka and Racheleh, he could not stay and resist evil. But at least his heart burned to do so. That was something.

At the end of the avenue, Ari found the shop he was looking for. He reached into his belt and withdrew a short dagger, forged of Damascus steel by Levi the bronzeworker. Ari had found a new improvement to get more carbon into the steel, and it was now more beautiful than ever, its ragged grain more chaotic, its cutting edge more savage.

Ari took a breath and stepped inside the small shop. "*Shalom,* Brother Gamaliel."

Gamaliel's head shot up from the ledger of accounts he was toiling over. "Brother Ari!"

"I have brought you something." Ari handed him the dagger. "A gift. Please, you will make good use of it." A small contribution to those who would oppose evil.

Gamaliel slipped the dagger inside his cloth belt. He clasped hands with Ari. "I thank you, my friend."

Ari drew in a deep breath. Now he needed a favor. "When will Brother Yoseph return from Rome?"

Gamaliel's eyes hooded with suspicion. "Who told you he went to Rome?"

Ari saw no reason to lie. "My woman told me. HaShem showed her."

Gamaliel nodded. "Brother Yoseph will return by fall, or next spring at latest."

"What did the priests do who are in prison?"

Gamaliel sprang away from him, shock shining in his black eyes. "Did your woman tell you about the priests?"

"Of course. What did they do?"

"Please, you will not speak of it." Gamaliel's face turned red.

"I need to know the truth," Ari said. "Many ten thousand lives may depend on it."

"Did your woman tell you so?"

Ari did not know if she had said any such thing, but he needed to know. "Yes."

Gamaliel was sweating now. "I . . . I am the cause of it. Because of me, the brothers are in prison. Yoseph means to find a way to gain their release, and then he will return."

Ari stared at him. "Brothers? These are Sons of Righteous Priests?"

Gamaliel nodded. "Please, it is a matter of grave dishonor. I did a foolish thing once, and on my account, they have been in prison these seven years."

Ari did a quick calculation. He had been here in Jerusalem for a bit more than seven years. "Please, you will tell me."

Gamaliel shook his head. "Another time. If Brother Yoseph — "

A shout outside jerked Ari's head around. He stepped to the door and peered out. A torrent of men came racing down the street toward him.

Ari ducked back inside and slammed the door. "Another food riot!"

Gamaliel was beside him in an instant. He slammed a thick bar into place, wedging the stout wooden door shut.

Seconds later, the street outside was alive with hate. Gamaliel leaned against the door, as if he could hold the door shut against the mob. Ari also leaned against the door.

The sound outside rose to a crescendo. Something heavy began pounding on the door. Ari's elbows stung at each blow. The shouts of men filtered in overhead through the thin window slits.

"If they throw in a torch, we will have to go out," Gamaliel said.

Ari waited, his throat dry with fear. Olive oil was flammable.

After a very long time, the shouting outside died down. Gamaliel waited, pressing his ear against the door. Finally he nodded. "I think it is safe."

They stepped back and unbarred the door. Outside, the street was carnage. A barrel of beer had been tipped over in the street. The cloth merchant two doors away had his entire inventory strewn in the street. Several doors had been smashed in, their shops looted.

Gamaliel locked his shop. "We must see what has happened."

Together, they walked up the street. It was the same story everywhere. The whole shopping district was wrecked. After walking five hundred meters, they turned left onto the broad avenue that led northwest for a full kilometer in a straight line to the city gate. This opened out quickly into a warehouse district. Gamaliel hurried forward. One of the large wheat warehouses had been destroyed.

Ari could not believe this foolish destruction. The large wooden double doors had been ripped off their iron hinges. Inside, emptiness. Great storage bins of many cubic meters were ransacked. Ari turned to Gamaliel. "Who owns this, do you know?"

Gamaliel was white-lipped with anger. "Naqdimon ben Gorion. He is a righteous man, a Pharisee. He sits on the Sanhedrin, like his father and grandfather before him, a pious man who gives many alms to the poor. This is a great evil."

Ari did not say anything. Yes, it was evil, but it was only hungry men stealing food to feed their families.

It was nothing to the horrors that were coming.

EIGHTEEN

Rivka

Rivka paced the streets of the New City, praying. Ari had come home yesterday after the food riot, shaken and angry. They had talked far into the night. Yes, he agreed with her at last, they must leave the city soon. In two years, this city would burn with zeal, and Florus would rampage through these streets. They must leave the city before then. According to Eusebius, the whole community of The Way would leave at the prompting of "an oracle."

Rivka had a hunch who that oracle might be.

But a hunch was not knowing, and she had determined never again to do anything without hearing from HaShem. If only she could hear better!

So every afternoon, she left Rachel in the care of Hana and came out to offer up a sacrifice of praise and pray over the streets of this city of God. She wanted desperately to save these souls, but she was going to do it God's way, or not at all.

Please, HaShem. Bless these people. Bless this city. Bless . . .

Rivka bit her lip. It was just so hard to pray for Hanan ben Hanan. He symbolized everything that was evil in this city. She hated him. And therefore she had to pray for him. If she could learn to love him, she could love anyone.

HaShem, thank you for putting Hanan ben Hanan in my life.

Rivka sighed. It made no sense to give thanks for Hanan ben Hanan. He didn't care about this city, about this wretched drought, about the fact that unemployment had gone through the roof when they finished construction on the Temple.

According to Josephus, eighteen thousand men were put out of work. Josephus was known to exaggerate his population numbers, but still. Probably thousands of day laborers had lost their jobs. The Temple hierarchy had asked Agrippa's permission to start up another work project in the Temple. He had refused, and there were no prospects for any other construction.

Rivka stopped. A cloud of dust swirled around her feet — the dust of a dry city, short on rain for the past two years. There *was* supposed to be another construction project. According to Josephus, King Agrippa was going to allow the Temple to finance a new public project. Paving the streets of Jerusalem with white stone.

Rivka hadn't heard a word yet about this paving project. Ari was always the first to know anything about construction in Jerusalem. If there was something planned, he'd have told her months ago. Had Josephus got it wrong? He wasn't even in town — he'd gone off to Rome.

An old line from *Star Trek* flashed through Rivka's mind. *Make it so.*

She stared up at the bright blue sky. The sun scorched down on her, but suddenly she felt very cold. *HaShem, is that you?*

Rivka began walking again. This whole business of listening to HaShem was so frustrating. Like God was playing peek-a-boo with her. She never knew if it was him or not. Why did it have to be so hard?

She turned right at the next intersection and headed south. Soon, she reached a broad avenue and turned left toward the market area near the Temple Mount. She scurried through the ruined market street. The mob yesterday had just gutted the place. Now she was running. Shopkeepers turned to stare at her. A woman didn't run in Jerusalem. It wasn't seemly. Rivka didn't give a rip anymore about what was seemly and what wasn't.

Just before Gamaliel's shop, she stopped and caught her breath. Then she wiped her sweaty hands on her tunic and stepped into the little shop.

Baby Eleazar looked up. "A blessed day, sister! I am glad you have come to visit me. You have been speaking with HaShem, I see."

"How . . . ?" Rivka stared at him.

"Your face is shining. You have been in the *Shekinah*." Baby Eleazar smiled. "It is good to be in the presence of HaShem, yes?"

Rivka felt a tingle in her heart. "Do you think I heard from HaShem?"

Baby Eleazar studied her. "Did you hear to follow other gods?"

"No."

"Did you hear to violate the commandments?"

Rivka shook her head. "No."

"To do a good thing?"

"I think so."

Baby Eleazar's eyes glittered, deep pools of knowing. "Please, you will do what HaShem has commanded you. Obedience is better than sacrifice."

"But I'm not sure I truly heard from HaShem."

"Please, you will do it anyway. When you hear to do a merciful thing, that is always at least a whisper from the heart of HaShem. Obedience will strengthen the ears of your spirit."

Rivka took a deep breath. "I will do it."

"Go in peace, sister."

It's called the ripple effect," Rivka said. She was lying on the couch in the garden of Berenike's palace and had spent half an hour trying to persuade her to get Agrippa to pay to pave the streets of Jerusalem. "You spend a *dinar* hiring a workman. He spends that *dinar* to buy bread from a baker, who spends it to buy sandals from a leather-worker, who spends it to buy firewood from a wood-carrier, who spends it . . . you get the picture. And all of those men are engaged in useful work, so they maintain their honor and they have no time for rioting, for plotting against Rome. Everybody wins."

Berenike looked skeptical. "Everybody? How is this possible?"

Rivka sighed. She remembered reading that in ancient cultures, people thought economics was a zero-sum game. Therefore, the poor hated the rich because they assumed that there was a fixed amount of money. Whereas modern people realized that you could actually create wealth, either by stimulating the economy or by enhancing productivity. But how to explain that?

Berenike studied her. "Do you know this on your own knowledge, or is this revealed to you from HaShem?"

"I know it from —" Rivka caught herself. She had been going to say that HaShem had told her. Which was a lie. HaShem had allowed her a view of the far future and a knowledge of economics, but it was lying to say that he had told her. She had to tell the truth. No more lying.

"I know it from my own knowledge." Rivka stood up. She might as well leave now. Berenike wasn't going to be convinced.

"I did not give you leave to go." Berenike pointed to the couch. "You will sit with me again."

Rivka felt her blood pressure notch upward. If Berenike was going to slap her, she wasn't interested.

Berenike snapped her fingers and pointed to the place beside her.

Rivka reclined.

"You have changed, seer woman. Before, you would have lied to me and said HaShem spoke to you."

"Yes, I've changed." Rivka felt her ears burning hot. "I'm sorry. I haven't always been very honest with you."

"You predicted Albinus. And Florus. Did you know those of your own knowledge?"

"Yes," Rivka said in a very small voice.

"And you told me my future. Was that your word or HaShem's?"

"Mine." Rivka felt like a fool. "But I know all that I foretold will happen."

"And if I decide no?" Berenike's eyes were hot lances, piercing Rivka.

Rivka did not know the answer. All she knew was that those things would happen. Josephus said so. They were ordained. Therefore, why did Rivka feel that she was personally responsible to make them happen? She put her hand on Berenike's arm. "I should never have told you your future."

"You told me some hard things."

"But not beyond your ability." Rivka smiled encouragement. "Perhaps beyond your brother, but not beyond you." *Good grief, I'm manipulating her again.*

Berenike's eyes flashed with anger. "If I wish to be flattered, I have many who are skilled at it. Leave me!"

"I'm sorry, I —"

Berenike rolled away from her. "You will go now."

"Will you think on the matter of the streets?"

"Leave!" Berenike shrieked.

Rivka hurried away, cursing her own stupidity. She had meant to do well, and she had blown it. Again.

Berenike

No, there is nothing to be gained by paving the streets," Agrippa said. "It is foolishness. You must give me a more persuasive argument."

Berenike did not know how to argue the case further. She had given the matter much thought all afternoon. The seer woman knew things. She admitting to lying. Yet she knew things that were to come. If she said that tomorrow horses would fly over the Temple, Berenike would not believe it, because horses could not fly. But if she said that tomorrow, a horseman would come with a letter from Governor Florus, Berenike would expect a letter, because it was the sort of thing that could happen.

The seer woman said that the streets would rise up in rage, and Berenike believed that, because the streets had already risen up. To say that they would do so again was plausible. To say that one could prevent this unrest by putting men to work — that too was plausible. The seer woman's ripple effect might be real. After much thought this afternoon, Berenike had decided that it was real. The seer woman spoke as one who has seen a thing, not as one who wishes for a thing. Berenike would wager many ten thousand *dinars* that this ripple effect was real, that it would smother the flames of discontent in the streets.

But it required money, and Agrippa did not like spending money on things that were merely useful. If it was a matter of building statues to beautify a city, he was happy to do so. He had commissioned much art in Banias and Caesarea this year. But paving streets? Where was the honor in that?

They had spent the whole evening meal arguing about the matter, and Berenike had a headache. They were reclining on a broad couch in their dining room, looking out over the Temple and enjoying the cool of the evening. Torches in the Temple courts flickered in the twilight — the Temple guards moving to their posts at the gates. The courts of the Temple were paved in white stone. It was the greatest Temple in the world, and all because their great-grandfather had been a man of vision, one willing to dare great things. Whereas Agrippa would not even dare small things.

"So you will do nothing then?" Berenike said.

"I did not say so." Agrippa's eyes glittered in the light of a dozen olive-oil lamps. "I said that you must give me a more persuasive argument."

That made no sense. Berenike had made her best arguments already. She was tired of this foolish game. The seer woman was right, but Agrippa did not care. Perhaps, once again, he did not wish to be told what to do by a woman. Berenike snapped her fingers. "Shlomi, come! Help me up!"

Her servant Shlomi extended a hand and pulled Berenike up. Berenike swung her legs over the side of the couch and stalked out. She had asked Agrippa a most reasonable thing, and he refused it, for no reason. Was there no way to resolve this muddle?

At midnight, Berenike woke from a light sleep. She lay for a time, tense as a tiger. On a small bedroll on the floor, Shlomi lay snoring. Shlomi was a heavy sleeper and she never awoke when Berenike rose in the middle of the night to pass water. Berenike rolled silently out of bed and stepped past Shlomi to her small latrine. She relieved herself, then stood for a long time at the window slits, staring out through the ivory shutters at the Temple.

The city lay sleeping beneath her, this city which looked to her for help. And she had none to give.

Except . . .

Berenike looked again at Shlomi. Still snoring.

She went to her large closet and selected a tunica. Berenike was not used to dressing herself — that was what servants were for — but she fitted it over her head and let it slide down her body. Carefully now.

Berenike tiptoed to the door of her sleeping chamber. She cracked the great oaken door ajar and peered out. The palace lay sleeping. Olive-oil lamps burned in a few niches in the walls, splashing pools of light in the dark hallway. Berenike eased out into the hallway and held her breath as she pulled the door shut. It was so rare for her to go anywhere without a servant that she felt naked when she was alone.

She glided silently down the hallway, steering around the patches of light as best she could. Several doors passed her on either side. She had done this once before. Only once, and it had ended badly, because it was for herself. This time, it was for her city.

Berenike reached the door.

Turned the golden handle.

Eased it inward.

Stepped inside.

She shut the door and dared to breathe.

Moonlight flooded in through the window. Berenike moved inward on silent cat feet. A great golden bed. A silent figure in the bed, breathing evenly.

Berenike sat on the bed. Her lungs were on fire now. She must not do this. She had to do this.

She lay down.

The even breathing became ragged and then . . .

A fierce whisper. "Berenike! What are you doing here?"

"To persuade you." Berenike felt sick at heart. She had promised herself never again.

Agrippa laughed softly.

Ari

Ari the Kazan!"

Ari turned at the shout. Two men hurried toward him. Ari had met them once in the Hasmonean Palace. Their names were Saul and Costabar and they were cousins of King Agrippa. Ari did not like them. They had a reputation as gamblers and idlers, and they treated Ari as scum, a commoner who actually *worked* for pay.

Ari waited. Saul was taller than his brother Costabar, and he had an auburn tint to his hair, though his beard was black. Costabar was the younger of the two, and he had a scar across his forehead for which Ari had never heard a satisfactory explanation. He understood that it involved an angry husband, but the details were vague.

"Ari the Kazan," Saul said again.

"Saul." Ari did not smile. "Costabar."

"You were speaking with Agrippa this morning in the palace." Saul said this as if Ari should be ashamed of it.

"Yes."

"On a matter of importance?" Saul's eyes gleamed. For him, a matter of importance could only involve money.

"Yes."

"He has commissioned you for a *task?*" Saul pronounced this as if it were a disgusting and fatal disease.

"What can I do for you?" Ari looked at both men. They were much shorter than he, but there were two of them and they had taken an intimidating stance, with Saul directly in front of him and Costabar to the side, slightly behind Ari.

Saul smiled as if Ari were a slow student. He took out a very short iron dagger and began cleaning his fingernails. "I have a minor debt — a foolish fellow won a sum from me at dice. I would consider it a service if you could make me a small loan."

"A loan." Ari knew that neither Saul nor Costabar ever repaid loans.

"A small one," Saul said.

"How small is small?" Ari said. "I have a few *dinars* with me now." This was a deliberate insult, but he was tired of their petty foolishness.

"Two thousand *dinars*." Saul smiled. "A small sum for one such as you, who deals in large contracts with our cousin, the king."

Costabar coughed gently. Ari turned to look and saw that Costabar had also taken out a short dagger and was calmly holding it in his palm.

It was a holdup, as simple and direct as the one Ari had seen once in Princeton, when a man walked into a bank with a gun and asked the teller for money. He could complain to King Agrippa, but the king turned a blind eye to his cousins and it would be two men's word against one. They would say that they had politely asked for a loan, that Ari the Kazan had misinterpreted their innocent request. And Ari would seem like a petty man, unwilling to help others when he had a contract for fifty thousand *dinars* for the paving of the streets of Jerusalem.

Sweat stood on the back of Ari's neck. He could not afford this foolishness. But to refuse them would be to ask for violence at the hands of these thugs.

"You will help us, yes?" Saul said, and the dagger gleamed in the blinding noon sun.

"Of course, my friends." Ari's eyes flickered from one man to another. "But I do not have two thousand *dinars* in cash. It would be foolish to carry so much."

Both men nodded, their cold eyes watching him closely.

Ari gave them a wry smile. "In fact, I have only two hundred *dinars* with me now. A trifling sum. I would not insult you — "

"It would be of some small value now," Saul said. "So long as the rest were forthcoming tomorrow."

Ari shook his head. "Two hundred *dinars* is nothing. Tomorrow — "

"Now." Saul's tone had gone flat and menacing.

"As you wish." Ari reached inside his cloth belt and pulled out a leather bundle. He unfolded it carefully, revealing a large and heavy dagger forged of Damascus steel. With two quick slashes, he knocked the light iron daggers out of the two men's hands.

Costabar leaped away, a thin red line dripping from his right hand. Saul was caught wrong-footed. Ari seized his beard and put the blade near his throat. "This blade is valued at two hundred *dinars*. Shall I give it to you?"

Costabar tried to circle around, but Ari stepped sideways, keeping Saul between himself and his brother.

"My friends," Ari gave them a savage smile. "You may be thinking that I have a woman and daughter."

Saul's eyes told him that this was exactly what he was thinking.

"If anything should happen to my woman or my daughter, I would hunt you down like rats. I have many friends and many eyes in this city. I have a weapon in my house that you have not imagined. It throws fire at a distance and no iron can stop it. There is no country you could flee to, not Babylon, not Rome, not Spain, that I would not pursue you. Do I make myself clear?"

Saul's eyes were white with terror. "Y–yes."

Costabar's teeth gleamed with malice. "Ari the Kazan, perhaps you have misunderstood."

"Please, you will enlighten me."

Costabar's eyes flicked to the dagger in Ari's hand. "We meant no harm. We took you to be a friend, a man of honor who might aid his friends in need. It is said that you are a generous man. Perhaps we were mistaken."

Ari pushed Saul backward hard. Saul stumbled against Costabar and both of them fell in the dusty street. Ari dropped to his knees and made two swift strokes with his heavy dagger, shattering the blades the two men had dropped. He stood up and stepped toward them, holding up his weapon. "I have many friends in this city and each of them carries a dagger like this. Do not trouble me ever again."

Saul and Costabar staggered to their feet and fled.

NINETEEN

Rivka

Several weeks after Ari was commissioned to pave the streets of Jerusalem, in the heat of a sleepy late summer afternoon, Rivka heard pounding on her door. She went downstairs and opened the door.

A servant boy of about fifteen stood with a folded piece of papyrus. He handed it to her. "Agrippa the king sends word to Rivka the Kazan."

Rivka examined the wax seal on the papyrus. It looked authentic, though she had no way to know for sure. She broke the seal with her thumbnail and opened the note. It was written in Latin, which told her that Agrippa did not wish the note to be read by anyone but her.

Marcus Julius Agrippa, king of Trachonitis, Batanaea, and Gaulanitis, to Rivka, the woman of Ari the Kazan, peace. You will come promptly with the messenger boy to my palace. My sister the queen and I wish to question you on a matter of importance.

Rivka folded the note and stuffed it in her belt. "Just let me get my daughter."

"You will hurry." The boy fidgeted, looking nervously up and down the street as if he expected to be waylaid by bandits.

Rivka closed the door and ran upstairs. "Rachel! Come, let's go see Dov."

Rachel was playing with a small carved wooden doll on the floor. Her face lit up. "Dov! He can be the *abba* and I'll be the *imma!*"

Rivka's heart did a little flutter, then tried to claw its way up into her throat. Rachel was almost six years old. In another six years, she'd be ready to get betrothed. And in the year Rachel turned twelve, destruction would come like a flood over Jerusalem. Rivka leaned against a wall, her head feeling light.

"*Imma?*" Rachel tugged at Rivka's tunic. "*Imma?* Why are you looking that way? It frightens me."

Rivka took Rachel's hand in her own and just held it. She knelt down and hugged her. "I'm sorry, Racheleh. I love you so much, and I'm frightened too. Bad things will happen and I don't want them to happen to you."

"Or Dov?"

"Not Dov either." Rachel stood up. "Let's go see him. You can play there and I need to go see somebody."

"Is it the queen?"

Rivka looked down at her. "What made you say that?"

Rachel gave her a pearled smile. "I don't know. Maybe HaShem told me?"

"Maybe." Rivka tugged her downstairs, wondering how Rachel was always so good at guessing things.

Outside, she locked the door and set off with the messenger boy. He kept hurrying ahead, then turning back and spearing her with impatient eyes. Rachel was dawdling along, stopping every few feet to look at a crack in a wall or a ragged weed or a dead rat in the gutter.

"Let's hurry," Rivka said. "So you can play with Dov."

Rachel hurried.

Eventually, Rivka got Rachel to Hana's place and then followed the boy to the palace of the king and queen. She was no longer awed by this place, these people. They were royalty, yes, but they were just people. The boy led her up to the highest floor, to the dining room Ari had designed for them years ago, which had caused so much trouble. Rivka had never been to this room. She gasped when she saw how high up she was, what a magnificent view of the Temple the room gave.

Agrippa stood at the window staring out across the narrow valley at the Temple. Berenike was pacing behind him. Tension crackled in the room like the last few seconds before kickoff at the Super Bowl back home in San Diego.

"What's going on?" Rivka said.

Berenike kept pacing. "Five years ago, you told us certain things to come."

Rivka nodded. "That's right. Was I wrong?"

Agrippa turned and studied her with black hawk's eyes. "You told true, so far as you told. Now a thing has happened which you have not told."

Rivka jutted her chin at him. "I promised you five years."

"And the five years ended after *Pesach*." Agrippa took a stance with his feet spread well apart, like a gunslinger.

Rivka's pulse notched upward but she met his gaze evenly. "You failed to keep your promise, and yet I kept mine." *And I'm not sure Berenike will keep hers, but she still has two years before the crunch comes.*

Agrippa leaned toward her, his face menacing. "You did not tell us what was to happen this summer."

"That wasn't part of the agreement."

Agrippa moved toward her. "You will tell us more now."

Rivka folded her arms across her chest. "I don't have to put up with your threats."

Berenike stepped between them and put a soothing hand on Rivka's arm. "Please, seer woman. My brother means you no harm, but we have heard word of a thing that has happened at Rome —"

Rivka gasped and felt her face go clammy.

"You know something?" Agrippa said.

Rivka's mind was spinning. She hadn't thought about it much, but yes, she did know something. This was the summer of the year A.D. 64, a terrible year. The year Nero would decide that Christians were not Jews. "There is to be a great fire in Rome." Her voice came out in a hoarse whisper.

Agrippa shot a quick look at Berenike.

Rivka read reams in that glance. "Has it happened already?" She remembered that the fire was set on the night of July 19, A.D. 64. Rivka tried to think what today was in the western calendar. Close to the end of August. So the fire had roared through Rome five or six weeks ago — enough time for a fast ship to bring news to Judea.

"Tell us what you know," Berenike said.

Rivka's throat felt raw. "There was a great fire. It burned for six days before the city fire wardens finally put it under control. Then it got past them again and burned for another three days. It destroyed two thirds of the city, but the Jewish districts were spared. Caesar Nero will take the opportunity to rebuild the city to his liking. He will build himself a new palace, the *Domus Aurea*, Palace of Gold."

"And what is to happen here in Jerusalem?" Agrippa said. "Seer woman, did you not think to warn us about this matter?"

"I . . ." Rivka felt like a fool. "I didn't think of it."

Agrippa looked like he might slap her.

Rivka pulled away from him, stumbled toward the door, tripped, fell.

Berenike interposed herself between Rivka and Agrippa. "Enough!" she hissed at her brother. "Seer woman, you should have warned us. There will be trouble over this."

Rivka raised herself off the floor. "Tell me what you know."

Agrippa held up a parchment document. "I had a letter from Governor Florus today by a fast rider, telling me just what you have said." He looked furious. "You will tell me what is to happen here."

Rivka gawked at him. The truth was, she didn't know. Josephus said little about this period, which only made sense, because he was gone to—

Rome.

To get certain zealous priests out of prison.

To spy out the land of Canaan.

The only districts not burned were those where most of the Jews and Christians lived, but the Christians would get the blame. And so would begin the first great persecution in Rome. The apostles Peter and Paul would soon be martyred. Hundreds more would also die, burned alive as human torches by Nero, who was hungry for a scapegoat. Others would die in the arena.

This was the year that the church of Rome would go underground, separating itself from the synagogue of Rome. And Rivka had a tiny little suspicion who was to blame. Yoseph. Of course she could never prove it. There would never be enough information to answer the question.

Rivka felt like somebody had just slugged her in the stomach, leaving her winded and gasping.

Berenike clutched at Agrippa's arm. "She saw something just now. HaShem showed her a thing."

Rivka shook her head. "No." She looked Berenike in the eye. "HaShem showed me nothing. I know certain facts and from these I can make guesses. But these are far away in Rome. I know nothing of what is to happen here."

"But you can guess?" Agrippa said.

Rivka staggered toward the window, her knees feeling like Jell-O. She leaned her hands on the sill and peered out. "Yes, I can guess. The same things you guess."

"When word reaches the streets, there will be a riot," Berenike said.

"Yes." Rivka's heart beat madly in her chest.

And you don't need a seer woman to tell you that.

Ari

The following morning, at the close of the morning prayers, the synagogue of The Way prayed the *Sh'ma* together. Ari thought it was a fine way to begin the day, as dawn broke over the city of HaShem, to say the *Sh'ma*.

The voice of Shimon ben Klopas began the prayer and all the others joined in. "*Sh'ma, Yisrael! Adonai, Eloheinu! Adonai echad!*" Hear, Israel. The Lord our God. The Lord is One!

Ari loved this prayer, which was already ancient and would live on without change into the far future. Jews for two thousand years would chant the *Sh'ma* as they died at the hands of Christians who insisted that God was not One but Three. But such evil was yet future. In this year and in this city, men who followed Rabban Yeshua found no contradiction to pray the *Sh'ma*, to affirm that HaShem was One. So long as they affirmed this, Ari would have no problem praying here with Baruch and his many friends, even though—

Shouts.

Shouts of joy out in the street.

Ari fought the urge to open his eyes, to run outside and see what was going on.

The brothers of The Way continued the *Sh'ma* without hesitating. "*Baruch, Shem K'vod, Malchuto, le'olam va'ed.*" Blessed be his Name of glory whose kingdom shall be forever—

The door of the synagogue flew open with a crash. Ari turned to look and saw a small wiry man run in. "Rejoice!" he shouted. "Rejoice that the Great *Zonah* is burned with fire! The Dragon is destroyed under the wrath of HaShem! The Queen of Heaven is no more!"

That ended the prayers. A hundred men clustered around the small man, hammering him with questions. Ari removed his *tallit* and *tefillin* and folded them inside his belt, next to his dagger made of Damascus steel. Then he pressed close to listen.

"—destroyed all the city of the Dragon! Our people were spared—the fire did not touch their neighborhoods, but the districts of the *goyim* are crushed!" The man's eyes burned with joy. "Be glad and dance! The Great *Zonah* is destroyed!"

The room shook with cheers.

Ari felt his jaw sagging. He would have expected the Sons of Righteous Priests to act this way, but followers of Yeshua? He pushed his way outside, needing air.

All up and down the street, doors were springing open and men were rushing out into the street, shouting, leaping, dancing, singing. A man held aloft a torch, swinging it around wildly, bellowing foolish words. Ari wanted to vomit. These people were fools. Rome had burned, but she still ruled the earth. Her legions had not burned, and a city could be rebuilt. Would be rebuilt, according to Rivka.

Rome would come back stronger than ever, and would burn this very city of HaShem. Ari sagged against the side of the synagogue. Far up the street, he saw a line of women, holding each other's shoulders and dancing like one of those ill-mannered celebratory snake dances at an American political convention. The women were screaming with joy, ululating in a frenzy that chilled Ari's blood. He closed his eyes. Rivka was right. They must leave this city. Soon.

A dozen men burst out of the synagogue of The Way, singing a war song. Baruch followed them, his arms raised above them. "My brothers!" he bellowed.

Nobody paid him the least amount of attention. More men poured out and formed into a circle and began dancing something that looked almost exactly like the *hora* that Ari had learned when he was growing up in Haifa.

Baruch's face was red with shouting. With anger. "My brothers, you must stop this foolishness!"

Again, no response from the joyful men. "*Mashiach!*" one of the newer men shouted. "Come, Yeshua!"

"The birthpangs are on us!" shouted another.

Shimon ben Klopas came out of the synagogue, and anguish covered his face. "My sons!" he shouted.

A few men stopped dancing.

"Stop this evil!" Shimon shouted.

A roar came from beyond the corner. Ari pressed himself against the wall.

A hundred men came dancing around the corner. "Burned! The Dragon is burned! The Queen of Heaven is fallen!"

A hand clutched Ari's. Shimon ben Klopas pulled himself close to Ari. "Ari the Kazan, does your woman have a clear word from HaShem on the matter we spoke of?"

"Not yet," Ari said. "But it will not be long, I think."

"Please tell her to ask HaShem again about the matter."

"Yes, my father." Ari felt a line of sweat running down his side.

Rome had burned. Now Jerusalem was burning too — burning with hate.

At home, after a quiet breakfast, Ari told Rivka about the celebration while Rachel played with her doll in the other room. Rivka sat in her rocking chair, her face drawn with anxiety. Ari saw wrinkle lines in her skin that he had never noticed before. He patted her arm. "I am sorry, Rivkaleh."

"About . . . ?" Her face betrayed that she knew what about.

"The men of The Way. I am sorry that they behaved with such hate."

Tears stood out in Rivka's eyes. "I had hoped Brandon was wrong."

"Brandon?"

"S. G. F. Brandon. A British scholar." Rivka brushed the sleeve of her tunic across her face. "He wrote several books about how the early church was not so lily-white innocent as a lot of Christians believe. That maybe most of them were mixed up with the right-wing zealots."

"And you find this surprising?" Ari said "In America, many Christians are, as you say, mixed up with the right-wing zealots."

"That's different." Rivka put on a defensive look. "This is the early church. It's supposed to be . . . I don't know. Different." She sighed deeply. "I just expected better."

Ari had learned not ever to expect better of anyone. "Shimon ben Klopas asks if you know yet when we are to leave the city."

Rivka gave a helpless shrug. "I'll know when I hear from HaShem. Until then, I'm not doing anything."

"Please listen quickly, Rivkaleh."

Which was foolishness, but Ari did not know what else to say.

TWENTY

Ari

Three days later, Ari sat sweating on a bench in the workshop of Levi the bronzeworker. Ari had designed an improved bellows system that could create a hotter fire. Levi was excited about the prospects of making even better quality steel.

A shadow darkened the open doorway of the workshop. Ari looked up in time to see Brother Eleazar's massive frame enter. His face was wound up tight and his whole body seemed charged with electricity.

"*Shalom*, Brother Eleazar!" Levi said. "Ari the Kazan and I—"

"Ari the Kazan, I wish to have words with you." Eleazar's black eyes glowed almost red, like the coals in Levi's fire.

Levi's mouth dropped open, but then he muttered something to himself and went back to his forge.

Eleazar turned and walked outside. Ari followed him.

Eleazar stood a few steps down from the shop door, his face dark as a thunderhead. It was the early afternoon lull, and the street was deserted.

Ari came up beside him. "Yes?"

"There has been another massacre in Caesarea." Brother Eleazar's voice was thick with emotion. "Our brothers there were rejoicing in the marketplace because of the burning of the Great Dragon. Governor Florus sent out soldiers and seized many of the men. He . . ." Tears streamed down Eleazar's face.

Ari swallowed hard, but a great stone had settled in the back of his throat. "Yes?"

"He crucified fifty men in the public square." Anguish shrouded Eleazar's eyes. "Fifty men. Men with wives and children. Men who were merely dancing in the streets."

Dancing over the misfortune of Rome. Ari did not know what to say. It was wrong of the men to rejoice over the fire in Rome. But was it not far more wrong to crucify such men?

"There is word also from Brother Yoseph," Eleazar said. His eyes turned hard now, black gems of obsidian. "He is delayed and will not return before next spring. There is a matter he must deal with, but his main business is accomplished."

Ari did not ask if Yoseph's main business was to free the priests who were in captivity or something more sinister. If Yoseph had been sent to set the fire, Eleazar would lie about it anyway, and Ari did not wish him to know of Rivka's suspicions. In any event, it was a relief to know that Brother Eleazar's deadline would not fall until next spring. That would give Ari more time. By next spring, perhaps he and Rivka and the brothers of The Way would be gone from this wretched city.

Eleazar grasped Ari's hand in a powerful handclasp. "Ari the Kazan, I must have an answer by *Sukkot*. You will delay me no more. Wheels are turning now. You will aid my cause or else you will be my enemy. How will you choose?"

Ari's heart shifted into overdrive. *Sukkot?* Could he be gone by *Sukkot?* Already, it was nearly Rosh HaShanah. He could not leave before then, nor could he persuade The Way to leave during the three weeks before the end of *Sukkot*. The next month was the most exciting of the year, like the month of December in America. He could not escape before Eleazar's deadline.

"Have you made up your mind on the matter?" Eleazar's words were intense, electric.

"I will discuss it with my woman."

Eleazar's eyes showed astonishment, then disdain, then . . .

Then something else, but before Ari could identify it, the shutters of Eleazar's eyes slammed shut.

"Ari the Kazan, we need you. *Mashiach* needs you." Eleazar's grip tightened like a vise. "You are sent to us from HaShem for such a time as this. Do not be found fighting HaShem."

Rivka

Do not be found fighting HaShem. Rivka paced the long avenue of the New City, praying her hopes, her fears. She had stayed up late last night, talking with Ari about Eleazar's words of yesterday. Ari was worried. He had lain in her arms, tense, talking much. Could they leave Jerusalem before *Sukkot?* Brother Eleazar insisted on an answer by *Sukkot*.

Rivka was beginning to hate Brother Eleazar. What right did he have to demand that Ari help him? He couldn't *do* that. Ari wasn't going to help him with his stupid war and that was that. No, they could not leave Jerusalem before Eleazar's deadline expired. Ari was just going to have to stand up to him.

Thank you, HaShem, for sending Brother Eleazar into our lives to test Ari and help him grow. Please give Ari the backbone to say no to the men of violence. And when it's time for us to leave, please show me clearly. Thank you for giving us this year in Jerusalem. It's been a hard year, but I'm glad I met Baby Eleazar.

Far up ahead, Rivka saw a crowd forming. They were bunched up around the gate leading out of the northwest corner of the city. This looked like trouble. She quickened her pace.

When she reached the gate, she saw that somebody was going to be crucified. Three somebodies — a squad of Roman soldiers was lowering the last of three vertical stakes into a hole in the ground, tamping in loose stones to wedge it firmly in place. Rivka wanted to leave, but she could not. At any execution, there was always the grim fear that she might know the victim. She had never yet known anyone who got crucified, but she knew plenty who would probably deserve it — at least in Roman eyes. Rivka stayed to watch, stuffing her knuckles into her mouth.

Several hundred people had gathered to watch the crucifixion. Rivka stood on her toes, trying to see over their heads, but it was useless. She would just have to wait.

Finally, an audible gasp came rippling back through the crowd, and Rivka knew that the first man was going up. Then she saw him and realized immediately that he was nobody she knew. Thanks be to HaShem. Two soldiers raised each end of the crossbar. The man's wrists had been tied to the bar, not nailed like in all the paintings. The Romans did it both ways, but today they were using ropes.

The victim was a short man, about Rivka's own height, brown as a bean, and writhing in anticipation of the agony to come. He was completely naked. Medieval artists always put loincloths on their crucifixions, but the Romans had no such scruples. Part of the punishment was the humiliation of hanging up there, totally exposed. Rivka stared in stark horror. The man's legs kicked wildly, seeking purchase to take some of the weight off of his arms. His face was already blue. Rivka had read somewhere that a man would asphyxiate quickly if you hung him by the arms at that angle.

But the soldiers had no intention of letting him die quickly. Two of them grabbed his ankles and slammed them roughly against the vertical beam. He immediately pushed up with his legs, sucking in a lungful of air, then sagging down again.

The soldiers twisted each foot outward and pushed them upward until his knees were spread obscenely wide. Rivka wanted to scream, to turn away, to run. But her legs were lead and she could not breathe. *Yeshua went through this for me.*

A third soldier lashed the man's calves to the upright stake. A collective hiss went up from the crowd. They knew what was coming next, just as Rivka did.

One of the soldiers ducked out of sight. When he reappeared a moment later, he had a rusted iron spike in one hand and a heavy mallet in the other. He put the spike up against the victim's foot, just below the ankle bone.

Raised the mallet.

Smashed it against the head of the nail.

The man's head jerked back and he screamed like a baby. Rage sank its talons into Rivka's skull. She tasted bile in the back of her throat.

The soldier swung the mallet again. Again. Again. The man's head was jerking back and forth now in a paroxysm of agony. He pushed up with his legs, took a breath, and screamed again.

The soldiers repeated the process on the other ankle. Tears swam in Rivka's eyes now, and she wanted to scream, to run somewhere, to beat her fists on the soldiers' backs, to do *something.* But there was nothing she could do, and her feet were encased in ice. She still hadn't seen the other two men. If she found that she *knew* one of them, she was going to vomit.

The first man was now doing a horrible dance. That was the only way Rivka could describe it—a death dance. His body weight hanging on his arms prevented his lungs from inhaling. When he could stand it no longer, he pushed himself up a few inches with his cramped legs, applying maximum pain to his shattered ankles. He drew a quick breath, then dropped down again to end the torture in his ankles. And there he hung until he needed another breath.

Over and over again. Rivka had heard of men lasting two or three days on a cross. It was evil unspeakable and she felt blind fury welling up in her heart. There was no *reason* to kill a man this way. None at all. The Romans were evil and she hated them with an everlasting hate.

Movement.

Rivka held her breath in an agony of suspense. Would she know the next man?

The team lifted the crossbar. This man was bigger. Half his beard was ripped off, and . . . he too was a stranger. The soldiers repeated the process of fixing his bar to the stake, tying off his legs, and nailing his ankles.

Rivka wanted to faint. She had heard of mass crucifixions, of hundreds of crosses littering a hillside, the air ripped by the screams of the tortured.

The soldiers disappeared again and now Rivka felt a terrible tingling in her skull. A wave of shocked hisses came rippling back through the crowd. Something truly evil was about to happen. Rivka did not know how it could be worse than what she had seen, but . . .

The soldiers stood up again.

Heaved the bar upward, displaying a naked . . .

Woman.

She was young, no older than Rivka, with long black hair that hung to her waist in a sweaty tangle. Blood gushed from her mouth, and her eyes were swollen shut. Rivka felt like fainting. She never forgot a face, and she recognized this woman. Her name was Yohana, and Rivka had delivered her first child a few years ago.

The soldiers hoisted the bar up and fixed it to the stake, facing Yohana's body away from the crowd in the token gesture of modesty that the Romans accorded women. Rivka whirled and staggered away, feeling sure she would throw up.

A scream shredded the afternoon sky. Rivka felt her insides tingling with electric rage. The soldiers had nailed one of Yohana's ankles.

Another scream.

Rivka ran.

Rivka walked the streets for two hours, weeping uncontrollably, stopping often to rest, praying her guts out. *Yeshua did that for me. Voluntarily. And he forgave the men who did it.*

She could not imagine how he could forgive them. The Romans were *evil*. The governor must have ordered those crucifixions himself. Governor Florus was Satan incarnate. Rivka knew that there would come a day when he would order many hundreds of those in a single day.

She and Ari would be gone from this city long before then, but many would not. Her people would be tortured, slaughtered, crucified.

An image formed in Rivka's mind, clear and cold. Years ago, in Berkeley, at an InterVarsity Bible study, she had been studying Matthew in a small group. And some guy had been rambling on about how "the Jews" rejected Jesus, and that's why God sent the Romans to burn Jerusalem forty years later. Rivka had been ticked off then at the jerk's insensitivity.

Now she was furious.

She was starting to understand Ari's rage about the blood curse. Any Christian who believed in corporate guilt was an idiot. A monster.

Forgiven.

The thought superposed itself over Rivka's consciousness, like an audible voice. She looked around, wondering if someone had really spoken to her. She was alone.

Rivka felt cold sweat down her back. Yeshua forgave his tormentors. And if he did that, wouldn't he also forgive idiots who taught the blood curse? She felt sick to her marrow. If Yeshua forgave them, then she had to also.

Please, HaShem, show those morons how wrong they are.

Rivka shook her head. No, that wasn't right.

Oh, Lord, change their hearts. Make them see that they're no better than these Romans who torture people.

But that wasn't the whole story, either. Rivka stopped and leaned against a wall, closing her eyes, letting the rough limestone press against her back.

Change my heart, HaShem. Teach me to love even the people who hate me. The Romans. Governor Florus. Even Hanan ben Hanan.

An image formed in Rivka's mind. A crushed reed, nearly broken. That was all, just a crushed reed. Rivka remembered something she'd read a zillion years ago. A passage from Brother Andrew's book *God's Smuggler.*

Strengthen that which remains.

Brother Andrew took that to mean that he should smuggle Bibles behind the Iron Curtain, should strengthen the church in Communist countries.

But what did it mean for her?

Ari

"... and then they crucified a woman." Ari felt his voice quivering with rage. "Rivka could not sleep all night. She knew the woman."

"This is a great evil." Grief darkened Baruch's face. It was early morning and they were walking together to the morning prayers. "It is not done, to crucify a woman."

"The governor is sending a message." Ari fingered the steel dagger nestled in his belt. "He is making an example. We must find a way to fight him."

Baruch spun his head and gave Ari a piercing look. "We must ask HaShem to fight him. The battle belongs to HaShem, Brother Ari."

"Of course. I misspoke." Ari felt heat in his veins, because he knew something Baruch did not. Rivka had told him all she knew of Governor Florus last night. There would come a day when two men and one woman on crosses would seem a small thing. Ari wanted to —

"Your thoughts are dark today, Brother Ari."

Ari said nothing. Brother Baruch would not understand. He himself did not understand. He was a pacifist. He had served in the IDF because he must, but he had hated being a soldier, hated the fact that he must go on patrols in the Palestinian territories, which right-wing politicians insisted were the ancient property of Jews to all generations. Ari did not believe this. It was extremists on the Israeli right — and Muslim terrorists — who prevented peace. Between them, the fringes conspired to make constant war. Ari had never wanted any part of that.

But this was different. This time, it was Jews who were the oppressed. They were Palestinians in their own country, tormented for no good cause by foreign imperialists. Rome was filth, a whore, a dragon. Ari did not wish to fight Rome, and yet . . .

And yet he wished to fight Rome.

He knew it was foolishness, that the stream of history was too strong to oppose. But a man who does not resist when all is at stake is not a man. If a Roman legion stood at his door, demanding to violate Rivka and Rachel, then Ari would fight them to the death with his bare hands, because that is what a man must do, hopeless odds or not. He would die before he gave up his woman and his child to evil men.

"Brother Ari."

Ari turned to look at his friend.

Baruch's eyes probed Ari's soul. "Brother Ari, your heart is not right before HaShem."

"You think it is wrong to defend the innocent?" Ari crossed his arms on his chest. "Father Avraham led his servants in battle against the four kings.

King David slew the giant and fought the Philistines. The prophet Eliyahu killed the prophets of the *ba'alim*."

Baruch's eyes gleamed. "All of these were called by HaShem to fight. Have you been called by HaShem to fight?"

Ari blinked. No, he had not heard an audible voice telling him to fight. "Is that required? If evil men seize your woman to rape her, will you wait for HaShem to tell you what to do?"

Deep pain washed across Baruch's face.

Too late, Ari realized his blunder. "I am sorry, Brother Baruch. That was foolish." He touched his friend's shoulder.

Baruch closed his eyes for a moment and his lips moved.

Ari's heart quivered. If he could take back the words, he would do so, but he could not.

Then Baruch's face eased and he opened his eyes and smiled. "The battle belongs to HaShem. Please, you will remember that."

"Yes, of course, Brother Baruch. Let us hurry or we will be late for the morning prayers."

The two men began walking again toward the synagogue of The Way. Ari's heart felt numb. Baruch was right. History said that Baruch was right. Rivka said that Baruch was right. Logic also.

But Brother Eleazar was right too.

It was a matter of right versus right, and Ari did not know which was more right. Deep dread filled his soul. HaShem had given him a Möbius strip, and however he colored it, he must fail.

TWENTY-ONE

Hanan ben Hanan

Hanan's feet had felt cold all day. Today, on this holiest day of the year, The Fast, all Yisrael went barefoot. Hanan had been up since well before dawn, helping with the sacrifices in the Temple. It was still early fall, but unseasonably cold, and the chill had not yet gone out of his bones. His lower legs ached, and he had no feeling in his toes.

He stood now in a patch of thin afternoon sunlight in the Court of Priests, supervising the cleaning of the marble slaughtering tables. Teams of priests lugged bronze buckets of cold water from the outlet of the aqueduct and sloshed them across the polished stone. Water covered the pavement all around to the depth of two fingers.

"Uncle, there is a matter to be dealt with."

Hanan turned and saw his nephew, Mattityahu ben Theophilus, who was *sagan* of the Temple. Mattityahu wore a look of great discomfort, and that was not usual. Like most men of the House of Hanan, Mattityahu was not easily unbalanced. "Surely you are competent to deal with this matter," Hanan said.

Mattityahu shook his head and looked around nervously. "It has to do with That Woman."

That Woman. Hanan grimaced. That Woman was their private code word for Marta, wife of the high priest, Yeshua ben Gamaliel. Hanan had counseled Yeshua not to marry her, but Yeshua had been stubborn. Marta came of the House of Boetus, and it was his marriage to her that gave Yeshua the wealth and prestige he needed to be high priest. It was dishonorable to depend on a woman for such things, but Yeshua was his protégé and Hanan could not say so. Sooner or later, Yeshua would come to his senses and divorce her, and then Hanan could give him his daughter — certainly a better match than Marta.

Hanan nodded to Mattityahu. "Show me."

Mattityahu jerked his head in the direction of the Nicanor Gate. Hanan followed him through it to the steps that led down into the Court of Women. Crowds were gathering for the afternoon sacrifices and . . .

All Hanan's breath left him. No, this was foolishness. Even That Woman would not be such an imbecile. Hanan's mind told him that she could not, but his eyes told him that she could.

Marta stood motionless in the middle of the court, waiting with an imperious attitude. She was barefoot, but standing on a thick woolen carpet, about four cubits square. Two large servants were lifting a similar square of carpet behind her. Grunting and sweating in the chilly breeze, they hauled it around in front of her. Without looking at the men, Marta stepped forward on dainty feet onto the next carpet. The men bent down and wrestled the previous one off the pavement. She must have walked all the way from home in this way, making mock of the custom to go barefoot.

Many dozen people gawked at Marta. Those in front of her looked properly respectful. Those behind her wore looks of revulsion. It was not done, to carpet the streets on Yom Kippur in order to walk barefoot in luxury.

Hanan hurried down the stairs into the Court of Women. On the bottom step, he trod on a small pebble. Pain lanced up through his foot. He stopped in front of Marta's carpet, unwilling to accept its softness beneath his aching feet. "Woman, this is foolishness. You will tell your men to return home with these" — Hanan gestured at the carpets — "frivolities."

Marta ignored him. The men had hefted the thick carpet behind her and now they stood there, stupid looks on their faces, waiting for Hanan to move so they could lay the carpet where he stood. Marta snapped her fingers at the men and pointed at Hanan's feet.

Hanan stood his ground. He would not allow her to advance one more step into the house of the living God like this.

Like any wealthy woman, Marta wore a veil, though hers was of such transparent silk that Hanan considered it indecent. Her face had gone very pink. She glared at Hanan. "You will move or I will call my husband." She crooked a finger at Mattityahu. "You there! You are *sagan*. Call the Temple guards and remove this man from my path."

Hanan turned to Mattityahu and gave him a tiny smile. "The woman has spoken."

Mattityahu spun around and disappeared up the stairs into the Court of Priests. Hanan knew that he would not reappear, and therefore Marta could not complain to her husband about his insolence.

Marta put her hands on her hips and stepped toward Hanan. "Did you not hear me? You will move or I will — "

Movement at the edge of Hanan's vision. The glitter of sunlight on metal. A dirty-faced man lunging through the crowd.

In an eyeblink, Hanan realized that he stood alone without his usual bodyguards in the middle of many hundred common folk. On just such a day, ten years ago, his brother Yonatan had been murdered in this court. But he also saw that the target of the dagger-man was not himself.

It was Marta.

Hanan dove forward, catching Marta at the waist with a thick arm. Marta screamed. They crashed together onto the carpet.

The dagger-man slashed his weapon in a wild sweep, just missing Marta's face but catching her veil with his dagger. The force of his swing twisted him around. He staggered to his knees on the heavy carpet, flailing his arms for balance, his blackened teeth frozen in a hideous smile.

Hanan pushed Marta away from the man and rolled to his feet in one continuous motion. He had once been *sagan*, had trained Temple guards, and he knew how to fight. He yanked his white turban off his head, shaking it out into a long length of strong linen.

The dagger-man pushed himself to his feet and rose to a fighting crouch, brandishing his gleaming dagger. "There is no Lord but HaShem!" he shouted.

Hanan looped the ends of his turban in his hands and moved to keep himself between the dagger-man and Marta, crouching on the balls of his feet, waiting, watching.

The dagger-man's eyes flicked left, then right. Hanan heard a shout from the Court of Priests. Mattityahu would arrive shortly with Temple guards. Where were Marta's fool servants? If they would simply stand on either side of Hanan, they would form a wall. But the cowards did nothing.

The dagger-man spit at Hanan's feet.

Then he lunged forward, slashing at Hanan's left side.

Quick as a cobra, Hanan threw up both his hands and caught the brunt of the thrust in the length of his turban. The dagger pierced the turban, but the strong cloth blunted its force. Hanan yanked down hard, turning the dagger away from himself and breaking the dagger-man's balance. The man staggered forward and then . . .

Then, *somehow*, he wrested his dagger free and slashed again at Hanan's face. Hanan pushed back at him and lost his footing. He crashed heavily onto the carpet. Pain hammered his bones. Fear shot through him. He had no defense now. The dagger-man raised his weapon and chopped downward. Hanan tried to roll to one side, but his head felt dull and heavy and the world had slowed down. He was going to—

A flash of white linen.

A crash. The dagger-man staggered sideways, the dagger flying out of his grasp. Hanan felt his heart pounding in his chest. He saw a large man on top of the dagger-man, heard him shouting for help. Now the bystanders joined in. One of them picked up the dagger. Others fell on the would-be assassin, pinning his arms and legs.

Shouts came from the direction of the Court of Priests. Four Temple guards arrived. Hanan tried to stand, but sweat clouded his vision and his muscles had become water.

"No Lord but HaShem!" the dagger-man shouted again.

Hanan heard the guards dragging him away. He groaned and wiped his eyes, blinking rapidly to restore his vision.

A face swam into view and a hand reached down to help him up. "Can you stand?"

Hanan took the hand, slowly pulled himself up, and found himself looking into the eyes of . . .

Kazan.

"Are you well, Hanan ben Hanan?"

At any other time, Hanan would have spit at Kazan's feet. Kazan was a man whom the people believed knew deep secrets of the universe. A magician from a far country. A messianic. Kazan stood for all that Hanan hated and despised, a man who did not love the Temple.

"I am well." Hanan turned away.

It was a lie, of course. Kazan, his enemy, had saved his life. Therefore, he owed Kazan a debt of honor.

He would not pay it. Never, ever, ever, while he walked under the sun. Better that he should have died than to owe a debt of honor to such a one as Ari the Kazan.

Rivka

It was awfully brave of you," Rivka said that night. Ari had told her the full story after they put Rachel to bed.

"Hanan ben Hanan still hates me," Ari said. "Some say I should have let the dagger-man kill him."

Rivka clutched him. She was thinking the same thing. Hanan filled her with revulsion. And yet . . . if the dagger-men weren't stopped, the city would fall into lawlessness and that would be worse than having a creep like Hanan walking around. Marginally.

"There is talk about Marta," Ari said. "People say that she paid many *dinars* to King Agrippa, and now see how arrogant she is, to carpet the streets on Yom Kippur."

"I read about that in the Talmud," Rivka said. "She's supposed to be the most spoiled little princess you ever heard of. Guess how she died. You'll laugh."

"Dying is not a matter to laugh at," Ari said.

At this point, Rivka didn't care. She was just relieved Ari hadn't got hurt today and if she couldn't let off steam by laughing a little, she was going to freak. "The Talmud says that during the siege of Jerusalem, Marta couldn't believe that there wasn't any food to be had, so she went out in the street to investigate and she stepped in a pile of donkey-doo, and it was such a shock to her system that the little wimp just died."

"Rivkaleh." Ari's voice sounded distant, sad.

"What's gotten into you? Don't you think it's funny?"

Ari's strong arms wrapped around her, and she smelled his tangy sweat. "Ten more days, and I must tell Brother Eleazar my decision."

"And you're going to tell him he's full of beans, right, Ari?"

Silence.

"Right, Ari?"

Another long pause. "Yes, of course. Sleep well, Rivkaleh."

Rivka kissed his chest. "I'm so proud of you, Ari. You sleep well too."

Berenike

You are missing the point." Berenike leaned forward on her throne and jabbed a finger at the high priest, Yeshua ben Gamaliel. Beside him, Hanan ben Hanan stood impassively, his face a study in controlled anger. Berenike saw that Hanan understood the matter, but Yeshua did not, and he must be made to understand.

Berenike looked sideways and saw that Agrippa seemed bored by the whole proceeding. Good, that left her free to do what must be done for the good of the city. "It is a matter of no consequence that your woman was attacked yesterday by the dagger-men. That is a danger we all face, and it is a result of Roman policies, not ours. We have no control over these wicked men."

Yeshua's face twitched. "But — "

"I did not give you leave to speak," Berenike said. "Your woman was a fool to flaunt her luxury yesterday in the Temple. The people are suffering. There is a drought. The Fast is a day on which even the wealthiest are expected to endure pain, or at least to give the appearance of enduring pain. And your foolish *zonah* came walking barefoot — on carpets! The Pharisees hate her already, because you married her when she was not a virgin. This morning they were beating on my gates."

Yeshua's face told her plainly that he was not interested in foolish Pharisees or in Berenike's gates.

Berenike leaned back and crossed her legs. "And they are right. They are fools, but even a fool is correct once in a lifetime. Your woman has cast dishonor on your house. You will divorce her." She smiled at him to let him know that now he might speak.

Yeshua's face hardened like clay in the sun. "No. The woman was a widow of unquestioned virtue when I married her. The Pharisees stretch Torah beyond all reason with their — "

"I am not concerned with her purity," Berenike said. "It is no concern to me whether she is virgin or a *goy* temple prostitute. She behaved like an imbecile yesterday." Berenike snapped her fingers at Hanan ben Hanan. "You will explain the matter to him."

Hanan took Yeshua's elbow and backed him toward the rear of the Hasmonean throne room. The two men spent a quarter of an hour speaking in low voices. Berenike could see that Hanan was angry. As he should be. A purple bruise covered his left arm, and he walked with a limp today. He was a brave man to have fought the dagger-man unarmed.

Brave and foolish. Had he done nothing, the woman would now be dead and there would not be this matter to deal with today. Hanan's problem was that he was too honorable. He was narrow, uncompromising, ambitious. For those things, Berenike hated him. But he was also a man of honor, and such a man did not stand by and leave a woman of his own class undefended. Berenike felt certain that he would likewise have defended her against such an attack. For that, Hanan ben Hanan had her respect.

Finally, Hanan finished instructing Yeshua on the matter. Yeshua strode back toward Berenike and Agrippa, and his face told that he had made a decision. Hanan stayed near the door, his dour face an unreadable mask.

When Yeshua stopped, Berenike leaned forward again. "You will divorce the woman."

Yeshua did not flinch. "No."

Berenike had not expected that, but she had prepared for it. She turned to look at her brother.

She tugged on her left ear.

A thin smile curved Agrippa's lips. He stood up and let the folds of his toga straighten out. "You are dismissed, Yeshua ben Gamaliel. Hanan ben Hanan, we will have a word with you privately."

Yeshua's eyes widened. He began spluttering, and finally forced out one word. "D–dismissed?"

"From the high priesthood. Now you will leave. It is urgent that we find a successor swiftly, and for that we require the services of Hanan ben Hanan."

Yeshua's face purpled. He made a gagging sound deep in his throat. Finally, he spit at Berenike's feet. "You vile woman! *Zonah!*" He spun on his heel and — contrary to all rules of royalty — turned his back on Berenike and Agrippa.

Berenike watched him stomp out. Yeshua was reputed to be an intelligent man, gifted in languages and the best expounder of Torah from among the Sadducees.

All of which showed that intelligence was not wisdom, and even a genius could be played for a fool when a woman was involved.

Hanan ben Hanan stepped forward. "My humblest apologies for the behavior of Yeshua. He is much taken with the woman."

Berenike sat down again, and Agrippa followed suit. She studied Hanan carefully. He had made a terrible mistake once, in the matter of the man Yaakov called *tsaddik*. Had he learned from his mistake? Of course she would not reappoint him, but she needed his help. Berenike did not know of a suitable man from the senior members of the Four Houses. It was time to move on to the next generation. "Hanan, your nephew Mattityahu — is he married to a virgin?"

Hanan's eyes flashed with understanding. "Yes, a modest woman who does not appear in public."

"And he is a man of means?" Berenike did not expect a large payment, but she wanted to get something out of this transaction.

Hanan coughed diplomatically. "Some means. The House of Hanan has been much depleted by the drought, but we have still something. Perhaps two talents this year and two more in two years?"

Berenike smiled. He was playing for the long term, and that was good. But of course he could do better. "Three talents this year and one in each succeeding year."

Hanan considered this for some time. Berenike wondered if she had squeezed him too hard. The drought had brutalized Judea, and even Hanan could not force water from a stone. Finally, he said, "Two and a half this year, and one and a half in each year following."

Which meant that he intended that his nephew should endure in office longer than had been usual lately. Berenike liked that. Too many men thought only of the next year, the next harvest. She looked to Agrippa and scratched her nose.

Agrippa yawned and gave a short nod. "Agreed. Send your nephew here and see to the money. You may go now."

Hanan bowed his head the merest fraction and backed toward the door. When he reached the door, he stopped for a moment, studying Berenike. Then he vanished, but not before she saw something in his eyes she had not seen before.

Respect.

TWENTY-TWO

Rivka

S*ukkot* arrived, and with it, the deadline Brother Eleazar had given Ari. Every day, Rivka walked the streets of the New City, praying that somehow Ari would find a solution. They could not leave the city and Ari could not knuckle under to Eleazar's demands. On the third day of the seven-day feast, Ari came home with the news that the new high priest, Mattityahu ben Theophilus, had just named Eleazar as his *sagan*, the captain of the Temple. By the last day of the feast, neither Rivka nor Ari was sleeping more than a couple of hours per night.

The feast ended, the city emptied of pilgrims who had come for the feast, and Ari heard nothing from Brother Eleazar. All Jerusalem was chattering about the upcoming wedding of the daughter of Naqdimon ben Gorion, one of the wealthiest men in the city. For three days, Rivka held her breath. Then the day of the wedding arrived.

The festivities would last a full week, and Rivka decided that Brother Eleazar would wait until after the wedding if he was going to make a scene. All day, the sun burned yellow in a cloudless sky. Rivka spent much of her daily walk praying for rain. Technically, you were supposed to wait three weeks after *Sukkot* to pray for rain, so as to allow visitors from Babylon to get home. Rivka didn't care. Judea needed rain *now*, and hang the Babylonian Jews.

But there was no sign of rain. When the sun went down, she and Ari dressed in their finest clothes to go celebrate the wedding feast. Because of the perfect weather — a balmy evening in early fall — the feast was held in the large courtyard of Naqdimon's palace. The wealthiest citizens of Jerusalem had come. Naqdimon's brother Yoseph, who with Naqdimon controlled much of the wheat and barley trade in the city. Their father Gorion ben Naqdimon, a distinguished man of about sixty, known for his shrewd business dealings and his hatred of Rome. King Agrippa and Queen Berenike and their royal retinue. The leading men of the Four Houses.

Dozens of U-shaped tables were set in rows, each with several dining couches.

Rivka had never seen such a feast. There were apples dipped in honey. Seven kinds of salad. Jericho dates. Honeyed figs. Roasted calf. Golden bread stuffed with falafel and cucumbers. Onion soup. Fat-tailed sheep. Twelve different kinds of wine. And that was all in the first hour.

Well before the midpoint of the feast, Rivka was wrestling with guilt at the extravagant cost of this feast — when children in the city were hungry. Just as in America, she had no idea what to do about it. Ari knew Naqdimon quite well, and the man would have been offended if Ari and Rivka had not come.

The meal went on until midnight, punctuated by the best entertainment a man of Naqdimon's wealth could buy. A troupe of a hundred and twenty dancing girls. An orchestra of flutists, harpists, trumpet players, and cymbalists. Six jugglers who drew gasps from the crowd with their colored balls and ceramic plates and flaming torches.

As the moon was rising, Rivka saw that many people had gathered around the table of Rabbi Yohanan. She grabbed Ari's elbow. "Let's go see what's happening."

Ari, who was quite drunk, lurched along beside her. Rivka was one of the very few who had drunk little wine.

" — us a story!" someone shouted.

"Yes, tell us a story!"

Rivka stood on her toes, trying to see. "Ari, who's going to tell a story?"

"Baby Eleazar." Ari elbowed his way into the crowd. "Come, Rivka. If you have never heard Eleazar ben Arakh tell a story, then you have never heard a story."

Rivka followed in his wake, but still she could not see anything.

An immense calm settled over the listeners. Rivka waited, closing her eyes so that she could listen without distraction.

"In the days of Honi the Circler, the rains failed for many months." Baby Eleazar's clear voice rang out through the courtyard. "Honi was an old man, no taller than a boy. His beard was gray and his hair was thin, but he was a man to whom HaShem listened when he prayed."

Rivka gasped. In her mind's eye, she could *see* Honi. Maybe not as clear as daylight, but certainly as clear as dreaming. In her mind, Honi turned and peered at her. His nose was scorched by the sun and his eyes were deep pools of knowing.

Rivka looked past Honi, and she saw a land shriveled under the heat of the sun. She saw the cruel blue sky, the pinched faces of children wailing for bread. The stench of dead and rotting cattle filled her nostrils. An arid wind blew dust in her face, sucking the moisture from her eyes. Its acrid tang parched her throat.

"How long, HaShem?" Honi shook his bony fist at the sky. In a rage, he seized a stick from the ground and scratched a circle in the dust. He flung the stick in the gutter and raised both hands to the heavens. "God of our fathers, Creator of heaven and earth, Lord of the harvest, I cry out to you to make rain! I swear by my life-blood that I will not leave this circle until it is mud!" Honi sat in the dusty circle and waited.

Children gathered around him, staring, laughing, pointing.

Honi sat.

Women came to look, and their mockery rained on him, bitter and cold.

Honi sat.

Young men came to laugh at him. Old men to reason.

Honi sat.

A night and a day passed, and the sun burned down from a molten sky.

Honi sat.

Another night and another day, and still nothing.

Honi sat.

On the third day, in the heat of the afternoon, a light wind sprang up, sharp and cool, a westerly breeze from the sea.

Honi sat.

Thin clouds formed on the horizon, gray and distant as death.

Honi sat.

The clouds blew in from the sea, rolling, rising, billowing, boiling. The people muttered and scowled.

Honi sat.

The wind blew harder, the clouds grew darker, and the hearts of the people beat faster.

Honi sat.

The sky became black overhead. Thunder shattered the silence. The first drops fell, heavy and hard and full of life. A shout rose up from the people. Joy danced in the streets.

Honi sat.

More drops, many drops, thick rain, a downpour. Rain gushed in the gutters. HaShem laughed in the thunder. The circle around Honi became thick mud.

Honi stood.

The rains continued to pour and the waters rose to Honi's ankles. People rushed to their rooftops, crying in fear. The water reached Honi's knees.

Honi raised his hands overhead. "Enough!"

And the rains ended.

The vision, or whatever it was, faded from Rivka's sight, and she found herself back in the land of the normal. She rubbed her eyes and looked around and saw that others had been caught in the same spell. Baby Eleazar's story had taken them to another place, another time, had given them hope, and now . . .

Now she saw that it was all an illusion. The same drought pinched the stony land, and no rains would come. Rivka wanted to weep.

She heard a gasp, then a whisper. "Honi! It is Honi!"

Rivka grabbed Ari's arm. "What's going on? Where's Honi?"

Ari pushed forward, pulling her behind him. They broke through into the circle.

Rivka saw Honi.

No, it was Rabbi Yohanan, but it was the Honi she had seen in her vision — an old man, tiny and thin, with a wispy gray beard and authority in his eyes.

"Honi the Circler!" somebody shouted. "Make rain for us, Honi!"

Rivka's heart lurched. She knew perfectly well that Rabbi Yohanan was no Honi. Honi was a man of legend, a Merlin-like figure who might never even have existed. Whereas Yohanan was a man of Torah, all too real and all too ordinary in his powers.

Rabbi Yohanan raised his hands to the sky. "I swear by my life-blood before the living God that I will neither eat food nor drink wine until HaShem gives us rain."

A hiss of astonishment ran around the circle. Rivka felt Ari's hand squeezing hers very tight. It was not yet the season for rain. In a month, yes, but not now. It was crazy to take a vow like that right now. Even crazier for a skinny old man without enough body fat to interest a vulture.

All around Rivka she heard whispering. "Foolishness!" "What if the rains are late?" "He must find a way to nullify his vow."

Rivka studied Rabbi Yohanan's face and read there a grim determination. Fear shivered through her, and then a sudden, fierce love. This little old man must know that he could not survive long without eating. Yet he had made himself a hostage before HaShem on behalf of his people. Unless HaShem sent rain soon, Rabbi Yohanan would die.

Around the old rabbi, several men reached out to touch his *tzitzit*, the ritual fringes at the four corners of his tunic. Admiration shone on their faces. Rivka looked past them to Rabbi Yohanan's disciples — and there she saw deep respect mingled with deep fear.

Behind Rabbi Yohanan, Baby Eleazar had collapsed onto one of the dining couches clutching his head. Rivka felt pain knife through her heart.

Baby Eleazar was weeping.

Ari

The next day, it did not rain. Ari found himself looking up at the sky five times in every hour, as though expecting to see clouds. But that was foolishness. It was yet early in the season, and rain was not expected for some weeks.

All the city was talking about Rabbi Yohanan's vow. Some thought it was very brave. Others thought it foolish. But none except Rivka knew what Ari knew.

Rabbi Yohanan could not die. He must not die, or who would save the nation after the coming disaster? He was destined to start a school in Yavneh after the war, a school which would produce the seeds of rabbinic Judaism. Jews would survive for twenty centuries and more because of this man. If he died on account of this vow, then Judaism itself would die.

Ari knew that it was the foolish rules of rabbinic Judaism that would keep his people alive. Without these rules — the kosher laws, the feasts, *Shabbat* — keeping them separate from other peoples, there would be no Jews surviving down the long centuries. Without the orthodox, there would be no Freud, no Einstein, no Salk, no Chagall, no Potok.

On the second day, there was again no rain. That evening, the third night of the wedding feast, Rabbi Yohanan did not attend and the mood was somber.

On the third day, a *Shabbat*, still none. The wedding feast that evening was a dismal affair. People muttered behind their hands. Ari felt guilty eating and drinking, knowing that Rabbi Yohanan was getting steadily weaker.

On the fourth day, Ari went to Gamaliel's olive-oil shop. Gamaliel knew Rabbi Yohanan. He could talk sense into him. This fast was a foolish gesture. HaShem would send rain or he would not send rain, and the fast of one old man would make no change.

In the shop, he found Gamaliel sitting with a gloomy look on his face.

"Gamaliel, my friend." Ari clasped his hand at the wrist. "You must speak with Rabbi Yohanan on the matter of his fast."

Gamaliel stared at him. "There is nothing to discuss with him."

"It is foolishness," Ari said. "If he continues, he will die."

"He made a solemn vow before HaShem." Gamaliel sighed deeply. "One cannot rescind a solemn vow."

"There are ways to rescind them," Ari said. He had heard his stepfather and his friends discuss Talmud on vows many times. If a man wished to revoke a vow, he could do it.

A very strange look crossed Gamaliel's face. Ari wondered what that might mean.

"This vow cannot be revoked," Gamaliel said. "Rabbi Yohanan would not revoke it, even if Torah allowed it."

Ari stepped outside and looked up at the bright blue sky. His heart quickened. "We cannot allow Rabbi Yohanan to die. Do you know how important this is?"

"We need rain," Gamaliel said.

"At the cost of a man's life?" Ari began pacing.

"Baby Eleazar says that sometimes when a great thing is needed, then a sacrifice is necessary," Gamaliel said.

"Necessary?" Ari's head snapped around. "It is necessary that a great man should die to change the mind of HaShem?"

Gamaliel gave him a cryptic smile. "Perhaps. Please, you will pray that HaShem will send rain."

For the next three days, Ari prayed for rain. All Jerusalem was praying for rain.

Nothing.

The heavens spread out in a bright blue canopy, mocking the city. The last day of the wedding feast came. Rumor told that Rabbi Yohanan would attend the feast, though he would not eat.

Ari and Rivka went to his house before the feast. A great crowd waited out in the street, watching for the rabbi. Ari prayed.

Shortly after the sun disappeared, the door of the rabbi's house opened. The crowd stepped back, murmuring in awe. A muscular young man, one of the rabbi's disciples, appeared in the doorway. When he came out in the street, Ari saw that he carried a makeshift bed, a litter bearing the wasted form of Rabbi Yohanan. Another of the rabbi's disciples carried the other end.

Ari's heart flip-flopped. If Rabbi Yohanan was too weak to walk, then he would not live much longer. Several more young men followed the rabbi out of the house. Baby Eleazar came last, and his tearful face told Ari that the situation was very grave.

The crowd trudged through the streets toward Naqdimon's palace, and their prayers ascended to the heavens like incense. Ari prayed also. Rivka clutched his arm, her eyes half closed, her lips moving. As they reached the gates, a great shout echoed through the streets.

"Woe! A voice from the east! A voice from the west! A voice from the bridegroom and a voice from the bride! Woe to this city! Woe — "

A shower of stones flew at the man. Ari recognized him, and felt a strange mix of fury and pity. The man was crazy, or possessed with evil spirits, or something. Ari no longer knew what was wrong with him, but this was not the time to broadcast his woes. He picked up a stone and heaved it after the crazy man.

Naqdimon ben Gorion himself came out of his palace to greet the people. Ari could see he was much displeased at having a gloomy crowd attend the wedding feast, but he could not turn them away and he could not force them to be happy.

Naqdimon saw Rabbi Yohanan, and concern washed across his face. He made his way through the crowd to the old rabbi. Ari pressed closer.

"Rabbi Yohanan, please you will eat tonight," Naqdimon said. "At a wedding feast, it is not fitting to fast."

The old rabbi shook his head, and his voice came out in a dry rasp that terrified Ari. "My son, do not ask me to break a solemn vow. HaShem will send rain, or I will soon have words with him in the World to Come."

Naqdimon looked sick at heart, but he nodded his head in respect. "As you wish, my father." He raised his hands to the people. "As for the rest of you, come! There is a feast prepared." He led the way into the outer court of his palace.

Ari and Rivka had been assigned places only two tables over from Rabbi Yohanan. The old sage was lifted from his litter to recline in the place of honor at his table. His disciples clustered around him, looking out of place, as students always do when they find themselves in high society.

Servants brought out the first course, huge clusters of grapes.

Ari reached for a grape and ate one. He saw that Rivka took nothing. "Something is wrong with the grapes?"

She shook her head. "They look fine. I just can't eat, knowing that Rabbi Yohanan is fasting. I think I'll just pray."

Ari looked around the table. Nobody else was eating either. He raised up on his elbow and peered across to Rabbi Yohanan's table. None of the rabbi's disciples were eating. It was the same at the next table, and the next. Ari rose off his dining couch and walked toward the eastern end of the courtyard, until he came to the tables occupied by the Four Houses. Hanan ben Hanan was eating. So was his friend Yeshua ben Gamaliel and his nephew Mattityahu, the high priest. At the next table, Hananyah ben Nadavayah and his brother and three of his sons were eating. His youngest son, Brother Eleazar, was not eating. King Agrippa and his sister Berenike and their wretched cousins Saul and Costabar were eating.

Rabbi Shimon ben Gamaliel was not eating, nor any of his disciples. At the next table, the zealous Rabbi Tsaduq was not eating. Table after table, Ari walked. The Sadducees were eating. The Pharisees were fasting. Ari decided he would not eat. He returned to his own table and reclined beside Rivka. She was still praying.

As the meal progressed, a low sound like buzzing filled Ari's ears. Its volume grew and grew. It was the sound of people praying, praying, praying for the life of Rabbi Yohanan. For a miracle. For rain.

Ari thought the true miracle was that so many people had been led to pray, only through the example of one old rabbi. Through one man's sacrifice of his own comfort, and perhaps his life.

Finally, Ari stood up and began to pray the standing prayer, the *Amidah*, including the words to be included after *Sukkot*, the request for rain in due season. "And give dew and rain for a blessing." As he reached the end of the prayer, he heard a voice.

It was the voice of a small boy who would someday be a great sage in Yisrael. Ari's eyes popped open and he craned his neck to see.

Baby Eleazar was kneeling in the courtyard with his head between his knees. Praying with an intensity Ari had never heard. The small hairs on Ari's arms stood out, and a quiver ran down his back. A sense of heaviness filled his being. Dread. Awe. And then . . . sweet delight.

Ari laughed out loud. The *Shekinah* was here.

Baby Eleazar's voice had become a mighty instrument, a trumpet, a ram's horn, calling on the name of HaShem.

A touch of coolness tingled on Ari's skin. The fresh feel of a morning in springtime, when the sun has just come up, and dew lies on the grass. Ari looked at the night sky and saw that many of the stars had disappeared behind a ceiling of clouds. A breeze sprang up, chilling his body.

Baby Eleazar prayed on.

Rivka stood up and clutched Ari's arm. A pinprick of moisture kissed his neck. Then another.

Ari stared up at the sky. A small drop hit his forehead.

"Ari, did you feel something too?"

"Yes." His voice came out in a hoarse whisper. "Rivkaleh . . ."

Another drop hit him, a true raindrop. Then another. Another. Far away, a thin bolt of lightning leaped to earth. Soon, the isolated raindrops became a steady drizzle, soft as a baby's laugh. Ari's heart leaped inside him.

Baby Eleazar prayed on.

A thunderclap smote the courtyard, leaving an electric taste in Ari's mouth. All around him, people screamed. The rain became a shower. Ari's tunic turned wet and cold, and he had brought no cloak. Beside him, Rivka shrieked with glee.

Baby Eleazar prayed on.

Now it was a downpour. All around, people were shouting, dancing, singing, screaming, running, laughing, crying. The rain drenched all, a stream, a river, a mighty torrent.

Ari took a handful of grapes and ate one. Its sweetness filled him with joy. He went to Rabbi Yohanan and put a grape in the old man's mouth. "Eat!" he said.

Rabbi Yohanan ate the grape.

Baby Eleazar stopped praying.

The city of God danced for joy.

Ari did not sleep all night. Before daybreak, he dressed and went outside. A fine drizzle was falling on the city. Ari pulled his cloak over his head and locked his house and slogged through the streets to Baruch's house. Baruch was just locking his door when Ari arrived.

"Brother Baruch, I have a question."

Baruch raised an eyebrow. It was not usual to break silence on the way to the synagogue.

Ari told him of the feast and the miracle of rain as they walked. Baruch nodded and smiled.

When he finished, Ari said, "Why does sacrifice release power?"

Baruch walked in thought for many paces. "It is a deep law of the universe."

Baruch was always saying things like that, but Ari still did not understand. "Perhaps so, but why?"

"Can you not guess?"

Ari had been guessing all night. "When Rabbi Yohanan showed himself willing to sacrifice his life, it inspired others to pray."

"And had nobody prayed for rain before last night?"

Ari shrugged. "Not with such desperation. Rabbi Yohanan was close to death."

"And desperation makes a prayer more powerful?" Baruch stepped over a large puddle.

Ari did not know, but he did not think that was the answer. "The boy prayed with great power. Rabbi Yohanan's sacrifice forced him to it."

"The boy did not pray for rain before last night?"

Ari knew that he did. He was out of guesses. "Tell me then, why does sacrifice release power?"

"I told you — it is a deep law of the universe."

"But why?"

Baruch thought for a long moment. "The uncertainty principle of this man Heisenberg — it is a deep law of the universe, yes?"

"Yes."

"And the equivalence principle of this man Einstein is likewise a deep law?"

"Yes."

"Why?"

Ari shrugged. "There is no why for such things. They are because they are."

Baruch smiled and said nothing more.

Ari did not know what to think of that. It was a strange universe, if such things were true — that HaShem should be swayed by the sacrifices of his children. But as Einstein and Heisenberg had shown, it was a strange universe.

When they reached the synagogue, Ari felt a deep sense of dread fall on his heart. These were men he had known now for more than seven years. He had prayed with them, feasted with them, laughed with them, mourned with them. According to Rivka, soon they would all leave this city for elsewhere, and they would never return. They would go into exile and so would end the synagogue of The Way in Jerusalem.

Meanwhile, the rest of his people would stay here a few years longer. They would battle the Great Dragon, would suffer, bleed, die. For four long years and more they would stave off the inevitable.

How was this possible? Ari pulled out his *tefillin* and *tallit* and mechanically put them on. Shimon ben Klopas began the mighty words of the *Amidah*. Ari followed along, but his mind was far away.

He had seen the power of Rome. Roman soldiers were well-equipped, well-trained, well-disciplined. They were all that the zealous young fools of Jerusalem were not.

Yet history said that the Jews would shock Rome. For no reason, in the early months of the war, a few ragtag Jews would destroy Roman forces far superior in strength. How?

The answer came to Ari without conscious thought. One minute he did not know. The next minute, he did.

All his flesh went cold.

For the rest of the morning prayers, Ari could not think, did not wish to think. His heart was lead inside his chest. When they finished, Shimon ben Klopas asked Baruch to come and pray for a man with a sickness of the lungs. Ari slipped outside, pulled his cloak tight around him, and hurried away.

He had never felt so alone. The streets were nearly empty. Rain rushed in the gutters, a muddy foaming mess that spilled over in places onto the street. Ari passed his house and continued north until he reached a gate in the First Wall of the city. He went out, then turned right and went in through a gate in the Second Wall. He turned left on the first street, passed a bakery, and saw the synagogue of the Sons of Righteous Priests.

Ari waited.

Shortly, the door opened and a number of men spilled out. Some of them greeted Ari. He nodded to them. Finally, he saw the giant frame of Brother Eleazar.

"Ari the Kazan."

Ari nodded. "We must talk."

Eleazar led the way back into the synagogue. Gamaliel and another young priest were locked in animated conversation near the door. Gamaliel grinned broadly. "*Shalom*, Ari the Kazan! Have you —"

Eleazar said something in a quiet voice to Gamaliel and his friend. Both of them nodded and went out.

Eleazar's eyes narrowed to dagger slits. "So, Ari the Kazan. Time is short. Have you decided what you will do?"

Ari swallowed a great lump in his throat. "I have."

Eleazar waited.

"I will help you prepare machines of war," Ari said.

Eleazar stared at him for a second, then let out a great bellow. He rushed Ari and wrapped him in a great bear hug, kissing him on both cheeks. "You are certain of your decision, Ari the Kazan?"

Ari nodded. He felt dizzy with anxiety, but he knew this was right. There was no reason his people would not be crushed in the first two weeks of the war that was coming. No reason at all, except that they would have a weapon the Romans did not have. But the Romans had all that an army of this world could have.

Therefore, the Jews must come against them with a weapon not of this world. They must have Ari Kazan. It was the only solution Ari could see. It was not logical to fight in this hopeless war. Ari knew it would end in defeat. Yet he felt certain, deep in his soul, that HaShem called him to fight. For what reason HaShem called him, Ari could not guess. Surely he would die in the war. A man could not fight Rome for four years and not be killed. That would be his sacrifice to HaShem.

Ari did not fear death. He had nearly died once, had stood before the throne of HaShem. There, HaShem had asked him to do a great thing. And he had challenged Ari to consider the Problem of Good.

At last Ari felt that he understood it. For long, he had wrestled with the Problem of Evil, with the reasons why HaShem allowed darkness in the world. But he saw now that darkness was the wrong metaphor for Evil. It implied that Evil was the mere absence of Good, that Good could drive out Evil by its very presence, as light drove out darkness.

That was wrong. Evil could exist on its own, just as Good could. When Evil arose, Good must arise also to give battle. And it would be a true battle. Light drove out darkness with no effort, but Good could drive out Evil only with great effort, and Good could even fail. Yet even if Good failed, it was better to fight Evil than to not fight Evil.

The Problem of Good was that Good shone brightest when it strove against the deepest Evil. It required great Evil to make great Good, and the greatest Good of all was that which presented itself in sacrifice against the greatest Evil.

HaShem's universe was twisted, just as Ari's.

Eleazar's voice broke in on his thoughts. "Brother Ari, you are far from this place."

Eleazar had never called him Brother Ari before. Ari blinked and the big man's face swam into focus.

Eleazar studied him closely. "What of your woman? I was given to understand that she opposes me."

Ari's heart was hammering in his chest. "I will not tell her of this matter. You will speak to the brothers."

"Of course." Eleazar pursed his lips. "What of this womanish friend of yours, this Baruch?"

Ari sighed deeply. "I will not tell him either. When the time comes, my woman and child will leave the city, and Brother Baruch will protect them. HaShem has given him to pray, and my woman to see visions, but he has given me to fight."

Eleazar bellowed with laughter. "Well said, Brother Ari." He thumped Ari on the shoulders. "Together, we will see the rising of *Mashiach*."

Ari clasped Eleazar's hand at the wrist and deep grief shrouded his heart. *No, my friend, you are wrong. Together we will die, but we will die opposing Evil.*

PART FOUR

ABOMINATION

Spring, A.D. 65

But when you see the abomination of desolation standing
  where it should not
(Let the reader understand)
Then let those who are in Judea flee to the mountains.

— Rabban Yeshua, Mark 13:14, author's paraphrase

The people belonging to the church at Jerusalem had been ordered by an oracle revealed to approved men on the spot before the war broke out, to leave the city and dwell in a town of Perea called Pella.

— Eusebius, Ecclesiastical History III:5

TWENTY-THREE

Rivka

Imma, why do we eat the feast of *Pesach?*"

Rivka squeezed Rachel's hand. "I'll bet Dov knows." They were on the way to the market with Hana and Dov to buy food for the feast. It was a brisk spring morning, and a sharp wind blew through the streets. The warm sun beat down on Rivka, doing its best to lighten her heart, and failing miserably.

"I know! I know!" Dov shouted. He scooted forward and turned around so he could walk backward, looking back at them. His little imitation *tefillin* slipped sideways and down on his forehead like an eyepatch, making him look like some sort of chubby pirate. "Somebody hated us."

Rachel began hopping up and down. "Then HaShem saved us!" She tugged at Rivka's hand, prompting her to finish the litany.

A smile forced itself onto Rivka's lips. "Let's eat!"

Hana twirled a woven shopping basket in her hands. "Dov, now tell Aunt Rivka who it was who hated us, that we should celebrate *Pesach.*"

Dov thought for a moment. "The king of Syria!"

Hana shook her head. "No, that is for *Hanukkah.*"

"Haman!" Dov shouted.

"No, that is for Queen Esther and *Purim,*" Hana said. "Racheleh, do you know?"

"Hanan ben Hanan!" Rachel said.

Rivka cringed. "Rachel, you know better than that."

Hana shot her a fierce look. Rivka felt herself blushing. They continued in silence until they reached the market square. Merchant stalls lined its edges, and a double row ran down the center. Hana pointed toward Herod's Palace at the far end of the square. "Dov! Rachel! Run to Herod's Palace and bring me back a small stone from the wall. Hurry!"

Dov raced away. Rachel followed in his wake, shouting, "Wait for me, Dov!"

Hana set her basket on a stone bench. "Rivkaleh, sit."

Rivka sat.

Hana put a hand on her arm. "You have been speaking evil of Hanan ben Hanan."

Rivka sighed. "I try not to. But it's hard to speak about him and not say something bad. He's an evil man."

"You have been praying for him as HaShem told you?"

"Sometimes," Rivka said.

Hana just looked at her.

"It's been awhile." Rivka put her face in her hands. "You don't understand, Hana. I *hate* him. He tried to kill Ari. Then Ari saved his life last fall and did he thank Ari? No, he treated him like scum. I wish . . ." Rivka didn't want to admit what she wished.

"You wish Ari the Kazan had let him be killed," Hana said.

Rivka nodded.

Hana stood up and took Rivka's hand. "Rivkaleh, please, you will not be offended, but you are a prisoner of Hanan ben Hanan."

"A . . . what?"

"A prisoner." Hana's black eyes were like lasers. "When you hate a man, then you are his prisoner. It is time for you to be released from prison. Come."

Rivka braced her feet. "Hana, you don't understand."

Hana raised an eyebrow. "You are not the first to ever hate a man."

"*Imma!*" Dov's gleeful voice rose above the market bustle. "Look what I found!" He raced toward them across the square, holding aloft a sweaty fist. His light brown hair flowed behind him, a golden mane. Rivka felt a stab in her heart. Of course Hana understood hate.

Dov crashed into Hana. She staggered back under his impact, then gave him a fierce hug. "Show me what you brought, little bear."

Dov opened his fat paw. Inside was nothing. Dov's smile vanished. "I had a stone, *Imma!* It was here!"

Hana tussled his hair and straightened his little *tefillin*. "Of course, little bear. You lost it in the wind of your speed, yes?"

He gave her one of those heart-stopping grins that showed he was going to be a star with the ladies in just a few years.

"*Imma!*" Rachel's voice, thin and squeaky and full of joy. "*Imma*, look what I found!" When she arrived, a shiny glow covered her face and a missing-tooth smile told Rivka that she had succeeded. "Look, *Imma*, I found a stone from the wall!" In her hand was a small piece of the white limestone used everywhere in Jerusalem.

Hana picked it up and showed it to Dov. "Less haste, little bear, and more speed, yes?"

"Yes, *Imma*."

Hana stood up and handed the stone shard to Rivka. "Yes, Rivkaleh?"

Rivka sighed. "Yes, Hana."

Hana took her hand and pulled. "Then come. It is time you were free from your prison."

Rivka followed. "Where are we going?"

But she knew.

When they reached the palace of Hanan ben Hanan, Rivka's heart was pounding. What was Hana planning?

Hana pulled her past the front gate and around the corner of the outer wall into a tiny alley. Rivka hadn't been here since the night Hanan ben Hanan had flogged Ari hard enough to kill him.

"*Imma*, why are we here?" Dov said. Rachel immediately squatted in the dirt and began playing with a line of ants.

Hana put Rivka's hand flat on the wall. "You will not take your hand away until you have forgiven the man."

The wall felt clammy and cold. "Hana, what is it you expect me to do?"

Hana looked exasperated. "You will pray for him, just as Baruch has told you many times."

Rivka gave her a blank stare.

Hana put her right hand over Rivka's and raised her left hand toward heaven. "Hanan ben Hanan, I bless you in the name of HaShem. I bless your sons and daughters to the last generation. I call on HaShem to fill your heart with peace and joy, to give you a long life, and at the end to welcome you into the World to Come."

Hana took her hand off Rivka's. "Now you will do the same."

Rivka wanted to scream at Hana, to tell her she couldn't possibly understand. Except that Hanan ben Hanan had also tried to kill Baruch. If Hana could do it, Rivka could.

But she couldn't. Rivka opened her mouth, but nothing came out.

"*Imma*, if you say the words, your heart will learn to mean them." Rachel put a grubby hand on Rivka's arm.

Rivka gave her a sharp look. Sometimes Rachel said things that were impossibly profound.

Hana narrowed her eyes. "Dov! Racheleh! Come, we have shopping. Rivka, please you will stay here until you are no longer a prisoner. I will be waiting for you at home."

"Hana, wait . . ." Rivka couldn't think of a single reason why Hana should wait.

Hana took one of the children in each hand and disappeared around the corner.

Rivka felt panic clutching at her heart. This was crazy. She couldn't do this.

She had to do this.

Hana was right. She hated Hanan ben Hanan's guts, and until she could let go of that, she was going to be his prisoner.

Rivka raised one hand toward heaven and pressed the other against the wall. "Hanan ben Hanan, I . . ."

Sweat sprang out on her forehead. This was hard, very hard.

"Hanan ben Hanan, I . . . bless you in the name of . . . HaShem."

Rivka closed her eyes and tried again. And again. On the fourth try, she got all the way through the blessing Hana had said. She didn't mean it, but she got through it. That was something.

Tears sprang up in her eyes, and she realized just how much she hated Hanan ben Hanan, and everything he stood for.

"Hanan ben Hanan, I bless you in the name of HaShem." She continued straight through to the end. And still she didn't mean it.

She said it again, the words boiling in her heart.

On the fifteenth time, she heard a voice in the street. "You there! Witch woman, what are you doing?"

Rivka's eyes jerked open. She wiped her teary eyes with her sleeve and saw a man in the street. Probably one of Hanan's servants.

Rage lit up his eyes. "You will leave now, witch woman, and never come back."

Rivka felt like an idiot. She turned and raced away up the alley toward the next street. This was horrible. Worse than horrible. She could only imagine what it looked like — the witch woman casting a spell on Hanan ben Hanan. If that man told Hanan, she was going to be in real trouble.

Rivka ran all the way to Hana's house. When she got there, her heart was thumping so hard in her chest she thought Baruch and Hana would be able to hear it through their thick wooden door. She twisted the latch and collapsed inward, falling headlong on the dirt floor, gasping for breath.

Upstairs, she heard Dov and Rachel singing a song. Then Hana's voice. "Children, hush! Did you hear something?"

Footsteps at the top of the stairs. A gasp. "Rivkaleh!" Feet thumped down the steps.

Hands caressed her face. "Rivka, are you well? Please, you will speak to me!"

Rivka fought to open her eyes. She smiled at Hana. "I'm . . . fine, Hana. I . . . did what you asked." *I tried, anyway. I didn't finish, but I started.*

Hana leaned close and peered into her eyes. A broad smile lit up the world. "Blessed be HaShem. You had hatred in your heart where it should not be, but now it has fled."

Before Rivka could say anything, the world seemed to change. The veil to the Other Side pulled back and all her senses opened to another reality. She felt hot all over, and a brightness filled her soul. Flaming words formed in her heart, and she heard them, felt them, saw them, smelt them.

When you see the abomination of desolation standing where it should not be, let those who are in Judea flee to the mountains.

Then the world darkened, and Rivka could see ordinary sights again, could hear ordinary sounds. Hana's face swam into view. " — you well, Rivka?"

Rivka took a deep breath, and realized she had not been breathing while she was gone. "Yes, I am well."

"Please, you will rest a little." Hana put Rivka's head in her lap and loosened her hair covering. "When you are ready, you will tell me what happened."

Rivka relaxed and let her body catch its breath. She told Hana about praying for Hanan ben Hanan. About getting caught, and running here, and collapsing. About the thing she had heard or seen or whatever.

"It is a vision from HaShem," Hana said. "What do the words mean?"

"It means it is time." Rivka had been waiting years for this word from HaShem. Now it had come in the last way she would ever have expected. "Hana, I think it's a sign that we need to leave Jerusalem. We knew it was coming. Now it's here."

"What is this abomination of desolation?" Hana's face sagged with grief. "What is this sign?"

Rivka realized that Hana did not know any home other than Jerusalem. They had talked about leaving many times, but that was just talk. Now it was real.

"Please, you will speak with Ari the Kazan on this matter." Hana's voice sounded thick with emotion. "And I will speak with Baruch."

That night, after they put Rachel to bed, Rivka took Ari up on the roof of their home and they looked at the stars and talked. She told him the whole story.

". . . and I'm certain it was a word from HaShem," Rivka said.

Ari folded her hands in his. "Yes, Rivkaleh, I believe you."

She heard tears in his voice and realized how much he loved this city. "What should we do now? I think HaShem wants all our people to leave."

"Forever?"

"Yes . . . forever. There won't be anything to come back to when the Romans get through."

"Of course." Ari's voice quivered. "Yes, of course, forever. We must speak with Shimon ben Klopas in the morning."

"We?"

"You and I," Ari said. "Baruch also. I feel in my heart this is a true word from HaShem. A year from now, the war will be upon us. We must leave soon, and find a place. Do you know where we are to go?"

"Eusebius says the community went to Pella," Rivka said. "It's a city on the other side of the Jordan."

"Outside the Land of Yisrael."

"Yes, outside."

Ari put a hand on her hair and stroked it gently. "Come to bed then. Tomorrow will take care of itself."

Rivka stood up and they went back downstairs, holding hands. She had been looking forward to leaving ever since she got here. Now she could not bear the thought.

Ari

The next morning Ari took Rivka with him to the morning prayers. While it was not forbidden for a woman to join in these prayers, such a thing almost never happened, since a woman was considered free from any commandment that would hamper her child-rearing responsibilities. During the prayers, Ari spread his *tallit* over both of them. A great well of sadness opened in his heart. This would be his sacrifice to HaShem, to be separated from his woman and child for the sake of his people.

By the time they finished the *Sh'ma*, Ari was weeping. Rivka clung to his arm, and Ari knew that she also wept to leave the city. She did not yet know that she would leave without him. Ari could not think how he would tell her, but he would find a way. Only not yet.

Ari folded his *tallit* and removed his *tefillin* and put them in his broad cloth belt. Baruch went to fetch Shimon ben Klopas. Half a dozen men clustered around Ari, sending sidelong looks at Rivka but refusing to ask the obvious question. Why had she come to morning prayers?

Baruch led Shimon over to Ari and Rivka. His wise old eyes ran around the circle. "My children, I will have a private word with Ari the Kazan and his woman and Baruch the *tsaddik*."

Eyes opened wide and the room began buzzing with excited whispers. As the men left, many of them looked back at Rivka.

When the meeting room was empty, Shimon shut the door and led them to a row of wooden benches along the side wall. "So." Shimon's eyes studied Rivka. "It has been many months since Ari the Kazan told me certain matters that would soon befall. He told of a man named Florus. He told of the burning of the Queen of Heaven. He told that we must soon leave this city. The first two of these have passed us. Please, you will tell me the word HaShem has given to you."

Rivka explained the vision she had seen.

"You saw this darkly or clearly?" Shimon asked.

"Clearly, my father."

Shimon closed his eyes and sat deep in thought for a long time. Ari wondered if he had fallen asleep. Finally, the old man's eyelids flickered open. "Please, you will explain again the matter of the abomination of desolation. This is a dark word that Rabban Yeshua spoke, and none have ever explained it. What is the meaning?"

"I do not know," Rivka said.

Baruch coughed lightly. "My father, if Sister Rivka has heard a true word from HaShem, then we will know shortly what is this abomination, yes?"

"Yes," Shimon said. "And if we learn what is the abomination, then she has heard a true word."

Baruch was nodding as if this made perfect sense.

Ari bit his tongue. Shimon had just committed a logical fallacy, and now Baruch had agreed to it.

"Very good then, my children." Shimon stood up. "Please, you will inform me promptly when you understand the matter."

TWENTY-FOUR

Rivka

That afternoon, Rivka left Rachel with Hana and visited Gamaliel's olive-oil shop. It was now only two days before *Pesach*, and the shop was crowded. Rivka waited patiently until the other customers left.

Baby Eleazar fixed her with a rapt expression. "Sister, I see that you have been in the *Shekinah*."

Rivka wished she could just look at a person and see that. "I heard a thing from HaShem that worries me."

Baby Eleazar said nothing.

Rivka picked up a small vessel of olive oil and examined it minutely. "Do you know the meaning of the abomination of desolation spoken of by the prophet Daniel?"

"It is the wicked king of Syria," Baby Eleazar said. "HaShem raised up the Maccabees to drive him out."

"Yes, but is there a second meaning? A meaning for a later time? I have heard of a word from HaShem that speaks of a second abomination standing where it should not."

"If so, then it is a deep mystery of HaShem," Baby Eleazar said.

Rivka put the vessel back on its shelf and turned to the door. Baby Eleazar didn't know any more about this than she did.

"Sister, please you will tell me of the far country from which you come."

Rivka wondered what she could tell him. "I come from a land where women are treated as men." *Almost like men, anyway.* "There, any person can learn whatever they wish in great schools of learning. They have libraries with ten thousand times ten thousand books. They have wise men who know the deep mysteries of the universe. They have machines which can think like a man, and other machines to do many kinds of work. They have machines to fly through the air, and to speak with people in other far countries, and to see things in yet others."

Baby Eleazar's face was shining. "I wish to see your far country some-day. Will you take me there? All people in your far country must be very happy."

Rivka hesitated. People back home lived longer, owned more things, ate better food. But were they happier?

"Did I say something wrong, Sister?"

"No." Rivka smiled at him. "People in my far country are often unhappy."

Baby Eleazar seemed puzzled. "But with so many wonderful things, they must be very thankful to HaShem."

Rivka did not know what to say. How could she explain that not all in her far country believed in HaShem, and of those who did, not all were thankful to him? It struck her that, given the choice to go back, she was no longer certain she would. She had grown to love this city of God, and now she was going to leave it, to abandon it to evil.

"I am sorry, Sister." Baby Eleazar looked distressed. "You are a stranger in a strange land, and you intend to leave, yes? I saw when you came in that you mean to leave Jerusalem."

His image blurred into a soft focus. "Yes."

"And you are going home to your far country?"

"No, I can never return there."

Baby Eleazar sighed deeply. "Then you are like me. You have no true home but the World to Come."

Rivka peered into his eyes. Someday, he would be recognized as a great rabbi, the greatest of his generation. Then something would happen and the other rabbis would exclude him and he would live out his life as an outcast. "Are you lonely, little brother?"

He bit his lip and looked down at the floor. "When will you leave? I will be sad of your leaving."

"When I understand what is the second meaning of the abomination of desolation."

Baby Eleazar's face brightened. "Then it will be long before you leave, Sister."

Ari

Ari loaded the last lead ball into the ballista. As a boy, he had been taught that such things were called catapults, but he had learned different here. A catapult threw spears. A ballista threw stones or other ballistic objects.

Brother Eleazar turned the winch and the ratchet clicked. The device was simple. It stored torsional energy in a set of ropes that twisted as the ratchet turned. When the ropes reached their full torsional compression, a switch could be activated to transfer the energy to the throwing arm, which heaved the projectile. The physics was easy but the engineering was not. Ari wanted to achieve maximum energy transfer and range, and that meant optimizing the mass of the projectile, its angle of launch, and the torsional energy of the ropes.

Ari had constructed a small ballista with the help of Levi the bronze-worker, using the best steel components he could build. The small scale made it easy to experiment. He had a theoretical model of how the device should perform, but now he needed data. They had come out here, two kilometers into the desert, where they could shoot projectiles as much as they wanted, with nobody to bother them.

Eleazar's thick muscles strained at the winch. "It is ready," he grunted.

Ari signaled downrange to make sure nobody was in line with the weapon. Small as it was, the device packed enough energy to kill a man at two hundred meters. "Fire the weapon."

Brother Eleazar flicked the switch.

The arm leapt up much too fast for Ari's eye to follow it. He heard the lead ball hum through the air, then watched the kick of dust far away. That was the tenth shot. Now came the part that mystified all the Sons of Righteous Priests, but which Ari knew was most important. They must collect and analyze the data. At the very least, he needed to measure the mean and standard deviation, and look for anomalies.

Ari pounded a short stake into the ground and began paying out a thin rope along the ground. He saw Brother Levi pounding in a stake where the projectile had hit. Ari and Eleazar walked toward him. Every ten cubits, a red silk thread was tied to the rope. Ari counted each one. At 352 cubits, they reached the first stake. It was marked with a number to tell which shot was fired.

"Write this," Ari said. "Projectile number ten at 352 cubits."

Brother Eleazar grumbled something and wrote it down.

Ari checked to make sure the numbers were correct, then moved on. The next projectile was number nine. And the next was number eight. This pattern continued all the way to the first, which had gone the farthest. Ari felt a surge of disappointment. The ballista was losing range with each shot. The problem was to figure out why.

The Sons of Righteous Priests collected the projectiles and they all walked back to the ballista. All of them looked thrilled that the device actually worked.

Ari was not happy. It looked as if the ropes were losing torsional strength with each shot. That was not acceptable. To be effective in battle, the weapon required repeatability from shot to shot.

"Ari the Kazan, the device throws almost as far as you predicted," Brother Eleazar said.

"Only the first time," Ari said. "After that, it loses elasticity. Are you sure the Romans use ropes in their ballistas?"

Brother Eleazar shrugged. "I have never seen one of their machines. When Brother Yoseph comes back, perhaps he will know."

"And when will he return?" Ari asked.

"Soon," Brother Eleazar said. "I had hoped before *Pesach*, but that requires good weather. He was shipwrecked on the way to Rome, and I think he will not wish to risk that on the way home."

Ari had not heard that Brother Yoseph had shipwrecked on the way to Rome. For the moment, his larger concern was to find a material that would not lose elasticity. He had a little more than a year to solve this problem and many dozen more. There were calculations to make on the optimal size of lead balls for slingers. Likewise, for the optimal length of mechanical arms for spear-throwing, for the optimal mass loading on the spears, for the best penetrating projectiles that could be mass-produced cheaply. He should have started years ago. The war, which had long seemed a far-off and indefinite thing, now loomed ahead of him, closer than he had imagined and rushing at him far too fast.

They reached the ballista. Ari examined it for signs of damage. The steel frame had many nicks at the release point, but it appeared undamaged. The ropes were visibly degraded. Either he was loading them too much, or the material was intrinsically defective.

"Shall we fire it again?" Brother Eleazar said. Like a small boy, he seemed very excited at the prospect of being able to throw kilogram-sized projectiles almost two hundred meters. He seemed not at all perturbed by the material-degradation problem.

"No, we will take it back to the shop," Ari said. "There is a matter to be solved."

"Very good," Eleazar said. "You will solve this matter and we will test it again tomorrow."

You are quiet, tonight, Rivkaleh." Ari lay in bed watching Rivka comb through her long black hair with a double-ended wooden lice comb. She rarely found any lice, but it was a necessary precaution in a crowded city, even though her hair was covered most of the day.

She pursed her lips and kept combing. "I talked to Baby Eleazar today. He doesn't think we're going to figure out that abomination of desolation thing anytime soon."

"So then we go to the Plan B, yes?"

She slumped onto the bed. "Ari, I don't have a Plan B. I just assumed that I'd hear from HaShem at the right time, and then it would all fall together."

Ari had never seen her so discouraged. "Nothing falls together without some difficulty. I heard today that Brother Yoseph was shipwrecked on his way to Rome. Did you know that?"

She looked at him. "Well, of course. Didn't I tell you? He was almost killed — had to swim for it. But it turned out for the best, because in the wreck or right afterward he met up with some actor who turned out to know Caesar's wife, and that's how he made the connections he needed to get those priests out of prison."

Ari had heard none of this.

Rivka turned up the very ends of her hair. "Who told you about the shipwreck? Gamaliel?"

"Brother Eleazar."

Rivka flinched. "I wish you would have nothing to do with that awful man."

Ari said nothing. He had spent many hours with Brother Eleazar over the winter. Brother Eleazar came from what Americans would call a dysfunctional family. His father was a tyrant and his mother a weeping zero.

Rivka finished her hair and lay down beside him. "So what did Eleazar want?"

"Want?" Ari gave her his most innocent expression.

She put her fingers in his beard. "Don't play dumb with me. You talked to Eleazar today and he told you about the shipwreck. But Eleazar doesn't hand out news for free. He always wants something."

"Yes, of course." Ari wondered if Rivka had ever studied weapons in archaeology school. "Eleazar wished to know what sort of materials the Romans use for the springs in catapults."

"Is he still harping about weapons?" Rivka looked disgusted. "Good grief, everybody knows what the Romans used."

"I do not."

"Every historian knows." Rivka knelt beside Ari and let her hair flop down loosely in his face. "Don't tell him, but it's this stuff."

"What stuff?"

"Hair, silly!" Rivka waggled her hair around, letting its silky softness enfold him. "When a Greek city was besieged in antiquity, the first thing that happened was the city officials went around asking women for their hair. It was the patriotic thing to do, you know. Cut off your hair so they could weave it into these big thick skeins. I don't know why they used hair."

"That much is evident," Ari said. "It does not lose elasticity over time."

Rivka raised her head and just looked at him.

He felt his ears turning hot.

"Ari?"

"Yes, Rivkaleh?"

"Please, please, please tell me you're not doing something with catapults."

Ari's throat felt very dry.

"Ari! Tell me you're not making some kind of military thing."

"Rivka, they are children. Fools. They will be sacrificed like lambs. Do you think they will last five minutes against a Roman army?"

Rivka's face turned white. "Ari, how long have you been doing this?" Tears formed in her eyes.

"Six months." He held his arms out to her. "Please, Rivkaleh. Try to understand—"

She slapped him hard, then rolled off the bed, her eyes furious. "Six months! You liar! You haven't said a word about this to me. That's horrible. How could you?" She stalked to the door.

"Where are you going?"

"To Rachel's room." She glowered at him. "If you think I'm going to sleep in the same bed with you, you can forget it." She stomped out.

Ari closed his eyes and listened to the swishing sound of blood racing through his temples. Deep regret surged through his veins. He had done wrong. Had lied to Rivka. Now she hated him and he deserved it. He had been a fool to withhold the truth from her. He would not make that mistake ever again.

But he was not going to stop working with Brother Eleazar, whatever Rivka said.

TWENTY-FIVE

Baruch

Baruch strode through the New City, looking for the construction site. Anger burned in his heart. This was a great evil, and he would not stand silently and do nothing. HaShem would not forgive him if he did nothing. A warm breeze blew through the city. By the time Baruch found the lot, he was sweating.

He spotted Brother Ari at the far end of the site, standing in the center of a circle of workmen holding a roll of papyrus. Baruch picked a way through the piles of stone blocks toward the men. Brother Ari spotted him and said something in a low tone. The men around him dispersed, leaving Ari alone.

Baruch stopped directly in front of him. "Brother Ari, there is a matter we must discuss."

Ari's eyes gleamed. "Speak."

Baruch crossed his arms on his chest. "Sister Rivka came this morning with Racheleh. She was crying. You are doing a great wrong, to give aid to the men of violence."

Ari tugged at his beard. "You know this of your own knowledge or you have a word from HaShem?"

"I heard from HaShem," Baruch said. "I am directed to tell you to have nothing to do with the men of violence."

Ari's left eyelid flickered, and he looked nervously at the sky. "I must think on this. I understood that HaShem wished for me to do what I could to battle evil."

"The battle belongs to HaShem, my friend." Deep heaviness weighed on Baruch's heart. How was it that Brother Ari had spent six months in this wickedness, and Baruch had not known? He had seen no outward sign. Nor had he heard a word from HaShem on the matter until now.

Ari sat on a pile of stone blocks. "My brother, the battle belongs to HaShem, but he gives each man his role to play in that battle. He gives you to pray. He gives another man to fight. He gives me to design —"

"No!" Baruch said. "You are a good man, Brother Ari. But good mixed with evil is evil. These are men of violence, and Rabban Yeshua commanded us to have nothing to do with them."

"Very well," Brother Ari said. "He commanded you so. Therefore, you must be separate from the men of violence. But I do not follow Rabban Yeshua, and —"

Baruch bent down and seized Ari's tunic, yanking him to his feet. "This is the way of death. HaShem says if you follow this way, you will find death. You *must* leave this path and follow the way of Yeshua."

Ari grabbed Baruch's hands and tore them away from his tunic. "You will not tell me what I *must* do, ever again." His voice sounded cold as iron and a spirit of anger filled his face. "I will fight evil in the way HaShem has commanded me. This is my decision, and you will respect it or you are not my friend."

Baruch felt a hard knot in his throat. Now he must choose whether to obey Ari or the word of HaShem.

"My way is set," Ari said. "There is a thing I must do for HaShem, and I will do it, whether it leads me to death or not. And you will *not* presume to instruct me. It was I who stood before the Throne, not you. HaShem asked me to do one thing for him, and I will do it."

Baruch clasped Ari's hand in his. "Brother Ari, please do not be offended, but this is not the thing HaShem has given you to do."

"Then you have not heard from HaShem." Ari turned his back on Baruch. "Now leave me."

Baruch felt his heart crushed. No, he could not leave. Not when Brother Ari was choosing death. Better that he himself should die. He walked around in front of Ari. "Please, my brother, hear my words —"

Ari spit at his feet. "Baruch, you have overstepped. Now leave me. You are no longer my friend." He spun around and strode away.

Black grief fell on Baruch. He had offended Brother Ari and lost his friendship, to no gain.

Except that he had obeyed HaShem. What more could he have done?

Gamaliel

On the eve of *Pesach*, directly after the afternoon sacrifices, the slaughter began. Gamaliel had been assigned a place on the south side of the *Khel*, the platform just outside the inner Temple, at the top of the steps that led up from the outer courts. By tradition, all families who meant to eat a *Pesach* lamb tonight must send a representative here to buy a lamb and slaughter it inside the Court of Priests between the ending of the afternoon sacrifices and the going down of the sun.

This required excellent organization, in order that the many ten thousand men should slaughter their lambs in good order. Today, Gamaliel was part of that organization. It was his job to direct men with their lambs through the broad gates into the Court of Women, where other priests would direct them in lines into the Court of Priests. When their lambs were slaughtered, they would then come out through one of the narrow gates and down the steps and out through the barrier into the outer court.

Gamaliel looked toward the sun and guessed there remained yet an hour before it would set. And still many lambs to be sacrificed.

On the portico roof on the western side of the Temple Mount, Gamaliel saw several Roman soldiers running north. Fear clutched at his heart. His own father had been killed here many years ago at *Pesach*. The last thing Gamaliel remembered seeing before he lost his father was soldiers on the portico roof. Running.

Heart thumping, Gamaliel strode west until he reached the end of the *Khel*. He turned right and headed north. Many soldiers were pouring down the steps from the portico roofs at the northern end of the outer courts. Gamaliel began running.

When he reached the northern end of the *Khel*, he turned right again and saw . . .

Confusion.

Many Jews were waiting with lambs to enter the inner Temple on this side also, just as on the south. But here, just outside the barrier wall, trouble waited.

A dozen Roman soldiers clustered in a circle, their weapons drawn. In the center of the circle stood a man wearing a toga with a thin purple stripe.

Governor Florus had come to watch *Pesach*.

Gamaliel tasted bile in the back of his throat. He raced down the steps and ran to the gate in the low barrier wall. The barrier was not so much an obstacle as a reminder. It stood only waist high and could easily be vaulted by a man. But its purpose was to demark the boundary beyond which *goyim* must not come — on pain of death. Once, two centuries ago, the wicked king Antiochus had come through the barrier and sacrificed a pig on the altar of the living God. That was an abomination that took years to purify from the land. The victory over Antiochus was the reason for celebrating the feast of *Hanukkah*.

Fear gripped Gamaliel's heart. When he reached the barrier, he skidded to a stop beside a small circle of priests at the gate.

"... is not permitted for a *goy* to enter." The priest at the gate was speaking loudly in Aramaic and making exaggerated gestures, as if that would help the foolish Romans understand better.

Gamaliel pushed forward. "My brothers, does nobody here speak Greek?"

The priests turned and smiled. "Gamaliel ben Levi! You will speak to the soldiers, please. The governor wishes to observe the sacrifices in the Court of Priests."

Cold terror ran a hand down Gamaliel's spine. Black spots formed before his eyes. If he could not speak reason with these men, something terrible would happen.

Gamaliel stepped forward and gave a slight bow with his head. He dared not look at the governor, so he found the centurion's eye and took a deep breath. "Sir, please may I speak with you? My brothers do not speak Greek."

The centurion gave him an impassive look. "The governor wishes to observe the sacrifices being made on behalf of Caesar. Inform your men that we will enter the Temple and escort the governor to the altar."

Gamaliel wondered if today he would join his father in the World to Come. "Sir, with respect, there is a legal matter. Caesar has declared our ancient religion to be a legal religion, protected by the Senate. Part of our law from many hundred years is that only circumcised Jews may come through the barrier." Gamaliel spread his hands apologetically. "Even Caesar himself is forbidden by the Senate from entering here."

Governor Florus pushed forward and he peered between the shoulders of two soldiers. "Stupid Jew! I do not require instruction in Roman law. Tell your men that we will enter the Temple and observe the sacrifices!"

Gamaliel felt light-headed. He gripped the top of the barrier wall and took a deep breath to calm his heart. "Excellency, please, it is not permitted by our law. If—"

Florus spit on Gamaliel's linen tunic. "Jew, did you hear me? I spit on your filthy laws. Tell your men to stand aside or I will have my men draw swords. How many of you wish to die today for the sake of your laws?"

Gamaliel jutted his chin at the governor. He would be killed for this, but there were some things a man must die for, or else not be a man. "Excellency, you may kill me if you wish. But you should know that you would need to also kill the priests beside me. Then you must kill the ten thousand men who stand inside the Temple with their lambs. Not one of us would refuse to die in order to protect our laws."

The governor's eyes narrowed to points. "You wish to die, Jew? Very well —" A look of shock rippled down his face.

Gamaliel heard the tramp of many feet behind him. He spun to look.

Fifty Temple guards raced down the steps from the inner Temple. Brother Eleazar ran at their head. They bore short swords and light shields, and grim determination set their faces.

Brother Eleazar arrived first, his great frame casting a long shadow to the east. He gave a slight bow to the soldiers. "I am Eleazar, son of Ananias, captain of the Temple," he said in rough street Greek. "With me are fifty picked men of my guard. On the walls behind me are a hundred men with slings, each of them a dead shot at a hundred cubits."

Gamaliel looked up at the walls, and saw many dozen men appear. Perhaps they were a hundred, and perhaps they were fewer, but Gamaliel knew they were not slingers. Six months from now, Ari the Kazan would have assembled a corps of slingers and outfitted them with slings and lead shot, but today they were a false show of strength.

Governor Florus looked like he might faint. The soldiers closed ranks in front of him and the centurion spoke with a quivering voice. "His Excellency withdraws his request."

Brother Eleazar showed no reaction. "May you enjoy a peaceful festival."

The centurion nodded and barked an order. The soldiers spun around and began marching back north toward the Antonia Fortress.

Gamaliel watched them until they had gone up the steps, across the northern portico roof, and into the iron door of the Antonia.

Brother Eleazar pounded Gamaliel hard on the shoulders. "Bravely done, Brother Gamaliel. You kept the abomination out of the Temple. You are a true son of your father."

Gamaliel felt fierce pride pulsing through his veins. "Yet a year and *Mashiach* will come and all the *goyim* will be pushed into the sea."

Brother Eleazar smiled.

TWENTY-SIX

Rivka

Eight days passed in unbearable tension. Baruch tried several times to speak to Ari, but Ari refused to see him. Every night, Rivka slept in Rachel's room, dreamed about the abomination in the Temple, heard a voice telling her it was time for The Way to leave the city. Every day, she begged Ari to take her to speak with Shimon ben Klopas about the matter. Ari refused, and that made her frantic. Shimon would never consent to speak to her without her husband.

By the last day of the Feast of Unleavened Bread, Rivka could stand it no longer. Early in the morning, while Ari was at morning prayers with Eleazar and his wretched crew, Rivka packed a bag with some clothes and sat down with Rachel at the kitchen table.

Finally, she heard the key scratching at the iron lock. Rivka stood up and took Rachel's hand. "Let's go see Dov, shall we?"

Rachel looked up with her mournful eyes. "Are we going away from *Abba* forever?"

Doubt pierced Rivka's heart.

The door opened and Ari stepped inside. He looked at Rivka, then Rachel, then the bag of clothes. "You are going somewhere?"

Rivka steeled her courage. She had to do this. "We're leaving you, unless you take me to speak with Shimon today."

Ari looked like she had kicked him in the stomach. He leaned against the doorframe and closed his eyes. "You could go with Baruch to see Shimon."

Rivka reached down and picked up her bag. "That won't work and you know it. If I want to talk to Shimon, I need you with me."

"And yet you believe Baruch is right and I am not, in the matter of the weapons."

Rivka said nothing.

Ari shut the door and stepped toward her, his eyes shadowed with grief. He clutched her to himself, stroking her long hair softly. "Rivkaleh, it is wrong that a woman should oppose her own husband."

Rivka felt her throat tighten like a fist and her resolve turned to water. She wrapped her arms around Ari's waist and buried her face in his chest. How could she not oppose him, when he was making a terrible blunder? Eleazar was going to destroy the city, the whole nation. He was evil. Helping him was dead wrong.

"Ari, I *need* to talk to Shimon. We have to get our people out of this city. I've been hearing from HaShem every night. We have to go soon, or it'll be too late. Innocent people are going to get killed if we don't go. Can't you just swallow your pride and help me?"

Ari held her. "Yes, many hundreds will die if you do nothing. That is a tragedy." His voice cracked. "But now please swallow your own pride and listen to me. Many ten thousand will die if I do nothing. Can you understand that? Or do only followers of Rabban Yeshua deserve to live?"

"Ari —"

"Not yet, Rivka. Let me say one other thing. I can understand that you do not wish to involve yourself with fighting. I also hate war. I am a pacifist. But I will not stand by while our people are destroyed. I do not ask for your help. Only that you respect me enough to let me do what HaShem has told me to do."

"Can't you talk to Baruch about it?"

Ari's body tightened. "Rivkaleh, I have nothing to say to Baruch. He has his battle and I respect it. I have my battle, and he does not respect it."

"Please, just talk —"

"No. If you intend to leave me, then you must leave me, but I will not be swayed. I must do this thing that HaShem has told me."

Rivka sighed and went upstairs with her bag. Ari had called her bluff. When she was five years old, her father had walked out on her and her mother. There was no way in the world Rivka was going to let that happen to Rachel. She dumped the clothes on her bed and put everything away on the shelf.

When she came back downstairs, Ari was sitting quietly on a stool holding Rachel on his lap. Rachel's lip trembled, and she had red eyes and wet-streaked cheeks. Rivka felt horribly guilty. She brought out unleavened bread and cheese and pickled cucumbers and beer, which she mixed with water. They sat on stools around the small stone table. Ari said the blessing before meals, and then broke off a piece of *matzah* for Rachel.

Rachel seemed dispirited and ate little, making a big pile of crumbs. Finally, she nibbled on a piece of cheese. "*Imma*, what's an abomination?"

"It's a man who fights against HaShem, sweetie. Eat your food, don't play with it."

Rachel wiggled one of her bottom teeth. "Is *Abba* an abomination?"

Ari's hand slapped on the table, making the food jump.

Rachel began crying.

Rivka took her in her arms. "Don't cry, sweetheart. Did somebody tell you *Abba* fights against HaShem?"

Rachel sniffed loudly. "Uncle Baruch said so."

Ari was pacing back and forth now, his face agitated.

Rivka took Rachel upstairs and found her doll. "Play up here for a little."

"Will *Abba* make peace with Uncle Baruch today?"

"Maybe." Rivka went downstairs. Ari looked ready to explode. She wrapped her arms around him. "Baruch loves you, Ari."

Ari's body felt tense, coiled to strike. "I do not say such things behind his back. Why does he say such things behind mine?"

"You two need to talk."

"Not until he stops speaking evil behind my back."

"He thinks you're doing the wrong thing."

"And I know I am doing the right thing. For this purpose, HaShem sent me back. If Baruch wishes me to do nothing, then let him discuss the matter with HaShem."

Rivka could think of nothing to say to that. According to Baruch, he *had* discussed it with HaShem. And HaShem said that Baruch must tell Ari to have nothing to do with the men of violence. Rivka had also prayed about the whole rotten mess, but HaShem had told her nothing except that the time had come to leave the city. Rivka wiggled free of Ari's arms and stumbled blindly upstairs, fighting tears. It wasn't supposed to be like this. They were supposed to be a team, a man and a woman, both doing what HaShem told them.

Rivka slumped on her bed and fell backward onto the covers. Her hair covering slipped loose. Furious, she flung it on the floor. Her hair was a mess today and she needed to talk to Shimon, and for that she needed Ari. Downstairs, she heard Ari pacing.

Finally, Rivka sat up on the bed and wiped her eyes. She reached for her brush and combed out the tangles in her hair. Mechanically, she began braiding it. When she first met Ari, she used to wear it in a French braid. She hadn't done that in years. It was too much trouble. Her fingers moved swiftly, binding her hair into a long thick braid which she would cover up all day. When she finished, she knotted the end with a short piece of wool yarn.

Rivka stood up, took a deep breath, and went into Rachel's room.

"Pretty, *Imma!* Will you braid my hair like that?"

"In a minute." Rivka rummaged around among her sewing things. Finally she found what she needed. *HaShem, I hope this is the right thing.*

She picked up the thick iron shears, placed them flush to the back of her head, and snipped off her braid in one quick motion.

"*Imma!*" Rachel looked horrified.

Rivka went back to her room, covered the ragged mess that was her hair, and then hurried downstairs.

Ari sat at the table with his back to her. Rivka wrapped her arms around him. She found his left hand and put the braid in it.

"Rivka?" Ari twisted to look at her, his eyes wide with shock. "What is this?"

"It's my hair, Ari. For your catapult."

Ari stood up and put his hands to her head, caressing the phantom locks that were no more. "Rivkaleh."

She buried her face in his chest. "Now, please take me to talk with Shimon. And do whatever HaShem tells you to do. I love you, even if you're wrong."

Ari

Rome is a decaying corpse," Brother Yoseph said. "The city lies in ruins and the people live in fear of Caesar, who is a madman."

Ari thought Yoseph had matured much in the past year. He had survived a shipwreck and the Great Fire of Rome, had made friends in Caesar's court, had brought back six priests from a living death in prison. Most important of all, he had brought back intelligence on the enemy. It was the evening of the last day of the Feast of Unleavened Bread, and Yoseph had arrived in Jerusalem today after a long journey.

"I visited the training camp for their army." Yoseph began pacing. "Romans are only men, like us. They take raw recruits and train them for many weeks. They provide them with weapons, teach them their uses, give them physical training, and ... "

Yoseph held up his index finger. "... and this is of first importance — they organize the men. This is the secret of the power of Rome. Many men, all trained to obey orders, and a few officers who are trained to give the correct orders. A squad of ten men, properly trained, has strength ten times that of one man with no loss in speed. Improperly trained, they have only the strength of one man and have a speed equal to the tenth part of one man. This is why Rome wins and her enemies lose. She is organized and they are not."

"What of the Jews in Rome?" Eleazar said. "When we rise up to throw off Rome, will they also rise up and slay the Dragon?"

Yoseph looked dubious. "They are grown soft and careless. They may rise up and they may not, but we cannot depend on them. They will not aid our enemies, but I think they will not fight them either."

"Will they send money?" Eleazar asked.

"No." Yoseph's word fell like a heavy stone on the floor. "We must request the help of the leading citizens here." He scanned the room, and his eyes fell on Ari. "How goes the work on the machines of war, Ari the Kazan?"

Ari pulled the braid of Rivka's hair out of his belt. "I have solved part of the problem with the ballista. Men, we require hair. If you have female slaves, you will cut their hair. If you have wives, mothers, daughters, sisters, you will ask them for their hair. My woman tells me this makes the best material."

Brother Eleazar's eyes went wide. "Your woman gave you that willingly?"

Ari pulled out a smaller braid. "Yes, and my daughter also. But I need more. Brother Yoseph, when you are rested from your long journey, I must question you closely on what you saw in Rome. Weapons, tools, training, tactics, strategy."

"I will be rested tomorrow." Yoseph pulled his steel dagger out of his belt. "But I will tell you that a Roman senator offered me an equal weight in gold for this dagger, and my own weight in gold for the secret of its manufacture."

"If he knew the value of Ari the Kazan, he would offer you ten times that amount." Eleazar stood up. "Men, there will be much to do tomorrow, but now Brother Yoseph is exhausted from his long travels. We will talk with him more after the morning prayers."

The meeting adjourned. The Sons of Righteous Priests filed out of the synagogue, talking excitedly in small clusters. Ari waited until only Yoseph and Eleazar remained.

"Ari the Kazan." Yoseph clasped his hand. "I am glad that you have decided to work in the service of *Mashiach*."

Ari smiled politely but he did not have the heart to say that there would be no *Mashiach*. "It is good that you arrived back safely."

Yoseph gave Eleazar a shrewd look. "And Brother Gamaliel is well?"

Ari realized he had not seen Gamaliel tonight.

"He is well." Eleazar's eyes flicked toward Ari. "He did a brave thing in the Temple on the eve of *Pesach*. It is well with the others?"

Yoseph nodded pensively. "They say so. We shall see, but yes, I believe so."

Ari could see that they were guarding their speech on account of him. Very well. If they wished to keep a secret, they could keep a secret. If he needed to know it, he would learn it in due time. "*Shalom*, my friends." He went out into the night chill, pulling his cloak tight and grasping his steel dagger in case of bandits. Tomorrow, he would take Rivka to see Shimon, and then he must begin building new weapons in the service of HaShem.

TWENTY-SEVEN

Baruch

On the *Shabbat* three days after the Feast of Unleavened Bread, Shimon ben Klopas told the congregation of The Way that HaShem had spoken through a prophet on a matter of grave interest to them all. Baruch's heart pounded like a war drum in his chest. This was the hour he had feared for more than three years. And he did not think Sister Rivka was ready for this test.

On the far side of the room, Baruch saw Ari and Rivka, and his heart ached. He would have done anything in the world to keep Ari as his friend. Anything except to hold silent when HaShem told him to speak.

HaShem had spoken clearly — that he must tell Ari to leave alone this man Eleazar, whose soul was dark and whose eyes were deep holes. Baruch had spoken the truth, and now Ari hated him for it, but Baruch could do nothing. That battle belonged to HaShem.

"My brothers, an evil time is upon us." Shimon looked around the room, and his face was somber. "You all know of the thing which befell in the Temple on the eve of *Pesach*. The governor took men of violence and tried to enter into the place he should not go."

Heads nodded around the room. It was a scandal, that the governor should attempt this, like the wicked king, Antiochus, in the days of the Maccabees.

Shimon tugged at his white beard and waited for complete silence. "My brothers, it was revealed to us already a few days before this event that the abomination of desolation would stand shortly in the place where it should not. Long ago, the Rabban warned that when we saw this sign, then we must leave Jerusalem, for sudden disaster is coming on the city."

All around the room, faces went pale.

"Brother Baruch, please you will come and tell us of this matter." Shimon extended a hand to Baruch.

Baruch stood up and moved to the front of the room. He scanned the faces of these men he loved. Sister Rivka's eyes were locked on him. Brother Ari stared at the floor. Baruch prayed in his heart that HaShem would give him the words to speak. "My brothers, you know how I have devoted myself to listening to HaShem since the evil priest killed Yaakov the *tsaddik* and the elders."

Heads nodded among the brothers. All knew Baruch to be a man of prayer. If he told them he had heard a thing from HaShem, then they would believe him. But Baruch did not know if they would believe Sister Rivka.

"HaShem spoke to me once and revealed to me that one of us would be specially chosen to hear his words in the end of days." Baruch licked his lips. His palms felt cold and clammy. "I have long warned this person to listen carefully to HaShem."

All around the room, Baruch saw suspicion rising in men's eyes. He pressed on. "My brothers, HaShem reveals himself often to the weak and dishonored of this world. Rabban Yeshua told us that those who were dishonored in the eyes of men would be honored in the eyes of HaShem. Was he not dishonored by the prince of this world? Was he not stripped naked and killed on a cross? Did not HaShem change his dishonor into honor by raising him from the dead?"

Baruch was sweating now. "My brothers, it is the man who is dishonored who seeks HaShem with the deepest yearning. This is the word of HaShem through his son, Rabban Yeshua, and it is the word of HaShem through Yaakov the *tsaddik*."

Baruch raised his arm in blessing toward Sister Rivka. "Who is of less repute in this city than our Sister Rivka? Men spit at her feet. Women whisper that she is a witch woman. Children throw stones at her. Even among the brothers of The Way, she is treated as a fool. But it is the weak and foolish of the world whom HaShem has chosen to confound the wise. HaShem chose Gideon, the youngest of his house. He chose Moshe the prophet, a man who could not speak. And in these last days, HaShem has chosen Sister Rivka, a woman."

Baruch felt a spirit of unbelief hovering in the room, pressing in on him. "My brothers, HaShem has given Sister Rivka to know that this city will be destroyed soon. She foresaw that Rome would burn. She foresaw that Governor Florus would be appointed to torment us. These things and many others, she told me six years ago. She also told me that in yet a year, men of violence in this city will rise up against Rome. There will be a time of trouble such as none here have ever seen. The Dragon will come and destroy our city and our Temple and our people. All who stay here will die or go into captivity and the city will burn. The word of HaShem came to Sister Rivka, saying that we must cross the Jordan and go to a city named Pella and be saved."

The air in the room became as the moment before lightning strikes. Baruch felt all the hair on his arms standing on end. He looked at these men he loved, and felt his heart breaking. "My brothers, who will follow HaShem away from this city of death?"

Rivka

Rivka had not known what to expect at this meeting. She knew how it would end, of course. History said that the congregation would leave the city at the words of an "oracle." The details were a little fuzzy, but the end was clear. Now, listening to Baruch, she felt very foolish.

Brother Yoni, one of the elders, stood up to speak. He seemed nervous, and his voice shook when he spoke. "My brothers, I would not have us disobey the word of HaShem. But I have this to say. Rabban Yeshua commanded us to beware of false prophets, who would lead us out into the desert. Some years ago, the Egyptian claimed to be a prophet and led many out to their deaths. Then came our own Brother Shmuel, who was once a true prophet but was led astray by a spirit of rage, and he also led many to their deaths."

Brother Yoni's eyes ranged around the room, and he seemed to draw courage from the others. "Sister Rivka also has rage in her heart. I counsel that we should not follow into the desert after one who nurses rage."

Brother Yoni sat down, and murmurs of agreement ran around the room.

Hot anger roiled in Rivka's belly. She wanted to stand up and tell Brother Yoni what an —

Shame slapped Rivka on both cheeks. She bit her tongue and leaned forward, covering her face with her hands. She felt so ashamed, because Brother Yoni was right. She did have rage in her heart. Baruch and Hana had been telling her that for years and she hadn't listened, and now it might cost her people their lives. *Please, HaShem, forgive me for being so awful. Don't hold it against your people. Don't hold it against Brother Yoni.*

Brother Levi stood up, and his eyes were steel. "Furthermore, Ari the Kazan does not follow after Rabban Yeshua. Why should we hear the words of one from the house of an unbeliever?"

Baruch held up his hands. "My brothers — "

A buzz throughout the congregation cut him off. Everybody knew that Ari had stopped coming to the morning prayers with Baruch.

Rivka felt sick to her heart. Sweat rolled down her sides. That was just so unloving, to call Ari an unbeliever. How did they think he'd ever come to follow Rabban Yeshua, when they treated him like dirt?

Ari put a hand on the back of her neck. Rivka felt peace flow into her. *Abba, I'm so angry, I could spit. Levi is driving Ari away from you with his hate, and I ask you to bless him with a spirit of love. Teach him to listen to Rabban Yeshua and learn to love even the nonbelievers. And teach me that too.*

"I also have something to say." It was Brother Mattityahu, a merchant and a Pharisee, who had much influence in the congregation. "It is dishonor to follow after the counsel of a woman. I will not accept the prophecy of a woman, nor will I do as she does. If she stands, I will sit. If she sits, I will stand. If she goes, I will stay. If she stays, I will go."

This met with much approval. All around the room, men were nodding, smiling at each other, talking.

Brother Mattityahu's words hit Rivka like a club. They weren't even logical. He was refusing the plain word of HaShem for no reason except that Rivka was a woman. *Just move to the back of the bus, little lady, and let the big boys drive.* It hurt so bad, Rivka couldn't breathe. Nothing had changed in Jerusalem. These fools hadn't learned a thing from following Rabban Yeshua. They were just as moronic as everybody else in this wretched city.

Rivka clenched her fists. Yeshua had treated women with respect, violating the norms of this culture. But he also taught that no one should pursue his own rights, which violated the norms of Rivka's culture. Shame cut through her. She was just as stuck on her culture as Mattityahu was stuck on his.

I'm so sorry, HaShem, I've ignored Yeshua's teaching. Forgive me again. And please forgive Brother Mattityahu for his ignoring your teachings too.

Bless his wife, and his family, his sons and daughters. Give him a long life full of joy. And thank you for sending him into my life.

"My brothers, please!" Baruch held up his hands for quiet. "Rabban Yeshua promised a sign long ago, that we would see the abomination of desolation standing where it should not. The Rabban warned that when we saw this, we should go out."

Rivka's hearing abruptly faded. Baruch's voice dulled to a whisper. Rivka heard Baby Eleazar's voice playing again in her memory. *"It will be long before you leave, Sister."*

And behind Baby's Eleazar's words, the deep rumbling voice of HaShem.

You will stay and strengthen that which remains.

It was the same word she had heard six months ago. A horrible realization hit Rivka in the gut. She knew what she had to do. Knew it with a certainty that came from HaShem. She didn't like it, but she knew.

Rivka pushed herself to her feet, brushing madly at the tears on her face. *Ari is going to kill me for this.* Baruch was waving at her with both hands to sit down.

Rivka ignored him. "Brother Baruch, I have something to say."

The whole room went silent at the sight of a woman who dared to speak to men.

Rivka steeled her heart. "All that Brother Baruch has told you is true. Rabban Yeshua commanded us to leave Jerusalem when we saw the abomination standing where it should not. This is the will of HaShem for you, but it is not the will of HaShem for me. HaShem says that I am to stay and strengthen those who remain."

Rivka looked directly at Brother Mattityahu. "Please you will go out with our father Shimon, my brother. I will remain and die in your place."

Shocked murmurs ran around the room. Brother Mattityahu looked like he was going to faint.

Rivka sat down, trembling. She clutched Ari's arm. "I'm sorry," she whispered. "I know that was stupid."

Shimon ben Klopas held up his hands for silence. "My children, hear now my decision. Yet six weeks and I will leave the city. I will take my family away after the feast of *Shavuot*. Those who will follow me will follow me. Those who will not will not. Each of you must choose as HaShem shows you. Please you will all pray on the matter."

That night, Rivka and Ari sat on their roof, watching the stars. Ari seemed deep in thought, but he held Rivka's hand in a fierce grip. Her heart roiled in confusion.

"Ari, what do you think it all means? Why did HaShem tell me to stay? I don't want to stay. I'm scared to death to stay."

Ari waited an age before he said anything. "Can you think of no reason?"

She looked at him sharply. "Do you know something I don't?"

"Perhaps."

Rivka waited for some sort of explanation, but he said nothing else. She scrunched closer to him. "I wouldn't mind if you'd enlighten me."

"Please think on it. I believe you know the answer."

Rivka stared up at the cosmic blackness, wondering what he could possibly be talking about, and why, oh why, she had ever married such an infuriating man. She puzzled on it until they went to bed.

Early the next morning, she woke up crying.

TWENTY-EIGHT

Hana

On the day after Shabbat, Hana waited until mid-morning and then took Dov to see Rivka and Rachel. By this hour, Ari the Kazan would be gone to his work and Hana would be free to speak to Rivka. Ari the Kazan was a man who prided himself in a foolish thing he called logic, but Rivka was a woman and therefore sensible.

Dov pounded on the door with his strong fist. "Rachel! Aunt Rivka!"

Hana put a hand on his shoulder. "Patience, little bear."

The door opened. Rivka's face lit up. "Hana! Please come in!" She held the door open. "Good morning, Dov. Rachel is up in her room."

Dov raced past Rivka and up the stairs, shouting, "Racheleh!"

Rivka led Hana into the kitchen and they sat down on stools at the table. Hana saw red streaks in Rivka's eyes and her heart felt heavy. She put a hand on Rivka's. "Why, Sister Rivka? Why have you decided to stay?"

Rivka shook her head. "I don't know. It must sound foolish, but I *have* to do it. HaShem commanded me to stay."

Hana narrowed her eyes. "Please speak sensibly. HaShem has told Baruch that you are not to stay. How is it that HaShem has told you to stay?"

Rivka wiped her eyes on her sleeve. "All I know is what I heard. Baruch was the one who told me to listen to HaShem. If it was up to me, I'd leave tomorrow. But HaShem told me to stay and I'm going to do what he told me."

Hana felt a tightness in her throat. "It is because of Ari the Kazan. If he decided to go, then HaShem would tell you also to go, yes?"

Rivka nodded her head. "I . . . think so." She squeezed hard on Hana's hand. "Ari needs me, but he won't go, and I can't make him go."

"Baruch says Ari the Kazan is doing a great wrong, to aid the men of violence. Baruch heard it from HaShem."

Rivka's mouth tightened into a thin line. "Hana, please don't try to drive a wedge between me and my husband. Ari believes he heard from HaShem also, that he is to stay and fight for our people."

"Do you believe this?" Hana did not see how an intelligent woman like Rivka could believe such foolishness. "Does HaShem tell one thing to Ari the Kazan and the opposite thing to Baruch?"

A thunder of feet on the steps. The children raced downstairs, holding hands. "We made up a song! Listen to our song!"

Hana's heart felt pierced that soon these innocent friends would be separated on account of the foolishness of Ari the Kazan. "Sing for us," she said.

Dov began singing very loudly a song about Rabban Yeshua. Rachel also joined in, but Hana could not hear her. Hana stood up and waved her hands. "Dov! Not so loud — you will wake the dead with such a voice. Racheleh, louder — you would not wake a mouse. Both of you sing again, from the beginning."

They sang it again. This time it was better, but still Dov sang much louder than Rachel.

Rivka hugged the two children. "Dov, you must sing very quietly. Rachel, I want you to sing as loud as you can."

They sang the song a third time. Now Hana could hear them both perfectly.

"Beautiful," Rivka said. She gave them each a handful of raisins from a clay jar in the pantry. They raced upstairs, with Dov in the lead, bellowing the song. Rachel followed him, her shrill voice squeaking.

Rivka sat down at the table. "Hana."

Hana did not know what to say. She sat staring at her hands for a long time. Finally she stood and hugged Rivka. "All is in the hands of HaShem."

Rivka kissed her softly on the cheek. "All."

A week passed, and Hana learned that the families of The Way were divided. Some chose to go, some to stay. Hana grieved for those who chose to stay. Most of all, she grieved for Rivka and Rachel and Ari the Kazan. But she did not argue with Rivka again, and Ari the Kazan refused to discuss the matter with Baruch. Dov cried every night, to hear that he must leave and Rachel must stay.

On the eve of *Shavuot*, Hana invited Rivka to go to the afternoon sacrifices with her. They purified themselves at home, left the children with a reliable neighbor woman, and walked together to the Temple. Hana felt that her heart would break. If Rivka and Ari the Kazan stayed in this forsaken city, they would die, and Racheleh also.

They went in through the Huldah Gates on the southern side of the Temple Mount. Eight years ago, when Sister Rivka came from her far country on the eve of *Shavuot*, they had come here together, had walked up through this same damp tunnel and out into the warm summer sunshine. Then, Rivka was the stranger and Hana the native. Now all things were reversed. Hana felt herself a stranger in her own city.

They reached the barrier and entered the holy area. Sister Rivka smiled at Hana when they climbed the steps together, as they had so long ago. They walked across the *Khel* and into the Court of Women. They had come early, and there were few in the court.

Many dozen priests stood on the steps before the Nicanor Gate, practicing for the worship. No, they were not priests; they were Levites dressed in the garb of priests. This was a new thing in the Temple, and Hana did not like it. The Levites should dress as Levites. Tales said that King Agrippa wished to gain favor in the eyes of the Levites by allowing them this liberty. Perhaps he had, but he had lost favor in the eyes of the priests.

The afternoon sun beat down on them. Hana wept. Rivka would not come out of the city unless HaShem told her to do so, and HaShem would not change his mind. Hana closed her eyes and clutched Rivka's arm.

"Sister Hana, are you well?"

Hana shook her head. How could she be well, when all around her the world was not well?

Rivka put both hands on her shoulders and prayed quietly. A spirit of peace settled on Hana. She waited quietly, and soon the Presence filled her soul, the *Shekinah* of HaShem. She knew that she must walk a long road, but with HaShem, it would be a road of peace. At last, she opened her eyes and kissed Sister Rivka on the cheek. "Thank you, my friend."

"The sacrifices are about to begin." Sister Rivka pointed up through the great gleaming bronze gates.

Hana saw the priests leading in a ram. The sun glittered off the roof of the Sanctuary. The great stone altar rose up to heaven. Tales told that it was here that Father Avraham had brought his son Yitzhak to be sacrificed to HaShem.

Hana shivered and closed her eyes. HaShem had asked a hard thing of Father Avraham, to give his only son. Some said that Father Avraham had killed his son, and then HaShem had raised him up again. Baruch said such tales were idle, that Torah taught that HaShem had held back Father

Avraham's knife. Hana did not think she could do such a thing, to sacrifice her own son for HaShem. Yet HaShem had done so. He had not held back the knife to save Rabban Yeshua. HaShem had given the Rabban as a sacrifice, a *Pesach* lamb for the sins of all the people.

Hana heard the ram bawl out, and her eyes flew open. The ram's horns were now bound to the brass rings in the slaughtering poles. One priest held a silver pitcher beneath the ram's neck. Another raised a flint knife to its throat.

A slash of blood.

The ram began kicking its hind legs furiously. Its hot life-blood gushed into the silver pitcher. Hana held her breath. Just so, HaShem must have held his breath when Rabban Yeshua sacrificed himself. Slowly, the ram's kicks grew weaker. His knees buckled, and he sagged to the cruel stone pavement.

The priests bled the life out of the ram and then cut loose his horns. More priests came and lifted the ram onto the stone table. Hana felt the power of HaShem sweep over her. She dropped to her knees and fell on her face to pray.

All the world became distant and she felt the *Shekinah* wrapping itself around her like a warm blanket. Soon, she would go to a far country to live out her life, far from this Temple, and yet not far from the *Shekinah*. Wherever she went, HaShem would also go. If to fire, HaShem would be in the fire. If to flood, HaShem would be in the flood. If to war . . . HaShem would be in the war.

From very far away, Hana heard the clang of the silver cymbals. The Levite singers burst into song.

> *God of all vengeance, Yahweh,*
> *God of all vengeance, shine forth!*
> *Rise up, judge of all the earth,*
> *Pay back in full to the haughty!*
> *How long will the evil ones, Yahweh,*
> *How long will the evil ones triumph?*

When the music ended, a deep peace filled Hana's soul. She was not afraid of the trouble to come. War would come to this city and consume it. From now until the end of days, evil and death would follow those who obeyed HaShem. If she went to the ends of the earth, death and war would follow her, but she would not fear it. HaShem held her in his hands.

Therefore ... why should she flee? HaShem had not told her to flee. Neither had he told her to stay. She had not inquired of HaShem at all. Why had she not inquired?

Sister Rivka had inquired, and HaShem had told her to stay. HaShem did not promise Sister Rivka that she would live, only that she must stay here, perhaps to sacrifice her own life on behalf of her people. It might be that HaShem would stay the knife, and it might be that he would not stay the knife. It was not given to Sister Rivka to know.

Nor was it given to Hana to know the day of her death. It was given to her to trust in HaShem, to do the thing which HaShem put in her hand.

If that thing was to sacrifice her own life, then Hana would do it gladly and enter into the World to Come. A woman who was in the hands of HaShem had nothing to fear.

A hand on Hana's back. "Sister Hana, the worship is over."

Hana pushed herself up and saw the bright sun shining and Sister Rivka smiling and she knew that all would be well. She would inquire of HaShem, and whatever he told her to do, that she would do.

Baruch

Early on the morning of *Shavuot*, Baruch pounded on the door of Ari's house. His heart ached with deep grief. This was great evil, and more evil would come of it.

The door opened. Brother Ari stared at him, his face astonished. Finally he said, "*Hag sameakh*, Baruch."

It was not a happy holiday, and Baruch would not pretend so. "Please, may I speak with you, Brother Ari?"

Brother Ari pulled the door open. Baruch saw Sister Rivka clearing away the remains of the morning meal. She said, "Baruch! How wonderful to see you this morning! You must be very excited about leaving soon."

Baruch could not bear to think about leaving. "I would speak with you also, Sister Rivka."

Rivka nodded and wiped the table with a rag. "Rachel, sweetheart, we need to talk with Uncle Baruch about something important. Run upstairs and play for a little."

Rachel came and hugged Baruch. "Uncle Baruch, can I be a *tsaddik* like you someday?"

Baruch pinched her cheek. "That is a thing you must ask of HaShem, not me." He bent down and kissed the top of her head. Her hair had grown out a little, but it cut Baruch to the quick to see what Brother Ari had done to his own daughter, for the sake of his machines of evil. "Now, please, you will allow me to speak with your *imma* and *abba*."

Rachel scampered up the stairs.

Brother Ari and Sister Rivka pulled up short wooden stools around their table. Baruch also sat down. Now the grief in his heart welled up through his eyes.

"Baruch!" Sister Rivka said. "What's wrong?"

Baruch's hands twitched, and he felt that his heart would burn through his chest. "Hana refuses to leave. She says she must stay here with you."

Brother Ari's breath hissed in the silence. Sister Rivka gasped. "Baruch! That's crazy! Where did she get that idea?"

Baruch shook his head. "She says it is a word from HaShem. Yes, it is foolishness, but she will not listen. Sister Rivka, she says if you go, she will go. If you stay, she will stay."

Sister Rivka put a hand on his arm, and her touch was fire. "Baruch, I ... I don't know what to say. I never asked her to stay. This is terrible."

"Rivka, you must speak to her," Brother Ari said. "She must not stay. It is too dangerous. Reason with her. This thing is not logical."

Baruch stared at them. "Please, Sister Rivka, Brother Ari. Listen to your own voices. Both of you would counsel Hana in this matter, but why do you refuse your own counsel? You yourselves gave the word from HaShem that we must leave the city, yet you mean to stay. It is death to remain here. Come out and be saved! Choose life! Then Hana will also come out."

Rivka shook her head. "Baruch, it is also the word of HaShem to me and to Ari that we must stay."

Baruch bit his lip. "It is death to stay."

Rivka's grip on his arm became painful. "If so, then it is a sacrifice we are prepared to make."

"And you will also sacrifice Racheleh?" Baruch put a hand on Brother Ari's shoulder. "Brother Ari, you will put your own child in danger?"

Ari's eyes were haunted. "I will do as HaShem tells me, and I will do all in my power to protect the child."

Sister Rivka put her face in her hands and her whole frame shook. "Baruch, all is in the hands of HaShem. I learned this from you and Hana. We will do as HaShem tells us, and trust in him."

Baruch stood up and began pacing. Anger flooded his veins. "You are wrong! Both of you have not heard from HaShem. The word of HaShem came to me clearly, Brother Ari. You must not become one of the men of violence! They are evil and will lead the nation to ruin, and you also with them. Is this the will of HaShem, that you should destroy our people by bringing on us the wrath of Rome? You must not answer violence with violence, or you will become evil also!"

"Baruch, you have overstepped again." Brother Ari's words were clipped and cold. "You will not insult me in my house, or else you will leave."

"Brother Ari, when you are wrong, it is no insult to tell you so. It is love. Because I love you and Sister Rivka, I will not endure to see you make this great error." Baruch stopped pacing and crossed his arms on his chest. "Please, Brother Ari, hear my logic. You must go out with us. You must!"

Brother Ari stood up, and he towered above Baruch. His eyes gleamed with black anger, and his face quivered. "Baruch, I have heard from HaShem and — "

"No!" Baruch jabbed a finger at Ari's chest. "I have heard from HaShem. Brother Ari, it is a simple matter of logic. If I am right, then you are wrong. If you are right, then I am wrong. It is you who taught me logic. Now explain the matter to me. Which of us is wrong?"

Fury blazed in Ari's eyes. He lunged at Baruch and wrapped him in his powerful arms. Baruch made no effort to resist. Brother Ari lifted him bodily and carried him to the door. He jerked it open and threw Baruch into the street. Baruch stumbled and fell heavily in the dust. He lay there, stunned by the foolish spirit of anger that had fallen on Ari.

Brother Ari leaned through the door and his voice hissed when he spoke. "You will not speak to me more on this matter, Baruch. This is no matter of logic, it is a matter of respect. I have made my decision at great cost to myself, and you will not dishonor me by demanding that I change it." The door slammed shut.

Baruch stood up and confusion fell on him. What had he done wrong? He had heard true from HaShem, there could be no doubt about that. Therefore, Brother Ari had not heard true. Likewise, Sister Rivka had not heard true. If they stayed, it was death. And more than death, because now Hana was caught in their foolish web. She would not leave until they did. Yet none of them would listen to the clear word of HaShem.

Baruch walked back home, and his heart was torn. HaShem had commanded the people to go. Even Sister Rivka admitted so, and Brother Ari also. Yet they would not leave. Hana would not leave.

And Dov?

If Baruch went out and Hana did not, then Dov would lack either father or mother. That would be unbearable. Yet he could not force Hana to go out. This city was turning now, turning from blessings to curses, from life to death. To stay here was death. To leave, life. *HaShem, show me the right way, when there is no right way.*

He arrived home and opened his door. Hana and Dov sat at the table, just preparing to eat the morning meal.

Baruch slumped down onto a stool. Discouragement gripped his heart like a fist.

Fear clouded Hana's eyes. "Did you speak to Brother Ari and Sister Rivka?"

Baruch nodded. "They will not go." He saw resolution in Hana's eyes and he knew she would not go either. Baruch sighed deeply and took Hana's and Dov's hands in each of his own. To stay was death, to go was life. But some things were worse than death.

"We will stay," he said, and his voice felt thick as blood. "All of us will stay, and may HaShem fight our enemies for us."

Dov's face broke into a great smile. "Somebody hated us! HaShem saved us! Let's eat!"

Baruch raised his eyes to heaven and said the blessing over the bread. "Blessed are you, Lord our God, King of the Universe, who brings forth bread from the earth!"

Ari

Ari slammed the door and stalked back into the kitchen.

Rivka's eyes showed her fright. "Ari, he means well. He was just trying to help us."

Ari glared at her. "There are some kinds of help I must refuse." He began pacing. "Baruch wishes to leave the city and I respect his decision. I believe it is the will of HaShem that he and the others should go out and live. But it is also the will of HaShem that you and I should stay. Yes, it is dangerous. Yes, we may be killed. But HaShem has called us, and it is our decision to stay. Yet Baruch does not respect our decision, and this is not acceptable."

"He loves you, Ari."

Ari reached into his belt and drew out the small olive-wood cross and felt the old familiar rage well up in his heart. "This is precisely the difference between the Christian and the Jew down the long centuries. Each believes HaShem has called him to his way of life. The Jew respects the right of the Christian to follow after HaShem as he has heard. But the Christian does not respect the right of the Jew to follow after HaShem as he has heard. The Jew allows for the possibility that the Christian may be a true follower of HaShem. The Christian insists that both cannot be right, and shoves his cross down the throat of the Jew."

Ari slammed the little cross on the stone table in front of Rivka. "Yes, Rivka? This makes sense to you?"

Rivka picked up the small cross and clutched it to her heart. "Ari, Yeshua sacrificed his life for you. Doesn't that mean anything to you?"

"And what if I do not accept this sacrifice?" Ari glowered at her. "Moshe did not accept this sacrifice. King David did not. The prophet Eliyahu did not. Will they burn in hell for this failure? If not, then why would HaShem send me to hell for following him in the same way as these righteous men?"

Rivka shook her head. "I haven't got any logic left, Ari. All I know is that Yeshua died for you, whether you accept that sacrifice or not." She stood up. "Please, let's not argue about it anymore. It hurts too much. Let's just give it to HaShem."

She stepped to the fireplace and wedged the little cross in a crack between two large stones. "Let's just leave it there, okay, Ari? I can't stand to have the cross between us anymore."

Ari felt the anger in his heart cool. It was not Rivka who enraged him. Not Rabban Yeshua, either. It was the cross. No, not even the cross. It was the evil that the cross stood for. The evil that men had made of it. Rivka was right about this one thing, that he must put it away from him.

HaShem must take care of this cross. Ari had a battle to fight. It was a battle that HaShem had called him to fight, and he would fight it until HaShem called him to stop fighting.

But no more would he fight the cross.

TWENTY-NINE

Rivka

After Shimon ben Klopas led out those who chose to go, the days and weeks passed with terrifying speed. Rivka saw the future hurtling at her, an unstoppable train coming to destroy her, and she was powerless to prevent it. Ari spent much of his time now working with Brother Eleazar and his weapons.

Through the long hot summer, Rivka spent many hours with Hana, praying about the troubles to come, and watching the children playing together. The new year came and went. On the day after Yom Kippur, they quietly celebrated Rachel's seventh birthday. Rachel lost another tooth. Rivka desperately wished she could raise this child in San Diego, could pretend that the tooth fairy had left a dollar under her pillow. Something normal. Next year at this time, the city would be at war.

The worst of it all was that Ari remained on bad terms with Baruch. He was icily polite when they crossed paths, but he did his best to avoid Baruch. It didn't help that Baruch kept telling him he was wrong, that HaShem said he must forsake the men of violence, that they should leave the city as soon as possible.

Fall came, and with it, the rains. This year, the rains were very heavy, and the muddy roads became impassable for weeks. Ari fretted that the rains kept him from field-testing the weapons he was working on. He paced the house, distracted. Rachel found it difficult to get him to play with her. Rivka exerted all her charms to turn Ari's thoughts away from his wretched machines.

Finally, a few weeks before *Hanukkah*, the skies cleared and Ari resumed his experiments. Rivka saw many women on the streets whose head-coverings seemed suspiciously empty, and her heart ached to know that she and so many others were contributing to machines of war. Had it truly been a sacrifice to save lives — or to destroy?

Three days before *Hanukkah*, on a day when Rivka found herself pacing the house in a state of high anxiety, a messenger came with a note informing her that her presence was required by Queen Berenike.

Immediately.

Berenike

Berenike stood alone at the window of her dining room, staring down at the public square in front of her palace. Far below, a team of workmen were laying a course of paving stones. The seer woman had told true about the work. The streets had not risen in revolt. But something worse was rising, and this she could not tolerate.

The door opened behind her. Berenike waited, but heard no step. "Seer woman?"

"Yes."

"Come in and shut the door behind you."

A soft click. Footsteps.

Berenike turned and glared at her. "I have heard an evil rumor."

The seer woman's face looked moist and pale.

"My cousin Saul saw your husband leaving the city yesterday with certain most interesting persons. Would you know anything of this matter?"

The seer woman's mouth gaped open. "My husband ... does not tell me all his business."

"Really?" Berenike let the word hang in the air for an age. "You know of a certain man whose name is called Levi, a bronzeworker?"

The seer woman nodded. "Ari employs him for various construction jobs around the city. Levi is said to be skilled in all kinds of metalwork."

"All kinds, yes. Bronze. Iron. Steel." Berenike took a step toward the seer woman. "You are aware that your husband and this man Levi have developed Damascus steel?"

"I ... had heard him mention it."

"And what uses might they have for such a metal?"

The seer woman looked ready to faint. "I am sure it has many uses for constructing machines of various types."

"Various types?"

"Cranes. Pulleys. Hooks. Levers."

Berenike noticed something now, and it enraged her. She took three steps and tore off the seer woman's head-covering.

The seer woman gasped. Her ragged hair hung barely to her shoulders.

Berenike threw the hair covering on the floor. "What is this? Your hair once hung to your waist."

"I . . ." The seer woman wobbled dangerously.

"You cut it off and gave it to your husband."

Silence.

"Do you know what my cousin Saul saw yesterday when he followed Ari the Kazan and this bronzeworker man out into the desert?"

The seer woman's face turned scarlet and she stared at the floor.

"A machine of war!" Berenike screamed. "A machine which throws metal balls five hundred cubits! Did you know of this thing?"

"Yes."

"Fool!" Rage clawed at Berenike's heart. "If the governor learns of this, what will he think? What will he do? Do you want him to come and destroy our city?" She backhanded the seer woman across the right cheek.

Tears sprang up in the seer woman's eyes. "Please, I am not well."

"You will be worse when I tell you what I have decided." Berenike spun around and strode to the window. Her breath was coming in gasps now. "Six and a half years ago, when you healed me of a desperate illness, you told me my future — on condition that I do you a service in seven years time. Do you remember this, seer woman?"

"Yes."

"You told me this was a thing HaShem would commend, something that would make the people love me. You said it would be an act of greatness."

The sound of quiet tears.

"I will not do it, seer woman! You have played me for a fool since you have known me, telling me things that suited you, withholding those that did not. Now your husband is building weapons of war and you have told me nothing! Why then should I help you? Such an oath is not binding, when one party violates the terms. Do you understand me, seer woman?"

A thump. The sound of retching.

Berenike whirled. The seer woman had fallen to her knees and was heaving out her insides on the clean mosaic floor.

Berenike screamed.

The door opened and Shlomi ran in. She stopped short when she saw the seer woman. "Rivka the Kazan! Are you ill?"

The seer woman retched again. And again. Finally she looked up at Shlomi, and her face was perfect misery. "I'm sorry, but I think I'm pregnant."

"Good." Berenike spat at the seer woman's head. "I hope the child dies and you with it."

Ari

Late that night, Ari lay in bed and held Rivka in his arms while she told him the story. Ari's heart was pounding. "Rivkaleh, when is the child due?"

"Next summer." Her voice sounded shaky.

"I am sorry. Please forgive me."

She buried her face in his chest. "No, I'm sorry. We've been so careful all these years, and now at the worst possible time ..."

"Rivka, the child is a gift from HaShem. I am sorry that the queen slapped you on my account. Please forgive me."

"Of course." Rivka clutched him, and her breath was hot on his neck. "Ari?"

"Yes?"

"Can we leave the city? Please? I can't bear the thought of having a baby right when the war's going to break out."

Something stole Ari's breath away. "Do you know when the hostilities will begin?"

She shook her head. "Nobody knows the exact date. I know that a month after *Pesach*, there's going to be a lot of trouble here in Jerusalem, but the real war won't start till late summer. Right after the baby's due."

Ari considered this for some time. The city would need him when the war began. He had designed tactics and weapons and instructed the Sons of Righteous Priests in their use. But when the battle began, both weapons and tactics would need to be reevaluated and corrections must be made instantly.

Now all was changed. A wife and daughter were one thing. A wife and daughter and newborn baby were yet another. They would have to leave, as soon as could be arranged.

Ari saw that it could not be helped. "Yes, Rivkaleh. I will take you to Pella. Please tell me when you wish to go."

Rivka clung to him, weeping. Ari stroked her ragged hair gently, knowing that these were tears of joy.

Finally, she wiped her eyes. "I'll be barfing for the first three months and I'll be a moose for the last three. The second trimester is always the easiest. Let's celebrate *Pesach* here in Jerusalem one last time and then we'll leave right afterward. That'll be the safest time to travel. Will that be okay?"

"Yes, of course." Ari's heart filled with deep sadness. He would take Rivka and Rachel to Pella and make a new home with them there in the community of The Way. Baruch and Hana and Dov would go also. In midsummer his new son or daughter would enter this most dangerous and hostile world. Ari would be there, rejoicing at the gift of new life HaShem would give him.

Then he would return here in time for the war, to do a great thing for HaShem. Alone.

PART FIVE

RETRIBUTION

Spring, A.D. 66

War broke out in the twelfth year of Nero's reign and the seventeenth of Agrippa, in the month of Artemisius. The ostensible pretext for war was insignificant in comparison with the fearful disasters to which it led.

— Josephus, Jewish War II XIV 4, translation by Gaalya Cornfeld

THIRTY

Rivka

Somebody hated us!" Rachel said.

Dov began hopping up and down. "HaShem saved us!"

Both of them looked up at Rivka.

Rivka didn't say anything. She was really not feeling well this morning. Her pregnancy was a bit more than four months along, and the last month had gone pretty well. Today was different — she'd been feeling a little . . . funny all morning. But shopping for *Pesach* wouldn't wait. The feast had crept up on her, and if she didn't get to the market today, she'd just get crushed in the last-minute crowds tomorrow.

"*Imma!* You have to say the rest of it!" Rachel tugged on Rivka's sleeve.

"You say it, sweetie. I'm — " Rivka stopped and clutched Hana's arm. Her tummy was doing something very weird, very not normal.

"Let's eat!" Rachel shouted. She seized Dov's hands and began dancing in the street.

"Eat! Eat!" Dov hollered so loud it made Rivka wince.

"Hush, children!" Hana put a hand on Rivka's cheek. "Sister Rivka, are you sick?"

Rivka leaned on her and shook her head. "No, I don't think so. But . . ." Her belly tightened up harder. She took a deep breath and willed it to relax. It had to be Braxton Hicks. *Please, HaShem, let it just be Braxton Hicks.*

Hana patted her on the back. "We will go home." She shot a sharp look at the children. "Now!"

Dov and Rachel sobered up instantly. They knew that tone in Hana's voice.

The tightness eased in Rivka's belly. "I think you're right, Hana. I need to rest a bit and I'll be fine."

Hana put an arm around her shoulders. "Slowly, slowly, Rivkaleh. Children, come!"

Two hours later, in bed in her own home, Rivka knew it wasn't just Braxton Hicks contractions. She was in labor. More than four months early, she was in labor.

Memories from home flooded through her. She had been nine years old that year. Mama had gotten remarried a year earlier to David, and she was twenty weeks pregnant when she went into preterm labor. It was the scariest thing that had ever happened to Rivka. They all went in to the hospital and the doctors put Mama in bed with her feet a little higher than her head and gave her a drug that made her very hot.

And it didn't work.

They tried another drug that made Mama feverish.

That didn't work either.

The doctors only had one other drug to try. If that didn't work, Baby Brother would be born and he would die. They tried it, and it made Mama hallucinate. After an hour of this drug, Mama's contractions stopped.

Over the next four months, Mama went to the hospital in labor five times. Rivka learned a lot that summer. Braxton Hicks contractions and real ones. Terbutelene. Twenty-four-hour bed rest. Uterine monitors. Ritodrine. Magnesium sulfate. She learned that nobody really knew what caused preterm labor, that there were about twenty suspected causes.

And she learned that it occasionally ran in families.

Rivka's heart was racing. "Dov! Can you run find your *abba?* I think we need him."

Hana began pacing. "We should find Ari the Kazan."

Rivka shook her head. "Get Baruch first. If I'm really in labor, we need to stop it as fast as possible. If we can't stop it, we'll have plenty of time to send for Ari before the baby comes."

Hana's face went white. "Dov, run home!" She snapped her fingers at him. "Bring *Abba* very fast!"

Dov raced out, shouting, "*Abba!*"

Rivka smiled. "He's a good boy, Hana."

Rachel whimpered and knelt beside Rivka's bed. "I'm scared, *Imma.*"

Rivka patted her head. "Everything is in the hands of HaShem, sweetie. There's nothing to be afraid of, as long as we trust HaShem."

Some minutes later, the door downstairs banged open. Dov's shout rolled up the stairs. "I found *Abba!* He's coming!"

Moments later, Baruch appeared. He knelt beside her, his face tight. "Please tell me what you know. Dov was quite confused about the matter."

Rivka explained quickly.

Baruch nodded. "Hanaleh, please, you will lay your hands on Sister Rivka's belly."

Rivka felt another contraction coming on.

Hana laid hands on her.

Baruch put his hands atop Hana's and asked for the Spirit to rest on them all. For some time, he was quiet, waiting. The contraction came and went. Rivka felt a blanket of peace enfold her. She closed her eyes and waited.

Another contraction came. Some minutes later, another.

Finally, Baruch said in a very quiet voice, "I command you to end your birthpangs."

Rivka opened her eyes, surprised. She saw that Baruch was not addressing her. He was speaking to her uterus.

Baruch took his hands away and waited.

Rivka held her breath. The contractions had been coming every five minutes or so, she reckoned. She counted slowly to a hundred. Two hundred. Three hundred. When she got to five hundred, she smiled at Baruch. "Blessed be HaShem."

She saw something new in his eyes, and it frightened her. "Baruch, really, it's over. I'm going to have to rest a lot from now on, but I'll be fine."

Baruch stood up. "Can you travel after *Pesach?*"

Rivka's heart began hammering. "That's going to be a problem. I don't think I can travel. I shouldn't walk at all. Walking is the worst thing for me."

"A donkey?" he said.

She shook her head. "That's almost as bad as walking. Or an oxcart. Any kind of traveling is going to be a major risk."

"If the birthpangs begin again, we could pray," Hana said.

Rivka knew that couldn't possibly work. "It isn't safe to travel without a caravan. And they won't let us stop every two hours so you can pray for me."

Baruch's lips compressed to a white line.

Rivka realized what he was worried about. "Baruch. Hana. Things are going to get bad in a month, but I can't leave the city. I think you should leave. Right after *Pesach*, you two should go. I'll be fine. I'll just stay here and keep on bed rest and . . ." She knew it was a lie. Bed rest or no bed rest, the contractions would start again.

"We will not go," Baruch said. "You must stay. Therefore, we will stay and trust in HaShem."

Ari

Brother Ari, do you see him?"

Ari squinted up at the roof of the northern portico of the Temple Mount. "Not yet." He and Gamaliel were packed in a crowd of anxious men in the northern end of the outer court of the Temple Mount, waiting to see if the rumor was true.

"There he is!" someone shouted.

Ari saw a squad of Roman soldiers coming down the steps from the Antonia Fortress onto the roof of the portico. Behind them walked Governor Florus, the man who had abused, cheated, tormented, robbed, and generally . . . governed Judea for nearly two years.

And behind Governor Florus came a stranger. He wore a gleaming white toga with a broad senatorial purple stripe. Cestius Gallus, governor of the large Roman province of Syria. He was the last hope for justice. Word had reached Jerusalem just yesterday that Cestius — a man of undisputed fairness — had come to visit Jerusalem with Governor Florus for *Pesach*. As a tourist.

As a boy, Ari had seen many ten thousand tourists, usually Christians, who came to the State of Israel to see the ancient sites. It had not occurred to him that in antiquity, there were also tourists who came to see the ancient sites.

Wealthy foreigners in this century traveled to Egypt to see the marvelous pyramids, to ask questions of the mysterious Sphinx, and to take pleasure cruises on the ancient Nile. Then they came to Judea and without fail wanted to see the greatest Temple in the world, where dwelt the mysterious *shekinah* of the invisible Jewish god.

Many such tourists came as far as this outer court of the Temple Mount where they discovered that they could not enter the Temple and offer sacrifices, because the Jewish god had decreed that none but the holy race of Jews might enter there. The inner Temple therefore carried a mystique unequaled in all the world. Men wondered what strange and savage rites were conducted in that terrible inner sanctum of the Jewish god. Such a god must be fierce and barbaric and powerful. Many tourists paid for a sacrifice to be offered to the Jewish god, a sacrifice which they would never witness, nor eat the meat, nor receive the skin. It was a place of fear to such foreigners.

Today, it was whispered in the streets that Governor Cestius would make his own pilgrimage to the Temple of the Jewish god. So all Jerusalem had come to see Cestius Gallus, the governor of Syria. Syria was a major power in the region, whereas Judea was a mere backwater province, lying in Syria's shadow. Governor Cestius was therefore in a position of power relative to Governor Florus.

The crowd surged forward. Ari moved with it in small, rapid steps, terrified that he would fall and be trampled. There was a spirit of rage on this crowd.

"Save us!" someone shouted in Greek.

Like many people in Jerusalem, Ari had picked up a bit of street Greek, but he was not fluent. Rivka was fluent, but he would not be so foolish as to bring her with him in a crowd like this when she was pregnant. Today she was shopping for *Pesach*, and the market was all the crowd he wished for her to deal with.

More people joined in. "Save us! Save us!" Then all the crowd was chanting, "Save us! Save us!" Ari repeated the words, wondering if they would do any good. He had discussed the matter with Rivka last night, and she had told him it would be safe to attend this demonstration, but that nothing would come of it.

Governor Florus turned very red in the face. Ari saw him speaking into the ear of Governor Cestius, who looked very perplexed. Finally Governor Cestius raised his right hand high overhead in a universally recognizable request for silence.

The chanting died away very quickly. In this culture, Ari had noticed that crowds behaved much more as a unit, were much quicker to discern the prevailing mood and to act on it. An American crowd would have quieted down to a dull rumble over the course of a minute or so. But these Jews cut to absolute quiet in a few seconds.

Governor Florus turned to one of the soldiers and said something in his ear. The soldier stepped to the edge of the portico and cupped his hands around his mouth. "Men of Jerusalem!" he shouted in Aramaic.

Ari guessed that he was one of the Samaritan auxiliary troops, since no Jew would join the Roman army.

"Men of Jerusalem!" the interpreter shouted again. "Governor Florus wishes to know what he can do to aid you."

"Tell him to cut his own throat!" shouted somebody near Ari. His booming voice echoed through the vast outer court.

Hoots of laughter greeted this, and the whole court rocked with the sound of stamping feet. Ari also stamped. It was a foolish gesture, but he must show solidarity.

"Save us!" A great wave of sound rolled across the crowd. "Save us!"

Ari found himself shouting as loud as anyone. "Save us!"

The interpreter held up both arms and crossed them at the forearms.

Evidently, this was his way of asking for silence. The many ten thousand angry Jews quieted again with extraordinary speed.

Governor Cestius stepped up behind the interpreter and spoke to him swiftly in an urgent tone. Ari thought Cestius had an honest look. He was said to be a good governor, a man who could rule a province without destroying it. Governor Florus was not such a man.

The interpreter nodded and cupped his hands to his mouth again. "Men of Jerusalem, you are many and the governor is one man. Send up a few picked men to discuss your request with him."

Ari could not believe what he was hearing. Governor Cestius actually wished to listen? Rivka had not told him of this. Perhaps, Josephus said nothing on the matter.

Several men near the front stepped forward. Ari did not know any of these men, but one of them recognized him. "Ari the Kazan! Come with us!"

Shouts of "Ari the Kazan!" rang all around.

Ari towered twenty centimeters above most of the men in the crowd. He could not hide. Gamaliel pushed him from behind. "Go, Brother Ari!"

Ari turned and grabbed Gamaliel's wrist. "Come with me. You speak Greek. It will help."

Hands around him pounded Ari on the shoulders. "Tell the governor, Ari the Kazan! Go with HaShem!"

Ari stumbled forward, feeling very foolish. He did not know what to tell the governor. Gamaliel followed tight behind him. They joined the men on the stairs. A great shout shook the court. Ari felt a visceral wave of power pushing him as he climbed. The portico roof was very high — Ari guessed it to be almost fifteen meters. When he reached the top of the stairs, he looked out and his heart shimmied.

He saw rage. It reminded him of pictures in the newspapers long ago, the funeral of some Palestinian terrorist. Many ten thousand angry young men, desperate in their fury. But these men were Jews, and their cause was Ari's. He turned to face the governor.

Roman soldiers were searching the delegates. Ari realized they were looking for weapons. Each of the Jews had one, mostly crude daggers. Ari took out his own dagger, a deadly blade of Damascus steel. When a soldier approached him, Ari handed it to him.

Half a dozen soldiers drew around, staring at the dagger, their eyes glowing with astonishment, fear, delight. This was a weapon none of them had ever seen, nor dreamed of. One soldier glared at Ari with hostile eyes. "What else do you have hidden, Jew?" He ran his hands over Ari's chest and shoulders.

Ari raised his arms and waited patiently. He had been through such things in Ben Gurion Airport many times.

The soldier was not gentle. He probed Ari's tender regions much harder than necessary. Ari groaned and nearly doubled over.

The Roman laughed harshly and said something in Latin, and his tone told Ari that he was jealous of Ari's dagger. He ran his hands down each of Ari's legs, then finally stood up. He was a full head shorter than Ari, and his eyes were marble beads of hate. "Pig."

A fist of rage twisted Ari hard in the gut. He should not have come. What would this accomplish? Nothing, except to frustrate him and all Jerusalem.

The soldier stepped aside and Ari saw the two governors waiting for him to join the other members of the impromptu delegation. He moved forward, feeling dizzy and exhausted. This was foolishness.

Governor Cestius looked at the half-dozen Jews. "Who will speak for you?" he said in Greek.

The other men all looked at Ari. "Ari the Kazan! Speak for us."

Ari swallowed his fear. "Brother Gamaliel, please, you will interpret my words into Greek."

Gamaliel nodded.

Ari began speaking. He told of the evils that had befallen Judea under Governor Felix, who was so bad that Caesar had called him back to Rome in disgrace and replaced him with Governor Festus. He told of the good that Festus had attempted, and how he had arrested many bandits and worked with the Jews to govern the province. He did not tell of the wild celebrations that came when Festus died. He told of the extraordinary evils of Governor Albinus, who made the crimes of Felix seem like schoolboy pranks. Finally, he told what he knew of Governor Florus, who arrested innocent men as bandits so that he might take bribes for their release. He told of the drought, and the insistence by Florus that no adjustment be made in the tribute to Caesar. He told of Jewish villages burned by Samaritans, of women violated, of mobs in Caesarea that destroyed Jewish shops. And he told of how Governor Florus winked at violence done on Jews, while crushing instantly any attempts at retribution by those same Jews.

Gamaliel translated each sentence into Greek.

Governor Cestius listened intently, and there was real anger in his eyes, genuine compassion at the plight of the Jews.

"There is not one Jew in all Judea who would not take back Governor Albinus instantly, if we could be rid of Governor Florus," Ari said. "Please help us, or we will all die."

Gamaliel repeated this in Greek.

Governor Florus stared at Ari with malevolent eyes. Ari felt very glad that he and Rivka and Rachel would be leaving this city immediately after *Pesach*. They would go to a village outside Judea, far from the jurisdiction of this animal Florus.

Governor Cestius nodded quietly. "You have finished?"

Ari understood this simple Greek sentence and he nodded. "I have told you a hundredth part of the crimes of Governor Florus, but they are enough. Please, you will save us or something terrible will happen. The people can bear no more."

Gamaliel translated this.

"You threaten me?" Cestius said.

Ari held up both hands, palm outward. "I am a man of peace and I would threaten no man. But if you beat a donkey, it will kick. The rage of the people will wait only a little longer. Save us, Governor Cestius."

Gamaliel translated again.

"I will think on the matter," Cestius said. He put a hand on Florus's arm. "And I will give Governor Florus an opportunity to explain the matter to me. Privately. You men are dismissed."

Ari turned away, wondering what he had accomplished. Nothing, of course. Rivka said nothing would come of this.

Ari walked woodenly back to the soldier who held the weapons. The soldier handed him a crudely made dagger.

Ari shook his head. "Gamaliel, tell him I wish to have my own dagger."

The other men joined them. Each received back his weapon. Ari gave the rough dagger to its real owner. Gamaliel spoke to the soldiers in Greek, and his face hardened with anger. He put a hand on Ari's elbow. "Brother Ari, they seem to have misplaced our daggers. Come, let us go. It is unwise to make an argument."

Black anger filled Ari's heart. He allowed Gamaliel to lead him away. As he descended the stairs, he looked back and saw the soldiers smirking at him. Ari stumped down toward the crowd of men below. A great shout went up all around him, thumping his ears.

"Ari the Kazan! Ari the Kazan! Ari the Kazan!"

Deep gloom fell on him. These fools might think he had accomplished something, but he knew better. There was no alternative now.

He must leave Jerusalem with Rivka and Rachel as soon as possible.

THIRTY-ONE

Berenike

What about those Jews, then?" Governor Cestius asked.

Berenike had spent the entire banquet wondering if he would raise this question. She had heard some interesting rumors about the incident in the Temple today, but she dared not humiliate Governor Florus by asking.

Florus guffawed loudly and put a honeyed date in his mouth. "Let me tell you something about Jews. These people are liars who think nothing of making up any outlandish story to tell a gullible foreigner. Do you know the saying that all Cretans are liars?"

"Who does not?" Cestius scooped up some peacock brains on a slice of flat bread.

"Have you heard the tale of the Cretan who told that all Cretans are liars?"

Cestius laughed out loud. "That is nonsense. If all Cretans are liars, then no Cretan would say so, since it would be the truth."

"Do you know who told me this tale?" Florus popped a roasted baby dormouse in his mouth and crunched it between his teeth. He washed it down with spiced wine.

The whole table looked at him expectantly.

"A Jew!" Florus said. "A Jew told me this idle tale. They are full of such foolishness. Do you know about this evil people who burned Rome? These *Khristianoi?*"

Cestius sipped his wine. "We have many such in Syria. There is much trouble because of them."

"And you know where this mischief arose, of course?" Florus said. "Here in Jerusalem." He inclined his head to Agrippa. "Am I right, my friend? This Jewish magician, this *Yesous*, was . . . executed here in this city, not far from here."

A shiver ran around the room. Florus had not said the word *crucified*, which was too disgusting to use in polite company, but everyone knew what he had almost said. Berenike suddenly felt ill. Florus should not have brought up the subject.

"Am I right, King Agrippa?" Florus said again.

Berenike could not believe any man could be so oblivious.

Agrippa gave him a thin smile. "Yes, it is well known."

"Well, there you have it then!" Florus gave a scornful laugh. "Have you ever heard such a fanciful tale? That such a man would be worshiped as a god. The thought turns my stomach. But Jews will tell any such lie that springs into their head, and some of them will even believe it. Lies, it is all lies. All Jews are liars, and the *Khristianoi* are the worst of them. Am I right, Agrippa?"

Grins passed around the table. Of course, Agrippa could not answer this question. If he agreed, it would make him as foolish as the Cretan who said all Cretans were liars. If he disagreed, then he would be saying that the *Khristianoi* were not the worst of the Jews.

Agrippa answered with a shrug that could mean anything.

Governor Cestius did not seem satisfied. "Who was that tall fellow this morning? The one with the extraordinary dagger?"

Berenike's ears perked up. She had heard nothing of this.

Governor Florus clearly did not wish to talk about the man. His face reddened and he took another date. "I do not know the man. An actor of some sort, perhaps. I despise actors. All of them prefer men to women, did you know that?"

"I have not heard that Jews were actors," Cestius said. "I have never seen such a tall man. He was very confident in his demeanor and spoke like a man of some education, though he was unlearned in Greek. Agrippa, do you know of such a man?"

Berenike felt her body tensing. She should have suspected something of the sort.

Agrippa gave a half-smile. "It sounds like a man whom we call in our language Ari HaKazan."

"That is the uncouth name I heard!" Florus said. "The people shouted it many times. He seems to be quite popular among the rabble. I know nothing of the man."

Berenike studied Florus intently, wondering what Ari the Kazan was up to. He was not content to build toys of war. Now he was stirring up the common folk, and that could only mean trouble.

"He is a brilliant man," Agrippa said. "A builder and a maker of clever things."

"My men were astonished with his dagger," Florus said. "They say it is harder than iron and cuts bronze like butter."

Governor Cestius was watching her intently, Berenike realized. He smiled. "You know of this man, Berenike?"

Berenike did not wish to tell them what she knew. She gave Cestius an innocent smile. "All Jerusalem knows of Ari the Kazan. The man is a builder, as my brother told you. He built our dining room and has a contract to pave the streets with white stone."

Governor Florus gave a raucous laugh. "You have seen the streets of this city? They are filled with dust. It is as I said. The man is a liar and a cheat. Agrippa, you should look into the matter."

Berenike saw that Governor Florus would keep hammering the same point until Cestius believed it — that the Jews were liars telling foolish tales. There would be no justice unless she and Agrippa could get Cestius alone and talk with him privately.

Talk now turned to other matters. Governor Cestius had been in Rome the previous summer, and he told of the devastation he had seen there. Whole sections of the city still lay in ashes, a year after the fire, while a great golden palace rose — a monument to Nero's greed.

Berenike had heard something of this, and she felt a sense of dread in her heart. The seer woman had predicted exactly this, down to the name the palace was given — the *Domus Aurea*.

Berenike did not know what to make of the seer woman. Her predictions were sometimes uncanny in their precision. Yet at other times, she seemed completely ignorant. Seven years ago, she had told Berenike many things that came to pass, including this day. Here was the vile man she predicted, Governor Florus. Here was Governor Cestius, also as predicted. Cestius would be taken in by the lies of Florus, again as predicted. The seer woman's word was gold on these points. And yet —

". . . saw your two sons in Rome," Cestius said.

Berenike realized he was talking to her. She had not had a letter from her sons in several years. They were loud and uncouth, and she had heard rumor that they were both . . . Herods.

Cestius was still looking at her, as if he expected her to say something. Berenike had never felt much of a maternal instinct toward the boys. They were sons by her uncle Herod, of whom she had evil memories. She had married him at the age of sixteen, and not willingly. When he died, she was not sad, and when his sons went off to Rome to finish their education, she did not miss them.

Finally, Cestius said, "And are they your only children?"

Berenike felt her breath taken away. She had been pregnant one other time. It would have been a daughter. She knew this with irrational certainty, only because she could not bear the thought that she would have another boy. A daughter who would have been a friend to her, the one soul on all the earth in whom she could confide. Someone to laugh with, cry with, scheme with. Someone to love.

Cestius was now looking at her with a very strange look on his face.

Berenike coughed to cover her wordlessness. She took a sip of wine and then gave the governor a weak smile. "Yes, my only children." Her skin felt prickly and hot all over her body, and she did not want to talk anymore with Cestius or Florus or any other man. Most especially, not with Agrippa.

My daughter would have been six years old now, if I had not killed her in the womb.

Rivka

Rivka lay very still in bed all day, waiting for Ari to come home. Baruch went out twice, looking for Ari, but he could not be found in the usual places.

When Ari arrived, Rivka heard Baruch speaking to him downstairs. Then Ari's steps thumped up the stairs and he burst into their room.

"Rivkaleh!" His face was a white panic and he knelt by her, clutching her hands. "You are well?"

She patted his arm. "I'm fine. Baruch prayed for me and the labor stopped."

"Please explain the matter to me," Ari said. "You are sure you were in labor?"

"I'm a midwife. I know what labor is." Rivka took fifteen minutes to explain to him about preterm labor. Sweat stood out on his face when she finished.

She ran her fingers through his beard. "Ari, the baby's going to be fine. My mother had this. She went to the hospital several times and they stopped it every time. It was kind of inconvenient, and I didn't know how to cook very well, so we wound up eating an awful lot of Tater Tots, but we got through it and my little brother was born as healthy as a horse. We're going to make it."

"Rivka, you do not understand." Ari's face had lost all its color. "An evil thing has happened. We must leave Jerusalem."

"Traveling is the one thing I can't do. What's gone so wrong that we have to leave?"

"I went to see what would happen with Governor Cestius today," Ari said. "You told me that it would be safe." He recounted the story of how he had met the governor.

". . . and now Governor Florus hates my name," Ari said. "Before today, I was unknown to him. I told Governor Cestius the truth, knowing that we were to leave after *Pesach*. You told me there are to be no troubles for yet a month."

Rivka's heart was now beating so hard it hurt. She breathed in deeply, trying to calm herself, but her whole body felt cold. "Ari, listen to me. We're going to be okay. I think. But I want you to stop hanging out with those friends of yours. Right now."

Ari looked pained. "I have just spent the afternoon with the brothers underground in the Temple. Brother Eleazar has many plans — "

"Ari, just stuff it, will you? You are not the *Mashiach*. You're my husband. You're a father. I'm going to need you around the clock. Rachel can't help me. She's too young. I need you, and I want you to promise you're going to be here with me. I can't cook. I can't shop. I can't even get out of bed to go to the bathroom. I'll need you here to help me on all that. If I go into labor, you'll need to run get Baruch right away. You need to choose. It's me and the baby, or it's your precious weapons. You can't have both. Now what are you going to do?"

Deep pain creased Ari's face. He lifted Rivka's hands to his mouth and kissed them. "Rivkaleh, that is no choice at all. I will inform Brother Eleazar that he will no longer have my services."

Rivka wept for joy. It was going to work out. Ari would quit helping the rebels. Maybe he and Baruch could be friends again. They would have four very horrible months, but they would get the baby. Blessed be HaShem.

THIRTY-TWO

Berenike

Pesach passed in a blur. Berenike's dreams were troubled with nightmares of her daughter, whom she had killed. She spent her days locked in a deep depression. Agrippa tried twice to send for Governor Cestius, but it was impossible to meet with him without inviting Governor Florus. Berenike had no energy to think of a ruse that might get Cestius away from Florus.

At the end of *Pesach*, the two governors left for Caesarea and Berenike knew that the word of the seer woman was again proved true. Panic gripped her heart. Her monthly time of *niddah* uncleanness arrived. Berenike waited out the days, but her uncleanness did not end. After two weeks, she was still spotting blood, and she knew that something very wrong had happened inside her body.

She sent for the seer woman, but the messenger boy reported that she was ill in bed and could not come. Berenike saw that she would get no help from the seer woman.

The time came for Berenike and Agrippa to leave for Egypt to congratulate Tiberius Alexander, a prominent Alexandrian Jew who had just been appointed governor of Egypt. Tiberius was the brother of Berenike's first husband, and an *apikoros* — a man who had renounced his Jewish heritage. Berenike had heard rumors that Tiberius had uncircumcised himself, a difficult and painful operation that she did not even wish to imagine. Berenike decided that she would not make the trip to Egypt.

This is foolishness!" Agrippa stood at the window of Berenike's chambers and stared out at the Temple Mount. "You will go to Egypt."

"No." Berenike leaned back in her soft padded chair. "The seer woman says — "

"Bring me this seer woman and she will change what she says." Agrippa spun around and glared at Berenike. "The woman is unreliable."

"She refuses to come," Berenike said. "Her husband sent word that she is having a difficult pregnancy." Berenike closed her eyes and remembered her own last pregnancy. If she could do it again, she would do something different. She would find a way to let the child live. Now HaShem was punishing her for her sin.

"You are obsessed with that woman," Agrippa said. "Are you of the House of Herod, or are you not? Come to Egypt. The change of air will do you good. This place is unwholesome."

"You can go without me," Berenike said. "I am not going until this bleeding is ended."

"You are taking too much arsenic." Agrippa picked up her bottle.

Berenike shook her head. "Papa took too little, and see what happened. Are you taking your daily dosage?"

"Usually." Agrippa put down the poison and began pacing. "And what will I tell Tiberius when he asks me why you have not come?"

"Tell him I am dying of a terrible contagious disease."

"The seer woman said you would live for many years yet."

"She is not always reliable. You have said so yourself." Berenike closed her eyes. She felt like she was dying. Every day she felt a little weaker. A woman was not meant to lose blood every day. HaShem was killing her. Slowly, slowly.

"You are not dying." Agrippa went to the door. "I will leave for Egypt in the morning, and you will be with me." The door clicked shut behind him.

Berenike felt so very tired and she did not have strength to argue with him. Agrippa would not believe she was truly sick unless she did something drastic. The seer woman had told her seven years ago that in this year and this month, she would do something drastic.

She had fought this foolish notion for years, and now she no longer had the will to fight it. If HaShem had spoken true to the seer woman, then there was only one way to receive back her health. "Shlomi!"

Shlomi had been hovering behind her the whole time, invisible as always until needed. "Yes, mistress?"

Berenike could not believe she was going to do this. She had told the seer woman she would not do it. But now she was sick, and it was clear that she must vow a vow to HaShem. The vow of the *Nazir*.

Berenike normally wore her hair in a braid which she coiled atop her head and fastened with silver pins. She released the pins and her hair tumbled down. In thirty days, when her vow ended, she would sacrifice her beautiful hair. Until then, she must do nothing to disturb it — she could not comb it nor braid it nor do anything that might violate the commandment to not cut her hair during the period of the vow. Icy calm settled over her soul.

"Mistress, what are you going to — "

"You are my witness," Berenike said. "Today, I take the vow of the *Nazir*."

Tears welled in Shlomi's eyes. "But mistress, your hair is so beautiful."

Berenike did not care. Yes, it would be a sacrifice to cut her hair. It wrenched her heart to give it up. But now she was committed.

Shlomi was still staring at her. "Will HaShem heal you, mistress?"

"The seer woman says so." Berenike steeled her heart. *And if the seer woman is wrong, at least I will not have to go to Egypt. When Agrippa hears that I have taken this vow, he will know that I am truly sick.*

Rivka

After *Pesach*, three weeks passed. Rivka had the occasional contraction, but labor did not restart. She grew increasingly tense. Ari stayed home with her around the clock, leaving only to go to the market or to fetch Hana. Baruch did not visit at all, and Rivka gathered that there was still tension between him and Ari. She felt helpless to mediate and decided it was not her battle. Right now, she had strength only to deal with this baby. Ari and Baruch would have to deal with their problems themselves.

In the outside world, Rivka knew things were happening, and she felt like she was flying blind into a hurricane. Josephus had provided only one date for this period, the sixteenth of the month Iyar. That was just about a month after *Pesach*, and she knew something terrible would happen on that date. But the troubles would begin before then, and she had no way of knowing exactly when. And she was helpless to prevent them. She spent much of her waking time praying. HaShem would have to deal with the problems of the world.

On the eighth of Iyar, the third day after *Shabbat*, Rivka heard a loud knocking downstairs at the door. Ari went to answer it. Rivka heard a man's voice, low and urgent. It was not Hana and not Baruch. "Rachel, sweetheart, run downstairs and see who's there."

Rachel went and came back smiling. "It's Uncle Gamaliel! Last night I dreamed he would visit us today!"

Rivka knew instinctively that something strange was going on. She was not going to let Ari get involved. "Rachel, find me a head-covering and then go ask Uncle Gamaliel to come up and see me. I never get any visitors."

Rachel found a hair-covering and then ran downstairs, yelling, "Uncle Gamaliel! *Imma* wants to see you!"

Rivka threw on the hair-covering and bound up her scruffy, sweaty hair. She hadn't bathed properly in weeks and she felt wretched and smelly. She pulled the covers up to her chin.

Two pairs of feet clumped up the stairs. Ari peeked in on Rivka. "Yes, she is quite presentable, Brother Gamaliel. Please come. She has not been outside the house in weeks and she would be glad of speaking with you."

Gamaliel came in, looking bashful. The *tefillin* on his forehead hung askew and he straightened them, looking like a self-conscious boy at a junior high school dance. He did not make eye contact with her. "Brother Ari, please give my greetings to your woman."

Rivka suppressed a smile. Dear, sweet Gamaliel. He wasn't being rude, he was being as polite as he knew how. His behavior no longer infuriated her. "Ari, please thank Gamaliel for coming to see me. And tell him also that I am much interested to know about the riot at the synagogue in Caesarea last *Shabbat*. Please, you will tell him that Governor Florus will never return the eight silver talents he stole."

Gamaliel's eyes nearly bulged out of his head. He had long known that Rivka was a seer woman. Still, he could not hide his astonishment. "Brother Ari, have you had other visitors who brought you this news?"

Ari shook his head. "Three weeks ago, my woman warned me that trouble was coming to Caesarea. She knew of the difficulties with the *goyim* over access to the synagogue. She also knew that our brothers would pay Florus a bribe of eight talents and that he would then leave the city and go to Sebaste. She did not tell me that *goyim* would be killed in the riot on *Shabbat*." He turned to Rivka. "Did you know this would happen?"

Pain gripped Rivka's heart. Josephus told of the insults on the Jews, but it looked like he had conveniently left out the facts that made the Jews look bad. "No, please you will tell me about it."

Gamaliel looked rather pleased that he knew something she did not. "On *Shabbat*, when our brothers tried to enter the synagogue, there were some worthless men blocking the way, killing birds on an upturned earthenware vessel and chanting a song that all Jews are lepers."

Rivka felt the insult like a knife in her heart. The sacrifice of birds in an earthen vessel was part of the ritual prescribed by Torah when a leper was declared clean. There was no worse insult you could call a Jew than "leper."

Gamaliel's black eyes flashed with fury. "Our brothers attacked the men and killed two of them. The *goyim* had brought Roman soldiers, who were waiting in hiding to see what would happen. They attacked our brothers and killed five." Grief shook Gamaliel's voice. "After the riot, the elders of the synagogue declared the place no longer a synagogue, and they withdrew the Torah scroll from the city to a safe place."

"Where?" Ari said.

Gamaliel looked uncomfortable. "Brother Eleazar warned me to tell nobody its location. Governor Florus thinks the Torah is a talisman of protection for the city, and he has demanded that it be returned to Caesarea. He has put twelve leading citizens of Caesarea in prison because they will not tell him where the Torah scroll is hidden."

"It was taken to Narbata," Rivka said.

Gamaliel's jaw dropped. He quickly recovered, and his face tightened. "Please, you will tell nobody. Much violence will befall our brothers if the governor learns where the scroll is and tries to bring it back by force."

Rivka had never understood the governor's motives until now. Florus, as superstitious as any Roman, was apparently terrified of making the local gods angry. He would do anything to make the Jews bring the Torah scroll back.

Gamaliel was looking at her, and now he blurted out a question without even bothering to go through Ari. "Rivka the Kazan, please you will tell me what is to happen next. What must be done?"

Rivka saw at once that nobody could fix this mess. Time had run out, and she couldn't do a thing, even though she knew exactly what would come next. If she warned Gamaliel, it would only make things worse.

Gamaliel was studying her intently. "You see a great thing. Please, you will tell me."

Rivka swallowed back her fear. Gamaliel was a nice guy. He was mixed up with some not-nice guys, but he deserved a warning if anyone did.

"Whatever you do, a week from tomorrow, don't go to the market near Herod's Palace."

Gamaliel's eyes were white with fear. "What will happen?"

Rivka closed her eyes to blot out the horrific images. A deep ache filled her heart. It was the worst thing in the world to know the future. "Great evil at the hand of Florus."

THIRTY-THREE

Gamaliel

Three days later, on the day before *Shabbat*, Gamaliel sat talking in his olive-oil shop with Baby Eleazar. "You do not believe she is a seer woman?"

Baby Eleazar shrugged. "I did not say so. There is a thick veil over her eyes and she sees little. But far, very far."

"She said that great evil will come next week in the upper market. Do you know anything of this matter?"

Baby Eleazar closed his eyes and his lips moved silently. Finally, he shook his head. "The matter is hidden from me. Therefore, it is better not to know."

"Will there be great evil?"

Shouts rang outside in the street.

Gamaliel stepped to the door and looked out. The street was alive with fear. A young woman nearby dropped her *Shabbat* shopping and ran toward Gamaliel. Behind her, from far up the street, a river of humanity flowed. As she passed his shop, she tripped and fell in the street. Her veil came loose and fluttered away.

Gamaliel raced out and hauled her to her feet. "Come this way!"

She moaned and her knee buckled.

Gamaliel dragged her into his shop. Baby Eleazar slammed the door and barred it. A thunder of feet pounded in the street.

Gamaliel put the woman on a low wooden stool. "Are you hurt?"

She looked up at him with tears in her eyes and Gamaliel saw that she was blushing. No, not blushing. Her left cheek was crimson but her right cheek was not. Gamaliel's heart quivered. Once, many years ago, his best friend's mother had been nursemaid to a baby girl with just such a birthmark. He studied her face intently. "Sarah?"

Recognition flooded her eyes. "Uncle Gamaliel?"

Gamaliel felt great joy. He had long ago forgotten about Baby Sarah, the only child of Hanan ben Hanan. "Yes, I was your uncle Gamaliel." He saw that she had grown into a beautiful young woman, and now he felt embarrassed. "Your veil!" Then he remembered that it was out in the street, being trampled by many hundred feet. He averted his eyes. She had worn a virgin's veil. It was not right for a man to look on the face of a virgin. Why was she not yet wed? She must already be in the fifteenth year of her age.

A rock settled in Gamaliel's throat. It was not fitting for him to speak with the virgin daughter of a man such as Hanan ben Hanan.

"Are you well, Uncle Gamaliel?" Sarah looked at him with anxious eyes.

"Yes." Gamaliel did not feel well at all. He fixed his eyes on the window slits. The sounds outside were rapidly dying away. "Is it safe now?"

Baby Eleazar unbarred the door. "We must see what has happened outside."

Gamaliel opened the door and looked out. Up and down the street, other shopkeepers were peering out of their shops. Gamaliel saw that it had not been a riot this time. It had only been a panic. He walked seven shops up the street to a seller of linen and bought a veil without bothering to haggle. Then he came back to his shop and found Baby Eleazar praying for Sarah's knee.

When Baby Eleazar finished, Sarah stood and her face lit up with astonishment. "It is well!"

Gamaliel gave her the veil. She put it on and then threw her arms around him and gave him a hug. "Thank you for saving me, Uncle Gamaliel!"

She had done this many times as a little girl, and Gamaliel had always returned her hug. Now she was not a little girl, and he felt a strange surge of excitement. He felt his ears turning very hot and he did not know what to say.

Sarah stepped back and looked at him, and then she seemed to realize what she had done. With a little squeal, she hurried outside and rushed away.

Gamaliel felt as if he had been struck in the head with a club. He saw Baby Eleazar smiling at him. "Something is funny?" he growled. His voice felt very thick.

Baby Eleazar shook his head and his smile broadened. "It is good, my friend. HaShem says it is very good."

Gamaliel did not care to ask what this might mean. "Please, you will watch over the shop. I wish to see what caused the panic."

An hour later, deep underground in the Temple treasury, Gamaliel saw with his own eyes what had caused the panic.

Brother Eleazar showed him the door that led underground to the Fortress Antonia. "The Romans came through here with many men. The priests on duty tried to fight them, but they were caught unawares and killed."

He led the way down a short passage into a strongroom. This was a temporary holding room where money was stored before being transferred to more secure locations further under the Temple Mount. Brother Yoseph, who had recently been appointed Temple treasurer, was kneeling on the floor poring over the record book. Other priests were counting stacks of silver *dinars*. Brother Eleazar swept his arm around the room. "They came in here and removed all the silver they could carry."

"How much?" Gamaliel asked.

"We are not sure," Brother Eleazar said.

Brother Yoseph looked up. "There were more than twenty-two talents when they came. They have not taken it all, but most of it is gone."

Gamaliel felt violated. If Romans could simply walk into the Temple and steal silver from the treasury, it was a great evil. Rivka the Kazan had predicted a great evil, but she had not said how great an evil. If she had told him, he would have made sure the place was better guarded. He would have stood guard himself.

And perhaps he would have been killed.

Gamaliel shivered. Yesterday, he would not have feared to die defending the Temple. Today . . . he wished to live.

But no, this was not the great evil Rivka the Kazan had predicted. That was yet five days away. Gamaliel wondered what evil could be worse than this, to have the Temple violated by *goyim*.

Brother Levi the bronzeworker rushed into the strongroom. "There is much trouble in the outer courts! Brother Eleazar, you must come and restore order!"

"No." Brother Eleazar's face was set like granite. "There is another way. Brother Levi, Brother Yoseph, Brother Gamaliel — you will summon all the Sons of Righteous Priests you can find in the Temple. Return here within the fourth part of an hour. There is a thing we will do to teach the *goyim* the meaning of their impiety."

Gamaliel hurried out, wondering what sort of thing Brother Eleazar meant to teach the wicked *goyim*.

Brother Eleazar opened a large cotton sack and began pulling out old, torn, ragged clothes and handing them to the fifteen Sons of Righteous Priests. "Put these on and be sure your faces are well-covered."

Gamaliel had no idea what Brother Eleazar intended, but he took a filthy tunic and pulled it over his body. He found a moth-eaten turban and wrapped it around his head. When he finished, he saw that Brother Eleazar had transformed himself. Rags covered every part of his body, even his massive arms. A dirty hood covered his head and face.

Brother Eleazar took a long Arabian face cloth and wrapped it around Gamaliel's head, leaving only enough space for Gamaliel to peer out through a narrow slit. "We must not be recognized, friends."

"What are we going to do?" Brother Yoseph asked.

Brother Eleazar threw a hood over him and drew it in tight. "We are going to mock the dragon," he said through clenched teeth.

Soon, they were all changed into anonymous beggars. Brother Eleazar scrutinized them carefully, then handed each of them a beggar's basket. "Alms for Caesar!" he said in a shrill voice, falsely high like a woman's. "Try it, each of you! Do not use your real voice."

The men all practiced several times, until Brother Eleazar was satisfied. "If we are recognized, it will go ill with us, so take care. Are any of you afraid?"

Gamaliel was terrified, but he would not admit it to his brothers.

"Follow me!" Brother Eleazar moved to the door of the chamber and peered out. They were deep under the Temple Mount, far from all eyes. The men followed Brother Eleazar out. Gamaliel's heart pounded in his ears.

They moved swiftly through the underground passages, climbing stairs now and again, until they came up into the Chamber of Wood, which stood at the northeast corner of the Court of Women. Eleazar stopped the group. "Remember, say only this — 'Alms for Caesar, alms for Florus!'"

The men nodded. Gamaliel wondered if he would be able to say a word around the large knot in his throat.

Eleazar went to the door and pushed it open. He leaped out and raced into the Court of Women. Gamaliel followed him at a dead run. They dashed to the northern gate of the inner Temple and rushed down the steps and out through the barricade into the outer court. "Alms for Caesar!" Brother Eleazar shouted in his false voice.

Gamaliel and the others repeated this, waving their beggar's baskets in the air. "Alms for Florus!"

Many thousand men huddled in small groups in the outer court, talking in angry voices.

"Alms for Caesar!" Eleazar shrieked again. Gamaliel and the others echoed it, but now some of the angry men did also. "Alms for Florus!"

Brother Eleazar continued running toward the northern portico. Gamaliel was breathing hard now, but he heard shouts of laughter all around the court, and now he understood Brother Eleazar's plan. The rage of the people could do nothing against the might of Rome. But mockery would be a grievous wound to Rome's honor.

"Alms for Caesar!" The shout echoed through the courts, and Gamaliel's voice was lost in the roar. It no longer mattered if he used his false voice or true.

Laughter rolled up against the portico. Gamaliel saw a long line of bored soldiers atop the portico suddenly come to attention and step forward to see this strange sight. Astonishment crossed their faces and then . . . rage.

Gamaliel smiled. "Alms for Florus!" he shouted.

Brother Eleazar led the stream of beggars to the very feet of the stairs leading up to the porticos, then veered to the right and past the steps. As Gamaliel ran by, he saw the soldiers staring down at him with fury in their eyes, and he felt grateful that his beggar's costume hid him completely.

The beggars ran east toward Shlomo's Portico, roaring "Alms for Caesar!" again and again. Now all the Temple Mount rocked with shouts of glee. Gamaliel was terrified. If the Roman officer gave the order to attack, the soldiers on the roof would come down and begin killing. At the northeast corner, Brother Eleazar turned right and raced down the long corridor under Shlomo's Portico, leaping past the startled eyes of many hundred students and sages. Gamaliel saw Rabbi Yohanan ben Zakkai with his students and he wondered what Rabbi Yohanan would say of this matter.

When they came level with the inner Temple, Brother Eleazar turned right once more and led the way in a straight line toward the Beautiful Gate on the eastern side. They reached the barrier and many dozen Jews at the gate sprang out of their way.

"Alms for Caesar!" Brother Eleazar screamed, and the whole court echoed with laughter. "Alms to the poor beggar, Florus!"

The men pounded up the steps and through the Beautiful Gate and back into the Chamber of Wood. Inside, Brother Eleazar counted them. "Sixteen! We are all here! Well done, men! Follow me!"

They descended into the bowels of the Temple Mount. Gamaliel spent the fourth part of an hour catching his breath as they worked their way back to the chamber where they had put on their costumes.

When they reached the chamber, Brother Eleazar slammed the door behind them. A great smile creased his face. "We are avenged a little on Governor Florus, men! You will say nothing to any man about this matter. If the governor learns our names, we are all dead men, so guard this secret with your life."

Gamaliel stripped off his rags, wondering what folly had come over his heart, that he should know fear.

Ari

By nightfall, all Jerusalem knew that Governor Florus had robbed the Temple treasury of many talents of silver, and that certain mysterious "beggars" had ridiculed Florus and Caesar. All Jerusalem was laughing at Rome.

When Hana brought food for Ari to make *Shabbat*, she told him the news, and he did not laugh.

Hana looked troubled. "Great evil will come of this, yes?"

Ari looked upstairs. Rivka had already told him this would happen. Now retribution would be swift. Finally, he nodded. "Great evil, yes. Buy food for many days, and do not go near Herod's Palace until next *Shabbat*. And warn Baruch also, that he should stay indoors all next week."

Her eyes glinted. "You should warn Baruch yourself."

Ari sighed. He did not wish to speak with Baruch. Baruch had far overstepped himself. A man had a right to decide what he would do. Baruch should not have told Ari that his decision was wrong.

Hana sighed and went upstairs. Ari put away the food and then went up to join the women.

". . . and none know who they are," Hana said.

Rivka's eyes filled with tears.

Ari knelt beside her. "Do you know who the beggars were?"

She shook her head. "Josephus mentioned them, but apparently nobody ever knew their names. Ari . . . it's the last straw. Governor Florus is going to hit the roof when he finds out about this."

Ari's skin prickled all over his body.

Hana leaned forward. "What does this mean, to hit the roof?"

Rivka wiped the sleeve of her tunic across her face. "It means you'd better stay indoors next week. Don't go outside for anything."

THIRTY-FOUR

Hanan ben Hanan

Governor Florus will arrive tomorrow." Hanan glared around his receiving room at the dozen chief priests he had called together. It was the morning of the second day after Shabbat and he had heard news from a fast rider from Samaria that the governor was marching on Jerusalem with a cohort of soldiers — five hundred men.

The former high priest Hananyah ben Nadavayah wore a disgusted expression. He was a severe man even by the standards of the Sadducees, and the only man Hanan feared. Hananyah said, "Who were the beggars? We must find them and give them up to the governor."

"That is the problem," Hanan said. "They were well-disguised. Nobody saw their faces."

"They were priests," Hananyah said. "They came out of the Chamber of Wood and returned there. Only priests would know the tunnels beneath the Temple Mount. Somebody must have seen them." He turned to the high priest, Mattityahu ben Theophilus. "Question every priest and ask who saw these ... beggars. If we find them and flog them, that will turn aside the governor's wrath."

Mattityahu nodded. "We are investigating the matter already." He turned to his *sagan*, Hananyah's son, Eleazar. "Have you learned anything yet?"

Eleazar's eyes were black ice. "When I find them, I will flog them with my own hand."

Hanan did not think this investigation would lead anywhere. The priests were a close community. They would not tell. He twirled a strand of beard in his fingers. "And what if the governor arrives before we find the beggars?"

"We will tell him that we are asking after their names," Hananyah said. "We will promise to punish the men severely when we find them."

"It will not be enough," Hanan said. "Florus is zealous for his honor. He will insist on taking his own retribution."

A hiss of fear ran around the circle.

"There is a possible solution, but it will require cooperation." Hanan paused, letting them think on this for a moment. "The beggars mocked Caesar. We must show Florus that our people honor Caesar."

"That is foolishness," Hananyah said. "Our people do not honor Caesar. The full measure of the theft is now counted. Florus stole seventeen talents of silver from the Temple treasury and claims it against the tribute the province owes. The people will not forgive this."

Hanan glowered at him. "Florus brings five hundred men with him. As many more are quartered in the Fortress Antonia. Do you want Florus to put a thousand soldiers to work savaging this city? Either we show him honor when he comes or he will show us blood. This man hates us. If he decides to attack the Temple, with what would we guard it? We have two hundred Temple guards, but they are not armed like Roman soldiers. We will submit or we will die!"

At last, they all understood. Hanan saw it in their eyes, the sudden look of a hunted animal caught in a pit, facing a ring of spears.

"What do you suggest?" Mattityahu said.

Hanan hesitated. "It is a risk, but it is all we have. We must organize the people. We will send them out to greet the governor when he arrives. We ourselves will lead the way, with dust on our heads. We will give salute to the governor. We will be obsequious in our honor to Governor Florus and perhaps he will not destroy us."

"Organize the people?" Hananyah said. "The people will not listen to Sadducees! We can command the priests in the Temple, but the idle scum of this city are deceived by the Pharisees."

"I said it would require cooperation," Hanan said in a very cold voice. "By this, I meant that it would require the Pharisees. Mattityahu, you will convene an emergency session of the full Sanhedrin. The Pharisees are fools, but they will understand that this is wisdom."

Hanan saw young Eleazar's cheeks flushing at this insult, but he did not care. It was on account of zealous Pharisees like Eleazar that a bad situation was now made worse.

"We will hold the meeting at noon," Hanan said. "Before that time, I expect that each of you will speak to your own houses. You will persuade your brothers, your sons, your sons-in-law, your friends, your neighbors, that this is the only way to survive the wrath of Florus. Then the Sadducees will speak with one voice in the Sanhedrin and the Pharisees will be persuaded and the city will be saved."

Gamaliel

We should stay and fight," Gamaliel said. It was nearly midnight, and he was walking with the other "beggars" toward the Essene Gate.

Brother Eleazar shook his head. "It is not the right time to fight. All the city is terrified of Florus, and they will not stand with us. My own father would give us up to the governor to be flayed, to no gain. We are not ready. Yet a few months, and then we will attack Rome at a time and place of our own choosing."

Brother Yoseph's head nodded in the light of the full moon. "Brother Eleazar is right. The time is not yet ripe. The men are not yet trained, and the rage of the city is not yet full. Only wait a few months, and then . . . *Mashiach.*" He smiled. "We know this from Ari the Kazan's woman."

Gamaliel did not like it. Better to stand and fight as men than to slink away like dogs in the night. But he could not fight the governor by himself, and he did not wish to die for something he had done at the instigation of others who would not fight alongside him. They would avenge the theft of the seventeen talents soon.

But not now.

The men reached the Essene Gate. Beside it was an iron door set in the wall. Brother Eleazar released the catch on it and the sixteen brothers slipped outside. The door closed with a loud grating noise. Gamaliel shivered. Now they were locked out of the city. By morning, they would be in hiding in Bethlehem. Brother Eleazar said they would be there only a few days, until the wrath of Governor Florus cooled.

Gamaliel had not told anyone he was leaving, not even his grandmother Marta. He would have gone by the house of Ari the Kazan to inform him of the matter, but Brother Eleazar had strictly charged him not to. Such information would be dangerous to whoever held it. Better that nobody know.

Hanan ben Hanan

Dust rose on the road leading north to Samaria. Hanan squinted his eyes against the late-afternoon sun, hoping desperately that his plan would save the city. At last a lone horsemen hove into view, riding hard.

Hanan saw that it was a Temple guard. The man reined the horse to a stop beside Hanan. "The governor is coming!" He brushed sweat out of his eyes. "He rides with a full cohort of infantry and fifty horsemen."

Hanan had gathered many thousand people along both sides of the road, including most of the chief priests and many of the rabbis among the Pharisees. The Pharisees were fools, but in this hour of crisis, there was no place for division. Fear hung over all the people.

Hanan knelt in the dust and took a double handful, pouring it over his head. Its acrid dryness nearly choked him. He stood up. "Warn all the people to do likewise, my son. Our lives depend on it."

The horseman guided his horse slowly forward, shouting, "Show acts worthy of submission! The governor is coming! Show acts worthy of submission!"

All down the road, man and woman, freeborn and slave, Sadducee and Pharisee, knelt and threw dust in their hair.

Hanan waited.

Soon a great cloud of dust appeared over the rise in the road. Spears appeared, poking their angry fists at the sky. Then men on horses — that would be the fifty that the Temple guard had spoken of. Behind them, many hundred men in full armor. Hanan's heart froze. If the governor chose, he could massacre them all now, helpless, with dust in their hair and no weapons in their hands.

The Roman cohort drew nearer.

Hanan stepped out into the center of the road to meet them. If his plan failed, it would be fitting that he should die first. He looked behind him and saw that many hundred Jews had also stepped into the road, their heads bowed in submission.

As the horsemen drew nearer, they took spears from the packs on their backs and leveled them at Hanan's chest.

Hanan could hardly breathe. The dust choked his throat. An image filled his mind — his daughter Sarah, alone at home. If he were killed now, she would be left alone, fatherless and unmarried. A terrible ache crushed his heart.

When the lead horsemen came within twenty paces of Hanan, an order rang out from the rear. The horses stopped. A rider came along the side of the road. His helmet had a transverse crest — he was the centurion. "What folly is this?" He drew his sword and pointed it at Hanan's heart.

Hanan stumbled forward and knelt in the road. "My name is called Ananus the son of Ananus," he said in Greek. "My people and I wish to give honor to the governor in token of apology for those foolish hotheads who —"

"Liar!" The centurion rode nearer, and anger glistened on his face. "If you think to mellow the governor's anger with soft words, falsely spoken, then you miscalculate."

Hanan's heart failed in its rhythm. "I beg you, please let us give proofs of our humility to the governor."

"You mocked him with hard words in his absence, and now you wish to mock him with a show of servility now?" The centurion gave a harsh laugh that slit through Hanan like a flint knife across the throat of a lamb. "Go, fools! If you will mock us with words, show your true selves and come out to us with weapons like men!"

Hanan stumbled to his feet and staggered forward. "We come in peace to salute the governor. Please give us leave to — "

The centurion stepped his horse to the left until he was just off the road. He raised his right arm and looked back at his horsemen. "Forward!" he bellowed. "Clear the road of this scum."

The horses sprang forward toward Hanan.

For a moment, fear paralyzed him. Then he dove to his right into the dirt. He heard the thump of hooves pounding past him. Hanan lay with his head in his hands, awaiting the thrust of a spear that would end his life. Screams rang out all along the road back toward Jerusalem.

No spear touched him. When the hoofbeats ended, Hanan dared to look. The centurion had moved back to the center of the road, awaiting the full strength of the cohort. Hanan saw the infantrymen marching, a long ribbon ablaze with color, and he realized that he had miscalculated. He had heard that Florus rode with a cohort, and had assumed it was the ordinary cohort of five hundred men. This appeared to be a first cohort — eight hundred men.

The centurion nudged his horse forward into a walk. Hanan rolled as far away from him as he could. As the centurion drew level, he spat at Hanan. "Do not insult the governor with your lying salute if you wish to live."

Hanan lay as still as a dead man.

Many hundred feet tramped past in perfect cadence. Hanan expected at any moment to be killed. Finally, the last of them ended and there followed the slow clop-clop of a horse's hooves. Hanan risked a glance and saw Governor Florus on a great black horse. He wore armor and a sword and shield.

For the first time since Hanan had met him, the governor was smiling.

Baruch

Baruch hesitated, then knocked on the door.

After some time, it opened. Ari stared at him. "Rivka is sleeping."

Baruch shook his head. "I have a word from HaShem for you."

Ari's face tightened. He did not open the door to invite Baruch in, but he did not close it either, and Baruch took that as permission. "Please, my brother, hear my words. The way of the men of violence will end in death."

Ari folded his arms across his chest and gave a loud sigh.

Baruch felt his heart breaking. "Our people went out today to give tokens of submission to the governor, but he refused them."

"As Rivka said." Ari looked unmoved.

"Yes, as Sister Rivka foretold. I will pray tonight that the hand of HaShem will protect this city. The governor brought many armed men with him."

Ari leaned against the doorpost and closed his eyes. "You will be careful tomorrow, please. It will be an evil day. Do not go outside."

"Brother Ari, it is for you that I fear. If it is known that you have done business with the men of violence, then it will go ill with you."

Ari's lips compressed in anger. "You are a man of prayer, and I respect that. I am a man of action, and you will please respect—"

"No." Baruch did not wish to confront Ari, but the word in his heart impelled him. "When you do wrong, it is my duty to say no. This battle cannot be won by acts of rage. This battle belongs to the Lord."

"And if we are all killed because nobody dares to act, what then?"

Baruch shook his head. "Then it is the will of HaShem. Brother Ari, I have a hard word for you."

Ari waited, his eyes narrowing to slits.

Baruch took a deep breath. "I forbid you to aid the men of violence. You will—"

Ari stepped forward and slapped him hard in the face. He seized Baruch's tunic. "You will not speak to me like this ever again." He pushed Baruch in the chest.

Baruch staggered backward and fell in the street. Before he could stand again, the door slammed. Baruch pounded on the door many times. "Brother Ari!"

No answer came.

Baruch did not know what he had done wrong. He had spoken the word of HaShem, and he had failed. He must pray on the matter. Yes, he must pray.

THIRTY-FIVE

Rivka

Rivka awoke the next morning with dread in her heart. Horrible things would happen out in the street today. She watched the pink glow of dawn light up the room and she prayed.

She had warned Baruch and Hana and her neighbors to stay indoors today. That was all she could do. When Ari woke, the sun was just up. He got out of bed and put on his tunic and his *tefillin* and his *tallit* and prayed the *Sh'ma*.

Rivka had heard him arguing last night with Baruch, and she wanted to ask him about it, but something told her he was going to have to work it out himself. She prayed about that while Ari went downstairs to fix some breakfast.

Soon enough, Ari came up with a tray of food. Rachel tagged in behind him and jumped on the bed. "*Imma*, is Baby Brother coming today?"

Rivka ruffled her hair. "No, silly, not for a long time. Months and months."

Rachel's face puckered in surprise. "I dreamed that he is coming today."

"We don't know it's going to be a boy, do we?"

Rachel looked at her with large brown eyes. "*Imma*, he will be a boy. We must name him after Uncle Baruch."

Rivka didn't think Ari would even consider that. "Let's bless HaShem for giving us food."

Ari prayed the blessing before meals with a wooden face.

"It will be hot today." Rachel broke off a piece of barley bread and dipped it in her beer. "But we must stay inside all day."

Rivka gave her a keen look. She had been trying to protect Rachel from knowing the horror that was coming, but she must have overheard something. Rachel was extremely perceptive for her age, and often picked up on things Rivka thought no child should know.

"Eat, Racheleh." Ari handed her and Rivka each a bowl of soured milk and some bread. "Yes, today, we will stay inside. It is a good day to stay in."

Rachel ate, prattling on about anything and everything. How surprised Dov was that she could read Torah. The fine times she would have playing with Baby Brother. How many hundred people would come to her wedding feast when she was grown.

Rivka ate, thinking how fast Rachel was growing up, and how she could not even imagine letting her get married at the age of thirteen, and wondering how she was going to put *that* off when everybody else seemed to think nothing of signing betrothal documents for their twelve-year-old daughters. Good grief, that was the age for junior high school, not weddings. And if a girl here wasn't pregnant by the age of sixteen or seventeen, everyone thought something was wrong. What would they say about *that* back home in California?

When they finished the meal, Rachel went to her room to play with her doll and Ari took the remnants of breakfast down to clean up. Rivka lay in bed doing nothing. Out there in the real world, things were happening. Scary stuff. Governor Florus had come to town to take retribution. She knew it from Josephus, and she knew it from the news Ari had brought.

Rivka's belly knotted.

For a minute, she didn't even realize what it was. Then it hit her. No, it had to be a Braxton Hicks. It had to be. She lay down flat in bed and put her hands over her uterus and prayed. All was calm for ten or fifteen minutes, and then ...

Another one.

It wasn't a very strong contraction, but it was real.

Be calm. Just relax and don't stress. HaShem won't let anything bad happen to me. Not today, of all days.

Hanan ben Hanan

Soon after dawn, a messenger arrived at Hanan's palace from Governor Florus. Hanan was to present himself at a tribunal before Herod's Palace to discuss a matter of grave import.

Hanan put on a rough mourning tunic made of *saq* and went out into his courtyard. He threw dust and ashes in his hair, then ordered six bodyguards to accompany him to the governor's tribunal. They went out through the great iron gate at the front of his palace courtyard. Hanan warned the gatekeeper to lock the gate and allow nobody in who was not known to him.

They strode quickly through the streets. The upper market area was already filling with shoppers. Hanan's bodyguards pushed through the crowded upper market. At the far end of the great square, he saw a low platform had been set up, with couches and a table. Overhead, workmen had constructed a framework for a shade-cloth so that the governor could conduct his business in comfort. The governor had not yet come out.

A circle of other chief priests were already there, shuffling on nervous feet and looking over their shoulders at the great iron gates of Herod's Palace. Hanan remembered that a first cohort was barracked in the palace now, not to mention the ordinary cohort that was garrisoned in the Fortress Antonia. If Florus wished to crush the people, he could do as he would. The city had no defenses. Was that a mistake — to leave a city to the mercy of a merciless man? Hanan's hands felt very hot.

Hanan joined the circle of chief priests. All the heads of the Four Houses were there, and most of the men of the Temple hierarchy. The *sagan*, Eleazar ben Hananyah, was not present. Hanan guessed he was in the Temple making inquiries about the beggars.

"Who is to answer the charges to the governor?" Hanan asked.

Nobody would look him in the eye. Hanan's nephew, Mattityahu, though he was high priest, did not appear eager to speak to Governor Florus. Hananyah ben Nadavayah had served nine years as high priest, and none of the other men had served nearly that long. Therefore, he was the senior man and should speak to Governor Florus. But Hananyah was sweating and his face looked waxy pale.

Hanan realized that they were all expecting him to be the spokesman. He had the best Greek among them. He was the head of the House of Hanan, the most prestigious of all the Four Houses. He had so far been the only one to think of any ideas for saving the city. Yes, he had failed, but at least he had tried. If he did not try again today, none of these mice would, and the city would be crushed.

The sound of many tramping feet.

Hanan turned and saw rank after rank of soldiers march out. They wore full battle dress, and their faces were flat and expressionless. Behind them came Governor Florus. He wore a toga and he was smiling the same smile he wore yesterday. Hanan felt his insides tighten into a hard knot.

The governor took his seat on the platform and scanned the little circle of chief priests. "Who will speak for you scum?" he asked in Greek.

The men around him all looked at Hanan, and he knew that he had no choice. Hanan wiped his hands on his tunic and stepped toward the governor. "Excellency, my name is called Ananus ben Ananus, and I will speak for — "

"Who are the men who mocked us?" Florus said. "Give me their names and where they may be found."

Hanan made a slight bow with his head. "Excellency, the evildoers disguised themselves as beggars, hiding their faces well, and they escaped in the confusion. We are making a thorough investigation but we still do not know the names — "

"Liar!" Governor Florus stood up and stepped down from the dais. He strode up to Hanan and glared into his face. "You know something. I see it in your eyes. Tell me what you know and I will show you mercy that you do not deserve. Fail to tell me, and you will learn the meaning of pain."

Hanan's stomach was on fire. He knelt in the dust at the governor's feet. "Excellency, I know nothing! Give us time and we will find the wicked men who insulted Caesar and you!"

Florus kicked him in the face.

Hanan fell on his side, clutching his jaw. Blood streamed through his fingers.

"Tell me their names!" Florus shouted.

"I do not know their names." Hanan's heart was beating a ragged rhythm now. "I swear by the Temple of the living God that I do not know the names."

"Liar!" Florus kicked him very hard in the groin.

Pain speared up into Hanan's belly. He turned his head and vomited in the dust. A roaring filled his ears and blackness covered his eyes. From very far away, he heard the voice of Florus shouting orders.

The tramp of many feet.

Hanan endured the pain for a long time. He guessed it was the fourth part of an hour before he could open his eyes. He saw a forest in the open square.

A forest of execution stakes. Many crews of soldiers had dug holes in the ground, dropped in heavy stakes, and wedged them in place with large stones.

Hanan realized that he would die today. Florus would kill him and the other chief priests and the city would be left without leaders. Or worse — in the hands of Pharisees. Could the Temple survive that?

Rough hands gripped Hanan's arms and yanked him to his feet. A fresh bolt of pain shot through his groin. Florus had damaged him and all movement was agony.

Two soldiers dragged Hanan to stand in front of the judgment seat of Florus. The governor was refreshing himself from a plate of fresh melons. He took a sip of wine, then favored Hanan with a malevolent smile. "Perhaps it is now clear to you that I mean what I say, Jew. Tell me the names of the men who dishonored us."

Hanan's mouth was full of dust. He leaned forward, retching.

A soldier jerked his head up and poured water mixed with vinegar into his mouth.

Hanan gagged and spit.

"Tell me the names, Jew."

Hanan took a deep breath. "I . . . do not know the names."

Florus smiled.

Only that. He smiled and gave a signal with his hand.

The soldiers holding Hanan turned him around. He saw a crowd of people. Ordinary people, shoppers taken from the market, huddled now in a circle, guarded by many soldiers.

Two soldiers stepped into the circle and selected a young man. He cowered away from them, but they seized his arms. A third soldier grabbed his beard and tugged.

The three soldiers dragged him out of the crowd. Behind them, a woman screamed, then rushed forward. The other prisoners tackled her and held her down.

The soldiers led the young man to the governor's dais.

Florus smiled at Hanan. "Tell me the names of the men who abused my name and Caesar's."

Hanan shook his head. "I do not know the names."

Florus flicked his fingers at the young man.

More soldiers brought up a crossbeam and laid it on the ground. "No!" The young man screamed like a woman. Now he became a madman, biting, kicking, scratching, cursing, shaking.

A soldier stepped forward, slipping on a leather glove with iron studs at the knuckles. He punched the prisoner three times in the face.

The young man's face went slack and his body hung limp. Blood streamed from his eyes and nose.

The soldiers ripped off his tunic, his loincloth, his sandals. They forced him to the ground and tied his arms to the crossbeam. Two men held down his legs. Two more brought iron spikes and a mallet.

Hanan felt rage like a river in his veins. "No! Excellency, please, no! We will find the men. Only give us a little time."

Florus was leaning forward now, and his eyes had a bloodlust in them. "You will give me the names of the men ... in a moment, when this business is finished."

A soldier set a spike at the prisoner's wrist and raised the mallet.

Hanan closed his eyes. He heard a thud and a scream simultaneously. Then another. Another.

When Hanan finally opened his eyes, the soldiers had nailed both wrists. The young man writhed in the dirt, his screams rising up to heaven, piercing Hanan's heart.

Two soldiers grasped the crossbeam on each end and lifted.

The screams rose a notch in intensity.

The soldiers lifted the man off the ground, leaving his feet kicking wildly. His screams cut off. The men carried the beam to an execution stake and heaved it on top, fixing it there with a spike set in a hole drilled through the beam. The prisoner's face slowly turned blue and sweat poured off his face. His feet kicked frantically at the stake, straining for purchase.

The soldiers grabbed his feet. The prisoner pushed himself up and his chest heaved. He gulped in air, and slowly his face regained color. Then he screamed again.

The soldiers released his weight and his scream gurgled to a whisper.

They forced his knees wide apart, brought his heels far up, almost touching his buttocks, and drove spikes through his ankles.

The man pushed himself up for a breath and screamed again.

"Now then, Jew," Florus said.

Hanan turned and saw that the governor's face was flushed, excited.

"Tell me the names of the men who dishonored my name and Caesar's."

Tears streamed down Hanan's face. "Excellency, please! I have no names to give you! I beg you to show mercy! Give us time and we will find the renegades!" Hanan's voice broke and he fell on his face in the dust.

"On your feet, Jew! Act like a man."

Hanan forced himself to stand.

Florus was still smiling. "Perhaps you are telling the truth and perhaps you are lying. It is difficult to be sure. You see these innocents?" He gestured toward the crowd of shoppers who stood in the circle. "Look at their faces. Look at each one."

Hanan looked. He saw defiant young men. Terrified women. Several children. An infant in arms. At least fifty innocent people.

"Remember this one thing, Jew. You have power to stop this at any time. Merely tell me the names and these will be spared."

"Excellency, please, I do not know — "

"Silence, pig. It is possible that you are telling the truth. That would be tragic, since then all these will die, and it will be necessary to seek out . . . more." Florus snapped his fingers.

Many soldiers stepped into the circle of prisoners and selected a dozen of them.

The whole market filled with the sounds of screaming.

Ari

Ari had spent a couple of hours cleaning the kitchen when he heard Rivka calling from upstairs. He hurried to see her.

Her face looked strained. "I'm sorry. I was hoping it would go away, but it just isn't. I've been having contractions since after breakfast and it's getting worse. Could you go bring Baruch?"

Ari's heart began hammering. "You are sure it is labor?" He knelt and put his hand on her belly.

"I'm sure. Just wait a minute and you'll see."

They waited a couple of minutes in tense silence. Then Rivka's whole belly knotted up.

Ari looked at her. "How often are they coming?"

"Every few minutes. They aren't bad yet. I think Baruch can stop them, but we need to do something soon."

Rachel came running into the room. "Is Baby Brother coming now?"

"We hope not." Ari stood up and went to peer out through the window slits at the street. All seemed quiet. "I must go find Baruch." He looked inside his belt, checking for the new dagger that Levi the bronzeworker had made for him.

"Bring Dov!" Rachel threw her arms around Ari's legs. "You will bring Dov, won't you, *Abba*?"

Ari knelt to hug her. "I am not sure it is safe to bring Dov." He looked to Rivka.

She shrugged. "It might be safer for Hana and Dov to be wherever Baruch is. Just hurry, okay? It's going to get dangerous out there very soon." Her face creased with something — tension or pain. Ari could not tell which.

He went to hug her. "Rivkaleh, it is in HaShem's hands. You will pray, please."

She kissed the end of his nose. "Okay. Now run. It'll be safer out there if you run."

Ari hurried downstairs and unbarred the door and opened it and peered out. The street was deserted. He stepped outside and locked the door. Then he ran for the safety of Baruch's house.

It was only two blocks over, but it seemed many kilometers. When he reached Baruch's street, he found it deserted. He pounded on the door. "Baruch! Hana! It is Ari! Please let me in!"

An age later, he heard footsteps. The bar scraped against the door. It swung inward and he saw Hana's frightened face. She pulled him inside and slammed the door. "Ari the Kazan! What —"

"Rivka is having birthpangs," Ari said. "We need Baruch!"

"He is sleeping," Hana said. "He spent the night praying for the city. There is a spirit of vengeance on the city and Baruch fought long."

Ari would once have considered this foolishness, but he knew better now.

"Uncle Ari!" Dov barreled down the stairs and flung himself on Ari. "Did you bring Racheleh?"

Ari tousled Dov's mop of light-brown hair. "She asked especially that you should come visit her." He looked to Hana. "Please, you will all come. Better that you and the boy should be with Baruch. Better that all of us should be in one place."

She nodded. "I will wake Baruch."

"Wait!" Ari did not know what to do. "Rivka begged me to return swiftly."

"Go then," Hana said. "Baruch sleeps like a dead man. It will take long to get him out of bed."

Ari turned to the door.

"I want to go now!" Dov shouted. "*Imma*, please?"

She gave him a distracted wave. "If Ari the Kazan will take you, then yes."

Ari took Dov's small hand in his. "Can you run fast?"

Dov nodded eagerly.

"Then we will run as fast as we can, yes?" Ari pulled open the door and looked outside.

Silent as *Sheol*.

He pulled Dov outside, tugged the door shut, and ran. Dov was indeed a very fast runner. His legs were half as long as Ari's, but they moved twice as fast.

At the first corner, Ari skidded to a stop. "Wait." He peered around the corner. Nothing. "Run, Dov!"

Together they ran down to the next corner. Ari again stopped, but Dov broke free and raced out into the intersection.

"Dov! Come back!" Ari looked around the corner. His heart stopped.

A Roman soldier was striding down the street toward them. Fifty meters behind him, others followed. Dov screamed and froze.

The soldier saw him and gave a shout. Then he ran directly toward Dov.

Dov bolted toward Ari's house. He tripped and sprawled in the dust. The soldier sprang toward him and pinned his legs.

Ari drew his dagger and raced at the soldier. He crashed into him from behind. The soldier staggered under his weight and both of them fell.

"Run, Dov!" Ari tried to drive his dagger into the soldier's neck. The man twisted at the last instant and Ari's dagger missed.

Dov leaped up and darted away.

The soldier rolled beneath Ari, lunged at his wrist. Ari brought the dagger down hard at the man's chest. The soldier deflected it into the dirt. The dagger leaped out of Ari's hand.

They fought for it, but neither could reach it.

Ari grabbed the man's wrists and pinned them both on the ground.

Something hit him in the back of the head and the world went dark.

THIRTY-SIX

Berenike

Berenike woke up screaming from an evil dream. She had been at a banquet with Governor Florus. He kept leering at her body with his huge gluttonous eyes and making rude suggestions. She hated him and struggled to leave, but found that her hair was woven into the dining couch. Finally, Florus signaled for the next course of the meal. Servants came in bearing a great silver platter. On it lay . . .

Berenike's daughter.

She screamed and that was when she woke up. Sweat shrouded her body and her heart was slamming in her chest and tears fogged her eyes.

Light streamed in through the cracks between the ivory shutters. She had slept late again, after another late night of sleepless pacing. Berenike remembered that Governor Florus had arrived yesterday and all the city was full of fear. None knew what he might do now, but he was a wicked man and such a man might do anything. If the seer woman had spoken true, then he would do great wickedness today, murdering innocent people.

Berenike covered her face in her hands. Florus would murder people he did not know, but she had murdered her own daughter. Which was worse? Because of her sin, HaShem had put his finger on her body and now she was cursed with a mighty curse. Unless HaShem showed mercy, she would continue in torment until she bled to death.

If she were HaShem, she would not show mercy because she did not deserve it. She was a Herod, and no Herod showed mercy nor accepted it.

As a girl, she had heard tales of her great-grandfather, King Herod, called Great. He destroyed his enemies without mercy. He killed many of his sons because he feared them or because they displeased him or for no reason at all. He killed his favorite wife in a fit of jealousy. Berenike had shivered in fear and delight when she heard these tales. She had vowed to be called Great herself someday, to be Queen of All the Earth.

She would give up all that for her daughter, but she could not. Even HaShem could not undo the evil she had done, nor could he forgive her sin. If she died, HaShem would not allow her to enter the World to Come. He would mock her and send her to Outer Darkness.

And she deserved it. She was all that the seer woman had warned her against.

Berenike rose and slipped to her window. She opened the blinds and peered out at the Temple.

A footstep behind her. "Mistress! You are awake!"

Berenike spun and saw Shlomi returning from the latrine in the next room. Shlomi ran to her and took her hand. "Are you well?"

Berenike shook her head. "I had an evil dream."

Shlomi's eyes filled with compassion. "I am sorry, mistress. I would give you my sleep if I could."

"What is happening outside?" Berenike said. Dread clamped her heart. "Dress me and then send some Germans out to see what is happening."

Shlomi looked at her vacantly. "Where should I send them?"

Berenike felt a wave of light-headedness sweep through her. This was foolishness. She could do nothing. Even the seer woman admitted she could do nothing. The woman asked too much, for no gain.

Shlomi was still looking at her. "Mistress, where should I send the Germans?"

Berenike sighed. "To the upper market, near Herod's Palace. I have a . . . premonition that much evil is to happen there today."

Ari

Ari's head seemed to be spinning. He struggled to remain standing. Something warm and sticky oozed down behind his left ear. His arms were bound tightly behind him, but his legs were free. He was one of about two dozen prisoners being herded by the soldiers toward the upper market. Ari had heard enough from Rivka to know that he was a dead man. The governor was killing indiscriminately, consumed by his spirit of rage.

Ari felt strangely at peace. He had married a good woman, had fathered a beautiful daughter, and perhaps another child, if Rivka's labor could be stopped. He had lived now almost four years longer than he should have. Those years had been a gift from HaShem, who had sent him back to do a great thing. Ari still did not know what that great thing would have been.

He had done his best, and yet failed. If HaShem was displeased, then he should have been more specific in his directions.

Ari prayed that Dov had escaped. The boy was not among the prisoners, and that was a good sign.

They reached the upper market and Ari saw a vision of evil. Many crosses stood in the square between the upper market and Herod's Palace. Screams ripped the sky. Ari saw soldiers pull the spike from the top of a cross. A dead body still hung on this cross. The soldiers pushed the crossbeam forward, and it toppled to the ground, carrying with it the corpse. The feet, still spiked to the stake, ripped through.

Ari vomited in the street.

The soldiers prodded him and the others through the forest of crosses. An old woman hung on a cross, her skinny nakedness exposed for all to see. The Romans had not even had the decency to turn her inward, as was always done with women. Her legs had been smashed with a heavy mallet so that she could no longer push herself up, and she was now blue-faced, suffocating or already dead. Tears blurred Ari's vision.

Then he saw the boy. A small boy, perhaps five years old. He was nailed at the wrists to the crossbeam but his legs hung free. He was screaming without ceasing.

Ari saw at once the horrible trick physics had played on this boy. His body weight was not sufficient to suffocate him in the normal way. Even if they smashed his legs, it would not hasten death, since he did not need to push himself up in order to breathe. Ari knew that a man could hang on a cross for more than a day without dying, so long as he could breathe. This boy would hang there all day in torment.

Rage filled Ari's soul.

Finally, they reached the governor's dais. He was reclining on a couch, eating honeyed figs and watching the crucifixions as if at a sporting event on which he had a wager. Before him, Hanan ben Hanan lay in the dirt. Weeping.

Ari had never thought he might see such a sight. Hanan ben Hanan was an evil man, but his evil was nothing to that of Florus.

Florus belched magnificently and said something to Hanan in Greek. Ari did not understand all the words, but it sounded like a threat. Hanan slowly stood up and looked at the new prisoners. His face registered recognition when he saw Ari.

Florus barked something to the soldiers. They waded into the crowd of prisoners and pulled Ari out of the group, prodding him over next to Hanan.

Florus jabbed a finger at Ari and shouted something in Greek.

Ari said, "Please, my Greek is very poor."

Florus shouted at Hanan.

Hanan cleared his throat and spoke in Aramaic. "Kazan, his Excellency demands to know if you were one of the beggars who insulted him and Caesar in the Temple."

Ari blinked. "You will tell him no, please. My wife is bedridden and I have been caring for her these many weeks. I have not been to the Temple since *Pesach*."

"But surely you must know who were the beggars? If you know who they were, you must tell their names!"

"No," Ari said.

Hanan spoke to the governor in rapid Greek.

Governor Florus eyed Ari and Hanan suspiciously, then barked an order to one of the soldiers beside Ari. By the look of him, the soldier was not a Roman. Probably a Samaritan auxiliary. The governor spoke to him.

The Samaritan stepped in front of Ari and looked him up and down, then began speaking in Aramaic. "What is your name?"

"My name is called Ari the Kazan."

"The governor wishes to know if you are known to this chief priest, Hanan ben Hanan."

Ari nodded. "We have a rather long acquaintance."

The Samaritan studied him with narrowed eyes. "The governor knows you are no innocent man. You are the tall man who insulted him at *Pesach*. Who were the beggars who insulted Caesar and the governor a few days ago?"

Ari shrugged. "I know nothing. My wife is bedridden, and I have been by her side for many weeks."

"You were not one of the beggars yourself?"

Ari shook his head. "No."

"You do not know who the beggars were?"

"No."

"Hanan ben Hanan thinks you know."

Ari shook his head. "I do not."

The Samaritan turned back to Governor Florus and spent several minutes in animated discussion with him. Finally he turned back to Ari.

"Perhaps you speak true and perhaps you speak false, Ari the Kazan. You will stand here beside Hanan ben Hanan and watch these people die. Then if you can name the beggars, you will live."

Ari's throat felt caked with dust. "And if I still cannot name them?"

The soldier gave him a thin smile. "Then of course you will die. Please think on the matter."

Baruch

Baruch had just finished saying the *Sh'ma* when he heard shouting outside in the street. Dov!

Baruch raced down the stairs. He saw Hana fling open the door.

Dov raced into the room, screaming, burying his face in Hana's tunic.

Baruch looked out into the street. It was empty. He slammed and barred the door, then knelt to wrap his arms around Dov.

Finally, Dov calmed down a little.

"Dov, where is Uncle Ari?" Hana asked.

Dov's tear-streaked face twisted in anguish. "He fought the bad men! They meant to catch me, but Ari the Kazan saved me!"

"What bad men?" Baruch's heart began racing.

"The soldiers! One of them chased me, but Ari the Kazan jumped on him and told me to run."

Baruch ran upstairs and looked down on the street from the window slits. The street was empty. *Please, HaShem, show me what I must do.*

Baruch went back downstairs. Dov was sitting on a stool drinking a mug of beer.

Hana was pacing back and forth. "Sister Rivka needs us. We must hurry."

Baruch went back upstairs and found his sword. He went to the door. "I will check the streets and come back for you."

Hana's face had gone white. She nodded and clutched Dov.

Dov finished his beer. "Will we visit Racheleh today?"

"Perhaps." Baruch unbarred the door and went out. The street looked empty, haunted. He hurried to the next street and peered around the corner. Nothing.

Baruch ran the length of the next block and came to the corner. He put his eye to the edge of the building and squinted down the long street.

Emptiness.

Something glinted in the dust. Baruch hurried to it. Almost buried in the dirt, a steel dagger peeked up at him. Baruch picked it up. There were no bloodstains, blessed be HaShem, but the ground showed signs of much struggle. Around the spot, Baruch saw many prints of the iron-cleated sandals that the Romans wore.

He ran to the next street and verified that all was emptiness, all the way to Brother Ari's house. Baruch turned and raced for home.

When he stepped through his door, he held up the dagger. "Brother Ari lost this."

Hana's knees buckled and she fell onto a wooden stool.

Dov said, "We have to give Uncle Ari back his dagger. He will need it to fight the bad men."

"Both of you, come now," Baruch said. "The streets are empty for the moment. We will go to Brother Ari's house and pray that HaShem has brought him there safe." He did not think this was likely, but if Brother Ari was taken, Sister Rivka would need the help of all of them.

Dov jumped up and began dancing in a circle. "Racheleh! We can play with Racheleh!"

Baruch knelt beside him. "Dov, my son, please you must behave like a brave man. We will run fast to see Racheleh, but we will make no noise, yes?"

Dov nodded gravely.

Baruch kissed him. "You will make a fine man, my son." He stood up and enclosed Hana in his arms. "Hanaleh."

She clutched him and whispered, "Where is Brother Ari?"

"In the hands of HaShem." Baruch released her. "Come, we need haste."

The three of them slipped outside. Baruch locked the door and gave Hana the key. She looked at him strangely and then hid it in her belt.

Baruch and Hana each took one of Dov's hands.

They ran.

When they reached Brother Ari's house, Baruch knocked loudly. "Brother Ari! Sister Rivka! Racheleh! It is Baruch. Open the door."

Nothing.

Baruch pounded on the door and called out again. After many beats of his heart, he heard a timid voice. "Uncle Baruch?"

Hana clutched his arm. "Baruch!"

"I know." He knelt and spoke in a quiet voice. "Racheleh! It is Uncle Baruch with Aunt Hana and Dov. Please, you will open the door."

The latch clicked and the door swung inward. Rachel's face was like an angel's. "Did you bring *Abba*?"

Baruch scooped her up in his arms and kissed her, pulling Hana and Dov inside. Hana threw the door shut and barred it.

"Where's *Abba*?" Rachel asked.

Baruch rocked her gently. "He was . . . delayed."

"You must pray for *Imma*! She is having many birthpangs."

Baruch set her down gently. "Dov, please you will stay here by the door and wait for Uncle Ari. If he comes, you must unbar the door and let him in quickly. Like a good watchman, you will not leave your post, yes?"

Dov nodded, his eyes solemn. He put his ear to the door, as if expecting Uncle Ari at any second.

Baruch felt his heart breaking. He took Rachel's hand and led her up the stairs. "Racheleh, run find your doll. Aunt Hana wishes very much to see your doll."

She ran into her room.

"Keep her there until I call for you," Baruch whispered to Hana.

Hana followed Rachel. Baruch strode into the room of Brother Ari and Sister Rivka.

Her face showed first surprise and then fear when she saw him. "Where's Ari?"

Baruch knelt beside her bed and told her all that he knew. Finally, he pulled out the dagger he had found. "This lay in the dirt where Ari saved Dov from the soldier." His eyes filled with tears. "I fear Brother Ari is taken."

Sister Rivka's face was the color of a corpse. Tears streamed from her eyes. "They are crucifying people in the upper market. Governor Florus is . . . evil. And he hates Ari."

Baruch put a hand on her forehead. "Peace, Sister Rivka. Brother Ari is in the hands of HaShem. There is another matter we must answer to."

Sister Rivka's face tightened, and her hands moved to her belly. "Another birthpang. I'm afraid Rachel was right. She dreamed the baby was coming today, and . . . it looks like it will."

"Only if HaShem allows it." Baruch studied Sister Rivka quietly for a moment, listening, listening. He was not sure, but . . . perhaps.

He stood up and went into Rachel's room. She was sitting in Hana's lap, laughing and cuddling her doll.

Baruch held out his hand. "Racheleh, my sweet, come. It is time you learned to pray for your *imma*."

Rachel's eyes gleamed with joy. She hopped out of Hana's lap and took Baruch's hand. "Did *Abba* come back yet?"

"Not yet. Hana, please you will keep Dov company downstairs while we pray." Baruch led Rachel into Sister Rivka's room. "Come, Racheleh, you will put your hands on Baby Brother, yes?"

She smiled at him and put her hands on Sister Rivka's womb. "Nobody except you believes me, that he is a boy."

Baruch put his hands above Rachel's. Not touching, but above. He saw Sister Rivka's eyebrows go up. "Say this, Racheleh." Baruch waited a moment to be sure she was listening. "Spirit of HaShem, come now with power on me and on *Imma*."

Rachel giggled and repeated the words.

Baruch waited, watching both of them. Presently, he saw a look of peace cover Sister Rivka's features. "Racheleh, please you will look at your *imma*," Baruch whispered. "Tell me what you see."

Rachel looked at Sister Rivka, and a look of delight filled her eyes. "HaShem is here," she whispered. "Uncle Baruch, do you see it? HaShem is here, holding *Imma* and making her glad."

Baruch nodded. "Yes, correct. Now you will listen to what HaShem tells you, and then you will pray that, yes? Only that, and nothing more."

Rachel squeezed her eyes shut and a look of fierce concentration filled her face. Nothing happened.

Baruch put his hands gently on Rachel's head. "A double portion, please, HaShem."

Something sparked in Rachel's face. Her eyes flickered open and she began praying. "HaShem says this to the little room where Baby Brother lives. You will be still now and you will keep Brother safe and warm. You will hold him there until HaShem calls him out. *Imma*, you will be at peace and you will rest from all your fighting, because the battle belongs to HaShem."

She waited for a long while, then looked up at Baruch with questions in her eyes. "Uncle Baruch, aren't you going to pray for *Imma*?"

"If HaShem tells me to pray for her, then I will pray for her." Baruch sat beside Rachel. "Please, you will remember this. Whatever HaShem tells you to do, that is what you must do. Next time your *imma* feels the birthpangs, you must pray for her instantly. You will pray just as I showed you, yes?"

Rachel stood up on the bed and kissed him on the cheek. "Yes, Uncle Baruch."

Baruch leaned close to Rivka's ear. "Are you well?"

Her eyes flickered open. "The birthpangs have stopped."

"You heard all that I told Racheleh?" he asked.

She nodded. "Thank you."

Baruch straightened. His back ached, and exhaustion lay on him like a shroud. He had spent many hours praying last night. Now Brother Ari was taken. "Sister Rivka, I must go out now and find Brother Ari."

"And . . . what do you intend to do?"

"Whatever HaShem gives me to do." He put a hand on Rachel's head. "Please, you and Hana and Racheleh must pray. Now I must speak with Hanaleh a moment alone."

Baruch went to the door and then stopped. "Sister Rivka, have you heard a word from HaShem lately?"

"Nothing. Not for a long time." Frustration knotted her eyebrows. "Why do I never hear from HaShem? You hear from him all the time. It isn't fair."

"I did not always hear the voice of HaShem." Baruch felt deep shame wash through his soul. "When I carried rage in my heart, I did not hear from HaShem for four years. HaShem stood outside the door of my heart, always speaking, but I heard nothing. When I opened the door to let my rage out, then the word of HaShem came in."

"Oh," she said in a very small voice.

"Sister Rivka, please you will pray for Hanan ben Hanan."

"Yes, Brother Baruch."

THIRTY-SEVEN

Berenike

Berenike felt naked going out like this, with her hair wild and unbraided, wearing only a plain and simple tunic, her feet unshod.

"Please, mistress, let me go with you," Shlomi said.

Berenike shook her head. "It is too dangerous. I will have the Germans to protect me. If something goes wrong, they will forget you and save me."

"Mistress, I still wish to go with you."

"No." Berenike tied a leather sheath on her forearm beneath the sleeve of her tunic. She slipped a small dagger into it and covered it with her sleeve. "You may come downstairs and see me to the palace gates."

She spun around and hurried out. Shlomi padded after her, making sniffling sounds.

Berenike had no time for such foolishness. She had sent out some Germans earlier to see what was happening. She knew that Governor Florus meant evil for the city, but she also knew that her Germans would be safe. Romans had an almost superstitious dread of Germans, a fear that went back many decades to the massacre of three Roman legions in the Teutoburg Forest by a savage German army. It was a disaster that grew with the telling, and Germans had attained a mythic, terrifying status in the Roman mind. For this reason, Caesar retained Germans for his personal bodyguard, and many in the Praetorian Guard in Rome were Germans. For this reason, Papa had used Germans for his own personal guard.

Therefore, Berenike had not feared to send Germans to spy out the upper market. They had returned with an evil tale, one which she would not have believed except that the seer woman had told it to her seven years ago.

Governor Florus was crucifying Jews in the public square. Men and women and children of her city.

These were her people, and she would be no queen at all if she did nothing. Governor Florus would listen to her. He *must* listen to her.

Berenike reached the bottom floor of her palace. Six Germans stood ready to go, each wearing a helmet and shield, each armed with a sword and a dagger and a mace. Berenike could not choose a safer escort unless HaShem himself came to protect her. She slipped into the center of the circle. "Take me to the governor."

The men strode out of the palace and across the courtyard to the great iron gate. When they passed through, Berenike ordered the gatekeeper to close the gate and be ready at the side door for her return.

They set off through the plaza, turning west at the street and heading uphill. The men moved swiftly, and Berenike soon found herself panting. She was not accustomed to walking barefoot and her feet felt every small pebble in the street.

They passed the palace of Hananyah ben Nadavayah and Berenike saw that it was locked up tight. The streets were completely empty, but she saw many eyes at the window slits of houses.

The further she walked, the more Berenike felt that her quest was hopeless. HaShem had not listened to her plea for help. Why, therefore, should Florus? HaShem was good, whereas Florus was evil. The seer woman had not promised she would succeed. The seer woman had not even explained why she should perform this foolishness.

At the top of the hill, they turned left toward the upper market. Fear hung heavy in the streets. She saw people now on the rooftops, peering down at her.

"The queen!" somebody shouted.

Soon, many fingers were pointing at her.

Berenike felt frightened. What if somebody decided to throw stones down on her? Her Germans would be no defense against stones.

"Save us!"

Berenike looked up, wondering who had shouted this foolishness.

"HaShem, save the queen!"

Berenike was sweating now. She wiped her face with the sleeve of her tunic.

"Blessed be the queen!"

Soon shouts rang through the streets. A great roar filled her ears. Heat filled Berenike's chest. Joy. It had been long since she had felt such pleasure. She reached the top of the hill and turned south into the heart of the upper city. She walked through empty streets, hearing the voices of her people shouting blessings down on her head.

Too soon, the streets ended and she found herself staring at the upper market. The stalls were deserted. Tables were turned over. Vegetables and fruit lay abandoned in the sun. And in the square before Herod's Palace . . .

Crosses.

Berenike had heard it already from her Germans. Still, the sight took her breath away. Many crosses, dozens, perhaps a hundred. Filled with the dead and dying. Screams tore at her heart. This was evil beyond evil, senseless evil.

At the far end of the plaza, Governor Florus sat taking his ease, watching the scene as if it were a Greek play put on for his amusement. Not a Greek tragedy. A comedy. The governor was laughing.

"Take me to him." Berenike pointed at the governor.

The Germans shuddered and then moved forward. Rage burned inside Berenike. She would carve out Florus's heart for this.

They began walking across the market, but Berenike stopped. This part of the market had many small stones and shards of pottery in it, and her bare feet were too tender to walk on them. "Find a way where I can walk!"

They backed up to the street. One of the Germans went to investigate and found that there was a clear path through the very center of the square, where the dust lay thick and soft. They took this path to the edge of the market. Berenike felt sick with grief. More than a hundred crosses had been raised up around the public square, and all bore a human cargo. Already, many dead bodies lay on the ground where they had been thrown down.

Berenike and her Germans threaded a path through the crosses and stopped before the dais. The governor looked at her with an amused expression on his face. "So very nice to see you, Your Highness! Your hair looks hideous. Have you come to join me in the festivities?"

"Stop this abomination at once!" she hissed. "Do you think Caesar will let you live when he learns what you have done?"

Florus gave her a paternal smile. "Caesar will thank me for defending the honor of his name."

"What foolishness are you talking about?" She pushed through the line of her Germans and stepped closer to the governor.

"Surely you know that certain young men mocked Caesar and me in the Temple, begging for alms as if we were indigents. When I learn the names of these men, then this little charade will end and I will punish the true culprits." Florus picked up a Jericho date with dainty fingers and popped it in his mouth. "Delicious! Would you like one?"

Berenike wanted to slice his throat, but she saw there was no hope of that. Two soldiers stood on either side of the governor's dining couch, and their ready posture told her she could not hope to reach him. She jabbed a finger at him. "I order you to stop this barbaric thing."

Florus laughed at her. "You dare lecture me about barbarism, you filthy Jew?"

Berenike felt the tight leather sheath on her wrist and wondered again if she could somehow find Florus's heart with her dagger.

A filthy smile crossed Florus's face. "You will take a message to Ananus, and then you will join me."

She glared at him.

"Tell Ananus that I am satisfied that he knows nothing. He may go home to his pigsty now. We have found a man who knows something, and he will talk."

Berenike put both hands on her hips. "What scum would tell you anything?"

Florus pointed toward the middle of the forest of crosses. "He is with Ananus and the others, enjoying the spectacle."

Berenike squinted in the direction pointed. She saw a dozen chief priests watching the soldiers crucify a woman. A little apart from the priests, standing in the center of four soldiers, stood a very tall man. Ari the Kazan.

Mesmerized, Berenike moved toward the scene. She could not believe Ari the Kazan would tell the governor anything. The men were just now nailing the ankles of the woman on the cross. Hanan ben Hanan knelt in the dust, begging for mercy. Tears streamed down the face of Ari the Kazan.

As Berenike drew nearer, the soldiers shifted slightly. Berenike gasped.

Ari the Kazan had both hands tied behind his back. They were going to crucify him also.

THIRTY-EIGHT

Ari

Ari's heart was filled with horror. He had never felt so helpless. The evil here was a hundred times greater than Rivka had told him, and he was a hundred times weaker than he had thought. Who was Ari the Kazan, that he should battle the Queen of Heaven?

"So then," said the voice of the Samaritan translator. "The governor wishes to speak with you again, Ari the Kazan."

Ari could see little through the tears in his swollen eyes. Rough hands seized his elbows and yanked him toward the governor's dais. Ari staggered along, guided by his captors. When they reached the governor, a slave appeared with a towel and wiped Ari's face and eyes.

Ari blinked several times and he could see again.

The governor said something to the Samaritan in rapid Greek.

"His Excellency asks if you have now remembered the names of the men who insulted him and Caesar."

Ari felt despair engulf him. He shook his head. "I told you, I know nothing."

"Please think again. We know that you know these names."

"I do not."

The Samaritan said something to Governor Florus.

The governor barked an order in Greek. "*Staurotheto.*"

Even Ari knew the meaning of this. *Crucify him.* Sick terror raced through his veins.

"Wait!" shouted a voice.

Ari spun his head to look, but he recognized the voice, even before he saw Baruch appear from behind a slashed tent at the edge of the market. *No, please, HaShem, do not allow Baruch to do something foolish. He is unskilled in fighting.*

But Baruch had come unarmed. He strode toward the governor's platform, his face unmarked by fear.

"Baruch, run!" Ari shouted. "They will show no mercy even to a *tsaddik!*"

Baruch ignored him. He marched past a dozen soldiers and stopped next to Ari. "Please, Excellency, hear me," he said in simple street Greek. "Do not kill my brother. Crucify me instead. Let my brother go free."

Pain unimaginable shot through Ari. "Baruch, no!" he hissed. "Run! This is foolishness!"

Four soldiers surrounded Baruch and seized his arms. Baruch did nothing to resist them.

The governor laughed, long and low. He beckoned the Samaritan translator. The two men held a long conversation in rapid Greek. The Samaritan nodded several times.

Finally, he turned to Ari. A smile twitched on his face. "This man is known to you?"

Ari nodded. "Yes." It would be senseless to deny the obvious.

"He wishes to take your place. Will you allow him to do so?"

Hot shame welled up inside Ari. For the last year, he had refused Baruch's friendship, had ignored him, treated him as an enemy. Yesterday, he had slapped Baruch and thrown him in the street. Now Baruch wished to take his place? A hard knot tightened in Ari's throat.

No, he could not do it. No man with a milligram of pride could allow it. That was the way of weakness, not the way of honor. A man who accepted such a sacrifice was not a Jew.

"No," Ari said. "I will not allow it."

"Brother Ari!"

"Shall we release him?" the Samaritan asked.

Ari could not look at Baruch. "Yes, please."

The Samaritan spun and gave an order to the soldiers holding Baruch. One of them pulled out his dagger and set it to the top seam of Baruch's tunic at the throat.

"No!" Ari lunged forward.

Strong arms jerked him back.

With one long slice, the soldier slit open Baruch's tunic all the way down the front. He went around behind and slit it at each sleeve. The tunic fell into the dirt. Another soldier yanked at Baruch's loincloth and it came undone.

Baruch stood naked before his captors.

Fury rose up in Ari's belly like a flood. "No!" he shouted again. He could not allow them to kill Baruch. "I refuse it! I refuse it!"

The Samaritan smiled at him. "We have already granted your request, Ari the Kazan. You refused that he should take your place. Very well, then he will not take your place. He is now a hostage, like all the others. You will give us the names of the beggars, or the man will die."

Hopelessness cut through Ari's soul. "Please, I do not know the names. Release him, I beg you. He is a good man, skilled in healing. He is a man of prayer, a *tsaddik*."

"That is a pity." The Samaritan turned to the soldiers holding Baruch. "Crucify him first, and then the tall man."

Eight soldiers led Ari and Baruch back into the forest of crosses until they reached an execution stake that was empty. Baruch's captors kicked him in the back of the knees. He collapsed in the dust and lay there without struggling.

Ari's heart was jack-hammering in his throat. *Please, HaShem, no. This is worse than evil. There is no meaning to this evil. Please, HaShem, take me, not Baruch. He has done nothing wrong. He gave himself for me and . . .*

The full horror of what he had done hit Ari in the belly. Baruch had come back for him. Had thrown himself into the jaws of the enemy. Had given himself willingly as a sacrifice for Ari.

And Ari had refused him.

Sorrow took Ari like a storm.

Berenike

Berenike turned her head and vomited. She recognized this man called Baruch. He was the pious man who had once healed her, seven years ago. Now he lay in the dust, naked as a newborn. His face was serene. "Courage, Brother Ari. The battle belongs to HaShem."

Ari the Kazan was weeping. "Brother Baruch, forgive me for the things I said to you."

"Of course, Brother Ari. HaShem also forgives you."

Two soldiers brought a crossbeam and dropped it in the dirt behind Baruch's head.

Baruch did not struggle against the soldiers who held him down. He tilted his head and looked at the man on his right hand. "I bless you and your sons," he said in very accented Greek. "May God grant you grace and peace."

The soldier's face went pale and he looked away as he raised Baruch's wrist and set it on the crossbeam.

Baruch said the same to the soldier on his left. This man's face filled with shame, but he pulled Baruch's left wrist onto the coarse wood.

Berenike felt a tingling in her heart.

Baruch blessed the two men who held his legs.

Tears sprang up in Berenike's eyes. She could not believe that a man would forgive those who killed him.

"Hanan ben Hanan," Baruch said. "I . . . bless you also. May HaShem give you peace."

Berenike turned her head and saw Hanan's face. Anguish filled his eyes. And astonishment.

Baruch gave a little gasp. Berenike saw that the soldiers were setting an iron spike to his wrist and raising a heavy mallet.

Berenike bit her lip.

"B—bless you, my son," Baruch said.

The soldier swung the mallet down hard.

The spike entered Baruch's wrist. Baruch's whole body spasmed. Berenike wanted to scream.

"Bless you, my son." Baruch's voice was a naked whisper.

The mallet swung again.

Baruch grunted in pain and sweat sprang out on his face. Ari the Kazan lunged forward again, but his captors yanked him back. One of them hit him in the face.

"Bless you . . . my son."

Berenike closed her eyes, feeling a dull ache in her heart. She heard the sound of the cruel mallet again.

"Bless you, my son."

Again the mallet thumped.

"May God fill you with peace."

At last, the pounding stopped. Berenike opened her eyes and saw that both of Baruch's arms were spiked. The four soldiers went to the ends of the crossbeam, counted to four, and lifted Baruch to a sitting position.

His face was now torn with pain. His gaze locked on Berenike. Compassion filled his eyes. "My daughter, HaShem says . . . this to you — that you are forgiven, that he wishes to hold you in his arms as his own daughter, if only you will come home to him."

Berenike covered her face with her hands and wept.

She heard the soldiers lifting again, heard their grunts, heard the thump of the crossbeam as it dropped onto the top of a stake. Heard a spike slide into a hole, locking the crossbeam in place. She dared to look again.

Baruch hung between heaven and earth. The soldiers made no move to spike his ankles. His face slowly turned blue, then purple. Berenike realized that the soldiers were taking mercy on him. They would let him die swiftly.

A centurion hurried up to the cross. "What are you doing, fools? Nail his ankles!"

The soldiers looked at each other. Berenike read their shame. Saw that they hated themselves. Two of them seized Baruch's feet and pressed them to the stake.

Baruch pushed himself up and began gasping for breath. Slowly the blue color left his face.

The soldiers brought spikes and a mallet. One held the ankles while the other pounded in the spikes.

"Thank you, my sons." Pain etched Baruch's face. He gulped for air.

One of the soldiers walked away a little, and Berenike heard the sound of retching. The other soldier's face hardened to granite.

Berenike found it unbearable to look. She turned around and nearly bumped into Hanan ben Hanan. She remembered the message Governor Florus had given her. "Hanan ben Hanan, the governor says that you and the other chief priests may go. He is persuaded that you know nothing, and he believes Ari the Kazan will give him the information he requires."

Hanan nodded and lurched toward the circle of chief priests. He spoke to them briefly in hushed tones. They all threw one last look at Baruch, and then hurried away.

Berenike had long prided herself that she could read the face of any man, but she could not read the look she saw now on the face of Hanan ben Hanan.

Hanan ben Hanan

Hanan should have been the happiest man in the world. Today, his long enemy Kazan would die. Also, the other man, Baruch, who had cursed him once, who had then escaped sentence of death.

Hanan did not understand what he had seen. This Baruch had . . . blessed him. Had forgiven the men who killed him. More extraordinary than that, this Baruch had offered himself in exchange for his friend. Hanan had no friend in the world for whom he would die. For the Temple, yes, he would die. For his daughter, Sarah, yes. But not for Hananyah ben Nadavayah. Not for Yeshua ben Gamaliel. Not for any of his friends. Nor would they die for him. A great knot rose in his throat. Hanan wondered what it might be like to have such a friend.

Hanan's bodyguards stood muttering quietly among themselves. Hanan rejoined them. "We will go home." He threw one long look back over his shoulder at the governor. Florus was shoveling some delicacy into his mouth. Hanan shuddered and hurried away.

Another face framed itself in his mind. The queen. Her head was covered in dust. Even so, she was a beautiful woman. Hanan had despised her for many years, and yet . . .

And yet she had risked her life to come here. The governor had not summoned her. She had come on her own, and that was an act of courage. Berenike was cast from different metal than her brother. Agrippa was scum. Berenike was . . . something more than scum.

She still looked like a *zonah*, but at least she had courage.

Hanan hurried through the empty streets. When he reached his palace, his doorkeeper pulled open the wooden door beside the gate and gaped at Hanan's dust-covered head. Hanan stormed past him and hurried across his open courtyard and into his palace.

"*Abba!*" Sarah's voice sounded horrified. She raced to him and threw her arms around him. "What happened, *Abba?*"

Hanan held her, and his heart ached. "Great evil, Sarah. Great evil."

Baruch

As the end drew near, despair pressed in on Baruch. He had known when he came for Brother Ari that he could not escape. Had sacrificed himself willingly for the sake of Brother Ari, who had yet some great thing to do for HaShem.

And he had failed. He had come to save Brother Ari, yet Brother Ari would still die. Hana and Rivka would be left widows, Dov and Rachel orphans. Was this the will of HaShem? It made no sense. Baruch knew that he had heard true from HaShem, to come and offer himself for Brother Ari. How could he have failed?

Or had HaShem failed him? Baruch could no longer evade this question. HaShem had sent him here, knowing that Brother Ari would refuse him, knowing they would both die. A great ache filled Baruch's heart. His head felt light-headed with grief. Why? The thing had no reason. He could accept it if only he knew the reason. A thing for no reason he could not accept.

A sacrifice of blood was a great and terrible thing.

A sacrifice of blood refused was a horror beyond imagining.

Baruch pushed himself up and gulped in air. The pain in his ankles tore at his soul. He sank down again, and now his wrists cried out and the black fist of death closed again on his chest.

Brother Ari was kneeling now, weeping. Baruch could think of no comfort. The evil men would do this same thing to Brother Ari. They were wicked — more wicked even than the men of violence.

Baruch saw now that he had been wrong and Brother Ari right. The men of violence were wicked men, yet they were innocent children next to Rome. If one must choose between the men of Rome and the men of violence, then the way of the men of violence was better.

Baruch pressed himself up again, sucking in another breath. "Brother . . . Ari."

Brother Ari looked up at him. Tears streaked his face.

Baruch was gasping feebly now. "I beg you to . . . forgive me . . . for my harsh words." He sank down again, and darkness crowded in.

Brother Ari gazed up at him. "Of course, my friend. The battle belongs to HaShem."

Despair deepened in Baruch's heart. He had believed this thing, had lived by it. Now he would die by it, and he . . . no longer understood. He had fought the battle as HaShem directed. He had warned Brother Ari away from the men of violence, as HaShem had told him. And he had been wrong. There came a time when a good man must fight evil, even with violence. Why had HaShem directed him to tell Brother Ari otherwise? Again, the thing had no reason.

Rage flared up in Baruch's heart. Rage at HaShem. When HaShem asked a man to do something, there should be a reason.

Black despair filled his soul.

"Brother Baruch." Brother Ari's voice.

Baruch said nothing.

"Brother Baruch!" Brother Ari grappled at his legs.

Baruch cracked his eyes open.

Ari was staring up at him. "A deep law of the universe, yes?"

Shame smote Baruch like a fist.

"Yes, Brother Baruch? A deep law?"

Baruch tried to press himself up, but he could not. His cramped legs cried out for mercy. He pushed again. His body rose a few finger-widths. He gulped in air. "Yes." His tortured legs failed, and he sagged down again.

Brother Ari was right. HaShem had a reason, even if Baruch could not know it in this world, even if he would not know it in the World to Come.

New strength entered Baruch's body. He pushed up again, though his ankles screamed and his thighs burned with deep fire. He took in a lungful of air and looked one last time at Brother Ari. "Blessed . . . be HaShem." *Reason or no reason.*

The *Shekinah* wrapped itself around Baruch, a mighty river of peace. "Blessed be HaShem!" he shouted. "Blessed be HaShem!"

Baruch heard voices. His eyes could not focus. A presence stood before him. Something swung at his legs.

Blinding pain shot up his right leg. He understood at once. The soldiers had decided to show mercy, to break his legs.

Another swing.

More terrible pain, this time in his left leg. Baruch slumped lower, no longer able to support any weight with his legs. Crushing darkness trickled into his chest, rising higher, higher. The world turned gray. A rushing sound filled his ears and darkness deepened around him.

Blessed be HaShem.

Baruch's head lolled forward and his lungs cried out for air, but there was no air.

With all that is within me . . . bless his holy Name.

Blackness devoured him.

Deep inside his soul, Baruch shouted for joy.

THIRTY-NINE

Rivka

Baruch had been gone for an hour and Rivka felt panic in her soul. She and Hana had spent the whole time praying that Ari and Baruch would be safe. Deep inside, Rivka knew that they were not.

Rachel huddled in bed with Rivka, her eyes wide with fright. "*Imma*, when is *Abba* coming back?"

Rivka clutched Rachel's little hand. "I don't know. Let's keep praying for him. Hana, I think I need some help again. All that water I've been drinking has gone right through me."

Hana brought a chamber pot to the side of the bed, then helped Rivka slowly climb out of bed. Rivka squatted down carefully and did her business. She flopped back into bed and lay there, terrified of what was going on out in the street. Ari was out there somewhere, probably captured. Baruch too. Rivka wanted to scream.

"*Imma*, aren't you going to pray for Hanan ben Hanan?" Rachel's eyes probed Rivka's face. "Uncle Baruch told you to pray for him."

Rivka didn't want to pray for Hanan. She wanted Ari and Baruch back safe. Hanan could throw himself down a deep well for all she cared.

Hana returned from emptying out the chamber pot. Her face was set. "Sister Rivka, Rachel is right. Baruch said you must pray for Hanan ben Hanan. Therefore, you must pray."

Rivka sighed. "I think we need to keep praying for Ari and Baruch."

Hana sat on the bed next to her. "Rivkaleh."

Rivka didn't say anything.

"Baruch and Ari the Kazan are in the hands of HaShem," Hana said. "Hanan ben Hanan is not in the hands of HaShem. We will pray for him." She took Rivka's hand and Rachel's.

Rachel took Rivka's other hand. "Uncle Baruch said so, *Imma*."

Rivka closed her eyes to shut out the screaming in her heart. She didn't know what to pray.

Rachel's voice filled the room. "Please, HaShem, send the Spirit here now and show us what we must pray."

Rivka waited.

Berenike

Berenike stood quietly in the circle of her Germans, watching the man named Baruch. Yes, he was a *tsaddik*, as Ari the Kazan said. Only a *tsaddik* could die in such a way, at peace with HaShem and the world, forgiving those who killed him.

The *tsaddik* had said HaShem forgave her sin. Was that possible? If an innocent man could forgive those who killed him, then could not HaShem forgive one who killed an innocent life? Berenike thought it might be so, but she could not *feel* that it was so.

A soldier came with a heavy mallet. Berenike held her breath. He swung it very hard, smashing one of Baruch's legs. He smashed the other one.

Cold washed through Berenike's heart. All was determined now. The man would die, and then what would become of his words? They were empty.

Baruch's head raised one more time. Berenike read his face, and she gasped. She saw joy.

Baruch's head sagged down. Ari the Kazan raised his voice in a long, agonized wail. Berenike found herself weeping again. She had never seen a man die like that, fully given to HaShem.

Something shuddered through her soul, and Berenike's whole body spasmed. She felt . . . light. Free.

Forgiven.

Ari

Ari's heart felt numb. He had lost all. Brother Baruch was dead. Now it was his turn. Rivka and Rachel must live or die without him.

The Samaritan translator came back and stood before Ari. "Will you now tell me the names of the men who insulted Caesar?"

Ari shook his head. "I do not know these men."

The Samaritan shook his head sadly. "The governor will speak with you again after his midday meal."

Ari felt a rush of hope. The governor would give him another chance.

The Samaritan pointed at four of the soldiers and spoke in Greek. "Crucify him. Do not break his legs."

A sheet of cold fear hit Ari. They would not break his legs. They would leave him to hang for hours, while the governor feasted. He would not die quickly, like Baruch. He would die slowly, like the boy.

A centurion came and issued a series of rapid orders. All but four of the soldiers trooped away to stand in front of the governor. Florus stepped down off his dais and the squad escorted him toward Herod's Palace.

The four remaining soldiers went about their work with grim efficiency. Two of them took out the top spike and shoved the crossbeam forward. It fell to the ground, dragging Baruch's body with it. His feet remained nailed to the stake. It tore at Ari's heart to see his brother hanging there, broken shards.

And yet ... that was not Baruch. Baruch was standing now before HaShem, at this very moment tasting the glory of the World to Come for the first time. HaShem would ask him if it was good. Baruch would say that it was very good. HaShem would explain to him about the matter of the Problem of Evil in a language far above the language of men. HaShem would teach him the deep things of the universe.

Deep longing filled Ari's soul. He could do nothing now for Rivka and Rachel. He would die like a man, and then he would go to HaShem, as he should have years ago. Except that he had not done any great thing for HaShem. Ari sighed deeply. It could not be helped. He would have done anything for HaShem, but now he could not.

The soldiers pounded and tugged on Baruch's feet until they broke free of the spikes. They did the same with his wrists.

When they finished, they gathered around Ari. None of them would look him in the eye. They had seen Baruch die, and perhaps they feared to see Ari die in the same way.

One soldier unsheathed his dagger and slit open Ari's tunic and tore it off. Another pulled away his loincloth. Ari flinched. He felt terribly exposed, defenseless. His arms were still bound behind his back.

The men led him forward and forced him to sit in the dirt. One of them held down his legs. Two others each seized an arm. The fourth went around behind him and looped a rope around his neck, drawing it back firmly, but not so tight that Ari could not breathe. The intent was clear. If Ari struggled, they would cut off his air. The soldier beside him began cutting the ropes that bound his arms. Ari gathered his strength. There was only a small chance, but he must take it. If he could not escape, at least he would force them to kill him quickly.

When he felt the ropes give way, Ari lunged forward.

The rope on his neck pulled him short. Ari wrenched one hand free and fought at the loop, but it tightened until black spots filled his vision and dizziness stole his strength.

The soldiers pulled his arms out to either side and lashed them to the crossbeam. Just as he began blacking out, the loop around his neck released. Ari had failed. They would not let him die quickly. They meant to crucify him slowly, in great pain.

When they finished tying his arms down, one of the soldiers went to help the one holding down Ari's legs. Ari's heart thudded like hoofbeats in his chest. Any second now, the other two soldiers would place a spike to one of his wrists and pain unendurable would follow.

But the men began arguing instead. Ari looked up and saw that one of them held a mallet, but no spikes. The other was looking around on the ground with an irritated look on his face. One of them pointed toward the dais, and then both of them strode toward it, still arguing.

Sweat bathed Ari's body. He closed his eyes. *Please, HaShem, I have not done the great thing you asked. Forgive me for my failure.*

One of the soldiers holding Ari's legs made a rude-sounding joke, and the other laughed. Unspeakable terror filled Ari's heart. He was not afraid of entering the World to Come. He was afraid of experiencing the pain to come. He tried to think of Rivka, of Rachel.

A woman's voice, low and harsh.

Ari's eyes flickered open. Two large blond men held daggers to the throats of the two soldiers holding his legs. The Romans released their grip. Ari drew up his legs, pulling himself into a defensive huddle.

Queen Berenike appeared and a small dagger flashed in her hands. "Your friend did not die in vain." She slashed at the ropes binding Ari's right arm.

Shouts from the direction of Herod's Palace. Ari saw the two soldiers who had gone off looking for spikes. They were running toward him, waving swords. The queen said something in Greek, and four more Germans moved to head them off.

Berenike finished cutting free Ari's right hand. Ari rolled to his left and tore at the rope binding his left hand.

"Leave it to me," the queen said. She slashed at the ropes, once, twice, three times. The ropes sprang free. "Run!" she said. "My Germans will protect me."

Ari ran.

Berenike

Gather around me!" Berenike said.

Four of her Germans sprang into a defensive circle around her, swords drawn and shields up. Berenike's heart was thumping now, but she felt oddly calm. The seer woman had told her she would live for many years after this day. Therefore, whatever she did, the governor would not kill her. Unless . . . the seer woman proved unreliable.

The two soldiers stared after Ari the Kazan, dismay in their eyes. Berenike suppressed her smile. Soldiers in battle gear could not outrun a naked man running in fear of his life. Ari the Kazan would live another day. That was Berenike's payment for the words of the holy man named Baruch, who had forgiven her sin. She would have saved Baruch also, but it had not been possible.

Berenike looked down at the two sweating soldiers who had held Ari the Kazan's legs. Her Germans held daggers to their throats. "Release them," she said. "It is a day for mercy, not justice."

The Germans stepped back and quickly joined the circle of guards around Berenike. She jutted her chin at the Romans. They could do as they wished, but they were only four, whereas she had six, and Germans into the bargain.

"We will return to the palace," Berenike said.

The six Germans began working their way through the forest of crosses, keeping a tight formation.

The Roman soldiers moved to block them. Berenike saw at once that they had stalemate. The Romans could move as single units, swiftly and easily. They could block her, but they could not attack. She and her Germans lacked the speed and agility to fight.

One of the soldiers retreated and then loped away toward Herod's Palace. Berenike began sweating. She could not move and soon reinforcements would arrive.

"Force a way," she said.

The Germans moved forward, their swords cutting a swath through the air. The three Romans fought a defensive battle, giving way slowly, playing for time.

Berenike looked back toward the palace, and her heart lurched. At least fifty soldiers were running toward her. They carried javelins. Behind them strode the governor.

He was laughing.

Berenike's mind raced, but she could not think what to do.

The soldiers surrounded her in a great circle, far enough away that her Germans' swords were useless, close enough that a single volley of javelins would kill them all. Florus stopped and studied her, licking his lips.

"My dear Queen Berenike, did I not invite you to join me?" His eyes gleamed with malice. "Now I see that you wish to leave the party early. How very rude."

Berenike spit in the dust. "You filth! You have murdered many innocents today, to no gain. Whoever those beggar men were, their names were not known. Do you not fear the gods?"

Fear spasmed across his face.

Berenike saw that she had struck a nerve. "You killed a righteous man."

"A weak man," Florus said.

"Stronger than any man I have ever seen." Berenike glared at him. "And you would have killed his comrade, who knew nothing and could not meet your demands."

Florus's face turned red. "He knew something and I would have learned it in a day or two. My men tell me that you had the ill manners to release him."

Berenike said nothing. She had spent her anger and she saw that Florus had not spent his.

The governor studied her for a time, and then a wolfish smile crossed his face. "If I give the order, my men will volley their javelins and you and all your Germans will die. Do you wish me to give the order?"

Berenike saw that he spoke true. "No."

His smile broadened. "Why die in vain, and six good men with you? If I promise that you will not be killed, will you come out peaceably?"

Berenike did not trust any promise he might make, but she saw no reason to force Florus to kill her, when there might be a chance of escape. "What will you do if I come out?"

His cheek twitched. "I will make you a ... sporting proposition. A wager."

Berenike felt light-headed with fear. She did not think any wager Florus might propose would be favorable to her, but was there any alternative?

"I promise you will not be harmed," Florus said. "A simple wager. On one chance, you will go free. On another chance ..." His eyes flicked over her body and he licked his lips. "... you will still not be harmed."

Berenike shivered with disgust and said nothing.

Florus stared at her, and his face hardened. He barked an order in Latin, and all around the circle, his soldiers cocked their arms, ready to launch their javelins. He smiled again at Berenike. "On both chances, your Germans will go free. Do you wish to accept my generous offer?"

Revulsion welled up in Berenike's heart. She did not think Florus would give her a sporting chance, and the thought of losing revolted her.

He raised his eyebrows. "Yes or no?"

Berenike's tongue felt like wood.

Florus's face flushed. "Do not make me lose my patience! Yes or no?"

"Yes." Berenike pushed on the burly back of two of the Germans. "Let me out."

The Germans refused to move.

"I order you to let me out!" Berenike screamed. "Now!"

Slowly, they stepped aside and she walked out of the circle. For good or ill, she would take his wager.

FORTY

Rivka

Rachel squeezed Rivka's hand. "Pray this, *Imma*. Please, HaShem, show mercy to Hanan ben Hanan."

Rivka felt rage heat up her insides.

Hana fell on her face. "Please, HaShem, show mercy to Hanan ben Hanan."

Rivka bit back her anger. "Please, HaShem, show mercy to . . . Hanan ben Hanan."

Nothing happened.

"Say it again," Rachel said.

Rivka said it again.

Still nothing.

"Another time," Hana said. "Please, you will say it fifty times if you must. You have opened the door to HaShem many times, but you have never kept it open. This time, you must keep it open until all your rage is gone."

Rivka took a deep breath. "Please, HaShem, show mercy to Hanan ben Hanan."

Something whooshed inside Rivka's head. Frightened, she tried to open her eyes. They were stuck tight. She felt like she was rising up, up, soaring high above the city of God. She could not breathe, could not think, could not feel. An instant later, Rivka realized what was happening.

She had crossed beyond the veil at last. She was going to the Throne.

Berenike

Florus gave Berenike an appraising smile. "You look young and healthy, Your Highness. I will give you a start and count to fifty. Run swiftly! If you arrive at your own palace safely, then you are free. If my men catch you, they will return you to me for your . . . reward."

Berenike shivered.

Florus turned to the three soldiers. "You will leave all your weapons here. She is not to be harmed. This is a sporting event. When I give the signal, you will pursue her."

Berenike felt a surge of hope. The men would be unarmed. They did not know about her dagger.

Florus was still talking. "If you bring her back to me, then you will enjoy her charms when I am finished."

The soldiers gawked at Berenike. Her heart pounded. She would cut their throats out before she let any of them touch her.

"Are we ready then?" Florus rubbed his hands together. "Even Caesar will see no better sport today." He stepped closer to Berenike, and his yellow teeth gleamed in the sun. "There is only one other thing, Your Highness."

She returned his gaze without flinching.

His hand snaked out and seized her left wrist. Before she could react, he twisted hard, bending her arm behind her back. Berenike cried out in pain. She heard the sound of her small dagger sliding out of its sheath.

Florus guffawed. "I am so very sorry, but surely you agree that it would be most unsporting to allow you a weapon when my men have none." His free hand ran over her body, checking for other weapons, lingering on the choicest areas.

Berenike recoiled at his vile touch. Now she would have no recourse if the men caught her. She could not fight even one man without a weapon.

Florus released her wrist from his sweaty grip and stepped away from her. "Now, I believe we are really ready. Berenike, you may begin running whenever you like and I will begin counting."

Berenike's heart was racing now. She tried to think, to map out strategy. The quickest way home was to cut diagonally across the market square. When she reached the streets, she would veer north, then east, and straight down the hill on the only avenue that would take her to her palace. It would be a race of perhaps half a Roman mile. The men would be wearing clumsy iron-soled sandals, whereas she was barefoot and lightly clad. If Florus gave her an honest count to fifty, then she had a chance.

She turned to look at Florus. He was still smiling. What did he know that she did not?

Berenike realized that there was only one way to find out. She would have to run, and if she failed, then she failed. *Please, HaShem, bring me home safe.*

She turned and fled.

Behind her, Florus began counting out loud in Greek. "One." A slight pause. "Two."

Berenike could not hear more, but her heart leaped. Florus was making a fair count. She had a chance.

She raced past the soldiers who still surrounded her Germans. They jeered at her, and several made obscene gestures. Berenike threaded her way through the crosses and broke free into the open square. After fifty paces, she dared to look back, and her heart shivered.

Florus had released her pursuers.

Berenike was already gasping. She tried to run faster. Then she saw the evil trick that the fates had played on her. She could not run across the diagonal of the market, on account of the stones and shards. Her feet would not bear it. She would have to run down the center lane, filled with soft dust. Berenike ran. When she had nearly reached the edge of the square, she risked a look back.

Her pursuers had cut diagonally across the market, their thick sandals making a mockery of the rough surface. She would reach the street first, but then she would have to turn left and she could not get past them before they gained the street. They would cut her off and . . .

Berenike ran faster. When she reached the street, instead of turning left toward home, she turned *right*.

Far behind her, she heard the men shout in dismay. She ran south, into the heart of the upper city. Here in the maze of streets, she would find a place to hide. Or she would pound on a door until somebody let her in. Or . . .

Or she might reach the Essene Gate and get out of the city.

Berenike darted left at the first corner. At the next, she turned right again. Her only hope was to lose her pursuers in the narrow twisting streets.

Now her heart was slamming in her chest, and she knew she must soon slow down. Berenike staggered along. Her right heel ached where she had stepped on a rock and her left calf felt like it would cramp soon.

A shout behind her.

Berenike looked back and saw one of the soldiers racing toward her. She turned and fled. If only she had the luxury of pounding on a door, any door, she could beg for a hiding place. But the soldier would see and force a way in and she would be trapped.

She passed the palace of Mattityahu the priest and turned left. Sweat stung her eyes, and then she tripped and fell.

Another bellow of triumph behind her. She scrambled to her feet and ran, throwing a glance over her shoulder. Terror seized her.

The soldier she had seen was much closer and gaining fast. Berenike heard his heavy breathing behind her. Despair filled her soul. She could not escape now. The man would run her down in the next twenty paces. She veered right at the next corner and saw a naked man crouched in the street, waiting. She stopped and stared.

The soldier came racing around the corner. Ari the Kazan rose up like a lion and hit the man very hard in the face. He staggered backward. Ari the Kazan hit him again.

The soldier turned and fled.

Ari the Kazan raced toward Berenike.

She gaped at him. "You should have gone home."

"I watched to see what would happen to you." Ari the Kazan grabbed her hand. "This way. We must lose him again."

Berenike ran.

A shrill, piercing whistle soared up to heaven.

Ari the Kazan looked back, and said something harsh in a language Berenike did not know. At the next corner, he yanked her to the right. "He is signaling the others. Hurry!"

They ran down the narrow alley between two large palaces. Behind these walls, on either side, Berenike knew, chief priests huddled in safety. Cowards. They were not the tenth part of such men as Baruch the *tsaddik* or Ari the Kazan. At the end of the alley, Ari the Kazan stopped and peered out into the long avenue that ran north and south.

Berenike looked also. Not far to the south, a soldier stood in indecision, his back to Ari and Berenike. He was standing at an intersection, looking down two streets.

Ari the Kazan looked at her. "If he leaves the street, we will go north," he whispered. "They will not expect us to double back."

Berenike nodded, waiting for the soldier to choose either east or west.

A shout behind them.

Berenike spun around and saw a soldier coming down the alley. He shouted again, and now the man out in the street turned, his eyes probing.

"Run!" Ari the Kazan took her hand and pulled her out into the street, turning north toward the heart of the city.

Two shouts behind them. Berenike's heart flogged her chest.

A whistle pierced the street. The third soldier dashed around the corner in front of them. He shouted in triumph.

Ari the Kazan and Berenike skidded to a stop. They were trapped, with two men behind and one ahead. They could not hope to fight three men.

Berenike clutched the arm of Ari the Kazan and pulled him to the side of the street. There was a great iron gate there, and beside it, a stout wooden door. She could not see a gatekeeper inside. She pounded on the door. "Help us!"

"Stop your useless shouting," Ari the Kazan said. "We will fight them and trust in HaShem." He stepped out into the middle of the street and waited, his head twisting first left and then right, watching the three soldiers approaching.

One of the soldiers laughed out loud and shouted a lewd remark in street Greek. Berenike pressed her back against the wooden door. Terror squeezed her insides so tight she could not breathe. A roaring sound filled her ears.

Ari the Kazan stooped in the street and began scooping up small stones. Berenike knelt down too, scrabbling frantically in the dirt for any stone she could find. She stood up to throw.

A hairy arm wrapped around her neck and pulled her backward.

Berenike screamed.

FORTY-ONE

Rivka

Rivka soared higher, beyond thought or fear. Cold welled up inside her, infinite cold. Her eyes were clammed shut. She fought to open them, fought to breathe, fought to feel. And then ... she was there.

Slowly, her eyes opened to a world she had never imagined. Cold mists swirled through her, chilling her heart. Rivka looked all around and saw nothing. An infinite sea of cold gray. She looked down and gasped.

She was naked. More than naked. Rivka held up her arms in wonder. They were nearly transparent. She stared in awe, watching the blood flow in her arteries, the muscles contract as she squeezed her hands. She peered into her belly and saw her baby. It floated upside down. She jiggled her tummy slightly and saw that it was a boy. Ari would be so proud if —

Greetings, Visitor! A cold, vacant voice echoed inside her head.

Rivka spun around and saw a man gliding toward her. From the voice, she knew it had to be a man. He was faceless, featureless, like an abstract sculpture in a white block of marble. His eyes were deep holes in his head, and he stared at her body hungrily, as if it were long since he had seen flesh, bones, blood, muscles, organs.

"Who are you?" she demanded.

I am your Guide.

"Guide?" She glared at him. "Where am I and why did you bring me here?"

His empty eyeholes glittered with something like mirth. *This place is called Outer Darkness, and you were brought here, but not by me.*

Rivka felt a crushing feeling in her gut. This was not the Throne. This was the other place. What was she doing here? "What ... what do you want with me?"

The Guide's formless face twisted into what might have been a smile. He took her hand in his cold, slimy mitt.

Rivka tried to yank her hand away. "Don't touch me!"

The Guide's hand held hers in a viselike grip. *Come with me. There is a thing He wishes you to see. It will amount to nothing, but He insists.*

Rivka was freaking out now. *Please, HaShem, get me out of here.*

The Guide gave her a horrible grinlike leer. *It will do no good to appeal to Him, since it was He who sent you here. Come with me.*

Rivka went, stumbling on wooden feet. HaShem had sent her here? For what purpose? Had she died or something? But no, that made no sense. She was alive. She could see her heart beating in her chest. This horrible *thing*, this Guide, was dead, or worse than dead, but she was not.

Yet.

They went in through a gate into the most wretched city Rivka could imagine. Gray stone buildings without windows lined both sides of a long avenue. The place was icy cold. Murky darkness hung over all. Along the sides of the street, dead souls squatted against the walls, gray shriveled beings, wailing in formless torment. As she passed by, they reached out to her like beggars, their hungry eyeholes taking in her fleshy reality. *Help us!*

The Guide squeezed her hand in clammy reassurance. *You can give them no help and they can give you no hurt.*

"I want out of here right now. I want to go home."

The Guide did his horrible mockery of a smile and said nothing.

They walked.

After many minutes, the Guide turned left down another avenue. Rivka felt dread clamp a fist over her heart. It felt like she had been here for years. She could not remember what light and hope were.

At last the Guide stopped in front of a building. *We have arrived.*

Rivka stared. There was an open doorway, but no door. Terror welled up inside her. "What . . . what do I do now?"

Go inside. There is a thing you must see.

Rivka breathed in deeply. The air hurt her lungs. She stepped though the doorway into a long room. At the far end, a shriveled old man huddled in the corner. An equally shriveled old woman was pacing back and forth in front of him, shaking her fist at him and shrieking in a language Rivka did not know. A long iron chain connected their ankles.

Rivka moved slowly toward them. What was this supposed to be?

Go closer. They cannot harm you.

As Rivka strode closer, the old woman turned. Red fear blazed in her eyeholes and she backed away from Rivka, nattering angrily and shaking her fist. The old man looked up at her and Rivka read hate in his formless face.

Rivka's eyes moved from one to the other. None of this made any sense. She turned to her Guide. "Okay, I've seen this thing you wanted me to see. Now can we go home?"

Her Guide released his grip and rubbed his hands together in slimy glee. *You may leave whenever you wish.*

Suspicious, Rivka stared at him. He wanted her to go. Why? She looked back at the old man, then at the raging old woman. Their blank and empty faces told her nothing. "Why are they here? What have they done?"

If you wish to know, examine their hearts. They are open to you.

Rivka knelt in front of the old man. He shrank away from her. She peered at his chest and saw that by concentrating, she could look inside him, could see his chest muscles, his ribs, his lungs, his . . .

Rivka gasped. "He hasn't got a heart." She stood up and went to look at the old woman. The woman cowered away, refusing to look at her.

"I won't hurt you." Rivka reached out to her. The woman shrank against the wall.

Rivka looked inside her and saw that she also had no heart. She stood up and turned back to her Guide. "Why don't they have hearts?"

Another shapeless smile. *They have no need of them here.*

"If they had hearts, could they leave this horrible place?"

No. The Guide was not looking at her. He rubbed his hands together again. *You are ready to leave now?*

Rivka did not trust him. There was a mystery here, and something told her that she had to solve it before she left. "I want you to give them a heart."

A smug silence. *I cannot.*

"Then why did you bring me here?" Rivka put her hands on her hips and glared at him. "What kind of game are you playing?"

I did not bring you here. It was at His insistence. You are free to go now. You will be taken back home, now that you have seen. Will you leave now? The Guide reached for her hand.

Rivka pulled away from his slimy presence, her heart thumping beneath her ribs. She put her hand on her chest as if to still its pounding.

A terrible idea formed in her head. She pressed hard with her fingers and her hand went inside her chest. Her ribs parted and she grasped her own hot, beating heart in her fingers. "Can I . . . could I give one of them my heart? Would it get them out of here?"

The Guide shook his faceless head. *Of course not. What foolishness. It is not possible.*

Rivka did not believe him. HaShem had sent her here, against the wishes of this Guide. If HaShem had sent her here, it had to be for a reason. But why? She had been minding her own business, praying to HaShem, when she ended up here. From very far away, she felt the faint echo of Rachel's voice and Hana's, repeating the same words over and over. "Please, HaShem, show mercy to Hanan ben Hanan."

Rivka said the words too. She felt a little heat in her hand. She said it again. More heat. Again. More.

Rivka repeated the words again and again, and as she did, compassion welled up in her soul. She gripped her throbbing heart and began pulling.

Pain shot through her chest. The Guide laughed an evil laugh. Rivka grimaced and pulled harder, ripping, tearing, severing. She sank to her knees, crying with the pain of it, and tore it out of her chest. She laid it down in front of the withered old man. "Here, take it."

He turned away from it. Rivka stared at her offering. Inside her chest, the heart had seemed a huge thing. Now it looked small and gray and stony. Horror filled her. What had she done? What crazy, stupid thing had she done?

Strong and gentle hands took her from behind and lifted her to her feet. Hands of flesh. "It was well meant, Little One, but your heart will do him no good. As you see, yours is as stony as his once was."

Shaking, sobbing, Rivka tried to turn.

The strong hands held her tight. "It was a gift well given, Little One. Now, perhaps you will have room for another. See what I give you." The hands gently turned her around.

Rivka was crying so hard, she could see nothing. Light filled all the room. She wiped her eyes and saw a strong hand holding a red, throbbing heart. A heart of flesh.

The hand entered her chest and put the heart in place. Swiftly, the hand repaired arteries, veins, muscles, tissues, ribs, skin. Rivka raised her eyes, but the brightness of the Man of Light's face was too much. She clamped her eyes shut. "Can't you . . . do anything for the old man?"

"Not unless he is willing to accept it, Little One."

Rivka did not know what to say to that. She wished she could make the old man take a new heart, a heart of flesh.

"Is there something you would give the man, Little One?"

Rivka could hardly think. She had meant to give her heart, but it was a little thing, stony and worthless and cold. What else could she give? She was nothing anyway. She was a phony, a fraud, a seer woman who couldn't see.

Rivka gasped.

"Yes, Little One?"

"Could I . . . could I give him my eyes?"

"If you wish. It will be painful."

"Would he take them? Then maybe he could see what a fool he is and take the heart you offer."

"Perhaps. He has a will of his own. But even a well-meant sacrifice may be refused."

Rivka screwed up her courage. She reached up and grasped her right eye and squeezed.

Horrible, blinding pain. Then Rivka felt the eye in her hand. She repeated the process with her left eye. An agony in her skull. She held them both out. "Please give them to the old man."

"As you wish, Little One."

Rivka felt the Man of Light brush past her. "The gift is given, Little One. Let us see if it will be accepted."

Behind her, the old woman shrieked in rage.

Rivka screamed, and then all the cold gray world disappeared.

Imma!"

Rivka opened her eyes and saw Rachel and Hana staring at her. Sunlight streamed in through the window slits, impossibly bright.

"Sister Rivka, are you well?" Hana's eyes showed her terror.

Rachel patted her hand. "You did well, to give him your heart and your eyes, *Imma*."

Rivka gaped at her. "You were . . . there?"

"No, silly. They wouldn't let me past the veil, but I saw."

Hana looked terrified. "Saw . . . what? What are you talking about?"

Rachel gave her a matter-of-fact look. "HaShem took *Imma* to a dark city on the Other Side to show her a bad thing."

"It was horrible." Rivka shivered.

"What dark city?" Hana said. "What is the bad thing you saw?"

Rivka shook her head. "A place called Outer Darkness. There was a horrible Guide who led me through the city and showed me two miserable people. I don't know why. None of it made any sense to me, but I think I learned a little about compassion. Maybe that was the point."

"*Imma*, don't you know who that poor old man was?"

"No," Rivka said in a very small voice.

Rachel gave her a gap-toothed smile. "Yes, you do! That was Hanan ben Hanan!"

Astonishment flooded through Rivka's soul. *That* was Hanan? That miserable, frightened, shriveled old man was Hanan ben Hanan? It seemed too huge for her to comprehend. It had to be some kind of metaphor. The great and powerful Hanan ben Hanan, eking out some miserable existence in Outer Darkness, hounded by that wretched old woman. Rivka felt light-headed. She had seen Hanan ben Hanan the way HaShem saw him, and he was pitiful. Rivka pulled Rachel close and hugged her. "I'm so glad to be back. Blessed be HaShem. I wonder who that horrible old woman was, who kept shrieking at Hanan."

Rachel broke free and looked up at her. "Oh, *Imma*, now you're teasing me! Of course you know."

"No, sweetie, I have no idea."

"*Imma*, that angry old woman was you."

FORTY-TWO

Hanan ben Hanan

After shaking the dust out of his hair and washing his face and immersing in his ritual bath, Hanan was still quivering with anger as he dressed. Governor Florus was evil. What would he do next? With two cohorts, he could destroy this city. No man was safe. Not the poorest man in his hovel nor Hanan in his palace. This city was naked and defenseless. Hanan did not like to admit it, but such men as Eleazar and Kazan might have a point. They were rash and insolent, but they might have a point.

In any event, Hanan needed information, and he did not wish to risk the lives of any of his servants by sending them out on the street. When he finished dressing, he went outside of his palace into the courtyard and climbed the stairs up onto his roof. He would be able to see much of what happened in the streets. If the Romans sent soldiers, he would know well in advance.

The sun stood high in the sky now. Hanan peered north toward the upper market. Nothing. East and west, also nothing. South toward the Essene Gate. Nothing.

By now, the governor's men would have finished killing the man Baruch. Perhaps, even now, they would be nailing Kazan's wrists to the crossbeam.

Hanan felt both anger and astonishment. Kazan was proud and arrogant and he lacked respect for the proper authorities, but he had done a courageous thing to refuse the sacrifice of his friend. It demonstrated honor. Many weak men of this city would allow another to die in their place. Hanan would never do such a thing, and he had no respect for any who would. Kazan had not. Kazan had great strength of will. Such a man might have been of some benefit in helping prepare the city.

The plan of Florus was clear now. To avoid prosecution by Caesar, he meant to provoke the people into revolt. Then Caesar would forgive all, if only Florus could quell the rebellion. Hanan clenched his fists. If today's evil did not provoke a revolt, Florus would double it tomorrow. If that failed, he would double it yet again, until all the people were killed, or until they struck back. Therefore . . .

Therefore, the only prudent thing was to strike back.

Quickly.

Hanan looked again to the north. When the soldiers finished with Kazan, they must seek out more victims. Florus could not stop killing now.

A swirl of dust.

Hanan squinted, cursing his old eyes. Sudden pain shot through his skull. He blinked and then . . .

He could see as a young man. He saw three soldiers racing across the square of the upper market. Suddenly, they shouted and altered course, running now straight south toward Hanan. He could see them clearly. What trick of lighting was this?

A woman. Hanan gasped. Not just any woman. Queen Berenike, unmistakable with her wild hair and bare feet. She reached the street and cut south toward Hanan. Shortly, she turned to her left on a narrow street, and a strange thing happened. Hanan could *still* see her, though many buildings blocked his view. He could see through the buildings. Of course, it was foolishness, a trick of his imagination.

But it was no trick of his mind that showed a naked man hiding behind a building, watching the queen. A tall man. Kazan! What foolishness was this? Kazan could not possibly have escaped from the Romans. Hanan rubbed his eyes and looked again.

The whole terrifying game played out for him as if he were HaShem, who sees all. The three soldiers split up, each choosing a different street. The queen turned left and right and left and right. Kazan kept ahead of her, now anticipating her movements, now hiding. Two of the soldiers took wrong paths. The third hesitated at an intersection. Hanan found himself holding his breath. And then . . .

The soldier took the street that would intersect with the queen. Hanan knew he could not warn her. The distance was too great. The man turned onto the street, saw the queen, and shouted. Hanan saw that the other soldiers were too far away to give aid. The queen began running toward the next corner. Behind that corner, Kazan crouched, waiting.

Fly, fool! Kazan could not know about the soldier, or he would be running also.

Berenike raced around the corner. The soldier followed after her. Kazan leaped up and hit him twice very hard, roaring in rage. Kazan's courage took Hanan's breath away. The soldier fled, whistling for help. Now Kazan and the queen came running south alongside the wall of Hanan's palace. Hanan marveled at this strange thing, that he could see through stone. Kazan and Berenike turned and raced west outside his southern wall.

Now Hanan saw the trap into which they had walked. To the south, one soldier. Behind them on the east, another. Hidden behind the north wall of the palace, a third. To the west, many buildings. Hanan strode toward his stairs.

He saw Kazan and the queen discover their danger on two sides. Saw them race out, hoping to break through to freedom by going north. Saw the third soldier appear, closing the trap.

Hanan ran down the stairs to his courtyard. Of course, it was foolish. He could do nothing. The queen backed up against the strong door next to Hanan's gate. Kazan stood naked in the street, appraising his enemies. The Romans came closer. Kazan knelt in the dust and picked up a few small stones. The queen did likewise.

Hanan moved to the wooden door.

Flung back the bolt.

Jerked open the door.

Grabbed the queen and hauled her in.

Kazan was throwing his stones now. Hanan gripped the edge of the door, ready to throw it shut. Kazan turned to look at him, and Hanan saw . . .

Joy.

Kazan knelt in the dirt and scooped up more stones. Hanan waited impatiently. What was Kazan playing at? Then he understood. Kazan's joy was to save the queen. He had no hope for himself.

Hanan strode out into the street.

Kazan threw another stone. One of the soldiers lurched backward.

Hanan grabbed Kazan's arm and yanked him toward the door. "In here, fool."

Together, they ran back inside. Hanan tripped and fell in the dust. Kazan flung the door shut and threw the bolt.

Three heavy thuds on the door.

Hanan looked and suddenly realized that he could no longer see through the door. His vision was that of an ordinary man again.

The queen had backed up against the wall of Hanan's palace, her face white and shiny.

Hanan pushed himself off the filthy ground and strode toward her. When he reached the queen, he turned and saw that Kazan was staring at him like an imbecile.

Hanan gave an impatient nod toward the palace. "Come along, fool, and cover your nakedness. Then we must talk."

Rivka

The day passed in dread. With each passing hour, Rivka's certainty grew. Ari and Baruch were dead. The hurt in Hana's eyes told Rivka that she also knew. Neither of them dared to say it aloud. Rachel sat quietly in a corner holding her doll and looking at the women with mournful eyes. Dov waited faithfully downstairs at the door, expecting his *abba* and Uncle Ari to arrive any minute.

All the fears Rivka had felt over the past four years came crashing in on her. She had been right all along. They should have left the city and gone somewhere, anywhere. Now Ari was dead and the war hadn't even started yet. He had died for no reason, and gotten Baruch killed in the process. Horror filled Rivka's soul. Now she and Hana were alone in a hostile city with two children and another on the way. They could not travel, had no source of income. Rivka had some money stored by, but she did not know how long that would last. How were they going to take care of Rachel and Dov through the next four years? And the baby that was coming? Yeshua was right. In these days, the barren woman would be called blessed.

Silence reigned out in the streets. A hot east wind blew in from the desert. Rivka lay in bed and drank cool water and prayed. Hana mostly stayed downstairs with Dov, but each time she came up, Rivka saw fresh tear tracks on her cheeks.

Dusk fell on the city of God, and with it, mourning. People came out in the street, talking in hushed whispers. Rivka sent Hana outside to hear the news. When she returned, her face was bleak, and she refused to tell Rivka anything until Rachel went downstairs to sit with Dov.

When they were alone, Hana sat on the bed next to Rivka. "The Romans crucified many hundred of our people in the market square. Rumor tells that they crucified also women and children. The bodies are piled in the square. We must go and . . . look."

Rivka's heart overflowed with grief. "I can't go." She held Hana's hand in hers. "Can you find somebody to go with you? I'll keep the children here."

Hana nodded. She kissed Rivka on the cheek. "Do not be afraid, Sister Rivka. We are in the hands of HaShem. If he takes us home tomorrow, we will find a golden city and be joined again to our men."

Rivka bit her lip and blinked to push back her tears. Hana was right. Dying was not the worst that could happen to her. Today she had seen a thing worse than death, and it terrified her. Yes, it was only a parable, a metaphor, but it carried a deep truth. She had passed some kind of test in that vision, but she knew in her heart that she was still chained to that horrible Hanan ben Hanan. If she could not break that chain, then a part of her would dwell in Outer Darkness all her days. Would she ever be free, really free?

A soft knock on the door downstairs.

Hana stood up and went out. Rivka listened to her soft footfall on the steps.

The door squeaked on its iron hinges.

Hana's voice pierced the night, wailing in anguish. Dov and Rachel screamed.

Rivka felt a knife in her heart. Somebody must have come from the market with news of Ari and Baruch. The pain took her breath away. She had to leave this wretched city that had so long prayed for retribution, and now had received it in full measure, pressed down, running over. This was only the first stroke of the war, and already she was a widow. How many more tens of thousands of women would lose their men before this horrible thing ended?

A heavy tread on the steps. Rivka stared at the door with bleary eyes. Would it be Gamaliel bringing the terrible news? Yoseph? Eleazar?

A shadow in the doorway. A tall man stepped through, carrying a shattered body. "Rivkaleh," Ari said.

Rivka screamed.

FORTY-THREE

Berenike

As evening approached, Berenike sent word to her palace by one of Hanan's servants. Soon, half a dozen Germans arrived to escort her home. Shlomi came with them. "Mistress! Are you well?"

Berenike did not know how to answer. Today had been a day of horror. Her people had been massacred by Florus and she had failed to prevent it. She had narrowly escaped capture and a fate too vile to think on. She had seen the torture of a good man, a *tsaddik* — a man who told her she was forgiven for her sin.

And she was healed.

Her flow of blood had stopped. It seemed impossible, and yet it was so. She felt new strength in her body. The seer woman had foreseen all, seven years ago. It was a gift from HaShem.

Berenike stepped out through the gate of Hanan's palace. "Come with us, Ari the Kazan, and we will see you safely home."

He shook his head. "I must find the body of the *tsaddik*."

"Then we will go with you and bear the body to your home."

The circle of Germans closed around Berenike. "Are you well?" Shlomi repeated. "We thought you were killed when the Germans came back without you and they could not tell where you had gone."

"I am well, thanks to Ari the Kazan." She snapped her fingers at the Germans. "Take us to the upper market. We must find the body of the righteous man."

They moved north in a tight cluster. Once past the palaces of the wealthy priests, they reached crowded streets. As Berenike approached, a hush fell. People turned and gawked at her.

"The queen!" somebody shouted. "Long live the queen, who defied Florus!"

Berenike felt a stone in her throat.

"The queen!" Others took up the shout. "Give honor to the queen!"

A man dropped to his face in the dirt, bowing toward Berenike. Then another. Then dozens, hundreds.

"Blessed be the queen!"

Berenike clutched Shlomi's arm and staggered on, unable to see a thing for the tears in her eyes.

Hanan ben Hanan

When the queen was gone, Hanan went up to his daughter's room. Sarah sat on her bed combing her thick black hair with an ivory lice comb. When she saw him, she covered her hair. "The queen is not so wicked as I imagined," she said.

Hanan could not think of an answer. The queen came of a vile house. Her brother was a true son of his father in the matter of women and wine, and yet was not the tenth part of his father in the exercise of power. Berenike was a true daughter of Herod in all respects, a woman of loose morals and scandalous dress, a brilliant thinker. Hanan did not like her, but he respected her wits and her courage. Finally he shrugged. "She did a bold thing today."

"Is it true that Ari the Kazan is a powerful magician?"

"He is a clever man." Hanan had not expected Kazan to show such courage. He would have given his life to save his friend, and that was an honorable thing. Kazan had defended the queen at the risk of his life, and that was yet more honorable, since the queen was no friend of his. Such a man of honor would defend the city, would guard the Temple with his life.

The time had come to put aside old rivalries. Hanan did not like Kazan, and Kazan did not like him. But now they were in desperate straits, with a mutual enemy who meant to destroy the city. Hanan had no knowledge of weapons, and for that he needed Kazan's expertise. Kazan had no experience in the exercise of power, and for that he needed Hanan. It was a strange thing HaShem had decreed, that Hanan and Kazan must knit their futures together, or else die separately.

To save the Temple of the living God, Hanan would work with even such a man as Kazan.

Hana

Wailing aloud, Hana fell on her knees beside the broken body of Baruch. Her heart felt crushed within her. Baruch had suffered much. His wrists and ankles were pierced, his legs broken. Yet there was joy on his face. He had gone into the Presence in great victory.

Baruch's left eye had fallen open and it stared blind at Hana. She shut it and kissed his face. Behind her, she heard Dov and Rachel screaming. Hana steeled her heart. It was not done to keep a body in the house overnight. They must wash Baruch and anoint him with spices and bury him outside the city. Immediately. Custom demanded it.

"Dov," she said. "You will come and kiss your father."

Dov stood there motionless, his huge round eyes spilling tears. Rachel took his hand. Tears streamed down her cheeks, but she knelt beside Baruch and kissed his face. "Come, Dov. Uncle Baruch is with HaShem."

Dov knelt beside her and kissed Baruch.

Ari the Kazan brought rags and a bucket of water. Hana's heart was stone within her, but she knew she must now wash the body. "Children, please, you will sit with Sister Rivka."

Dov and Rachel climbed onto the bed and huddled beside Rivka.

Hana dipped a rag in the water and swabbed Baruch's face. "Ari the Kazan, please you will find spices and a shroud."

"I have seen to it already," Ari the Kazan said. "Only wait a little."

Hana continued washing. Tears flowed down onto Baruch's body as she worked.

Ari the Kazan told them all that he had seen. How the Romans killed many without mercy. How they meant to crucify him also. How Baruch offered himself in exchange for Ari the Kazan.

How Ari the Kazan refused him.

Hana's heart raced at this. It must have broken Baruch's spirit, to have his sacrifice refused.

Ari the Kazan told how they crucified Baruch, and how he won a mighty victory. How the queen was healed and Ari the Kazan was saved and the heart of Hanan ben Hanan was changed. "It is a deep law of the universe," he said. "Sacrifice releases power."

A loud pounding downstairs.

Ari the Kazan went to answer it. He returned shortly with an expensive linen shroud, linen strips to bind Baruch's hands and feet, and a veil for his face. Also nard — the costliest of all burial perfumes.

Hana stared at the alabaster flask in wonder. "From where did you get nard?"

Ari the Kazan disappeared downstairs. A moment later, he returned with a woman of extraordinary beauty. "Queen Berenike," he said.

Hana had heard many evil rumors of the queen. She eyed the woman darkly.

Queen Berenike knelt beside Baruch's body and kissed his forehead. Tears dripped down onto the floor. "I never saw a man of such courage." She broke open the flask of nard and gave it to Hana.

Hana poured the nard over Baruch's body, rubbing it into his skin. The sweet scent of the World to Come filled the room. Ari the Kazan laid out the burial shroud on the floor and lifted Baruch's body onto it. Hana bound Baruch's hands and feet and laid the veil over his face. A sob spilled out of her mouth. She had done all that was needed for burial.

"I have a burial cave outside the city," the queen said. "Please, you will take him there. I would be honored to have him rest in my cave."

Hana bit her lip and nodded. She stood up and held out her hand to Dov. "Come little bear. We must take *Abba* to his resting place now."

"I want to come too," Rachel said.

"You must stay with your *imma*," Hana said. "In case the birthpangs come again."

Ari the Kazan picked up Baruch's shrouded body and carried it downstairs. Outside in the street, several of the queen's servants stood waiting. They had a funeral bier and six flute players. Ari the Kazan laid Baruch on the bier. He took one end. Hana and the queen took the other end. They all lifted together. Dov came alongside and clutched the dead hand of his father.

The flute players began a slow dirge. Hana lifted up her voice and began wailing.

They walked north a little way, then turned west toward the Temple. Many people came outside to see. Hana heard many shouts of "Baruch the *tsaddik!*" When they reached the bottom of the hill, Hana looked back and saw many dozen mourners following. Men whom Baruch had healed. Women who had been barren until Baruch prayed for them. Children who loved Baruch. Hana's heart felt cold.

They turned south toward the gate near the Pool of Siloam, and more mourners joined the throng. It was now dark, and some mourners brought torches to light the way. When they reached the pool, Hana saw that the gatekeepers had not closed the city gates for the night, on account of the many dead who required burial. Hana's heart became ice in her chest.

They went out through the gate and followed the road up through the Kidron Valley as far as the Temple. Here they turned west and climbed partway up the slopes of the Mount of Olives until they came to the queen's burial cave. Ari the Kazan and the queen's servants rolled back a great stone. They carried Baruch into the tomb and laid his body on a stone bed. Hana's heart was a great gaping empty hole within her.

Ari the Kazan prayed a prayer he called the *Kaddish*. It was a beautiful prayer. Hana had heard something similar before, only not so beautiful.

When Ari the Kazan finished, there was silence. The flute players had put away their flutes. The mourners were ready to go home. Now Hana would go home and she did not know what would become of her. All was in the hands of HaShem, but her road was dark.

Hana took Dov's hand. "Come little bear, we must—"

"Wait," Ari the Kazan put a hand on her arm.

Hana stared at him. It was not done, for a man to touch another man's widow.

"There is a thing I must say." Tears streamed down the face of Ari the Kazan. "I said harsh words to Brother Baruch in the past year. I begged his forgiveness today and he gave it gladly. Now there is another I must ask for forgiveness."

Hana could not breathe. Ari the Kazan was a proud man, a man of logic.

Ari the Kazan knelt before her. "Sister Hana, I wronged you also." He bent his head to the ground and kissed her feet. "Will you forgive me?"

Hana stared at him in wonder. Baruch's death had worked a miracle. "Yes, I forgive you, Brother Ari."

Brother Ari stood up and took Hana's hand and Dov's. "Today you are my sister. You and your son will live in my house and eat my bread as long as I live. Yes?"

Warmth filled every corner of Hana's heart. "Yes."

FORTY-FOUR

Ari

Ari woke up as dawn was breaking over the shattered city of HaShem. Rivka was still sleeping. They had stayed up very late talking last night, after he and Hana and Dov returned from burying Baruch. Ari felt exhausted, but he dressed and went downstairs into the small room he used as an office. He prayed the *Sh'ma*, but the prayer was ashes in his mouth.

Ari could not comprehend all that had happened yesterday. Brother Baruch was dead, along with many hundred other Jews. The governor meant to make war on the city, and now the city meant to make war on Rome. Rivka could not leave the city until the child was born. Ari stared numbly at his wooden writing desk, littered with many pieces of papyrus, designs for devices for Brother Eleazar. The men of violence.

Ari's heart ached. His life was shards and who could mend it?

On impulse, Ari took a pair of iron shears and cut a long strip of papyrus. He twisted one end and joined it to the other with paste, making a Möbius strip. He stared at it. This was his life, neither one thing nor the other. Rome would not allow him to be a man of peace, yet his conscience would not allow him to be a man of violence. HaShem was making a joke of him.

"What are you making, *Abba?*"

Ari turned and saw Racheleh come in clutching her doll, her eyes still crusted with sleep. Ari scooped her up in his arms and handed her the Möbius strip. "This is my life, Racheleh. See, it seems to have two sides, yet it is not so. There is one side only, and even HaShem cannot make it two."

Rachel looked at it with wide eyes. "HaShem can do anything, *Abba*. Please explain why HaShem cannot make it two."

Ari set her down. "Let me show you." He sharpened a reed pen, set a little cube of dried ink in a shallow inkwell, and mixed it with water to make ink. "Now see the puzzle HaShem has made for me. I draw a line down the middle of the Möbius strip to mark one side, yes?"

Rachel watched intently while Ari drew one long continuous line down the middle of the Möbius strip. At last he came back around to the starting point. He turned the strip over. "See, Racheleh? It only *seems* to have two sides, but you see that it has only one."

Rachel looked up at him. "HaShem can make it two."

He shook his head. "No. Even HaShem cannot do so. It is a logical impossibility."

"HaShem can make it two."

"Racheleh, it is a matter of mathematics."

Stubbornness crept across her face. "HaShem can make it two."

He smiled. "Show me."

"I do not know how." Rachel closed her eyes. "HaShem, please you will show us how to make it two."

A long silence.

Ari bent down to kiss her cheek. "When a thing is impossible, even HaShem cannot make it so."

Rachel picked up the iron shears in her small hands and began cutting along the central line Ari had drawn. She pursed her lips in concentration as she worked. Ari's mouth went dry as he watched her work. A curious fact about the Möbius strip was that it had only one edge. If you traced the left edge around the loop, it became the right edge because of the half twist. Tracing it around yet a second time, it became the left edge again.

Rachel was now cutting a new edge straight down the middle. She finished cutting and held it up. The strip of papyrus now made a full twist.

And it had two edges, two sides.

"See, *Abba?*" Rachel put down the shears and picked up her doll. "HaShem says that there is a deep thing for you to understand, if you will think on this matter."

Ari took the strip and stared at it. A deep thing? He bent and kissed the top of Rachel's head. "Go and see if *Imma* and Aunt Hana are awake yet."

Rachel skipped out of the room.

Ari went out in the street and looked up at the sky, wondering what this could mean.

The way of Brother Eleazar was the way of violence. Violence for the sake of violence. Eleazar loved the sword and the sling and the bow because they gave him the power he craved. Ari saw now that he could not take the side of the men of violence. Baruch had been right in saying so.

The way of Brother Baruch was the way of peace. Baruch counseled that a man should passively accept evil without fighting back. A man could live such a way, but a nation could not. In the World to Come, there would be no evil and no need to fight it, but in the World that Is, there was evil. The good man must fight evil, or else it would triumph. Eleazar had been right in saying so.

Both Baruch and Eleazar were right, and both were wrong. And both of them had been necessary to keep Ari from wrong. Had it not been for Baruch, Ari would have become a man of violence. Had it not been for Brother Eleazar, Ari would have never developed the defenses which the city now required.

Ari looked at the Möbius strip again. Racheleh had cut a line down the middle and solved the riddle. Just so, he must walk the middle road. He would fight evil, but he would not become evil to do so. Perhaps, like the Möbius strip, he also would be cut down the middle, but that was a sacrifice he was prepared to make. A *deep law of the universe.*

"*Abba?*"

Ari turned and saw Rachel standing in the doorway with Dov.

"*Imma* is awake now, and Aunt Hana is also awake and making breakfast."

"I will come."

The five of them ate up in the bedroom. Rivka sat in bed, with Rachel and Dov on either side of her. Ari sat on one side of the bed, Hana on the other.

"Ari, are you really going to cooperate with Hanan ben Hanan?" Rivka's voice sounded anguished. "I don't think you should trust him."

Ari sighed. "He saved my life."

"Only because you saved his life once," Rivka said. "He was obligated. It was a matter of honor. Now the score is even."

"Please, Rivkaleh."

She bit her lip. "I'm just being realistic. He killed Yaakov the *tsaddik.* His father sent Yeshua to the cross."

The cross. For all Ari's life, the cross had been a sign of rage. Christian rage against all Jews, Christ-killers. Jewish rage against all Christians, Jew-killers. The cross was the blood curse and the blood curse was the cross. The cross was retribution.

But no more.

Ari could never again see the cross as a curse. The cross was Baruch, giving himself freely for his friend, dying in despair because his sacrifice was refused, changing the hearts of all who saw, ascending in glory to the World to Come.

The cross was life, not death. A blessing, not a curse. Victory, not defeat. Reconciliation, not retribution.

A *deep law of the universe*. Ari saw it at last, the meaning of Baruch's death. Baruch had absorbed the twist in the universe into his own body, turning all things upside down.

Ari stood up abruptly, and now he knew what he must do. An action he must take, not merely a thing he must say. The first step on the middle road. And Rivka must take it with him.

Rivka looked at him in surprise. "Are you going somewhere?"

Ari pulled back her covers. "Yes, and you also. Up, children. *Imma* is going on a journey."

"Ari, I need to stay in bed. I'm not going—"

Ari bent over and picked her up.

"Ari! What are you doing?" A nervous laugh filled Rivka's voice. "I can't go outside. I'm not dressed for it."

Ari nodded to the children. "Dov, Rachel, Hanaleh, come with us."

"Ari!"

He carried her down the stairs and set her gently on a low wooden stool in the kitchen. "The doctor does not forbid you to sit, am I correct?"

"No, but would you please explain—"

Ari went to the fireplace and laid in a few pieces of wood and some kindling. He took the burning olive-oil lamp from its niche in the wall, twisted a handful of straw into a tight bundle, and lit it from the lamp. The straw flared into an open flame. He set it gently under the kindling. In minutes, he had a fire going in the fireplace.

Rivka looked perplexed. "Ari, it's hot outside. We don't need a fire. What's all this about?"

Ari reached up to a tiny wooden cross wedged between the stones of the fireplace. He pulled it out and knelt before Rivka. "Rivka, I must ask you to forgive me. All my life, this cross has been a sign of evil to me, a token of rage. I have allowed it to come between us and I am sorry."

Rivka's eyes glimmered with tears. She threw her arms around Ari. "Yes, Ari, I forgive you. I'm so sorry for what it's meant to you."

He put it in her hands and looked into her eyes.

Her eyebrows went up. "Is there something else?"

"Is it not also a token of rage for you?"

She gave him a perplexed look. "I don't understand."

Ari put his hand over hers. "For many centuries, this cross was the token of rage for Christians, the proof that all Jews were Christ-killers, the sign of the blood curse."

"Ari, you know I don't believe that way — "

"Rivkaleh." He put a hand on her cheek. "It is true that you do not participate in this lie. Yet you hold the cross against the House of Hanan. You hate and fear Hanan ben Hanan for no good reason."

"His father killed Yeshua!"

Ari narrowed his eyes. "The son is not the father."

"He killed Yaakov the *tsaddik*."

"The past is not the future. This one man, you will never allow to change. All others, yes, but not him. You saw a vision yesterday and gave a token of reconciliation, but already you regret your generosity. You are bound to Hanan ben Hanan with a chain of rage. Will you break it now, or will you be bound to him all your life?"

Rivka's face shattered in grief. She pulled Ari toward her and gripped him tight, her hot breath coming in little gasps. Her fingers traced the long scars on Ari's back, wounds received at the hands of Hanan ben Hanan.

"Ari, you're right. I've been trying and trying to pray for Hanan, like Baruch told me, but it's so hard." Rivka's tears streamed down Ari's neck and her body convulsed in sobs.

Ari patted her on the back.

Rivka wept for some minutes. Finally she sniffed loudly and wiped her nose on her sleeve. "I never thought about it, but I *have* believed in the blood curse, only I focused it all on one man. On Hanan ben Hanan. I'm sorry. That was so wrong."

Rivka's words cut Ari like a whip. Deep shame welled up in his heart. "Rivkaleh, I too have focused my rage on one man — a good man who never caused the blood curse. I was wrong to blame him."

Rivka's eyes sparkled. "You mean . . ."

"I will think on the matter."

Rivka threw her arms around him again and wept.

Ari hugged her tight. He swallowed back a great lump in his throat, marveling that HaShem could remove this last twist in his universe. "Blessed be HaShem for this cross."

"Blessed be HaShem." Rivka kissed him. "Ari, I think I know what I want to do."

He released her and leaned back. "I also wish to do this thing."

They stood up.

Walked together to the fireplace.

Threw the tiny cross into the fire.

And watched the flames devour the token of their rage.

Somewhere, deep inside Ari's soul, HaShem laughed for joy.

Glossary

Abba: Papa.

Aliyah: Emigration to the modern State of Israel.

Amidah: Literally, "standing." A traditional daily prayer of nineteen separate benedictions, chanted while standing. Often called "the Eighteen Benedictions."

Anshei Hamas: Literally, "men of violence," a term used in both the Bible and Talmud.

Apikoros: Renegade. May be a Hebrew transliteration of "Epicurean."

Chiton: A typical sleeveless Greek garment for women.

Dinar: The "denarius" of the New Testament. Nominally a day's wage for a working man, enough to feed twelve people for a day.

Flagrum: A Roman whip used for flogging. Had bits of bone or metal embedded in multiple strands of leather.

Gehenna: A Greek term meaning, approximately, hell. Derived from the Hinnom Valley, a place of refuse and burning pits.

Goy: Gentile. Plural, *goyim.*

HaShem: Literally, "The Name." Used instead of "God" out of respect for his holiness.

Havurah: A fellowship of Pharisees in ancient *Yisrael.*

Hanukkah: Feast of Hanukkah, usually in December.

Imma: Mama.

Ishah: Woman, wife.

Kaddish: A Jewish prayer with several variations. One form is used in Jewish funerals. Some form of the prayer was used in antiquity, but not as a prayer for the dead.

Lepton: The smallest copper coin, the "widow's mite" of the New Testament. Plural: *lepta.* One-hundred-twenty-eight lepta made one *dinar.*

Lictor: One trained in flogging.

Mamzer: Bastard.

Mashiach: Messiah.

Meshugah: Craziness. Foolishness.

Mezuzah: Literally, "doorpost." A small case attached to a doorframe, containing a tiny scroll with certain biblical passages inscribed.

Mikveh: Ritual bath.

Nazir: Nazirite. One who takes a vow to abstain from the fruit of the grapevine and the cutting of the hair. The vow could be either temporary or lifelong.

Ossuary: A bone-box, used for storing bones. In October 2002 a bone-box bearing the inscription "James, son of Joseph, brother of Jesus" was discovered in Jerusalem. The box has been acclaimed a relic by some and denounced as a fake by others. Both sides have overstated their case and there is no proof one way or the other.

Palla: A typical garment of a wealthy Roman woman.

Pesach: Passover, usually in March or April.

Python: A spirit of divination common in the Greek world, used by oracles such as the one at Delphi.

Rabban: Literally, "Our great one." Applied to a very few rabbis — Gamaliel, Shimon ben Gamaliel, Gamaliel II, and Yohanan ben Zakkai. In view of John 20:16, it is plausible that Jesus of Nazareth was called Rabban Yeshua.

Rosh HaShanah: The New Year, usually in September.

Sagan: Captain of the Temple guards, second only to the high priest in the Temple.

Savta: Grandma.

Shabbat: Sabbath.

Shalom: "Peace." Used as a greeting and a good-bye.

Shavuot: The Feast of Pentecost, usually in June.

Shekinah: Literally, "Presence." The physical presence of God.

Sheol: The grave.

Shofar: A ram's horn, blown at festivals.

Sh'ma: Literally, "Hear!" Traditional daily prayer affirming the One-ness of God.

Sukkot: The Feast of Tabernacles, usually in September or October.

Talent: A unit of weight, variously estimated between about sixty and one hundred pounds. A silver talent was 10,000 *dinars*, a lifetime's wage for a working man.

Tallit: Prayer shawl. Worn draped over the head and shoulders during prayers.

Tefillin: Phylacteries. Small leather boxes containing Torah inscriptions, worn during daily prayers (and all day by the pious), but not on *Shabbat* or other holy days.

Tevul yom: A lenient rule of the Pharisees allowing one to immerse after a ritual impurity and then get on with the day's business. Not allowed by the Sadducees.

Tsaddik: Literally, "Righteous one." Used among modern Jews of exceptionally holy men.

Tunica: The standard tunic worn by a Roman woman.

Tzitzit: Ritual fringes, made with blue and white twisted thread.

Yisrael: Israel.

Zonah: Prostitute. Plural, *zonot*.

HISTORICAL CHARACTERS

The following characters are based on real historical persons. I interviewed none of these for this book, and with some, I took a fair bit of literary license. Rivka's comments on each should be understood as the conventional judgment of history, when that differs from my presentation in the story. Spellings for each name have been chosen from Latin, Greek, Hebrew, or English as seemed appropriate.

Agrippa: Marcus Julius Agrippa, also called Herod Agrippa II, last Jewish scion of the Herod family. Born about A.D. 27.

Albinus: Lucceius Albinus, governor of Judea A.D. 62–64.

Berenike: Agrippa's oldest sister. Born about A.D. 28. Rumors of incest dogged her and Agrippa. Intensely jealous of her younger sister Drusilla.

Cestius: Cestius Gallus, Roman governor of Syria. Jews begged him for relief from Florus when he visited Jerusalem at Passover, A.D. 66.

Costabar: A cousin of Agrippa and Berenike, noted for his street brawling.

Eleazar ben Arakh: The greatest and most mysterious of the five disciples of Rabban Yohanan ben Zakkai.

Eleazar ben Hananyah: Son of high priest Hananyah ben Nadavayah. Captain of the Temple in early sixties. Born to a Sadducean family, apparently became a Pharisee, sparked the Jewish revolt in A.D. 66.

Felix: Marcus Antonius Felix, governor of Judea approximately A.D. 52–59. Lured Agrippa's youngest sister Drusilla away from her husband.

Festus: Porcius Festus, governor of Judea approximately A.D. 59–62. Died in office, leaving Judea temporarily without a governor.

Florus: Gessius Florus, governor of Judea A.D. 64–66. Crucified a large number of randomly chosen Jews in the spring of A.D. 66, prompting the Jewish revolt.

Hanan ben Hanan: "Annas, son of Annas." A Sadducee, youngest son of the "Annas" who presided over the trial of Jesus. Became high priest in A.D. 62 and promptly executed James, son of Joseph, brother of Jesus.

Hananyah ben Nadavayah: "Ananias, son of Nedebeus." A Sadducee, high priest circa A.D. 52–59. Widely hated for stealing tithes.

Honi the Circler: A mysterious legendary holy man who once drew a circle and refused to leave until God sent rain to end a drought.

Josephus: See Yoseph ben Mattityahu.

Marta: A wealthy and spoiled widow of the House of Boetus who married Yeshua ben Gamaliel. She once carpeted the streets on Yom Kippur so she could go to the Temple barefoot.

Mattityahu ben Theophilus: A Sadducee, high priest A.D. 64–66, nephew of Hanan.

Mattityahu ben Yoseph: "Matthew, son of Joseph." The father of Josephus. The names "Mattityahu" and "Yoseph" recur many times in this family.

Menahem ben Yehudah: "Menahem, son of Judas the Galilean." A bandit revolutionary who captured Masada early in the war.

Naqdimon ben Gorion: A wealthy man of Jerusalem who supported the war effort. May be the grandson of the "Nicodemus" of the New Testament.

Polemon: King of Pontus A.D. 38–64. Agreed to circumcision in order to marry Berenike, but the marriage soon failed.

Rambam: An acronym for "Rabbi Moshe ben Maimon," the greatest of all Jewish commentators, also known as Maimonides.

Saul: A cousin of Agrippa and Berenike, noted for his street brawling.

Shimon ben Gamaliel: A famous rabbi and friend of Yohanan ben Zakkai.

Shimon ben Klopas: A cousin of Jesus of Nazareth. Leader of The Way in Jerusalem after his cousin Yaakov was murdered. Led his flock to safety in Pella before the war.

Tsaduq: Rabbi Tsaduq, a Pharisee rabbi noted for his zeal.

Yaakov ben Yoseph: "James, son of Joseph." Brother of Jesus, leader of The Way in Jerusalem, murdered in A.D. 62 by Hanan ben Hanan.

Yeshua ben Dannai: "Jesus, son of Damneus." A Sadducee, high priest A.D. 62–63.

Yeshua ben Gamaliel: "Jesus, son of Gamaliel." A Sadducee, high priest approximately A.D. 63–64. Friend of Josephus and protégé of Hanan.

Yeshua ben Yoseph: "Jesus, son of Joseph." Jesus of Nazareth.

Yeshua ben Hananyah: "Jesus, son of Ananias." Peasant who shouted obscure oracles in the Temple from A.D. 62–70.

Yohanan ben Zakkai: A Pharisee, one of the most influential Jews of all time, the traditional founder of rabbinic Judaism after the war. Once prayed for rain to end a drought.

Yoseph ben Gorion: A wealthy man of Jerusalem who supported the war effort. Brother of Naqdimon ben Gorion.

Yoseph ben Mattityahu: "Joseph, son of Matthew." Born A.D. 37/38, aristocrat, priest, soldier, historian. Main historical source for this period, also known as Josephus.

Premonition

City of God Series

Randall Ingermanson,
Christy Award-Winning
Author of Transgression

An extraordinary stone box was recently discovered in Jerusalem—the bone-box of "James, son of Joseph, brother of Jesus." This is his story . . .

It's the year A.D. 57 and Jerusalem teeters on the brink of revolt against Rome. James, leader of the Jewish Christian community, has an enemy in high places. And two very strange friends . . .

Rivka Meyers is a Messianic Jewish archaeologist from California, trapped in first-century Jerusalem by a physics experiment gone horribly wrong.

Ari Kazan is her husband, an Israeli physicist slowly coming to grips with his Jewish heritage—and with a man named Jesus he was raised to hate.

With no way back to their own century, Rivka and Ari seek their niche in this doomed city of God. Rivka knows that an illegal trial and execution awaits James, son of Joseph, brother of Jesus. Can she prevent this disaster? Will James believe her "premonition"? Or is Ari right that Rivka's meddling in history will only . . . make matters worse?

Softcover: 0-310-24705-5

Pick up a copy today at your favorite bookstore!

ZONDERVAN™

GRAND RAPIDS, MICHIGAN 49530 USA

WWW.ZONDERVAN.COM

We want to hear from you. Please send your comments about this book to us in care of zreview@zondervan.com. Thank you.

ZONDERVAN™

GRAND RAPIDS, MICHIGAN 49530 USA

WWW.ZONDERVAN.COM